DORIS LESSING was born in Persia in 1919 and moved, at the age of five, to Southern Rhodesia (now Zimbabwe), where her father went to farm. She lived for a while in what was then Salisbury and in 1949 came to London, where she has lived ever since. She is the author of more than thirty books—novels, stories, reportage, poems, and plays.

BY DORIS LESSING

FICTION

The Grass Is Singing
This Was the Old Chief's Country
The Habit of Loving
The Golden Notebook
A Man and Two Women
Briefing for a Descent into Hell
The Temptation of Jack Orkney and Other Stories
The Summer Before the Dark
The Memoirs of a Survivor
African Stories
Stories
*The Diary of a Good Neighbor
*If the Old Could . . .
The Good Terrorist
The Fifth Child
The Doris Lessing Reader

Children of Violence

Martha Quest
A Proper Marriage
A Ripple from the Storm
Landlocked
The Four-Gated City

Canopus in Argos: Archives

Re: Colonised Planet 5, Shikasta
The Marriages Between Zones Three, Four, and Five
The Sirian Experiments
The Making of the Representative for Planet 8
Documents Relating to the Sentimental Agents in the Volyen Empire

NONFICTION

In Pursuit of the English
Going Home
Particularly Cats
A Small Personal Voice
Prisons We Choose to Live Inside
The Wind Blows Away Our Words

POETRY

Fourteen Poems

*Under the pseudonym Jane Somers

LANDLOCKED

A COMPLETE NOVEL FROM

Doris Lessing's *MASTERWORK*

CHILDREN OF VIOLENCE

A PLUME BOOK

PLUME
Published by the Penguin Group
Penguin Books USA Inc., 375 Hudson Street, New York, New York 10014, U.S.A.
Penguin Books Ltd, 27 Wrights Lane, London W8 5TZ, England
Penguin Books Australia Ltd, Ringwood, Victoria, Australia
Penguin Books Canada Ltd, 2801 John Street, Markham, Ontario, Canada L3R 1B4
Penguin Books (N.Z.) Ltd, 182-190 Wairau Road, Auckland 10, New Zealand

Penguin Books Ltd, Registered Offices: Harmondsworth, Middlesex, England

Published by Plume, an imprint of New American Library, a division of Penguin
Books USA Inc. Published by arrangement with Simon and Schuster, Inc.

First Plume Printing, September, 1970
15 14 13 12 11 10 9 8 7

 REGISTERED TRADEMARK—MARCA REGISTRADA

LIBRARY OF CONGRESS CATALOGING-IN-PUBLICATION DATA

Lessing, Doris May, 1919-
    Landlocked : a complete novel from Doris Lessing's masterwork Children
of violence.
      p.   cm. — (Children of violence)
    ISBN 0-452-25775-1
    I. Title.   II. Series: Lessing, Doris May, 1919-   Children of violence.
PR6023.E833L36   1991   90-22678
823'914—dc20   CIP

Printed in the United States of America

Book 4

LANDLOCKED

part one

The Mulla walked into a shop one day. The owner came forward to serve him.

"First things first," said Nasrudin; "did you see me walk into your shop?"

"Of course."

"Have you ever seen me before?"

"Never in my life."

"Then how do you know it is me?"

THE SUFIS; Idries Shah.

1

The afternoon sun was hot on Martha's back, but not steadily so; she had become conscious of a pattern varying in impact some minutes ago, at the start of a telephone conversation that seemed as if it might very well go on for hours yet. Mrs. Buss, the departing senior secretary, had telephoned for the fourth time that day to remind Martha, her probable successor, of things that must be done by any secretary to Mr. Robinson, for the comfort and greater efficiency of Mr. Robinson. Or rather that is what, she said and possibly even thought, the telephone calls were for. In fact they expressed her doubt (quite justified, Martha thought) that Martha was equipped to be anybody's secretary, and particularly Mr. Robinson's—who had been spoiled (as Martha saw it), looked after properly (as Mrs. Buss saw it) for five years of Mrs. Buss's life.

Mrs. Buss said, "And don't forget the invoice on Fridays," and so on; while Martha, fully prepared to be conscientious within the limits she had set for herself, made notes of her duties on one, two, three, four sheets of foolscap. Meanwhile she studied the burning, or warm, or glowing sensations on her back. The window was two yards behind her, and it had a greenish "folkweave" curtain whose edge, or rather the shadow of whose edge, chanced to strike Martha's shoulder and her hip. At first had chanced—Martha was now carefully maintaining an exact position. Areas of flesh glowed with chill, or tingled with it; behind heat, behind cold, was an interior glow, as if they were the same. Heat burned through the glass on to blade and buttock; the cool of the shadow burned too. But there was not only contrast between hot heat and hot chill (cold cold and cold heat?), there were subsidiary minor lines, felt as strokes of tepid sensation, where the shadow of the window frame cut diagonally. And, since the patches and angles of sunlight fell into the office for half of its depth, and had been so falling for three hours, everything was warmed—floors, desks, filing cabinets, flung off heat; and Martha stood, not only directly branded by sunlight and by shadow, her flesh stinging precisely in patterns, but warmed through by a general irradiation. Which, however, was getting to be too much of a good thing. "Actually," she said to Mrs. Buss, "I ought to be thinking of locking up." This was a mistake; it sounded like overeagerness to be done with work, and earned an immediate extension of the lecture she was getting. She ought to have said, "I think Mr. Robinson wants to make a call."

At this moment Mr. Robinson did in fact put his head out of his office and frown at Martha, who was *still* on the telephone. He instantly vanished, leaving a sense of reproach. Martha just had time to offer him the beginnings of a placatory smile of which she was ashamed. She was not going to be Mr. Robinson's secretary, and she ought to have told him so before this.

She should have made up her mind finally weeks ago, and, having made up her mind, told him. She had not, because of her tendency —getting worse—to let things slide, to let things happen. It had needed only this: that she should walk into Mr. Robinson's office and say, pleasantly, absent-mindedly almost, "I'm sorry, Mr. Robinson, I've decided it would be better if I weren't your secretary." At which he would nod, say, "Of course, Mrs. Hesse, think no more about it."

This unreal conversation was why Martha had not in fact gone in before now to make her stand on a refusal; and why she had spent so much of her time in the last week or so marvelling at the complexities behind such a simple act.

Mrs. Buss's husband had decided to take a job on the Copper Belt. Mrs. Buss did not want to leave this job, which fitted her soul like a glove, but being nothing if not an expert on what was right knew it was right to follow her husband wheresoever he would go. Although she was not married to her husband but to her work, or rather, to her boss—for the past five years, Mr. Robinson. This did not mean, far from it, that her relationship with Mr. Robinson was anything it should not be; her duty was to the idea of what was right from a secretary. In the Copper Belt, she would, after an agitated fortnight or so of writing letters to Martha telling her how to look after Mr. Robinson, transfer herself to her new boss, whoever he was, and around him henceforward her life, her time, her being, would revolve.

As for Mr. Robinson, he understood not the first thing about this phenomenon over which Martha pondered still, after years of working beside it.

What would he say, for instance, had Martha told him: Mr. Robinson, did you know that Mrs. Buss tells Mr. Buss, on the nights when her shorthand book is full, "You know I can't tonight, I've got two memorandums and a company agreement to type tomorrow morning." And Mr. Buss understood his position in her life so well that he knew (as Mrs. Buss said, with a nod of satisfaction) where he got off. What would Mr. Robinson say if told that Mrs. Buss went to bed early refusing sundowners, the pictures, a dance, anything at all, on the nights before an audit, a big court case where Mr. Robinson would have to appear, or even a particularly heavy mail?

Well, Martha could not conceive of telling him, he simply would not believe it. He would go crimson, she knew that; the lean "likeable" lawyer's face would grow sulky while the blood darkened it. Because, of course, he would not understand how impersonal this passion was, and that in two weeks' time, in Lusaka, Mr. Buss would be "told where he got off" just as strongly but in relation to another job, another boss.

The door flung open again, and again Mr. Robinson appeared, this time showing annoyance. Martha covered the mouthpiece, saying, "It's Mrs. Buss," relieved that Mrs. Buss was definitely "office-work."

"Does she want to speak to me?"

"Do you want to speak to Mr. Robinson?"

"Oh, no, I wouldn't disturb him in his work," came the prompt, admonishing reply. "I'll ring you tomorrow, Matty, in case we've forgotten anything."

The door to Mr. Robinson's office was a plane of orange-coloured wood, unmarked by mouldings, grooves, panels, patterns, marked by nothing but the tree's grain. It was teak, showing the—how many?—years of its growth in irregular concentric lines. With half-shut eyes, the orangey-brown became sand over which water had ebbed, leaving lines of foam, or debris. Stared at, unblinking, with concentration, the door seemed to come closer, became cliffs of weathered sandstone, weathered rock, eroded in patterns where water had run—or like the irregular concentric lines of growth in wood. ...

But all this was no use, for she had to go in and tell Mr. Robinson she would not be his secretary. He was at this moment sitting behind his desk waiting for her to come in, and confirm it. Reasonably enough: it was a post much better (she agreed) than she deserved.

Martha, now released from the tether of the telephone wire, was standing behind her desk, not looking at the door. The sun was on her back, but the patterns of heat had shifted. A few minutes ago she was confirming: edge of window curtain, window frame, glass, lines horizontal and diagonal, areas small and large. But now her flesh was confused. It had charted, most accurately, for some unvarying minutes, degrees of heat, of cold, and now it was sulking. It was being asked to register too much too quickly—her whole back, and the backs of her thighs and arms, flamed at random with heat and with cold. As if she were in a fever. It occurred to Martha that perhaps she was—she might have burned herself. After all, glass could act like a burning glass; perhaps a knot or a whorl had focused heat on to . . . She bent back her head, held forward her shoulder. It emerged smooth from a sleeveless pink cotton dress, but it was reddened.

She was standing in a dislocated position, trying to see her own back down through the gap in pink cotton where it fell away from her shoulders, when Mr. Robinson came in and caught her. He went red and so did she. With a muttered "Like to see you, Mrs. Hesse," he returned to his office. But now the door was open. A sweet grass-smelling air came wafting through from his office, his open windows—a smell of cool watered grass. This fresh smell mingled with the smell of hot glass, of heated metal, of hot paint, of warmed varnish. Martha put her palm on her own desk where the sun had been falling, and withdrew it quickly, as if away from a hot plate. Following the smell of newly cut grass, more than her will, she went into Mr. Robinson's office. Beneath his windows, Rhodes Street, pouring with traffic, a jangle of warmed metal in movement. But beyond two roofs and an Indian store was a parking lot fringed with grass, where a black man scythed the loose fronds of jade-green grass, which was frothy with white grass-flowers, and the scent of it showered over all the lower town.

Martha put her left hand up, backwards, under her left armpit, and said, to explain her tortured position, "I think I've burned myself—from the window you know," she added. Then added again, still smiling, afraid now that this might sound like a complaint, because the main office was so exposed to the sun, "I'm an idiot."

Mr. Robinson let out a laugh, most false, except in his desire to show willingness to laugh, and said, "Do sit down, Mrs. Hesse."

Mrs. Hesse sat, knowing that sitting in the clients' chair was going to make it more difficult to refuse.

Now Mr. Robinson offered her a cigarette, shooting out a brown athletic hand (he played golf or tennis and swam every Sunday) with the silver case at the end of it, in a level, pistonlike movement. There he sat, smooth, well tailored, healthy, intelligent, his lean, good-looking face waiting in a smile for Martha to make a formal acceptance of his offer that she would be his secretary.

These two human beings had shared all their working days for years, off and on, and they knew nothing about each other, had never had any real contact, and in fact, as Martha knew, did not like each other. He was asking her to remain as secretary because of an indolence that matched her own: better the devil one knows. At least she had been with him (as the phrase is) for all that time and presumably she would be irradiated with the reflected efficiency from Mrs. Buss?

"Look," she began awkwardly, "I'm terribly sorry, Mr. Robinson, but I can't be your secretary." Already he had turned on her an affronted stare which caused her to stammer as she went on, "For one thing, there's my father, he's terribly ill, and it wouldn't be fair, because I couldn't give my whole attention to the job."

He was red with annoyance, and also with heat—his office, sheltered from the evening sun by the outer office and a wall, nevertheless glittered and gleamed from every surface because the windows of the tall building opposite flashed red and gold rays into it. The heat in this room had a cooked composted smell of tobacco, of smoke, of stale pipe ashes, of heated wood and metal and hot flesh.

"Well, I don't see that as an obstacle," he said. He was annoyed because Mr. Quest's illness had been incorporated, so to speak, into this office system already. Several times in the past few weeks Martha had had to leave precipitously, summoned to the sick bed by Mrs. Quest, who had taken to ringing up Martha with the announcement that she would not answer for it if Martha did not come at once.

And besides, what about that long period (past, but it had certainly existed) when half the telephone calls were for Martha, in her capacity as secretary of half a dozen "Red" organizations? Mr. Robinson had swallowed all that too, out of sheer decency, for in his capacity as future member of Parliament, he denounced Communism with vigour. "I'm not going to have all you people upsetting our blacks"—as he put it to Martha, from time to time.

Martha thought: I've made a hash of it already. Why can't he see that we could never get on? Besides, I simply will not *be* a secretary —the essence of a good one being (and he most particularly will demand this from now on) that she should deliver herself to the work heart and soul. I'll stay on as a typist or something, but that's all.

Mr. Robinson was still waiting for her to produce a more sensible excuse. By now he had understood she would not be his secretary, but was going to show his annoyance by insisting on explanations.

"Damn that sun," he muttered, half-glancing at Martha to suggest she should draw the curtains. She had already risen, when he remembered that her sitting there before him, in the clients' chair, meant she was temporarily in a different role. He jumped up and tugged oatmeal coloured curtains across the whole wall; so now the sun showed in a thousand tiny lines of sharp yellow light crisscross over darkish linen.

He sat down again, smiling a small quizzical smile. Martha noted it with dismay, noted she was softening. The smile said: Are you being difficult perhaps? Do you want to be persuaded into it? Do tell me . . .

She felt absurd, theatrical, ridiculous. She knew if she said "yes" to this job it would be one of the bad, serious decisions of her life. She did not know why; it simply was so. Her life could be changed by it—in the wrong way. She *knew* this. And it was also pompous and melodramatic to refuse, and she felt silly.

"Listen, Mrs. Hesse, the war's on its last legs, that's obvious. The senior partners will be coming home any minute now. In a year from now this firm will have taken all this floor and the floor above—it will be the biggest legal firm in the city. There'll be five working partners and that'll mean five personal secretaries and I reckon about ten typists and a couple of accountants." His voice was full of pride. A long way was Mr. Robinson from the shabby old building in Founders' Street (still only four or five hundred yards away in space, however), the shabby old rooms, the half-dozen typists. And a long way was he in imagination from the present arrangement of two smart rooms filled by Mr. Robinson, Mrs. Buss, Mrs. Hesse. No, he was already the conqueror of two large modern glass-spread floors filled to the brim with lawyers, accountants and secretaries: "the biggest legal firm in the city."

And he wanted Martha to be thrilled with him. The trouble was, she *was* thrilled. If she wasn't careful, she was going to give in.

"I'm awfully sorry, Mr. Robinson," she said, awkwardly, but firm enough. He looked at her, hurt. To hide the red that flamed over his face, he jumped up from his chair and began rooting in a filing cabinet. "I can't find," he muttered, "the Condamine Mining Company file."

Martha sat on a moment, looking at the Condamine file, which was immediately in front of her on his desk. Then she stood up. "Look, Mr. Robinson," she was beginning, when he bent down to pick up a paper lying on the floor. As he straightened again, he banged his head hard on the sharp corner of a projecting drawer.

The bang went through Martha in a wave of sickness. As for him, he stood gripping the drawer with both hands, swaying with faintness, his face white, his closed eyelids squeezing out tears of pain. Martha's teeth clenched with the need to comfort, her arms were held in to her waist to stop them going around him—and she said nothing, not a word, nothing. She stood like a pillar of cold observation. At least, she thought, I must avert my eyes from . . . She turned herself, went to the window, twitched back a corner of the oatmeal linen, and looked out over the stream of cars and lorries, over roofs, over to the black man who steadily bent and straightened, bent and straightened, the sun glinting red on his black polished chest and back, and sliding red streaks along his scythe. The grass fell in jade-green swathes, frothy with white flowers, on either side of him, and the smell of cut grass wafted in over the thick sweet smells of tobacco, sweat, ash, heated wood—Martha heard Mr. Robinson's breathing steady and settle. She felt sick with his sickness, but could not think of anything to do. If he hated her for her detachment from his pain, he was right. "Are you all right?" she asked at last, and he said, with difficulty, "Yes, thanks." Off he went, out of the office, striding with his long springlike stride, and she thought: Of course, he's gone to get himself some water, I should have thought of it.

When he came back, he gave her a look of cold dislike, which she knew she had earned.

"Do you want to leave altogether?" he asked, sliding himself back into his chair, and slamming in drawers everywhere around him. On his forehead was a red bump in the middle of which was a blackish contusion, oozing blood. He sat dabbing at it.

"Not unless you want me to," she said, remaining where she was by the curtains.

"If you think I'm not offering you enough money, then I think you're being unreasonable."

Since he was offering her Mrs. Buss's salary, he was more than reasonable.

"It's not that—look, it's like this, I don't think you quite realize just how marvellous Mrs. Buss is—was. I don't think you've got any idea."

He gave her one of his quick assessing glances, quick from shyness, not from acuity, and concluded that the awkwardness of her manner meant insincerity. He said coldly, "My dear Mrs. Hesse, you aren't suggesting I don't know Mrs. Buss's worth, surely? I've never in my life had anyone like that working for me, and I'm sure I never will. But now she's gone, I can confess in confidence that sometimes it was too much of a good thing. I mean, sometimes I didn't feel good enough for her—as for being late in the morning, I wouldn't have dared!" He gave a hopeful laugh; she joined him emphatically. "I'm not asking you to be Mrs. Buss, believe you me!" Here he began a hasty uncoordinated shoving about of his files and papers all over the big surface of his slippery desk, which meant, as Martha knew (with an increasing exasperation which was compounded strongly, against her will, with affection) look, this is what I want, I want to be looked after as Mrs. Buss did, just look at the mess I'm getting into! The papers, pushed too hard, went fluttering off to the floor, and Martha bent to pick them up, feeling ridiculous, because now Mr. Robinson got up and bent too, cautious of his head though, and even giving the dangerous drawer humorous glances for Martha's benefit, just as she had put up her hand backwards to touch her shoulderblade, in a sort of explanation to him. For a few moments, these two bobbed up and down, like a couple of feeding hens, Martha thought, picking up the papers that lay everywhere, in the most touching scene of mutual harmony and goodwill. Luckily the telephone in the outer office rang, and Martha was released to answer it. "Robinson, Daniel and Cohen," said Martha, into the black tube, and Mrs. Quest said dramatically, "Matty, is that you? You must come at once!"

Martha sat down, enquired, "Is he ill again then?" and drew towards her a sheet of paper, adding pennies to pennies, shillings to shillings, and—since this was one of the firm's big accounts—hundreds of pounds to hundreds of pounds. Mrs. Quest had already rung twice that day, first to say that Mr. Quest was having a bad spell and Martha must be prepared to come at any moment; and again to say that Mr. Quest had turned the corner.

Martha was thinking that something had been forgotten in the interview with Mr. Robinson: she was being paid an extra ten pounds a month to do the books. But now there would be accountants, and he would be entirely in the right to deduct ten pounds from her salary.

"Matty, are you there?"

"Of course I'm here."

"I'm waiting for the doctor."

"Oh, are you?"

"Well, if you've got things to do, do them quickly, because you did say you'd come, and what with one thing and another I'm run off my feet. And I suppose you haven't had any lunch again either."

The sheer lunacy of this conversation went no deeper than the surface of Martha's sensibilities. "I'll be over on the dot," she said soothingly, and would have continued to soothe, if Mr. Robinson had not abruptly arrived in the central office exclaiming, "Mrs. Hesse!" before he saw she was still on the telephone. Martha covered the mouthpiece and said, "Yes, Mr. Robinson?"

"When you've finished," he said, and went back in.

The sun was burning Martha's burned shoulder. She drew the curtains right across, as Mrs. Quest said, "And so he can't keep anything down at all, so the doctor says it will be a question of rectal feeding soon. Did you enjoy yourself last night at the pictures?"

"I didn't go to the pictures. What did you ring me for?"

"Oh, by the way," said Mrs. Quest, after a confused pause, her breath coming quick, "I thought I should tell you Caroline is here for the afternoon and so you should be careful she doesn't see you."

Of course! thought Martha. That's it. I should have guessed. "Since I told you earlier I couldn't get to you until eight, and since Caroline will have gone home long before that, I don't see the point."

"Well, you might have come now, you bad girl, if you weren't so busy." Mrs. Quest now sounded playful, even coy, and to forestall anger, Martha said quickly, "Tell my father I'll be there at eight, goodbye, Mother." She put down the receiver, trembling with rage.

This situation had arisen: Mrs. Quest had taken to appropriating

her granddaughter several times a week for the day, or for the afternoon. The little girl played in the big garden with her nurse while
Mrs. Quest supervised from the windows of the room where Mr.
Quest lay ill. And why not? Martha considered it reasonable that the
Quests should have their grandchild, while she, the child's mother,
who had forfeited all right to her, should be excluded. It was quite
right she should never be seen by the child; it would upset Caroline,
who was now "used to," as everyone said, Elaine Talbot, now Elaine
Knowell, the new mother. All this Martha agreed to, accepted, saw
the justice of. But on the afternoons Caroline was with her grandmother, Mrs. Quest invariably telephoned Martha to say: Caroline's
here, I can see her playing near the fish pond, she does look pretty
today. Or: Be careful not to drop in, Matty, Caroline's here.

And Martha said, Yes, Mother. No, Mother. And never once had
she said what her appalled, offended heart repeated over and over
again, while she continued to say politely, "Yes," and "Of course":
You're enjoying this—you love punishing me. This is a victory for
you, being free to see the child when I am not—sadistic woman,
cruel sadistic woman . . . So Martha muttered to herself, consumed
with hatred for her mother, but consumed ridiculously, since the
essence of Martha's relationship with her mother must be, must,
apparently, forever be, that Mrs. Quest "couldn't help it." Well, she
couldn't.

Now Martha sat, rigid, trembling, seething with thoughts she
was ashamed of, knew were unfair and ridiculous, but could not
prevent: "And now my father's ill, really ill at last, and so I have to
go to that house, and she's got me just where she wants me, I'm
helpless."

Mr. Robinson came out of his office.

"Mr. Robinson?"

"I was going to say: advertise for a new secretary, you know the
sort of thing we want."

"I'll put it in the paper tomorrow. And about that ten pounds?"

"What ten pounds?"

"If we're going to have proper accountants, then . . ."

For the hundredth time that day (it seemed) he went red and so
did she.

"Forget it," he muttered. Then, afraid he had sounded abrupt, he
smiled hastily. She smiled brightly back. "Thanks," she said. He
rushed out of the office, slamming the door. Doors slammed all down
the centre of the building and then a car roared into movement.

Martha now shut drawers, doors; opened curtains again, exposing yards of heated glass; threw balls of paper into the baskets. The telephone began ringing. It was five minutes after time, so she left the instrument ringing in the hot, glowing room, and walked down the stairs, round and round the core of the building after her employer—probably now several miles away, at the speed he drove. The washroom was empty. Six basins and six square mirrors and a lavatory bowl stood gleamingly clean. The old man who was the building's "boy" had just finished cleaning. He went out as Martha came in, saying, "Good night, missus." Martha stood in front of a mirror, and lifted brown arms to her hair, then held them there, looking with a smile at the smooth, perfect flesh, at the small perfect crease in her shoulder.

The smile, however, was dry: she wiped it off her face. It was there too often, and too often did she have to push it away, and make harmless the attitude of mind it came from. She had to survive, she knew that; this phase of her life was sticking it out, waiting, keeping herself ready for when "life" would begin. But that smile . . . there was a grimness in it that reminded her of the set of her mother's face when she sat sewing, or was unaware she was being observed.

Martha made up her face, smoothed down pink cotton over hips and thighs, combed her hair. She could *not* prevent, this time, as she leaned forward into the mirror, a pang of real pain. She was twenty-four years old. She had never been, probably never would be again, as attractive as she was now. And what for?—that was the point. From now, four-thirty on a brilliant March afternoon until midnight, when she would receive Anton's kiss on her cheek, she would be running from one place to another, seeing one set of people after another, all of them greeting her in a certain way, which was tribute to—not only her looks at this time—but a quality which she could not define except as it was expressed in reverse, so to speak, by their attitude. Yet she remained locked in herself, and . . . what a damned waste, she ended these bitter thoughts, as she turned to examine her back view. To the waist only, the mirror was set too high. Because of all the "running around"—Anton's phrase for it; because her life at this time was nothing but seeing people, coping with things, dealing with situations and people, one after another, she was thin. She was "in a thin phase," she was again "a slim blonde." Well, almost; being blonde is probably more a quality of texture than of colour: Martha was not sleek enough to earn the word blonde.

And besides, what was real in her, underneath these metamorphoses of style or shape or—even, apparently—personality, remained and intensified. The continuity of Martha now was in a determination to survive—like everyone else in the world, these days, as she told herself; it was in a watchfulness, a tension of the will that was like a small flickering of light, like the perpetual tiny dance of lightning on the horizon from a storm so far over the earth's curve it could only show reflected on the sky. Martha was holding herself together—like everybody else. She was a lighthouse of watchfulness; she was a being totally on the defensive. This was her reality, not the "pretty" or "attractive" Martha Hesse, a blondish, dark-eyed young woman who smiled back at her from the mirror where she was becomingly set off in pink cotton that showed a dark angle of shadow in the angle of her hips. Yet it was the "attractive" Matty Hesse she would take now to see Maisie; and it was necessary to strengthen, to polish, to set off the attractive Matty, the shell, because above all Maisie always understood by instinct what was going on underneath everybody's false shells, and this was why Martha loved being with Maisie, but knew at the same time she must protect herself . . . there were fifteen minutes before Maisie expected her. Martha lit a cigarette, propped herself on the edge of a wash basin, shut her eyes, and let bitter smoke drift up through her teeth. She felt the smoke's touch on the down of her cheek, felt it touch and cling to her lashes, her brows.

She must keep things separate, she told herself.

Last Saturday morning she had spent with Maisie, relaxed in a good-humoured grumbling gossip, a female compliance in a pretence at accepting resignation. And what had been the result of that pleasure, the delight of being off guard? Why, the situation she was now in with Maisie, a false situation. She had not kept things separate, that was why.

Martha's dreams, always a faithful watchdog, or record, of what was going on, obligingly provided her with an image of her position. Her dream at this time, the one which recurred, like a thermometer, or gauge, from which she could check herself, was of a large house, a bungalow, with half a dozen different rooms in it, and she, Martha (the person who held herself together, who watched, who must preserve wholeness through a time of dryness and disintegration) moved from one room to the next, on guard. These rooms, each furnished differently, had to be kept separate—*had* to be, it was Martha's task for this time. For if she did not—well, her dreams told her what she might expect. The house crumbled drily under her eyes into a pile of dust, broken brick, a jut of ant-eaten rafter, a slant of rusting iron. And then, while she watched, the ruin changed: it was the house on the kopje, collapsed into a mess of ant-tunnelled mud, ant-consumed grass, where red ant-made tunnels wove a net, like red veins, over the burial mound of Martha's soul, over the rotting wood, rotting grass, subsiding mud; and bushes and trees, held at bay so long (but only just, only very precariously) by the Quests' tenancy, came striding in, marching over the fragments of substance originally snatched from the bush, to destroy the small shelter for the English family that they had built between teeming earth and brazen African sky.

Yes, she knew that—Martha knew that, if she could not trust her judgement, or rather, if her judgement of outside things, people, was like a light that grew brighter, harsher, as the area it covered grew smaller, she could trust with her life (and with her death, these dreams said) the monitor, the guardian, who stood some-where, *was* somewhere in this shell of substance, smooth brown flesh so pleasantly curved into the shape of young woman with smooth browny-gold hair, alert dark eyes. The guardian was to be trusted in messages of life and death; and to be trusted too when the dream (the Dream, she was beginning to think of it, it came in so many shapes and guises, and so often) moved back in time, or perhaps forward—she did not know; and was no longer the shallow town house of thin brick, and cement and tin, no longer the farm house of grass and mud; but was tall rather than wide, reached up, stretched down, was built layer on layer, but shadowy above and below the shallow mid-area comprising (as they say in the house agents' catalogues) "comprising six or so rooms" for which this present Martha was responsible, and which she must keep separate.

Keeping separate meant defeating, or at least, holding at bay, what was best in her. The warm response to "the biggest legal firm in the city;" the need to put her arms around Mr. Robinson when he hurt himself so cruelly on the drawer; the need to say yes, to com-ply, to melt into situations; the pleasant relationship with Maisie—well, all this wouldn't do, she must put an end to it. She had simply to accept, finally, that her role in life, for this period, was to walk like a housekeeper in and out of different rooms, but the people in the rooms could not meet each other or understand each other, and Martha must not expect them to. She must not try to explain, or build bridges.

Between now and twelve tonight, she would have moved from the office and Mr. Robinson, up-and-coming lawyer, future member of Parliament, with his wife, his two children, and his house in the suburbs, to Maisie; from Maisie to Joss and Solly Cohen; from them, the Cohen boys, to old Johnny Lindsay; from the old miner's sickbed to her father's, nursed by her mother; from the Quests' house to Anton. None of these people knew each other, or could meet with understanding. Improbably (almost impossibly, she thought) Martha was the link between them. And, a more violently discordant association than any of these, there was Mr. Maynard. Mr. Maynard was after Maisie, he was on the scent after Maisie, through her, Martha—which brought her back to her immediate preoccupation.

It was her duty to explain to Maisie, to warn Maisie . . . the cigarette was finished, and she must leave. She left the washroom door swinging softly behind her, and ran down the wide bare steps, and into the clanging, shouting, sun-glittering street. Her bicycle was in the rack on the pavement. She dropped it into the river of traffic, slid up on to it, and was off down the street, but turned sideways to detour past the parking lot whose edges were now loaded with great mounds of jade-green frothing grass, like waves with white foam on them, past the gum trees whose trunks shed loose coils of scented bark; past the Indian stores and then back in a great curve into Founders' Street. It was, in fact, as the crow flew (or as a young woman might choose to bicycle straight along the street, instead of detouring past grass verges where midges danced in a swoon of grass scent and eucalyptus) only a few hundred yards from Robinson, Daniel and Cohens' new offices to where Maisie lived. Founders' Street had not changed. On the very edge of the new glittering modern centre, it remained low and shabby, full of odorous stores, cheap cafés, wholesale warehouses, small grass lots with bits of rusted iron and dark-skinned children playing, full of the explosive vitality of the unrespectable. There was a bar called Webster's on a corner, which Martha had never been in, since women did not go into the bars of the city, and besides it was ugly, and besides it usually had groups of men standing about outside it, with the violent look of men waiting for bars to open, or hanging about in frustration because a bar has closed. But Maisie now lived over this place, in two rooms directly above the bar, and she worked in Webster's as a barmaid.

Martha came to rest at the curb, lifted the bicycle up on to the pavement, then left it leaning, locked with a chain like a tethered dog, while she squeezed back against the wall past a dark glass window that had Webster's on it in scratched white paint. Half a dozen Africans lifted crates of beer from a lorry which had the name of the city's brewery on its side, to the pavement, and from the pavement to the open door of the bar. It was nearly opening time, and a couple of youths in khaki, farm assistants, from the look of them, hung smoking by the open door, watching the crates being shouldered in past a red-sweaty-faced, paunchy man in shirt-sleeves who frowned his concentration that the beer handlers should not crash or damage the great bottle-jammed crates. As Martha went past him to the small side door that led to Maisie's rooms, a violent crash, a splintering of glass, angry shouts from the red-faced man, who was presumably Mr. Webster, and complaints, expostulations, even a laugh from the watching farm assistants. A sudden sour reek of beer across the sun-baked street. Martha ascended dark wooden stairs fast, away from the beer stench. She knocked on Maisie's door and heard, "Is that you, Matty? Come in then." She entered on a scene of a small child being put to bed for the night.

The two rooms, small and crammed, but very bright, had in them Maisie, a black nurse-girl, and the baby girl Rita, now about a year old. The child did not want to go to bed. She was fighting the nurse. "I-don t-want-nursie, I-don't-want," while the girl, indefatigably good-humoured, was trying to push windmilling arms and legs into scarlet pyjamas. "There Miss Rita, there now Miss Rita."

Maisie surveyed this scene from the doorway between the rooms, smoking; the soft blue of her cotton dress pushed out in a great bulge by the hip she rested her weight on. She wore a white wool jacket, and as Martha came in, dusted ash off it with one hand, while she raised her eyes with the same cosmos-questioning gesture and shrug she had once used for, "And who'd be a woman, hey?" But now she was saying, "Well, Matty, who'd be a mother, man? Just look at her."

Nevertheless, she smiled, and the nurse-girl smiled, having safely accomplished the task of getting all four dissident little limbs disposed in the scarlet arms and legs of the pyjamas. Now Rita stuck her thumb in her mouth and blinked great black eyes fighting each heavy blink, blink, with an obstinate tightening of her face. She was fighting sleep. Peace. Silence. The black girl smiled at Maisie, and began picking up garments from all over the room. Rita was scooped up by her mother, where she stood to attention, as it were, in her arms. Maisie tried to rock and cradle the child, but Rita would not go limp. A little stubborn bulldog, she tightened her lips in a determination not to sleep. Meanwhile Maisie, a cigarette hanging from her lips, blew smoke out above the small head. Suddenly, the child went limp, she was half asleep. Maisie looked down into the child's face, thoughtful, frowning. Martha came up close to look too. Martha did not touch the child. Last Saturday, when Rita had put her arms around the knees of her mother's friend, Maisie had called her away and said, "Yes, I can see it must be hard for you, when you've not got your own kid, I can see that." Maisie was winding a piece of Rita's black hair around her finger. But the hair was straight, and simply fell loose again. Maisie stood with a cigarette in her mouth, Rita cradled in one arm, trying with her free hand to make ringlets in Rita's hair. Then she put up her hand to wind a strand of her own fair hair around her forefinger. It sprang off in a perfect ringlet. Ash scattered on the red pyjamas, and Martha rescued the cig- arette. "Thanks, Matty, you're a pal." The child sucked her thumb noisily, the small pink lips working around the white wet thumb. She blinked, blinked. Maisie gave up the attempt to make the heavy black hair curl, and took a cautious step towards the small bed be- side her big one. The child opened her eyes and started up, strug- gling to stand in her mother's arms.

"Let me," said Martha, and nodded in response to Maisie's quick look of enquiry. Rita went into Martha's arms, staring in solemn curiosity into the new face close to hers.

"She's old for her age," said Maisie. "Do you know what, Matty? I think they're born older than they used to be. Sometimes Rita just gives me the creeps, watching me, you'd think she knew every- thing already." Certainly it was a serious and knowledgeable look. Martha did not feel she held a tiny child in her arms, and it made things easier, for this was the first time she had held a baby since she had left her own. She held the solid heavy little girl, while Maisie stripped off her dress and said, "Poor Matty, but perhaps one of these days you'll have another baby and then you'll forget all your sorrow."

"Yes, I expect I will," said Martha. She sat on Maisie's bed, hold- ing the child carefully. Rita was at last going to sleep, at last she seemed a baby—small, warm, confiding. Maisie stood in her pink satin petticoat, her strong white legs planted firmly, and frowned into a mirror, while she wet her eyebrows with a forefinger. The nurse came in and said, "Can I go home now, missus?" "Yes, you go home, nursie." "I'll do Miss Rita's washing in the morning." "Yes, that's fine." "Good night, Miss Maisie." "Good night, nursie." The girl nodded at Martha, with a quick unconscious smile of love for the sleeping child, and went out.

"She's a good girl," said Maisie. "She's got two kids of her own, she leaves them with her mom in the Location. I tell her she's lucky to have her mom near her, I wish I did." She frowned, stretching her mouth to take lipstick. "Her husband, or so she calls him, has gone to the mines in Joburg. Well, I tell her she's lucky to be rid of him, men are more trouble than they are worth."

Now she put on a cocktail dress, suitable for her calling as a barmaid. It was a bright blue crepe, tight over the big hips, pleated and folded marvellously over the breasts, showing large areas of solid white neck and white shoulder. She put on diamanté earrings, a diamanté brooch. She inspected herself, then used thumb and forefinger to crimp her pale hair into waves around her face. Martha thought: I wonder what Andrew would say if he could see Maisie now, and this apparently communicated itself to Maisie, for she turnéd from the mirror, smiling unpleasantly, to say, "If Andrew could see me, he'd have a fit. Well, that's his funeral, isn't it?" She now came over to Martha, lifted the baby, and slid her under the covers of the little bed. Off went the light. The room, dimmed, seemed larger. Except for the child's bed, it was exactly the same as the bedroom in the flat where Maisie had lived with Andrew. The same plump blue shining quilt, the same trinkets and pictures. A girl's bedroom. But no photographs—not a sign of them: Binkie and Maisie's three husbands were not here.

"Have you heard from Andrew yet?"

"Yes, strangely enough. He said would I come to England to live. But I can't see myself. Of course you want to go to England and I can see that it takes all sorts."

She now sat near Martha on the bed, offered her a cigarette, lit one herself, and said, "Everything's nuts. When the war was bad, well we used to think, the war will be over soon, and so will our troubles. But it just goes on. Well, they *say* it's going to be over soon but why should it? I mean, they had a war for a hundred years once, didn't they? But Athen says it will be over soon."

"Have you seen Athen?"

Maisie's face changed to an expression Martha had seen there before, when Athen was mentioned. A new look—resentment. "He came in to see me last week. Well, he's too good for this world, I can tell you that!" Then she sighed, lost her bitterness and said, "Yes, it's a fact, he's not long for this world." At Martha's look she nodded and insisted, "Yes, it's true when they say the good people go first. Look at my two first husbands, they're dead, aren't they?"

"And Andrew's bad just because he's still alive?" said Martha, smiling.

At this Maisie jumped up and said, "We'll wake Rita if we natter in here." She pushed open the window and instantly the room reeked from the spilt beer on the pavement just below. She shut the window again, saying, "Well, lucky it'll be winter soon, I can have the windows shut. Sometimes I can't stand the smell, and then the men from the bar start fighting and being sick so I can't sleep sometimes."

She went into the other room and Martha followed.

"I'm late for the bar," said Maisie, and sat down calmly, to smoke. "Athen says he wants to see you, Matty."

"Well, I'm always happy to see him."

"Yes, he's one of the people . . . " Again resentment, a sighing, puzzled resentment. "All the same, Matty. He said I shouldn't be working in a bar. I said to him, 'All right then, you find me a job where I can have my baby, just above my work all the time, you find me that job and I'll take it.' And then he went on and on, so I said, 'And what about your mom and your sisters? Didn't you tell me the things they had to do because they were poor? They had to do bad things. And your sister married a man she didn't love because he said he'd pay your mom's debts. Well, you said that didn't you?' And he said, 'Yes, but they were poor and you aren't.' Well, Matty, that made me so mad . . . " Her voice was shaking, her eyes full of tears. "Excuse me a sec, Matty." She went to the bedroom to fetch a handkerchief, and came back saying, "Well, who'd be a woman, eh?" exactly as she used to; and Martha saw the old, maidenly, fighting Maisie in the fat barmaid dressed garishly for her work.

Martha said, with difficulty, "You know, Maisie, I used to think you could love Athen if . . . "

Maisie gave Martha a look first conscious, then defiant. "Love. That's right. Well, he's the best man I've ever known in my life, I'll grant you that much. But what would he do with me in Greece? He doesn't even know when they're sending him back. There are six Greeks hanging about here, all trained to the ears to be pilots, but they don't send them to Greece. Athen says it's because of politics. Well, but he won't be a pilot after the war, and he used to be a newspaper seller. But anyway, I wouldn't be good enough for him would I? I told you, he's too good for this world and I told him that too."

"So he's coming to see me?"

"He's got a message about something. Something political about the blacks, I think it was. He told me but I forgot. He said he'd come this week so expect him. And you can tell him from me I'm not a bad girl just because I work in a bar."

"Well, Maisie, I don't believe he really thinks so."

"He says it, doesn't he?" Maisie lit a new cigarette, said again, "I should go down," but remained where she was. "There's some brandy in the cupboard if you like, but I can't stand drinking myself any more, after having to smell it every night down there." Martha got herself a brandy, and did not offer Maisie any; but when the bottle was put back, Maisie got up, went to the cupboard, poured herself a large brandy, and stood holding the glass between two hands against her breasts. The light fell through the rocking golden liquid and made spangles on the white flesh, and Maisie looked down, smiled. A great fat girl peered over a double chin and giggled because of the spinning lights from the liquid.

Giggling she said, "Well, let's have it, Martha. It's no good us sitting here and chatting about this and that just because we don't like thinking about it."

"It" was Mr. Maynard, the Maynards, and their pressure on Maisie.

Some weeks before, Mr. Maynard had telephoned Martha, demanding an interview. Martha had said that, since she had been told it was the Maynards who had arranged for Andrew, Maisie's husband, to be posted from the Colony, she never wanted to see or hear of the Maynards again. And had put down the telephone.

Mr. Maynard was waiting for her on the pavement when she left the office that evening. She tried to walk past him, but found her path blocked by a large, black-browed urbane presence who said, "My dear Martha, how very melodramatic, I am extremely surprised."

He then proceeded to talk, or rather, inform, while she stood, half-listening, wishing to escape. When he had finished she said, "What you mean is, you want me to go down to Maisie's, spy on her, find something wrong, and then come back and tell you so that you can persecute her."

"My dear Martha, the mother of my grandchild is working as a barmaid. You can't expect me to like that. My grandchild is being brought up in one of the most sordid bars in the city. I'm not going to stand for it."

"The only thing is, it isn't your grandchild."

At which he said, calm, forceful, his handsome dark face compressed with determination, "That child was fathered by my son. She is my granddaughter."

Martha could not stand up to him. She said, "I've got to go"—and literally ran away from him. That evening she had come to Maisie's

rooms late, when the bar was closed, to tell her that Mr. Maynard
was still on the scent.

Some hours later, waking at five in the morning, she realized,
appalled at her's and Maisie's readiness to be bullied, that there
was one simple way of defeating Mr. Maynard—and that was to take
no notice of him. She had telephoned Maisie that morning to say so.
Maisie said she had written the old bastard a letter which would
put him in his place forever. "But, Maisie, that's just where we
make our mistake, that's what I'm telephoning for. You shouldn't
have written because he has no right to a letter, that's the whole
point."

"Oh don't worry, Matty, I said what was right."

The letter Mr. Maynard got read:

Dear Mr. Maynard,
    My friend Mrs. Martha Hesse told me what you said. Please
don't worry, my Rita is being brought up properly. Just as well as
Binkie would, I'm sure of that. Binkie had his chance and lost it.
And there is another thing I want to say. I know who it was who
had my husband Corporal Andrew McGrew sent away to England. And I wish to have nothing to do with you or with Binkie
either. Please tell him so when he comes home.
                                Yours truly,
                                MAISIE McGREW.

This letter, written at white-heat, was pondered by the Maynards
for some days. Mr. Maynard then again waylaid Martha outside her
office.

"Well, Martha, you seem to be playing some kind of double
game."

"What do you mean? You know I'm with Maisie." She knew it was
a mistake to say this; she should simply have walked past him.
Now he smiled.

She said, "Mr. Maynard, you haven't got any legal right to that
child. You haven't got a moral right either."

He smiled again, the commanding face presented to her so that
she could feel the full pressure of its assurance. Again she walked
off, thinking: There wasn't anything he wanted to say, there was
nothing new to say, so what was he waiting there for? At last she
understood: Of course, he wants to know whether I can be bullied.
And I can be. And so can Maisie.

She had therefore gone down to spend an afternoon with Maisie.

It was a Saturday. They had walked in the park with the child, then gone back to the rooms and played with her. When she went off to sleep, they talked. Mr. Maynard seemed remote. They laughed a great deal and said how ridiculous the Maynards were, pushing people around and thinking they could get away with it.

And again it had been only afterwards, waking in the night, that Martha understood the whole pleasant easy afternoon was in fact another victory for Mr. Maynard. For one thing, his name, the Maynard name, had scarcely been off their tongues. Yet the essence of defeating Mr. Maynard was to forget him.

And Martha's being here now with Maisie was because Mr. Maynard telephoned yesterday, "How's my grandchild?" "She's not your grandchild, Mr. Maynard."

"Maisie, the Maynards haven't a legal right, they haven't even a moral right to Rita. You've got to see it."

"They didn't have a legal right or a moral right to send my husband away from this country. But they did it, didn't they?"

"That was because Mrs. Maynard's a cousin of the Commanding Officer."

"You know what I am saying, Matty, and it's true."

"Yes, I know. But look, what do you suppose the Maynards could do? They can't do a damned thing."

"After I posted that letter to Mr. Maynard, I saw I'd put it into print."

"But, Maisie, when you married Andrew, he became Rita's father. The Maynards are out."

"But I'm divorced from Andrew."

"It doesn't matter."

"So you say. All I know is, the Maynards do as they like. And he's a magistrate too. I lay awake last night thinking . . . "

Maisie stood in the middle of the little room, holding the glass of rocking liquid against her breasts, smiling, smiling nervously, while her serious blue eyes stared ahead, sombre with fear. She sipped brandy nervously, held the glass against her breasts; sipped, smiled, pressed the glass against her flesh so that the white and gold and green lights made jewels on her flesh above the glitter of the diamanté brooch. She talked on, obsessively, "When Binkie gets back I'm going to see him and ask him to stop his parents driving me mad. He's a decent kid, he'll know it isn't right. After all, it's not his fault he's got those old bastards for parents, he'll tell them off, when I ask him."

"What'll happen if Binkie still wants you back?"

"He's a decent kid, he's not their kind, he'll see right done. And anyway, he won't be back for ages yet. Perhaps years. How do we know how long the war'll go on? Perhaps he'll be killed, how do we know? Anyway, I've got to get down to work. My boss will be flaming mad as it is. You're a pal, helping me like this, and I don't like turning you out, but money's got to be earned, when all's said and done."

Martha got up, the two young women kissed, and Martha went out, saying, "Yes of course," in reply to Maisie's anxious, "If Mr. Maynard comes after you again, you'll let me know, won't you?"

In every city of the world there is a café or a third-rate restaurant called Dirty Dick's or Greasy Joe's. In this case Dirty Dick's was called so because Black Ally's, beloved of the R.A.F., had closed down last year and there had to be somewhere to feel at home. The old one had been run by a good-humoured Greek who served chips and eggs and sausages and allowed the local Reds to put newspapers and pamphlets on the counter for sale to anyone interested. This restaurant was run by a small sad grey-haired man who was going home to Salonika when the war was over, and who would not allow his counter to be used as a bookshop because, as he said, he had a brother fighting against the Communists in Greece at that very moment—and where was the sense in it? No hard feelings against you personally, Mrs. Hesse . . .

When he knew that his place was called Dirty Dick's, his sound commercial sense exulted and he at once made plans for taking the floor over his present one; which second restaurant, to be on an altogether smarter level than this, would be called "Mayfair" to distinguish it from "Piccadilly," the name which was painted in gold on the glass frontages that faced a waste lot where second-hand cars were sold.

He nodded at Martha as she came into the large room, recently a warehouse, which had one hundred tables arranged in four lines. Every table was occupied by the R.A.F., so that the place looked like a refectory or mess for the armed forces. "Mr. Cohen is in the back room," he said.

"You don't mind us plotting in your restaurant, but you won't sell our newspapers?"

"I can't stop you plotting, but I won't sell your newspapers."

The private room at the back had a large table in its centre, covered with a very white damask cloth on which stood every imaginable variety of sauce and condiment. Solly was waiting.

"I can't sit down," said Martha, "because I'm late."

"Oh, go on . . . " Solly pushed forward a chair, and Martha sat, suddenly, closing her eyes, and scrabbling for a cigarette which Solly put between her lips already lit. "If you'll take a cigarette from a dirty Trotskyist."

"I thought Joss was going to be here?"

"Ah, you'll take a cigarette from a dirty Trotskyist if protected by a clean Stalinist?"

"Oh, Lord, Solly, I've only just come, have a heart."

Here entered Johnny Capetenakis, smiling.

"What have you got to *eat*?" asked Solly.

"Fried eggs, chips and sausages," said Johnny, wiping the glittering white of the cloth with another cloth.

"I mean food."

"Ah, why didn't you say so? A nice kebab? Saffron rice? Stuffed peppers?"

"How about you, Matty?"

"I've got to go."

"Everything you've got that's food—twice. My brother'll be here in a minute."

"Right, Mr. Cohen."

He stood smiling, but Solly had turned to Martha, and the Greek switched on a couple more lights and drew a curtain across panes that showed a sudden dark where the stars already blazed.

He stood looking out, his hand on the sill, an ageing man glad of a moment's chance to rest. Solly turned to see why he was still there and said, "Sit with us a minute, Johnny?"

"Thanks for inviting me, but I'm a cook short tonight."

"Heard anything from home?"

Johnny shook his head. "Nothing good for your side or for mine and nothing will be."

"There'll be a Communist government in Greece after the war," said Solly. "But I'm as much against it as you are."

Johnny looked to see if he were joking; then he shrugged. "My brother was always the one for politics. It's not for me. My brother's wounded."

"I'm sorry," said Martha, politely.

"My cousin in Nyasaland got a letter but it was from last year, it came down from Cairo. My brother was wounded, but only in his leg."

As Solly said nothing Martha said, "I'm sorry," again, and took Solly's critical look with a smile.

"Yes, Mrs. Hesse, I suppose the good God knows what he is doing.

But there's not much left of my family, there's not much left of Greece by the time the war ends. Communist or not Communist. If the war ever does end." He nodded at them, sombre, and went out.

"All right then," said Martha, "but then why do we use this place practically as another office?"

"Get as much out of the dirty little fascists as we can, that's why."

"Oh, is that it? Well, what did you get me here for?"

"Don't be in such a hurry."

"I am in a hurry." She got up, to prove it.

"All right all right. I'm in contact with some contacts in the Coloured Quarter. As of *course* you know. There's a group of decent types. The point is, they've got a study group going with some Africans. Joss and I met them."

"*Joss?*" said Martha, disbelieving.

Here Joss came in, with a brief smiling nod at both of them. He sat down opposite his brother. He was in civilian clothes. The only sign he had been in the army was a red scar down his right hand—a gun had exploded in Somaliland last year and for him the war was already over. Four years in the army had burned out his youth. He had been an earnest student: now one could already see what he would look like in middle age. Except when you looked him straight in the eyes, you were looking at a Jewish business man.

Solly on the other hand had not changed at all: he was still like a student.

"I've ordered," said Solly to his brother.

"Good."

Joss waited, smiling. Martha waited. Solly said nothing.

"I'm in an awful hurry," Martha said.

"O.K., O.K., so you're in a hurry," said Solly.

She understood suddenly that this meeting was some sort of joke, or private triumph of Solly's, and that Joss did not know she was here "for a serious discussion."

"Oh, it really is *too* bad," she said, and her voice shook, although she tried to make it "humorous."

"What's going on?" said Joss. He spoke gently. He had understood, already, that she was on edge through one of the intuitive flashes of understanding by which human beings in fact understand and regulate their behaviour with each other. He, too, now lit a cigarette and handed it to her. "Keep your hair on and tell your Uncle Joss all about it."

"It's so damned silly," said Martha. "For months and months, nothing happens. Suddenly it seems the Africans are really starting something at last. Then we hear that there is Solly, with his oar well in, having his say. Well, naturally I suppose."

"Naturally," said Solly.

"Yes. But here *you* are, it seems you're with Solly?"

"God forbid," said Joss, humorous. But Martha kept her eyes on him and at last he said seriously, "If you're asking my advice, I think the *contradictions* should be kept out of it." This word contradictions was shorthand in this time for everything the Soviet Union did which went against what might be expected of that nation in her socialist aspect. Which meant, of course, everything. Except winning the war.

"Ah," said Martha thoughtfully, and looked at Joss with interest. He smiled, as if to say: Yes, I mean it.

"Except that it's not for you to keep the *contradictions* out of anything," said Solly. "You don't even know who these Africans are."

"Then why did you ask Matty here at all?" said Joss.

"An interesting point," said Solly, grinning. She looked at him— at first incredulous, then reproachful, then, seeing nothing but triumph, angry. She was blushing.

"Nonsense," she said energetically to Joss.

Joss had looked carefully at Solly, then at Martha, noting his brother's air of triumph and Martha's annoyance. He came to conclusions, and inwardly removed himself from the situation. "All that's got nothing to do with me."

"*Oh*," said Martha, furious. "How absolutely—Solly said I was to come here because of some African group."

"Awfully touchy, isn't she?" said Solly to his brother, echoing, for Martha, a situation a decade old, and arousing in her a remembered confusion of bitterness that made her pick up her bag ready to go. She was white, and she trembled. Anybody would think something serious had happened.

"Ah, Matty, man," said Joss gently, "relax, take it easy. Don't take any notice of my little brother. Everyone knows he's just a troublemaker." With which he offered his brother an unsmiling smile; he stretched his mouth briefly across his face and let it fall into seriousness again. Solly sat and grinned, rocking his chair back and forth.

"Look," said Martha direct to Joss, "I think your attitude is awfully . . . but I suppose you can't help him being your brother. The point is this. Solly's got this contact with an African group. But one of our people has a contact with it too, and he's—Solly is—trying to blacken us. Well, I think he is," she added, fair at all costs, and even looking at Solly in a way which said: I hope I am not maligning you. Which look Joss noted, and so, Martha felt at once, misinterpreted.

"Which one of us has got a contact with this group?" Joss asked Martha. She stared back in embarrassed amazement. Joss was asking her in front of Solly? Had Joss gone crazy? Or—was it possible?—had Joss, too "gone bad"?

"It is none other than Athen, your Greek comrade," said Solly, for Martha.

Here Johnny Capetenakis came in, with two plates balanced on his two held-out palms, his face offering them a gratified smile which preceded the food like its smell—a hot teasing aroma of garlic, lemon and oil. He set before Joss, before Solly, spikes stuck with glistening pieces of lamb, lightly charred onion rings, tiny half-tomatoes, their skins wrinkled and dimmed with heat and their flesh sprinkled with rosemary, smooth whole mushrooms, curls of bacon striped pink and white. These were displayed on large mounds of yellow rice.

"Without you, we'd die of hunger," said Joss.

"I'm still using the saffron from before the war," said the Greek. "When it's finished, then I really don't know."

"You'll have to grow it," said Martha.

"The war's going to end, cheer up," said Joss.

Johnny stood smiling benevolently as the brothers began to eat. Then he went out.

"Athen and Thomas Stern," said Solly.

"Oh, is Thomas back in town, good," said Joss. He looked up for some bread and there was Martha, still standing and waiting. "I'm here," he excused himself, "to eat kebab with my little brother. I didn't know there was anything else."

"Then, I'm going."

"Yes. I'll deal with my ever-loving brother for you."

"Obviously."

"What do you want me to do? If the Africans have started something—then about time too, and we should help them. And keep the nonsense out of it—the contradictions."

He did not look up—his head was bent over his food. Martha stood watching the brothers eat. She was hungry, but she had promised to eat with her mother. Inside her opened up the lit space on to which, unless she was careful (this was not the moment for it) emotions would walk like actors and begin to speak without (apparently) any prompting from her. This empty lit space was because of the half-dozen rooms she had to run around, looking after. The tall lit space was not an enemy, it was where, some time, the centre of the house would build itself. She observed, interested, that it was now, standing there looking at the Cohen boys, the antagonists, that the empty space opened out under its searchlights.

Feeling her silence, first Joss, then Solly, lifted their heads to look at her. She saw the two men, both with loaded forks in their hands, their heads turned sideways to look at her. She began to laugh.

"She thinks we are funny," said Joss to Solly.

"She's laughing at us," said Solly to Joss.

"Well, I'll see you around, anyway," she said to Joss.

"I don't think you will."

"Why not?"

"I'm thinking of settling up North. I'm going up to spy out the land tomorrow."

"Ah, I see!" Everything explained at last, Martha began to laugh again. She stopped, as she felt this laughter begin to burst up like flames, in the middle of the great empty space.

"She sees," said Solly to Joss.

"But what does she see?" said Joss to Solly.

"I might have known," said Martha. "Joss is leaving the country, and so of *course* he doesn't care. And neither would I, in his place."

"Speak for yourself," said Joss, suddenly, not looking at her, but filling his mouth.

"There won't be anybody left in this place a week after the war ends. Off you all go, and the moment you leave, it's just too bad about us." She left the intimate, odorous little room with the two men bent over their places, pressed her way through the tables crammed with the R.A.F., said goodbye to Johnny at the entrance desk, and gained the fresh air and her bicycle. She was thinking: Damn, Joss. Suddenly she remembered his "speak for yourself." It occurred to her for the first time, that perhaps *he* was there under false pretences too, and that in fact he was concerned to stop Solly knowing what he was up to. In which case, she was an idiot, had proved herself an utter . . . She bent to unlock her bicycle, and Solly's arms came around her waist from behind.

A couple of weeks ago there was a meeting on the Allied invasion of France—"Second Front, at last!" Solly had been there, heckling. He had waited outside afterwards, to heckle again, privately. He and Martha had walked through the emptying streets, in bitter argument, their antagonism fed by their ten years' knowledge of each other. Outside Martha's door they had embraced, violently, as if they had been flung together.

"Sex," Solly had said, "the great leveller," and she had laughed, but not enough.

Now she turned, swiftly, putting the bicycle between herself and Solly. Grinning, he laid his hand on her shoulder, where it sent waves of sensation in all directions.

"Surely, you'd admit there's some meeting ground?"

"No, I wouldn't."

"Liar."

"What did you have in mind, that we'd go rolling around over the pamphlets in the office, in between calling each other names like dirty Trotskyist?"

"Dogmatic Stalinist, these things can always be managed, if there's a will."

"But there isn't."

Martha knew she was smiling, direct into his smiling face. She could not stop. Their faces approached each other as if a hand behind either head pushed them together. They stood on the pavement, the bicycle between them, and a third of an inch of glass between them and the customers inside the Piccadilly. The bicycle pedal grazed Martha's bare leg, and she said, "Damn," and pulled herself away.

"What a pity," said Solly softly.

"Yes, I daresay."

She got on her bicycle and pedalled off.

If she lived, precariously, in a house with half a dozen rooms, each room full of people (they being unable to leave the rooms they were in to visit the others, unable even to understand them, since they did not know the languages spoken in the other rooms) then what was she waiting for, in waiting for (as she knew she did) a man? Why, someone who would unify her elements, a man would be like a roof, or like a fire burning in the centre of the empty space. Why then, was she allowing herself to respond to Solly as she had the other night, and would again, unless she made certain she wouldn't meet him? What had she got in common with Solly—except sex, she added, but couldn't laugh, for the truth was she was in a flaming, irritable bad temper. She cycled like a maniac between lorries, cars, bicycles, the headlights dazzling, scarlet rear-lights winking. She did not like Solly, apart from not approving of him.

Two blocks down from the Piccadilly was an Indian grocer and over it the new office, held in the name of the departed Jasmine

Cohen. It was used by half a dozen organizations who shared the rent. Martha let herself up dark unlit stairs, and opened, in the dark, a door, and turned the light on in a dingy little office which was the same as every political office she had ever seen. A small dark dapper man in the uniform of a Greek officer rose from a bench by the window. Athen smiled and said, "Matty, I'm glad it was you who came in."

"What are you doing sitting alone in the dark?"

He did not answer, she looked quickly at his face and went on, "I've come to pick up some books for Johnny Lindsay, and I'm late."

"But I must see you. When shall I see you?"

"Tomorrow?"

"But I have to go back to camp tonight."

"After Johnny Lindsay I must go and see my father and then I suppose I've got to go home."

She heard her own voice, desperate rather than angry, and raised her eyes to the grave judging eyes of the Greek.

"Your father is very ill," he said, in rebuke.

"I know that."

"And how is your husband?"

He had said your husband, instead of Anton, deliberately, and she smiled, freeing herself from his judgement. "Ah, Athen," she said affectionately, "you know, meeting you I'm always remind-ed ..."

He smiled and nodded, and did not ask what she had been going to say. People know what their roles are, the parts they play for others. They can fight them, or try to change; they can find their roles a prison or a support: Athen approved his role. Possibly he had even chosen it. He was a conscience for others. He burned always, a severe, self-demanding steady flame, at which people laughed, but always with affection; from which they took their bearings.

"Sometimes you seem to me almost impossibly naïve," she said apologetically, and he went on smiling, looking closely at her.

"Naïve? Because I remind you of your marriage with Anton?"

"I'm *not* married."

"Martha, are you well?"

"Yes, of course," she said, irritable. But his look refused this and she said, "I may be well, but I'm certainly in a very odd state. I don't think I understand anything." Tears filled into her eyes, frightening her because they came so often.

Athen took her by the hand, sat her on the wooden bench by the wall, sat by her, stroked her hand. "Martha, dear Comrade Martha, do you know something strange? I was thinking just as you came in, you know when I was a poor boy selling newspapers on the street in Athens, if someone had told me then that a white person in Africa could be a socialist and that I would be the comrade of such a person, then I should have laughed."

"Well, you would have been right to laugh."

"Why do you say that? You have many bad thoughts, Martha."

"Is that a bad thought? Why? When the war's over, you'll go back and sell newspapers and you'll live on tuppence-halfpenny. You'll be poor again. Suppose I never leave this country, suppose I never can get out? Well, what do you imagine we'd have in common then?"

"Martha, Martha. Why do you supose this and that? After the war we will fight till we have Communism in Greece, and then you will come to visit me in Greece and be my friend."

"Perhaps so."

"I wanted to see you and talk. Now you have to go."

"Yes. I'm late. I always seem to be late."

"How is Johnny Lindsay?"

"He's very ill. I do nothing but run from one sickbed to another. And I hate it and resent it, I hate illness."

Athen sat smiling, his small neat hand enclosing her hot one.

"My father's dying. He lies and thinks of nothing but himself and his medicines. And Johnny's dying—but he's a *good* man, so he thinks of other people all the time."

"Well, then, Comrade Martha?"

"Nothing. That's all. My life's always like this, it's always been like that—very crude and ridiculous."

After a minute he took his hand away from hers and sat, straight, his two hands on his knees, looking at the wall. She felt rejected, but could not withdraw anything.

"Well," he said at last, "it's time I went home. I live from day to day, waiting to be sent home. I am so much with my friends, in. my mind, that perhaps I cannot be a good friend to my friends here."

"Haven't you heard anything?"

"They won't send us back unless they have to—why should they send back six fully trained pilots when they know we'll escape and join the Communists the moment we get home? Of course not, if I were in their shoes I would keep us here too."

"I'm sorry, Athen. I suppose it's the same for everyone—we just have to wait, that's all."

"I want to talk with you about something important. If you have time when you have visited your father, then come to the Piccadilly."

"I'll try. What is it?"

"I've been talking to a man who lives in Sinoia Street. I want you to help him and his friends."

After a moment, she laughed. He waited, smiling, for her to explain.

"*You* have been talking to a man who lives in Sinoia Street. I've just come from Solly and Joss. *They* told me about contacts in the Coloured Quarter with the right sort of idea who have contacts with Africans."

"Well, perhaps I might have said that too," he said, laughing.

"Oh, no, oh, no, you wouldn't, and that's the point. Anyway, I'm going." From the door she said, "I saw Maisie this afternoon."

"That reminds me, Martha. I would very much like to talk to you about Maisie." She could not prevent herself searching his face to find out what he felt about Maisie, but he quickly turned to the window, away from her gaze.

She found the books Johnny wanted, and went out. In the street she looked up; the window was already dark, Athen had turned the light out again. A hand fell on her shoulder, at which she remembered Solly's touch and knew that this solid pressure was not his. She turned to see a brown stout young man smiling at her. "What are you doing, Matty? I was wondering who'd be in the office, and here you are standing gazing up into the sky with your mouth open."

"My mouth wasn't open! How are you? I heard you were back."

"Only for a week. It's still my fate to be banished in W . . . "

"Then that's a pity. Your study group's collapsed."

Thomas Stern had been in this city the year before, for a couple of months, during which short time his energy had created a state of activity not far from "the group's" achievements at its height. Study groups, lectures, etc., flourished for a few weeks, and stopped when he left.

"If a study group's dependent on one person, then it's not worth anything."

This didacticism was so like him that she laughed, but said, "I'm late, Thomas."

"Naturally. But when you're finished what you're late for come and have supper at Dirty Dick's."

"I can't. But if you want company, then Athen's sitting in the office all by himself." She cycled off, calling back, "Next time you come up, give me a ring." But he had already gone inside the building.

In a few minutes she was there. In the squalid night of this part of the city, the little houses of the poor street Johnny lived in blazed out light, noise, music. Children ran about over the hardening mud ruts from the recently ended rainy season; or carried long loaves of bread to their mothers from the Indian shop where a portable gramophone stood jigging out thin music on an orange box outside the door. The gramophone was watched by a small and incredibly clean little Indian boy whose white shirt dazzled like a reproach in the dirty gloom.

The verandah of the house was nothing but bricks laid straight into the dust with a few feet of tin propped over it. Martha chained her bicycle to the yard fence. The door from the verandah opened direct into a brightly lit room which had in it a great many books, a straw mat over a rough brick floor, a table with four chairs all loaded with papers and pamphlets, and a bed where Johnny Lindsay lay, very still, very white, his eyes closed, breathing noisily. Beside him on one side sat Mrs. Van der Bylt, her large firm person held upright on a small wooden chair; on the other was Flora, knitting orange wool which was almost the colour of her flaming shiny hair. At the foot of the bed a young man of twenty-two or -three sat reading aloud, from a long report in that day's *News* about conditions in the mining industry.

Flora, the pretty, blowsy middle-aged woman with whom the old miner had shared his life for ten years now, counted stitches and was obviously following her own thoughts. She smiled briefly at Martha, but it was Mrs. Van who nodded at Martha to sit down. The young man, a teacher from the Coloured School, half-rose, and looked at Mrs. Van whether to go on or not. Johnny opened his eyes to discover why the reading had stopped, saw Martha, filled labouring lungs and said, "Sit down, girlie," patting the bed. "They are making me stay in bed," he said, with the naughtiness of an invalid disobeying overprotective nurses. But in fact he was very ill, as Martha could see. She said, "Don't talk. Look, here are the books." She laid them on the thin, white counterpane, beside the old man's very large hand where pain showed in the tense knuckles. Everything in this room was most familiar to Martha from her father's sickroom: the smell of medicines, the attentive tactful people sitting around it, the invalid's overbright smile—and above all the look of shame in his eyes, the demand which said, This isn't *I*—this humiliating noisily suffering body isn't me.

"Johnny, I'm terribly late, I must rush off."

Mrs. Van frowned. Martha said, "I'm expected at my father's," and Mrs. Van smiled. Martha saw the fat old woman examining her—"like a headmistress" she could not help thinking. The small, piercing blue eyes that rested their steady beam on her had missed nothing—not even the small smudge of oil from the bicycle chain on her leg.

"Before you run off, I think Mr. de Wet would like to meet you, Martha," said Mrs. Van.

The young man rose, as if he had been ordered—well, he had been, in fact. He smiled politely at Martha, but waited for Mrs. Van to go on.

"Clive has a contact, an African contact. He wants to start a study group of some kind and I thought it would be useful if he could discuss things with you—you could order books for them. And so on."

"We have started the study group," said Clive abruptly. He sounded annoyed, though he had not meant to. Mrs. Van said quickly, "Well, in that case perhaps it's all right."

Martha thought this all out: Clive was Clive de Wet, the "man in Sinoia Street" mentioned by Athen, the "contact" mentioned by Solly. He also knew Thomas Stern. Mrs. Van could not know he was already the happy recipient of so much attention. The fact that he had not told Mrs. Van he already had at least three white people ready to supply "books and so on" meant that he did not trust her? Certainly he did not trust her, Martha, since Solly would have seen to it that he did not.

Martha said to Clive, "If you want to see me at any time, here is my telephone number." She scribbled her office number on a scrap of paper and handed it to him. He took it with a tiny hesitation which said that Martha had been quite right in diagnosing a dislike of so much interest.

She noted Mrs. Van's shrewd face accurately marking and analyzing all these tiny events and knew that she could expect from Mrs. Van, not later than lunchtime tomorrow, a telephone call enquiring, "Well, Matty, and what *is* going on with that study group? Why haven't I been told?"

Martha, Clive de Wet and Mrs. Van were watching each other, thinking about each other, all as alert as circling hawks. Meanwhile Johnny lay, eyes closed, on his pillows, and Flora clicked her needles. She was quite absorbed in her orange wool, and would have understood nothing of this scene.

Martha finally nodded and smiled at Mrs. Van, nodded at Clive de Wet, and tiptoed to the door over the slippery grass of the mat.

In the street the children were swooping and darting like so many swallows through the dusk and the little Indian boy was winding up his gramophone, which played Sarie Marais.

Now she must visit her father and then, thank goodness, she could go to bed early.

She made the transition from one world to another in fifteen minutes, arriving in the gardened avenues as they filled with cars headed for the eight o'clock cinemas. Everything dazzled and spun under racing headlights, but the Quests' place had trees all around it. It had always been a garden which accommodated a house, rather than a house with a garden. The stiff, fringed, lacy, fanning and sworded shapes of variegated foliage, shadowed or bright, hid the bricks and painted iron of an ordinary, even ugly house from whose windows light spilled in dusty yellow shafts through which moths fluttered. The strong shafts from the busy headlights swept across the tops of bushes, the boughs of trees. But at walking level, everything was dark, quiet.

Martha dumped her bicycle on gravel and ran up shallow steps where geranium spilled scented trails. No one on the verandah, but from a window which opened off it the sound of a child's voice, "Granny, Granny, I don't want pudding."

Martha's heart went small and tight; she fixed her smile neatly across her face, and went into the living room, on tiptoe. It was empty but the radio was on, the gramophone played the Emperor at full blast, and a small white dog rose to yap pointlessly, its tail frantically welcoming. Martha shushed the dog, turned off the gramophone, and received news of the war in Europe: Starvation was killing off the Dutch people. The Allies had made 70,000 prisoners. The Düsseldorf bridges had been blown up. Only forty sorties were flown by our Tactical Air Forces today, though medium bombers made a successful attack through ten-tenths cloud on a marshalling yard at Burgsteinfurt. The Germans' sense of war guilt was growing, and their nerves were "shot" as a result of the bombing. Behaviour of German civilians in the Rhineland was so servile that words like "cringing" were frequently and not unjustifiably used. Tommies and G.I.'s alike were developing the deepest contempt for the "herrenvolk." Life had almost stopped. Fields where corn should be growing were deeply marked by the tracks of manoeuvring tanks or were pitted by thousands of shell and bomb holes. It would need four years to get the Ukraine, our gallant Ally's granary, going again. Never before in this war had the Allies had such favourable weather before a major operation. The vastly superior number of Allied tanks and armoured vehicles, once across the Rhine, should find good going on the hard dry plains of the Northern Ruhr. A Liberator pilot said today, "Hundreds of fighters were strafing and diving below over what was the most tremendous battle I ever hope to see." There were still hundreds and thousands of Germans living among the ruins of Cologne. The whole central part of the city was a chaos of debris. There were riots in Czechoslovakia.

Perhaps she could see her father before her mother knew she was there?

She went quietly down the passage to the room at the back of the house, and knocked gently. No reply. Inside a scene of screened lights and the smell of medicines.

An old, neat, white-haired man lay on low pillows, his head fallen rather sideways, and his mouth open. His teeth were in a glass of water by the bed, and his jaw had a collapsed graveyard look.

Martha said, softly, "Father," but he did not move, so she went out again.

Mrs. Quest came down the passage with her hands full of ironed white things. There was a hot clean smell of ironing.

"Oh, there you are," she began, "you're late, aren't you?"

"Yes, I'm sorry."

"Just as well really, because I've only just this moment got Caroline off to sleep."

"I thought you said she was going home?" said Martha, automatically joining battle.

"Yes, but she looked a bit peaky, and I thought a bit of proper looking after would do her good."

The monstrous implications of this sentence caused Martha to flush with anger, but Mrs. Quest had already gone on to worse, "Better be quiet, keep your voice down sort of thing, because she doesn't know you are here."

Martha went straight past her mother, containing futile anger, to the living room. Again the little white dog leaped down off a chair, and began bounding like a rubber ball around Martha, yapping incessantly.

"God help us," shouted Martha, at last finding a safe target for anger. "That damned dog has seen me most days for three years and it still barks."

"Down Kaiser, down Kaiser, down!" Mrs. Quest's fond voice joined the symphony of yaps, and a little girl's voice said outside, "Granny, Granny, why is Kaiser barking?"

"Out of sight!" commanded Mrs. Quest dramatically.

Martha turned a look on her mother which caused the old woman to drop her eyes a moment, and then sigh, as if to say: I'm being blamed again! She whisked out of the room, and Martha heard, "Oh, Caroline, you wicked girl, what are you doing out of bed?"

But Mrs. Quest's voice, with the child, had the ease of love, and Caroline's voice came confidently, "I'd like it better if I could have Kaiser in my room, Granny."

"Well, we'll see."

Do you suppose, Martha wondered, that when I was little she talked to me like that? Is it possible she liked me enough?

The telephone rang, Mrs. Quest came bustling in to answer it, the cook announced from the door that the meat was cooked, and from the end of the house sounded the small bell that meant Mr. Quest was awake and needed something. Martha was on her way to her father, when Mrs. Quest came past her at a run, and the door to the sickroom opened and closed on her father's voice, "Oh there you are. What time is it?"

Martha went back to the darkened verandah, and peered into the room which held her daughter. A small dark girl squatted in the folds of a scarlet rug, fondling the ears of the white dog. "Your name is Kaiser," she was saying. "Did you know that? Your name is King Kaiser Wilhelm the First. Isn't that a funny name for a pooh dog?" The dog rolled adoring eyes, and flickered a pink tongue at the child's face. Martha heard her mother charging down the passage, and she withdrew from the window.

"I'm sorry about that, Matty, but I gave him a washout earlier, and as I thought, he wanted the bedpan."

"Oh, it's really all right. I'll see him tomorrow."

"I really don't know what I'm going to do if it goes on like this. It's been five days without any real result and I gave him two washouts yesterday alone. Yes, cook?"

"Missus, the meat's ready, missus."

"Well, I think you'd better try to keep it hot. The doctor's coming, he might like some supper."

Martha tried not to show her relief. "But, Mother, I can't wait for supper for hours."

"I wasn't expecting you to," said Mrs. Quest, hoity-toity, but triumphant. "Anton has telephoned me three times, he was expecting you hours ago."

"Then he must have misunderstood."

"One of us certainly did, because I got in a beautiful bit of sirloin, and now it's going to be wasted, unless the doctor eats it."

"I'll get home then," said Martha. She almost ran down the steps to her bicycle, with Mrs. Quest after her, "I had a letter from Jonathan today."

"Oh, did you?"

"Yes, he's got sick-leave in Cairo, but he's being sent to a hospital in England."

"What's wrong?"

"He didn't say."

Jonathan had been wounded slightly in the leg at El Alamein, but recovered. Recently he had been wounded again in the arm, and the arm showed no signs of properly healing, much to everyone's relief. As Mr. Quest said, "If he gets out of it with nothing worse than a gammy arm, he'll be doing quite well."

"Shhhhh," said Mrs. Quest suddenly, as Caroline said from the window where she was swinging from the burglar bars, "Who's that lady, Granny, who is that lady?"

Martha picked up her bicycle, jumped on it, and cycled fast through the bushes to the invisibility which would enable Mrs. Quest to turn the child's attention to something else. At a telephone box, Martha rang the Piccadilly. Johnny was happy to bring his compatriot to the telephone. Martha told Athen she could not see him that evening.

"I'm sorry," came Athen's voice, raised against the clatter of a hundred eating humans. "Well then, I'll see you in about a week, and in the meantime, will you please see my friend Clive de Wet?"

"I met him this evening at Johnny's. I don't think he wants to see me. I'm sure of it."

"No, I spoke to him about you. He wants to see you."

"When did you speak to him?"

"I've just been to his house, he was there and I spoke to him. He said he thought you were associated with Mrs. Van."

"I don't understand, he was reading to Johnny, doesn't he approve of Johnny?"

"He does, very much. But he does not trust Mrs. Van, I think."

"That's ridiculous—how can he like Johnny and not like Mrs. Van?"

"At any rate, it would be helpful if you explain things to him. They need much help—they have no books, and wish to be taught many things."

"Oh, well, in that case . . . and I'll see you next week."

"Yes. And give my greetings to your husband."

And now, at last, she must go home to Anton. Home was a new place, half a flat, half a house—two little rooms, a bathroom and a shared kitchen that was really a screened-off verandah over a patch of shared dirty lawn. The woman they shared with was a Mrs. Huxtable. Martha did not like her, but as there was never any time for cooking anyway, it didn't matter.

Anton had telephoned her three times. Three times. The information had been received apprehensively by her nerves. Her emotions repeated, with monotony: It's not fair, it's not fair—meaning that this kind of demand, or reproach, was not in the bargain of her marriage with Anton. Meanwhile her brain was sending messages of warning that she was scared to listen to. For months now there had been a kind of equilibrium in the marriage. Having acknowledged it was a bad marriage, that they had made a mistake, that they would split up again as soon as the war ended, a sort of friendliness even kindness, even—perhaps?—a tenderness was established. But while, for Martha, this new relationship was welcome because it softened an intolerable strain, it seemed that for Anton it meant a new promise. At any rate, three different telephone calls in one afternoon was a language, a demand, Martha could not begin to answer.

Cycling past McGrath's Hotel, she remembered that after all she belonged to a world where people might sit drinking in large rooms, served by waiters; they might dance; they might even eat dinners (bad dinners, but formal, that was something) in restaurants. She would ring up Anton from the foyer and ask him to join her for a drink, and perhaps dinner. He would say, humorously, "And what are we celebrating, Matty, have I forgotten your birthday?"

He would protest at having to come, but he would be pleased. They could drink for an hour or so, have dinner, listen to the band, and in this way both could forget (Martha hoped) the implications of the fact that practically everything he said, or did, these days, was really a reproach for her not doing, or being, what he now wanted her to be.

2

It was almost seven. Martha had been waiting since five. Waiting now being a condition of her life, like breathing, it scarcely mattered whether she waited for an interview or for when peace would be restored—the new phrase, which showed that the old one "when the war ends," had proved inadequate. She waited with the whole of herself, as other people might pray, yet with even prayer become something to be practised, kept in use merely, since it could be effective only with the beginning of a new life. Waiting for her life to begin, when she could go to England, she waited for "the contact from the African group," and with the same ability to cancel out present time. She read half a pamphlet about Japanese atrocities with an irritated boredom with propaganda which did not mean she disbelieved what she read. She absorbed a column or so of statistics about African education but with the irritation of impotence. She filed her nails, brushed her hair as she never had time to do in her bedroom, fifty strokes on each side, tidied a cupboard full of pamphlets that dealt definitively with affairs in at least a hundred countries, and finally sat down with deliberately idle but restless hands on a bench under the window over Founders' Street.

The heat of a stormy day had drained into the scarlet flush that still spread, westwards, under bright swollen stars only intermittently visible. Hailstones from the recent storm scattered the street and lay on the dirty windowsill, and gusts of sharp cold air drove from racing clouds across the hot currents rising from the pavements. It would be winter soon, the ice seemed promise of it. Martha's calves sweated slipperily against the wood of the bench, and she sucked a bit of ice as an ally against heat, watching her smooth brown skin pucker under the golden down on her forearm into protest against cold. There was a blanket folded on top of the wooden cupboard. The blanket was because friends in the R.A.F. sometimes slept here if they were too late for the last bus to camp. Martha now spread it on the bench against the unpleasant slipperiness of sweat, and wrapped her legs in it. The hailstones, even under a crust of dirt, sent forth their cool smell, and Martha twisted herself about to watch the sky from where the winds of a new storm already poured over the town. Sitting with her back turned, she did not see that Solly had come in, and missed the moment when she could judge why he was here. For a moment the two stared deeply at each other. She broke it by saying, "I'm waiting for a man to come from the African group." She had decided on this admission to save half an hour of fencing. A bad liar, she knew it, and had thus acquired the reputation: Matty is *such* a sincere person. Meanwhile, part of her mind juggled to find convincing lies to put him off.

"It's such a pleasure having dealings with you, Matty, always as honest as the day."

"It occurred to me recently there's no point in being anything else, living in this—ant nest." Her voice was shrill, and she set guards on herself; noting meanwhile that "enemy" Solly ceased to be one when she thought of him as a fellow victim of the provinces. She smiled at him: as a cat which has been scampering about a crouching tom suddenly rolls over and lifts meek paws. Not quite, however. But the flash of seriousness on this young man's face (whatever the reason for it) when he had first seen her under the window had after all weakened the force of her decision not to like him. So would he look into her face from a few inches distance *if*. But he was now saying, vibrant with sarcastic hostility, "You have a point, I grant you. Yesterday I met a comrade of yours from the camp who said, how was Matty? I said what did he mean? It seems our liaison is common gossip."

"What fun for you."

"Well, I do hope so, Matty."

"The thing is, I have to meet Athen at seven and it must be that now."

"Well, I would be only too happy to wait to seduce you until you had finished conferring with Comrade Athen."

He was on the bench beside her. His face grinned into hers from not six inches away. Luckily, however, not at all "serious," far from it, so she was saved. She got up and began piling pamphlets about the Second Front (now unsaleable) into the cupboard.

"Solly, are you seeing Clive de Wet?"

"Why should I tell you, Comrade Matty?"

"Well, if you want to be childish."

"It's you who are childish. This is Solly Cohen, the Trotskyist."

"But it looks as if the African group want help?"

"There isn't an African group."

"But a group of Africans?"

"What can you do for them I can't do?

She shrugged and then laughed. The laughter was because of a picture so sharp to her imagination it was hard to believe it wasn't in his also: "the African group," like a small starving child, its hands held out for help, was being torn to pieces by a group of adults fighting for the right to help it.

At which moment came a knock on the door. Martha shouted, "Come in" and a small black boy came in, looking nervously from one to the other of the two white people.

"Missus Mart," he said.

"No Mrs. Mart here," said Martha.

"Idiot, it's you."

Solly was already grinning; he knew what was in the dingy envelope that the small boy held out.

A single sheet of exercise paper said:

Dear Mrs. Martha,

   I apologize for not coming this afternoon, I have been prevented by unavoidable circumstances. Hoping I may have the pleasure of your acquaintance at another time.

                           Yours sincerely,
                                 Signature illegible.

Probably purposely so.

"Who sent you?"

The little boy shifted his feet and his eyes and said, "Don't know, missus."

Martha gave him a shilling and he started to run off. She said, "Please tell whoever sent you that I will be here tomorrow afternoon at the same time."

"Yes, missus."

He vanished and Solly jeered, "Ever faithful Matty, waiting day after day in pursuance of duty. But he won't come, I've seen to it."

"Luckily you're not the only influence abroad. There's Athen and Thomas as well."

He grinned. "Dear Matty. What makes you think it's the same group?"

"Oh, isn't it? Well never mind, I'm late for Athen."

"May I have the pleasure of walking you to Dirty Dick's?"

"How do you know it's Dirty Dick's?"

"Where else?"

On the pavement large drops of warm rain fell all about them. She wriggled her shoulders inside damp cotton. The warm wet was lashed by cold. Overhead, miles overhead, very likely, air masses had shifted, had clashed, and here spears of acid-cold water mingled with fat warm drops from a lower region of sky. Lightning splurged across the dark, and Solly pulled Martha under an awning. He put his hot arms about her, and dropped a hot cheek close to hers, while ice from the clouds bounced around their feet.

"But, Solly, there's absolutely no point in it."

"Look where all this high-mindedness has got you? The arms of Anton Hesse. Not to mention the divorced arms of Douglas Knowell. Why didn't you listen to Joss and me? We told you, didn't we, and you'd never listen."

"All right. But I'm late for Athen."

The Piccadilly was empty. Rather, it had half a dozen civilians in it. Unpredictably the R.A.F. flowed in and out of the town, and tonight the tide was out—not a uniform in sight. The big oblong room, with its shiny yellow walls, that were usually hung with hundreds of caps, jackets, coats, its hundred tables tightly massed with grey-blue uniforms, was empty. At the end of the room, a neat dark little man in a light suit rose to meet them. Athen himself. Martha had never seen him out of uniform and she examined him while Solly said to Johnny, "Where are all our gallant boys?" But Johnny spread out his palms, empty of information, and shrugged.

"Any news from home?" Martha asked politely, as usual.

"It'll soon be over now. We've offered them . . ." here he nodded towards Athen, ". . . an amnesty. Yes, Elas and Elam will give themselves up now, you'll see."

Athen watched Martha approach and smiled. But he saw Solly and his face went on guard. Athen despised Solly. Not for being a Trotskyist: Solly was not a serious person, said Athen. Before taking a person's beliefs seriously, he must be worthy to have beliefs. At any rate, when Solly was mentioned he simply shrugged. As for Solly, since it was not possible to despise Athen, he regarded him as the dupe of Stalin. Martha was angry with herself for letting Solly be here. It was going to be another awful evening, another among hundreds. It was her fault. She could never remember that because she "got on" with people, it didn't mean they should "get on" with each other. She was always creating situations full of discordant people. It did not flatter her that she could: on the contrary. If such tenuous ties she had with people, easy contact, surface friendship, yet had the strength to bring them together, what did that fact say about them, about her, and—she would not be Martha if she did not go on —about associations, groups, friendships generally? And it was no quality to be admired in herself that made her a focus. She was, at this time, available. That was all. If not her, it would be someone else—just as, before her, it had been the du Preez and before them Jasmine Cohen.

Very well then, it seemed that for this period of her life, her role was to . . . Well, this evening, for instance, a group consisting of Athen and Solly and herself, and then these three (unless she could shed Solly and there seemed no likelihood of that) and Anton and Joss and Thomas Stern would all go to the pictures. And afterwards everyone would come home to their flat (Anton's and hers) and she would cook eggs for them. This was friendship. She reminded herself that ten years before she had been saying critically, in such different circumstances: This is friendship! and made herself pay attention to her present scene. Solly was looking at her, very close, across the table, reminding her with his eyes why he was here. And Athen was standing by his chair, face to face with Johnny Capetenakis, and the two men spoke low and fast in bitter Greek, their eyes burning hatred. Martha had never seen this Athen, and she thought that if these two men were now, this evening, standing in the same way on their mother soil, it would be to kill each other. Athen's eyes blazed murder; Johnny's eyes blazed back. Athen's fist trembled as it hung by his side. Johnny Capetenakis spat out a last low volley of hate and turned and went off to his desk by the door of the restaurant.

Athen sat down. "He says our people should give themselves up to the amnesty, they would be safe. I told him, it's not the first time. There's a clause, criminals will be shot. I told him, we know who these criminals will turn out to be. He tells me I am a traitor to my country."

He sat, sombre, looking about him with dislike, then he said, "I cannot stay here, I am sorry, but it is too much to sit here, in this man's place."

"Well, we're late for the pictures anyway."

Martha led the way out, greeting Johnny at the desk, not knowing whether she should feel disloyal for doing so or not. But she noted that Athen nodded at Johnny, and that Johnny nodded briefly back.

The rain had gone, the stars were washed clean, steam rose from the Tarmac that shone like dark water, reflecting rose and blue and gold. It was nearly eight. Main Street was filled with groups of civilians moving towards the cinema. No R.A.F., absolutely none.

"It might just as well be peace time," said Martha.

"There is a big man coming tomorrow," said Athen. "Everyone has to polish their buttons tonight."

"What big man?"

"From England. An Air Vice-Marshal."

"Why are you allowed out then?"

"All the Greeks have got weekend leave, all of us. They have worked it out: the Greeks are all Communists, and the Communists are anti-British, therefore the Communists will try to assassinate the Air Vice-Marshal."

Athen sounded bitter, and Martha who had been going to laugh, stopped herself.

"What are you complaining about," said Solly, "if you've got the weekend?"

Martha had never seen Athen like this: the gentle controlled little man was beyond himself, he was flushed with anger, he looked humiliated and his hands shook.

"This proves what I always said about the reactionaries. They always know *facts*. They always know who is a member of what. They know who has written letters to who. They know who has attended this meeting, that meeting. They know who is a man's relatives and who can be made to talk. This they know because of their spies. But they can never interpret these facts, because they put their own bad minds into our minds."

Athen stood bitterly on the pavement, talking—not to them. Martha and Solly stood on one side waiting.

"I used to say to our comrades in the mountains. If it is a question of fact, they will know. Yes. Be frightened of that, and guard against it. But if it is a question of intention—if they interrogate you and say: You mean this, you want this, then keep your mouths shut and do not worry. They know nothing. They are too stupid. Their Air Vice-Marshal is safe from us," said Athen, his white teeth showing in bitterness.

"Athen," said Martha gently, but he was going on. Probably, she thought (since he spoke often of that time) he was in a freezing cave above a pass as narrow as Thermopylae. Tomorrow, or next week, they—he and his soldiers—would roll boulders down bare brown hillsides patched with snow to crush one hundred and fifty of their countrymen who, in British uniforms and British-officered, were hunting them out. "I tell them," Athen said softly, "I tell them always: Remember who you are, comrades. Now we are like criminals hunted over the mountains, but soon that will end, and we will be men."

"We are going to be late," said Solly. He went on ahead, having decided to take the others on the offensive of his effrontery. Martha heard him say, "Good evening, comrades, one and all. And good evening, brother Joss!"

Athen had taken Martha's hand. "Martha, I have to ask you something serious."

From fifty yards off, Solly, then Joss called, "Come on, you two, it's late."

"Have you noticed a change in me?"

"Yes, I have."

"Thank you for saying so. It is true."

"Athen, have you seen Maisie?"

Athen let Martha's hand go and frowned. "I know why you ask me that, Martha."

More shouts from outside the cinema.

"I must talk about this with you, Martha."

They ran towards the cinema and the waiting group.

There was a girl in the group—a red-haired girl in a white dress. Whose? Not Solly's, this evening; so that meant she must be Joss's, or Thomas Stern's. Probably Thomas's—he liked thin girls. As Martha decided this, Thomas took both her hands—Martha's, announced that she looked terrible, very pale, and much too thin, and that while he was always her slave on principle, tonight, because of her irresistible look of illness—she was irresistible. So she must be Joss's girl? No time to find out, no time even to be introduced—Martha and the red-haired girl smiled goodwill, and then the group joined the crowd that was being sucked into the cinema, quickening as it went, like bath water into a hole. The manager stood by the box office, his smile benign, but not enough to conceal his disappointment at the absence of his best customers. He kept darting glances at the entrance in case at the last minute the familiar blue-grey uniforms would appear, and all his seats be filled. But there were, after all, many R.A.F. present, in ordinary clothes, like Athen, and soon the manager was smiling and urging his flock into the dark with smiles, a pressure of the hand, a pat on the shoulder. To Martha, who after all he had been welcoming for five or six years now, he said jovially, "And how are you these days, Mrs. . . .?" But he was unable to remember her current married name.

The programme had started. Across the screen that was lifted high in the big dark space over the crowded floor, moved a file of soldiers which, seen in the confusion, the jerking about of finding seats, then sitting, then finding places for handbags and jackets, looked like the columns which, in one Allied uniform or another, had marched, flown, parachuted across that screen for the last five years. But suddenly they understood the great, staring hollow-cheeked face they looked at was a German, and the uniform he wore, which was worn into rags, was a German uniform. The announcer's voice had a note they had not heard before. It was jeering: "And so here he is, the übermensch, the superman, the ruler of the world, here he is, and take a good look at him." The German on the screen was eighteen? A starved twenty-year-old? A bit of rag fluttered wildly on his shoulder, and he shivered so that it seemed as if the whole cinema shivered with him. He stared into the cinema crowd with eyes quite empty of expression. So he had stared a few days ago into the camera which took pictures of the defeated armies—he had stared probably not knowing what the machine was doing there or what it wanted. He stared, his cheekbones speaking of death, into the faces of a thousand full-fed people, his victorious enemies, in a little town in the centre of Africa.

The cinema was very silent. They were shocked, or in a state of mild shock, for a few moments. Then they began to realize, slowly. For the five years of the war, they had seen the faces of the enemy at a distance, had seen aircraft spinning down in flames and smoke; seen corpses like photographs in the newspaper—pictures of corpses; seen the posturing faces of enemy leaders; seen massed troops, massed tanks, armies, men in the mass, men on the move in columns, men in uniforms. Now they saw this face, close, close; and it was a shock, because the minds of the men who organized newsreels, war films, "propaganda," had taken care that this face, the face of a shocked frightened boy, should not stare, as close as a lover, into the face of a cinema audience.

"Yes, take a good look," went on the commentator in the same calculatingly sneering sarcastic tone. "You'll not see anything like this again in your lives. The Allies have fought this bitter terrible war so that it will be impossible, ever again, for Germany to threaten the world. So look closely at victorious Germany, look at the superman."

The Horst Wessel song, played fragmentarily and in leering, jeering, sliding discord, accompanied the newman's voice that went on, with its bought sarcasm, while the small whirling beams of light from the projectionist's cabin created on the blank uplifted wall of the cinema men, defeated men, men in the last extremity of hunger, cold and defeat, thousands and thousands of hollow-cheeked ghosts, a ghost army, limping, their feet in rags, rags binding hands, shoulders, heads, bits of cloth fluttering in the cold cold wind of that frigid spring at the end of the European war. They limped slowly, in a frightful ominous silence strong enough to drown the ugly voice of the commentator. They drifted slowly across dark air while a thousand or so of their victorious enemies watched in absolute silence.

"Take a good look, ladies and gentlemen. We have fought the good fight and we have won. Take a look and never forget: here they are, the herrenvolk, the master race, the rulers of the world."

And the frozen defeated men limped away across the war-torn countryside of Europe, their eyes black with pain and with shock. "Yes, that's the end of it, that's the end of the dream. That's the end of the conquest of the world. You have paid for this victory in blood, sweat, tears and suffering. Take a good look for that's the last you'll ever see of Germany, and the menace of Germany in Europe. We have fought the good fight together and we have won—the free countries of the world."

Beside Martha, Thomas Stern shifted about in his seat and said steadily under his breath, "Bastards, bastards, bastards." On the other side, Solly Cohen very softly whistled the Internationale between his teeth. Leaning forwards, Martha looked for Anton. How did he feel, the German, looking at his ghostlike countrymen, listening to the cheap easy sneer? His regular profile, like one on a coin, showed beside the pretty upturned profile of the red-head. Neither face said anything, they were people at a cinema, and so, presumably, was she, Martha, though she raged with useless protest which expressed itself, "I bet that commentator was making his voice say three cheers for Chamberlain at Munich, I bet he was."

"Well, of course," said Solly, and whistled the Internationale more loudly. Joss leaned forward to ask Martha, "Whose idea was it to bring my little brother to the pictures?" And Solly laughed aloud as Martha said, "Mine."

"Shhh," said someone in front; and someone else let out a sudden loud raspberry—the whole cinema seethed frustration, anger, resentment, discomfort. Suddenly, from somewhere at the back, there was a shrill whistle, and then a shout, "*Up* the R.A.F."

"Trust them," said Joss approvingly, as the tension broke.

"We shall miss you," said Solly loudly to the R.A.F., invisible tonight in their mufti.

A scuffle. The manager appeared, an outraged presence; torches swung agitatedly; the whole cinema turned to watch a couple of men, their faces the broad you-aren't-fooling-me faces of the North English, being escorted to the door. "All right, I can walk, thank

you very much!" Then a last muffled shout, "The R.A.F. forever,
I don't think."

When everyone again turned to see what was going on a small
dark aircraft sped, turned, soared, across skies lit with fire, while
tiny dark eggs spilled into a dark city which flung up great showers
of spark and flame.

Solly said, loudly, copying the practised jeer of the announcer
(who was, however, saying in a voice unctuous with victory that
the city—which?—was now without water supplies, sewage or railways as a result of this successful bombing raid)—"And see how
they run, the filthy vermin, away from the cleansing bombs of our
gallant boys."

A man turned around from the front and said, "If you haven't got
any patriotic feelings why don't you go home where you came
from?"

"Thanks," said Solly, "I will." He unwound his long thin person
from the discomfort of the seat and made his way out, whistling
the Internationale. "Jesus," said Joss, moving up to fill Solly's seat
near to Martha, "I suppose one day he'll grow up." He was embarrassed for his brother. "I don't know," said Martha, "I felt the
same."

On the other side of Martha, Thomas Stern sat, silent. But his
hands gripping the arm rests vibrated with tension. He muttered,
steadily, "Bastards, bastards, bastards."

When Martha turned to look at him, he said, "And you shut up.
All of you shut up. You can keep out of it."

Martha said, "Who?"

Joss's restraining hand came on her forearm and he said, "Better
leave Thomas alone. A friend of his was with the people who entered Belsen, he had a letter today."

On the screen now appeared shots of jungle—a lush scene, which
might have done for a musical. But flames engulfed it. Flames from
a flame-thrower seared the flesh of men, the substance of trees and
plants. Black ash crumbled where men, trees, and plants had been,
and drifted across the screen in greasy smoke which could almost
be smelt in the cinema. An island in the Pacific. After all, it was only
the war in Europe that was due to end any day. The war in the Pacific was being fought from island to island still, while Europe
crumbled in famine, cold, and ruined cities. Which island was this?
But Martha had missed its name, she would never know which
island she had watched being scorched by the flame-throwers,

just as she would never know which German city she had seen
being pulverized to ruins.

This was the main film now. A thick slow tune began to pulse
through the cinema. It was music easy and sexual which would, in
a moment, have welded the thousand people in the cinema into a
whole. A heavy velvet curtain swirled across the screen and back
again, and there appeared the apparently naked back of a blonde
woman. She stood in a doorway over which was a sign in electric
lights: Stage Door, and when she turned to smile at a group of soldiers (American) and at the audience (in central Africa) it became
evident that she was not as naked as it had at first appeared: her
dress was held up in the front by a ribbon which tied it around her
neck. Sequins flashed and glittered as the flames had flickered a
moment before, and her great friendly mascaraed eyes were as close
as the hollowed staring eyes of the frozen German soldiers. Her
homely breasts bulged almost into the teeth of the audience, and
the music intensified as half a dozen G.I.s filed grinning shyly past
the naked shoulders and sequined breasts of a famous film star
(acting as hostess for the sake of the war effort) into the club.

"I thought we were seeing the Seventh Cross," said Thomas. "For
crying out loud. I've got work to do."

It was Martha's fault—she had brought them to the wrong film.
Thomas had already stood up and was on his way out. Joss followed.
Anton got up, with the red-haired girl. In a moment they were
all on their way out, and people shushed and said, "What did you
come for then?"

They assured the manager they had only come for the news, so
upset was he that six patrons were leaving all at once, and found
Solly still on the pavement. Apparently he had known all the time
that the main film was bound to send them out of the cinema, and
he had been waiting for them.

The seven stood on the pavement. The Cohen boys, Solly and
Joss, both finished with uniform, both about to start life in peace
time. Athen the Greek, far from being finished with war, his life was
consciously planned for years of war, civil war, revolution. Thomas
Stern, frowning on one side of the group, obviously wanting to
leave it and be alone with his anger. He saw Martha looking at
him. He said in a low violent voice, "All right, Martha. But I tell you,
I'd torture every one of them myself, with my own hands."

She said, "Some of them looked about fifteen."

"Well? They should simply be stamped out—they should be wiped out, like vermin." But as he stood, sombre, apart from them, he made himself smile and said, "All right then. I'll shut up. I'll shut up for now, anyway."

Anton, the German, who waited day by day for the moment he could go home to Germany, was talking to the red-haired girl. She was looking up at him with self-conscious glances of admiration.

And suddenly Martha understood that this girl was Anton's girl. For Anton was self-conscious about her, was flattered that this girl, or woman (she was vivacious rather than pretty, with green eyes too quick and wary for youth) had publicly claimed him. She was now taking his arm. Just so, Martha thought, a young man publicly announces, without saying it in words, "This is my girl." He stood smiling, while the others looked on, *not* looking at Martha. And Anton did not look at Martha. The girl did, however. Not more, though, than she did at the others; she included Martha in her rapid self-conscious glances, while she kept laughing up towards Anton's pale and handsome face.

Martha felt, as she knew she was bound to feel, a pang. But she suppressed it: I don't want him, I don't enjoy him, but if someone else takes him then I start crying! She was thinking: Well, and so the conversation we had last week was meant to be taken seriously, was it? He really does mean to get himself a woman? Well, good for him.

The group was drifting across the street to a tea room. Martha was introduced, at last, to Millicent. Millicent, Martha. Hello, how are you?

Martha thought: Thomas and Solly and Joss are going to feel sorry for me because Anton has a girl! This caused Martha genuine pain, genuine resentment. She was furious with herself.

Outside the tea room, the group hesitated, not knowing whether it would remain a unit for another hour, or allow itself to separate into its parts. Martha arranged a smile and looked towards her husband and Millicent. But their arms were no longer linked. Anton stood on one side, apparently embarrassed. Solly bent over the girl, or woman, who stared straight up at the tall young man, her face almost flat under the white lights of the tea room entrance, as if she had had a tuck taken in the back of her neck, or as if her head had been cut off and carelessly laid on her shoulders. At any rate, what with her red beads, and her agonized smile (from which Martha gathered that she had not known until now that Anton was married, or at least had not known that Martha, so very much present, was his wife) and a white pleated dress which carried out the same innocent sacrificial theme, she looked like a victim. Anton stood quietly apart, smiling, smiling. But socially—just as if nothing had happened, as if he had not been on show with a young woman not his wife. Solly's face was ecstatic with jeering triumph; it shouted to everyone: "Look, this old stick Anton's got a girl." And, of course, "Martha's free!" For his eyes were alive with dramatic intention, playing over Millicent's face, darting sideways at Martha, to see how she took it, swivelling to the others, to make sure they understood. "You can't go yet," he said to Millicent. "What is all this? The night's yet young."

She protested and said that she must. Her eyes were almost closed in the energy of her outstretched painful smile, which pride forced her to maintain. Anton stood silently by, waiting for Solly to put an end to it. Athen, Joss, Thomas Stern stood watching. Athen as usual looked from a distance: it was not for him to criticize, his attitude said. Thomas Stern, disapproving, juggled objects in the pockets of his khaki shorts—uniform shorts still, they would be for months yet. Joss stared at his brother as Martha felt he must have been doing all his life, with an affectionate but bitter smile of criticism. During the few moments of this cruel scene under the white harsh lights of the Old Vienna Tea Room, Martha repudiated Solly forever; his childishness, his open jeering triumph, and above all, his humiliation of the unfortunate girl, lost him any possibility (if there had been one, Martha defended herself, hastily) of ever, at any time, having an affair with Martha. Then Joss put out his hand, laid it on Martha's shoulder, and said with a smile clumsily tactful, "Well, Matty, and what are we all going to do with you, taking us to the wrong film?"

He took Martha into the tea room with him, and by the time they sat side by side, the group had come in after them. Millicent was not with them. Anton sat opposite Martha, giving her a smile both triumphant and apologetic. Athen sat near Anton, and began talking to him, which was his way of saying he did not propose to pass any judgement on what had been happening. Thomas Stern sat on the other side of Martha and he said again, "Well, Matty, I always thought you were attractive, but not for me, man. I'm a peasant myself, and so are you. But now you're sick, you've got everything—as far as I am concerned, I'm telling you, you can have me any time!"

They all laughed, even Athen. But there sat Thomas, leaning forward to look into Martha's face, absolutely serious. Martha thought that he spoke as if they had been alone. Her nerves were telling her he meant what he said.

She said, joking to lessen the tension, "So I'm a peasant?"

"Yes," he said, still with the same straight pressure of his strong blue eyes. "Yes. But don't you get well too quickly. I like you all strange and delicate."

"It's the first time I've heard that Matty is ill," Anton said, on a humorous grumbling note that restored normality.

"Where's Solly?" asked Martha quickly, to stop them examining her.

"I told him to get lost," said Joss.

"Who was eating all those kebabs with him last week?"

"Look," said Joss, suddenly very serious—with an intensity not far off that which Thomas had shown a few minutes before. "Listen. He's my brother—for my sins. I see him for meals, etcetera. For my sins. After all, when he's at home we even live in the same house. But I tell you, keep clear of him! He's one of the people to keep clear of."

Martha said, after a moment, "Well, well!" meaning to remind him of what he had said about "contradictions."

Again he looked at her, straight and intent, determined to make her accept what he was saying. "He's the kind of person things go wrong for. Always. If you tell him to bring a tray in from the kitchen, he drops it. If he drives a car to the garage, he'll take the wrong turning. I tell you, better watch out, I'm warning you."

They all began to laugh, because of his intensity, because they thought: families! Joss maintained his calm while they laughed, and when they had finished, "All right. But remember when I've gone I said so."

Of course, Joss was going; Martha had forgotten. The fact that she was disappointed was announced by her flesh, which had been relaxing in the most pleasant of understandings with Joss. Good Lord! she said to herself. Quite obviously I'm determined to have an affair with somebody. And I've only this very moment realized it. Well—if Joss is going, then it's a pity, because this is the first time since we've known each other that he's actually been attracted to me—I can feel he is.

"And now," remarked Athen, "we shall all eat cream cakes and drink real coffee." He meant to remind them of the newsreel they had just seen. They looked towards Anton, towards the fair and handsome German. The waitress, a pretty woman in a frilled lace pinafore and a frilled mob cap designed to remind customers of the films they had all seen of Old Vienna, stood smiling by their table, and Anton said, "Coffee, with cream, and cakes." Having made his point, he looked at his friends, and made it again, "I'm not going to starve myself for them. They deserve a good hiding, and that's what they are getting."

"It's natural you should feel like that, comrade," said Athen, in gentle, sorrowful rebuke.

Thomas Stern said, "If we all ate fifty cream cakes each, what difference would it make to them?" His *them* were the victims of the concentration camps, and as the plate of cakes descended between them from the manicured hand of the waitress, he took an éclair, making a public statement, and instantly bit a large piece out of it. Anton took a cake, so did Joss, so did Martha. But Athen shook his head and sat frowning, suffering.

"Have a heart," said Thomas. "You're making us feel terrible."

Athen hesitated, then he said, "Yes, I know, and I'm sorry for it. But recently I understood: these days, after being with you, I find myself thinking, this wine is bad, or this wine is good, I can't eat this meat, this is a bad meal. I find myself going into a good restaurant."

"Cheer up," said Joss. "There aren't any good restaurants. You couldn't corrupt yourself if you tried."

They all laughed, wanting to laugh. They were irritated by Athen, and ashamed that they were. And, now that he was forcing such thoughts on them, they sat and looked at him, elegant in his new cream-coloured suit.

Anton said, smiling, reaching for another cake, "I see you have found yourself a tailor, Comrade Athen."

This could have been taken as small talk. But they all knew each other far too well. They knew, almost before Anton had finished speaking, that Athen would go pale, would suffer, could be expected to lie awake that night, that tomorrow he would come to one or another of them and say, "But I couldn't send the money home to my family. And it was not an expensive suit."

And Martha, at least, knew that Anton was teasing Athen (as Anton would describe it), attacking Athen (as Athen would feel it), because he felt guilty over Millicent.

Suddenly Thomas got up saying, "I've got work. Matty, I want to see you. I'll ring you at your office. I've got something to talk over with you. Solly's up to something and Clive de Wet says he needs our help." Normally, Thomas would have made a joke for Anton's benefit: If your husband will give me permission—or something like that. But he nodded briefly at Anton, laid his hand on Athen's shoulder as if to say: Take it easy, for Heaven's sake! smiled at Martha, then at Joss, and went out.

"I suppose it's one of his girls," said Anton.

"No," said Joss. "He's upset. A friend of his was with the troops that went into Belsen. He got a long letter. I read it."

"Oh, well then, that's different," said Anton, almost in the tone he would have used as a chairman, accepting someone's excuse for leaving early.

Meanwhile Martha sat, registering the fact that Thomas's going off had upset a pleasant tension: she had been sitting, equally weighted, so to speak, between Joss and Thomas.

Athen got up, saying, "I'm sorry, comrades, but I must leave you. I am sorry that tonight I am such bad company." He went off by himself.

Anton took the bill to pay at the cash desk. Joss and Martha, alone, turned towards each other.

"You're having an affair with Solly?" said Joss, direct.

"No."

"It looked as if you were."

"No."

Now Joss examined her with the intimate frankness licensed by their long friendship, and then glanced at Anton's tall, correct back.

"You two not getting on too well, is that it?"

"Not very."

He said, in exactly the same tone of raillery as Solly, "Well, we did warn you, didn't we? You just wouldn't listen to us, that's your trouble."

Martha smiled, decided against telling him that the despised Solly had used almost the same words earlier, and said, "Yes, you did."

"Well," said Joss, practically. "It's a pity I've got to love you and leave you. But *when* the authorities get around to letting me have the right bits of paper, I'm off up North."

Here Anton came back. Joss said, rising, "Matty, can you have the office open for me tomorrow? I'll ring you."

He went off, as she nodded.

Now Anton and Martha walked together out of the Old Vienna Tea Room. She was thinking, as she sent glances at his pallor, the tension of his mouth: Is he upset because of Millicent or because of Germany? Last week he had sat silent on the edge of his bed, holding a small scrap of newsprint. Later she had found it in a drawer. It described how in a panic flight from Eastern Germany, away from the advancing Russian armies, women had left the train at the stops, carrying the corpses of babies that had died of hunger wrapped in newspaper. The women buried them in the snow by the side of the railway tracks. Famished dogs came afterwards, and dug up the half-buried babies. The mass bombings of German cities, the atrocities, the concentration camps, the frightful destruction of his country, the fact that his countrymen fled like guilty ghosts before the armies of half the world, the fact that they struggled and died and starved like animals—all of this, which surely must have reached the very essence of the man, was received by him with no more than the comment: They deserve a good hiding. But over this, the small scrap of newspaper about the babies wrapped in newspaper, he had sat and wept secretly, the tears running down his cheeks, then he had dried his cheeks carefully, with a large white handkerchief—then sat again, silent, crying.

Martha put her arm into her husband's arm, and let it drop again as he said, "What does Thomas want to see you for?"

"I don't know."

They found the car, an old Ford, parked among the lorries and wagons of the farmers who had been in the cinema, and began the half-mile drive back to the flat. They drove under banks of deep trees that were silvered by intermittent starlight, darkening and lifting into light as big clouds drove overhead. The Tarmac shone white, like salt or like snow, then was very dark under the trees.

"Well," said Anton at last, "What have you decided?"

Martha knew quite well that the right answer to this was that she should touch him, or kiss him. But she said stupidly, "What about?"

He let the car slide gently into a ditch filled with dry leaves, and neatly pulled in the brake before turning his pale eyes on her, "I want to know whether I should give you another chance or not."

Martha raged with resentment at the phrase; she could not dispel it, even though she knew that phrases like "give you another chance" or "give them a good hiding" should be calls on her compassion rather than triggers towards anger.

She walked quickly up the path away from him, listening to his crunch, crunch behind her on the gravel. In the tiny room that was their bedroom, she switched on the lights and at once winged insects began circling around it, their wings rustling and clicking.

She was thinking: There's something in this conflict with Anton that reminds me of the horrible cold arguments I have with my mother. She's always in the right—and so am I. And Anton and I

are both in the right. There's something about being in the right
. . . She felt positively sick with exasperation already—because of
the banality of what they were going to say. Both Anton and she
would be *thinking* quite sensible, even intelligent thoughts—but
what they said would be idiotic, and their bad temper, their unpleasantness would be because both knew they could not express
their sense in their words, let alone actions. Martha even felt as if
this conversation or discussion (if the coming exchange could be
dignified by such words) had taken place already and there was no
point in going through with it again.

However, she stood drawing striped cotton over the windows,
thereby shutting out a sky where the storm clouds still swept and
piled in great, dramatic silver masses, and folded back the thin
white covers of the two beds in which both were going to sleep so
badly. Meanwhile, Anton untied his tie before a glass and
watched his young wife in it, his face hard.

"Well, Matty, I'm waiting?"

"What for?"

"There was a discussion, *if* you'll be good enough to search your
memory."

"It looked to me this evening as if you've already made up *your*
mind," Martha said casually. She was pulling off her dress. The
solid brown curves of her legs, her arms, thus revealed, suddenly
spoke to her, and with a total authority. Thomas Stern said she was
a peasant, did he? She looked at her fine strong body, smelled the
delightful warm odours of her armpits, her hair, and thought: So he
thinks I am a peasant, does he?

"I don't know what you mean."

"You know quite well what I mean. What's the red-head's other
name?"

"I'm not going to deny that I find Millicent attractive, Matty!"

"Well, I should hope not."

Anton, a tall overthin man, his flesh glistening fair, his blond head
gleaming, the fine hair on his thighs and belly shining gold, stood
naked before stooping to pull up his pyjama trousers.

That's my husband, thought Martha. What nonsense! She watched
the fair fine flesh of her husband vanishing behind dark green cotton and her flesh said, He's got nothing to do with me, that man.

Aloud she said, "We agreed that if I . . . " She had been going to
say, took a lover, but that was too literary, even though he had
used the phrase first. Very European you are, she had said to herself, derisively, Take a lover! Good lord, who do you think I am?

Madame Bovary? Well, I wish we had her problems. And it was not possible with Anton, for some reason, to say: get myself a man, find myself a man—that would be a sort of insult to him. "We decided that if I decided to be unfaithful to you then I should be honest with you, and you would take a mist . . . get yourself a girl —at any rate, we'd both get other people."

"Quite correct," said Anton, standing upright, startlingly handsome in his admirable dark green pyjamas. He was tying the cord of his pyjama trousers.

This was the moment when Martha should go to him, naked as she nearly was, and put her arms around him. That was what he was waiting for, and why he tied his pyjama cord so slowly. If she did this, if she played her role properly, as a good wife should, then by midnight, or at the very latest, tomorrow morning, Millicent the red-head would have become one of the little married jokes that act as such a delightful lubricant. Too bad for Millicent, too bad for whatever expectations she might, at this moment, be cherishing of Anton. If things went one way, she might reasonably hope to be Anton's mistress, girl friend, at any rate, have an affair with him. If Martha now played her part properly, all warm and feminine and coaxing (Martha could see herself, and shuddered with disgust), then very soon Millicent would be "the red-head, Anton!"—and greeted with an understanding smile by Martha, a rather proud self-conscious little grin by Anton. She would be a married joke, a little joke to smooth the wheels of matrimony. Lord, how repulsive! How unpleasant the little jokes, the hundred dishonest little lies, the thousand sacrifices like Millicent (or like Solly if it had come to that) which marriage demands.

If Martha played her role one way, then tomorrow or the next day Millicent, throwing away her pride to ring Anton, or to run into him in the street, would be encountered with: "Hello, Millicent, how are things, all right?" "Fine, Anton how are you?" "See you some time, Millicent." If Martha went on behaving as she was now, obedient to her peremptory and at least entirely honest body, Millicent could confidently expect a probably very romantic and satisfactorily painful affair.

Anton stood upright, his head bent as he examined his fingernails. Martha discovered she was feeling uncomfortable—it was because she was standing naked in front of him. She did not belong to him! She pulled off her brassière, her back to him, delighting in a quick glimpse of her shoulder, at the fine curves with the perfect crease and dimple between them. Hastily she tugged on a nightdress. She went quickly into the bathroom to clean her teeth. She was crawling with shame because of the stupid scene they had just enacted. At the same time her flesh was exulting because next day she would see Joss—damn it, he was going to leave soon. But how lucky Joss was, she thought, sensing all of herself, her whole delightful sweet-smelling person.

She could not go back to the bedroom yet. Anton would still be waiting for her to come back. Perhaps he was sitting on the edge of the bed reading that bit of newsprint about the women burying their dead babies in newspaper in the snow? Oh God, if he was, then there'd be no help for it, she would have to put her arms around him, comfort him . . . she simply would *not* go back to the bedroom yet.

After a great deal of splashing and drying and brushing of her hair—for the second time that day it got the old-fashioned fifty strokes on each side—she went back to find Anton in bed, his bed-light off, his back to her.

She turned off her light. The room, in the dark, was not dark. It seemed that through the thin curtains, even through the walls, fell the cool brilliance of starlight, which shifted, lightened, darkened, as the clouds drove overhead. For a few minutes the insects maintained their circles around the dark focus of the light, then there was an interval of small uncoordinated bangings, slidings, fallings-away. The moth and insect noises stopped altogether. Martha knelt up in bed to look past the edges of the curtain at the dark pillars of the verandah. A black sky. Black trees, in pools of black shade. Ghostly white lilies in dark shade. Fragments of white gravel. Leaves turning and tossing under starlight in a rippling silver movement.

Tomorrow she would see Joss. No, it was Thomas she was going to see. From the sinking of her exultation she knew she would prefer Joss—*safer*, he would be. What on earth did she mean by that?—safer! There was no doubt the thought of Thomas confronted her uncomfortably, peremptorily. All right then, not Thomas. But somebody, and it would be soon.

3

On the morning peace was celebrated (or, as Mrs. Quest saw it in her mind's eye, Victory Morning) she was up before six. In order, she told herself, to have plenty of time to get Mr. Quest ready for the Victory Parade. But she had slept badly, waking confused, every muscle tensed and painful, and with an aching head. It was not until she had gone out into the exquisite morning to pick up the newspaper where it had been flung by the delivery boy on the verandah steps, that she remembered the dream which had woken her.

The sun on that May morning rose from wisps of rosy vapour and shone on Mrs. Quest where she stood in her flowered cotton wrapper on her steps, in the middle of a garden shrill with bird song. She shivered, for while the great red ball was presumably pumping out heat on other parts of the world, here it was winter. The air, the sky, each leaf and flower, had a cool sharp clarity. The garden was steeped in cold. Frosty water gemmed the lawn. Dewdrops hung from the roses and from the jacaranda boughs until shaken free in bright showers by the birds who swooped from bird bath to branch, from shrub to lawn.

Mrs. Quest noted with satisfaction that the newspaper confirmed her sense of what was right by stating it was VICTORY DAY in Europe, and the black print was six inches deep. She had dreamed, hadn't she? Oh, yes, and her head ached from it. It had been a terrible dream.

Her nights were always tense, peopled with regrets, fitfully menacing, unless she drugged herself. She had years ago justified the pills she took by the claim that she slept badly; her doses grew heavier, and still she slept badly—worse, she was convinced, than Mr. Quest, who was her patient.

Oh, what a dream, what a dream! Mrs. Quest turned her back on her garden, and went into the fusty living room, where the little dog leaped on to her lap. Dear Kaiser, there there, Kaiser, she whispered to the animal's pricked ears and wet muzzle. She let him out into the verandah, and walked around it into the kitchen. The servants were not in yet. Mrs. Quest made herself tea, keeping her mind occupied with cups, water, sugar, planning: if I dress now, then I might get dirty again, if I have to do something for him—but surely not, I've got everything ready; yes it would be more sensible to dress for the Parade now. The tea was ready, and the decision to dress taken. But Mrs. Quest returned to the living room, and switched on a coil of red electricity, and sat by it, shivering. Her old face was set with unhappiness. The little white dog bounded back—he knows how I feel, thought Mrs. Quest, fondling the silky ears. She bent her face to the warmth of the dog's fat back and remembered the dream.

Her mother, reaching down from a high place which Mrs. Quest knew was Heaven, handed her three red roses . . . the old lady was crying, thinking of her mother, who had died young. She had not known her. All through her childhood and youth her mother had been mysterious, not only with the brutal pathos of her death in childbirth, but because of a quality that for a long time the young girl had sensed as dangerous. There was something about her mother never explained, never put into words, but there always, like a sweet and reckless scent hidden in old dresses, old cupboards. Some things had been said. She was pretty, for instance. She was clever, too, and gay. She was brave—had ridden to the hounds on a great chestnut horse, jumping fences where no one would follow her. Had been strong—she went to balls and danced all night, and then teased her husband to walk home with her through the dawn while the carriage came behind. But she had died, after all, leaving not only three small children, not only the sting of resentment earned by those who die with all their qualities intact but—what *was* the thing that no one put into words but which the young girl felt so strongly?

Grown up at last, she understood that her mother had been beautiful. Not pretty. The grudging little word made her look again at the tall cold disciplined house she had been brought up in. Long concealed pictures came to light and the dead woman was revealed to be beautiful, and with the sort of beauty not easily admitted by that house whose chief virtue had been respectability, described as "a sense of proportion," as "healthy."

Did that mean her mother had been morbid, selfish, wrongheaded? The girl decided this must have been the case, even while she remembered that as a small girl she had started up in bed from a nightmare screaming, "They wanted her to die," and to the servant who came scolding in with a candle shielded behind a hand that smelled of hot dripping from the kitchen, "You all wanted her to die."

She knew, when she put her hair up, deciding that she would *not* be a Victorian young lady, but must fight her stern father so that she could be a nurse (which no real lady was, in spite of Florence Nightingale), that her childhood had lacked something which she craved. Beauty, she told herself it was, clinging to that word, refusing "morbid" and "selfish" and "wrong-minded."

But her life had gone—nursing. She had got her way, had fought her father, who would not speak to her for months, had won her battles. She had nursed—as a young woman, then through the war, and then her husband. She had nursed all her life. But never had she known "beauty." It seemed that her mother had taken this qual-

ity with her when she had died, selfishly—it was all her own fault,
they said, because she had insisted on dancing all night when she
was five months pregnant:

And now Mrs. Quest's mother had handed Mrs. Quest three crimson roses to which the old lady's memory added the crystal drops
of a winter's morning. The beautiful young woman had leaned
down, smiling, from Heaven, and handed the daughter she had
scarcely known three red roses, fresh with bright water. Mrs. Quest,
weeping with joy, her heart opening to her beautiful mother, had
looked down and seen that in her hand the roses had turned into—
a medicine bottle.

Yes, the dream had the quality of sheer brutality. Nothing was
concealed, nothing glossed over for kindness' sake. Mrs. Quest, an
old lady, for the first time in her life gave a name to that thing her
mother had possessed, which no one had spoken of, and which she
herself had described as "beauty." The beautiful woman had been
unkind. Yes, that was it. She had been pretty and reckless—and
unkind. She had had charm and a white skin and long black hair,
but she was unkind. She would dance in memory always like a light
burning or like the sunlight on the glossy skin of her wild chestnut
horse. But she was unkind.

Mrs. Quest put her withered face close to her little dog, who still
shivered from the garden's frost, and wept. She wept at the cruelty
of the dream. Medicine bottles, yes; that was her life, given her by a
cruel and mocking mother.

Three days ago, on to the polished cement of the verandah had
slid an official letter, bidding Mr. Quest to the Victory Celebrations
for the Second World War (in Europe) as a representative of the
soldiers of the First World War. Mr. Quest had been in a drugged
sleep when the letter came. Mrs. Quest, long before he had woken
up, had worked out a long and careful plan that would make it possible for her husband to attend. She yearned to be there, on that
morning of flags and bands, her invalid husband—the work of so
many years of devotion—beside her, his illnesses officially recognized as the result of the First World War. But she had been afraid
he would refuse. In the past, he had always laughed, with a bitter
contempt that had hurt her terribly. Or, if he had gone, it had been
(or so it seemed) only for the sake of the angry nihilism he could
use on the occasion after it was over.

In 1922 (was it?) she had stood by the Cenotaph in Whitehall
with the handsome man who was her husband, and her soul had
melted with the drums and the fifes and the flags of Remembrance

Day. Afterwards Mr. Quest had indulged in days of vituperation about the generals and the government and the type of mind that organized Remembrance Days and handed out white feathers—he had been handed a white feather on the day he had put off his uniform after the final interview with the doctors who said he would never be himself again. "We are afraid you will never really be yourself again, Captain." He mocked everything that fed the tender soul of Mrs. Quest, who had always needed the comfort of anniversaries, ceremonies, ritual, the proper payment of respect where it was due.

But—and here comes something odd that Mrs. Quest was quite aware of herself. There was something in her that liked her husband's mockery, that needed it. Something older, more savage, more knowledgeable in the tidily hatted matron who let her eyes fill with tears at The Last Post waited for and needed the old soldier's ribaldry. Three days ago, when she had taken the official letter to him, she had expected him to laugh.

But he had lowered faded eyes to the government letter, and remained silent, his lips folding and refolding as if he was tasting something from the past. Then he looked up at his wife with a face adjusted to an appropriate humility (a look which appalled Mrs. Quest, so unlike him was it) and said in a voice false with proper feeling, "Well, perhaps if I wrap up, how about it?"

Mrs. Quest had been shaken to her depths. Perhaps for the first time she really *felt* what the nurse in her had always known, that her husband really was not "himself." Not even intermittently, these days, was he himself, and for hours they had discussed in every painful detail how it could be possible for him to attend the ceremony, while his face preserved the terrifyingly unreal expression of a man who has given his all for his country and now submits in modesty to his country's thanks.

There were two main questions involved. One was, sleep or the absence of it. The other: Mr. Quest's bowels. But the problem was the same, in effect: it was impossible to predict anything. The point was, Mr. Quest's body had been so wrenched and twisted by every variety of drug, that drugs themselves had become like symptoms, to be discussed and watched. It was not a question of Mr. Quest's having taken so many grains of—whatever it was, which would have a certain effect. A sleeping draught, an aperient, might "work" or it might not, and if it did work, then it was unpredictably and extraordinarily, and information must be saved for the doctor, who would be interested scientifically in what surely must be unprecedented, from the medical point of view.

The Parade was at eleven, and would be over by twelve. During this hour Mr. Quest would be in a wheel chair with his medals pinned to his dressing gown—permission had been obtained for him to appear thus. But he must not fall asleep. And he must not . . .

They had discussed the exact strength of the dose appropriate to make Mr. Quest sleep all night yet wake alert enough to face the ceremony. It had been decided that seven-tenths of his usual dose would be right, if the doctor would agree to give a stimulant at ten o'clock. As for the bowels—well, that was more difficult. An enema at about nine-thirty would probably do the trick.

So it all had been planned and decided. And Mrs. Quest, last night, kissing her husband's cheek as he sank off to sleep already in the power of the drug that would keep him unconscious till nine next morning, had looked young for a moment, fresh—tomorrow she would be at the Parade, and she would be taken by Mrs. Maynard, who had been so kind as to offer them a lift.

For this, the Maynards' offer, Mr. Quest had been duly grateful, and had not made one critical comment. Yet he did not like Mrs. Maynard, he said she put the fear of God into him, with her committees and her intrigues.

Mrs. Quest had noted, but not digested, her husband's compliance. She had told Mrs. Maynard that they would be ready at ten-thirty. Mrs. Maynard had been "infinitely kind" about drugs and arrangements.

To get Mr. Quest to the Victory in Europe Parade had taken the formidable energies of one matron, and the readiness to be infinitely kind of another. But of course he wasn't there yet. He was still asleep.

Seven in the morning. Mrs. Quest, having decided that she might as well get into her best clothes, did nothing of the kind. She dressed rapidly in an old brown skirt and pink jersey. The bedroom she still shared with her husband was dim, and smelt of medicines, and he lay quite still, absolutely silent, while she banged drawers and rummaged in the wardrobe and brushed her hair and clattered objects on the dressing table. Partly, she was deaf, and did not know what noise she made. Partly, it was because it did not matter, "he would sleep through a hurricane when he had enough drugs inside him." Partly, this noise, this roughness of movement, was a protest against the perpetually narrowing cage she lived in.

When she was inside her thick jersey, and she felt warm and more cheerful, she went into the kitchen for the second time and told the cook to make some more tea. Letters lay on the kitchen table. Mrs. Quest trembled with excitement and took up the letter from her son in England and went back to the verandah. The sun was above the trees now, and sharp cool shadows lay across the lawns.

Mrs. Quest read the letter smiling. Before the end she had to rise to pin back a trail of creeper that waved too freely, unconfined, off a verandah pillar. She had to express her pleasure, her joy, in movement of some kind.

Jonathan, the young man convalescing in a village in Essex, had written a pleasantly filial letter, saying nothing of his deep feelings. He had been very ill with his smashed arm, had been frightened he would lose it. He did not want to worry his mother by telling her this, and so he chatted about the village, which was charming, he said; and the doctors and nurses in the hospital, who were so kind; and the village people—"really good types." He allowed his own emotions to appear for half a sentence, but in reverse, as it were: "Perhaps I might settle here, I could do worse!" What this meant was that he had a flirtation with the doctor's daughter in the village, and for an occasional sentimental half-hour thought of marrying her and living forever in this quiet ancient place that in fact spoke to nothing real in him. For he longed for Africa, and for a farm where he would have space "to be myself"—as he felt it.

But before Mrs. Quest had read the letter twice, old daydreams had been revived. She had worked it all out: they—Mr. Quest and herself—would go to England and take a little cottage in the village where Jonathan would settle with his wife—for of course he had a girl, perhaps even a fiancée, the letter could mean no less!—and she and Mr. Quest would be done forever with this country where the family had known nothing but disappointment and illness. Besides, the English climate would be better for Mr. Quest, it might even cure him.

The servant brought tea, and found Mrs. Quest smiling out at her shrubs and lawns. "Nice morning," he ventured. She did not hear, at first, then she smiled: she was already far away from Africa, in a village full of sensible people where she would never see a black face again. "Yes, but it's cold," she said, rather severely, and he went back in silence to his kitchen.

When Mr. Quest woke up, she would tell him about going to England. She ached with joy. She had forgotten about the ugly dream, and the three days of miserable planning for the Parade. She was

free of the patronage of Mrs. Maynard (now she was free, she
acknowledged that Mrs. Maynard was patronizing). She would
find her old friends and "when something happened" (which meant,
when her husband died—the doctor said it was a miracle she had
kept him alive for so long) she would live with her old school
friend Alice and devote herself to Jonathan's children.

At which point Mrs. Quest remembered the existence of her
granddaughter Caroline. Well, she could come and spend long holi-
days in England with her, Mrs. Quest, perhaps she should even live
there, because the education was so much better there than in this
country where there were no standards . . . as for Martha, well she
said she was going to England too.

Her wings were beginning to drag. She remembered the dream.
Her face set, though she had no idea of it, though she was planning happily for the Parade, into lines of wary resignation. She
ought to go and dress properly. She stayed where she was, an old
lady with a sad set face looking into a beautiful garden where a
small dog pranced around a dry white bone. She sat, shivering
slightly, for the cold was sharp, and thought—that she would give
anything in this world for a cigarette.

The longing came on her suddenly, without warning. At the beginning of the war, when her son went into danger with the armies up North, Mrs. Quest gave up smoking. "As a sacrifice for Jonathan's getting through the war safely." Mrs. Quest did nothing if
not "live on her nerves" and smoking was a necessity for her. It had
been for many years. To give up smoking was more painful than
she could have imagined. Yet, having once made the bargain with
God, she stuck to it. She had not smoked, except for five anguished
days when he was first wounded, and they had not been told
how badly. Then no cigarettes for days, weeks, months. Today was
Victory Day, the war was over (in Europe, anyhow) and she was
now free to smoke? No, for the bargain she had made with God
was that she would not smoke until he was home safely. Yes, but in his
letter he had said he might stay in England for good? Therefore she
was free, released from her part of the bargain? No, her conscience
told her she was not. And besides, an old mine, or floating explosive
of some kind might blow up the ship Jonathan came home in. She
must not smoke yet.

Mrs. Quest went into the living room where a carved wooden
box held cigarettes for visitors, and her hand went out to the lid.
The small bell tinkled which meant that her husband was awake.
Immediately her spirits lifted into expectation: yes, it was just

right. Eight o'clock in the morning, that meant she could talk, and gossip and coax him into wakefulness in good time for the car's arrival at ten-thirty.

When she reached the bedroom, it seemed that he was asleep again, his hand around the little silver bell. She fussed around for a while, looking at her watch, trying to make out from his face in the darkened room how he would feel when he woke.

Then he started awake, on a groan, and wildly stared around the room. "Lord," he said, "that was a dream and a half!"

"Well, never mind," said Mrs. Quest, briskly.

She moved to straighten the covers and help him sit up.

"Lord!" he exclaimed again, watching his dream retreat. "What time is it?"

"It's after eight."

"But it's early, isn't it?" he protested. He had already turned over to sleep again, but she said swiftly, "What would you like for break-fast?"

He lay seriously thinking about it, "Well, I had a boiled egg yes-terday, and I don't think the fat if I had a fried egg . . . how about a bit of haddock?"

"We haven't got any haddock," she said. She realized he had for-gotten all about the Parade, and from her spirits' slow fall into chill and resignation knew more than that, though she had not admitted it yet. She said brightly, "Well, if you remember, we had decided it would be better if you just had a bit of dried toast and some tea?"

He stared at her, blank. Then, horror came on to the empty face. Then it showed the purest dismay. Then came cunning. These ex-pressions followed each other, one after another, each as clean and unmixed as those on masks for an actors' school. Mr. Quest, totally absorbed in himself, never thinking how he appeared to others, ut-terly unself-conscious in the way a child is—was as transparent as a child.

He said in a voice which he allowed to become weak and trem-bling, "Oh dear, I don't think I really feel up to all that."

"Well, never mind, it doesn't matter," she said. But her eyes were wet, her lips shook, and so she went out of the room so as not to upset him. Of course he was not going. He had never really been ready to go. How could she have been so ridiculous as to think he would? For three days she had allowed herself to be taken in . . . she stood in the stuffy little living room, trembling now with dis-appointment, her whole nature clamouring because of its long deprivation of everything she craved: the fullness of life, warmth, people, things happening . . . her body ached with lack and with loss. She had lit a cigarette before she knew it. She stood drawing in long streams of the acrid fragrance, eyes shut, feeling the delicious smoke trickle through her. But her eyes were shut, holding in tears, and she put down one hand to pat the head of the little dog. "There Kaiser, there Kaiser."

She thought: I'm breaking my bargain with God. Almost, she put out the cigarette, but did not. She went back into the bedroom where her husband was dozing. She looked quietly at the grey-faced old man, with his grey, rather ragged moustache, his grey eyebrows, his grey hair. A small, faded, shrunken invalid, that was her handsome husband. He opened his eyes and said in a normal, alert voice, "I smell burning."

"It's all right, go to sleep."

"But I do smell burning."

"It's my cigarette."

"Oh. That's all right then." And he shut his eyes again.

Wild self-pity filled his wife. She had not smoked through the war, except for those five days—could it be that Jonathan's arm had taken so long to heal because—no, God could not be so unkind, she knew that. She felt it. Yet now her husband, whose every mood, gesture, pang, look, she knew, could interpret, could sense and foresee before it happened—this man knew so little, cared so little for her, that he did not even remark when she had started to smoke again.

There was a long silence. She sat on the bottom of her unmade bed, smoking deliciously, while her foot jerked restlessly up and down, and he lay, eyes shut.

He said, eyes shut, "I'm sorry, old girl, I know you are disappointed about the Victory thing."

She said, moved to her depths, "It's all right."

He said, "But they're damned silly, aren't they, I mean, Victory Parades . . . in the Great Unmentionable, medals, that sort of thing, it was all just . . . I don't think I'll risk haddock, old girl. Just let me have a boiled egg."

She immediately rose to attend to it.

"Well don't rush off so. You're always rushing about. And you've forgotten my injection."

"No. I haven't. I've had a letter from Jonathan."

"Oh, have you?"

"Yes. He says his arm is clearing up at last." She could not bring herself to say: He'll be coming home soon, thus putting an end to her brief and, after all, harmless dream about England.

"He's a good kid. Nice to have him back again," said Mr. Quest, drowsily. He would be asleep again, unfed, if she did not hurry.

"When is Matty coming?"

"She was here last night, but you were asleep."

She boiled the egg, four minutes, took the tray in, gave him his injection, sat with him while he ate, chatted about Jonathan, gave him a cigarette and sat by while he smoked it, then settled him down for his morning's sleep.

She then telephoned Mrs. Maynard: so sorry, but he isn't well enough. Mrs. Maynard said it was too bad, but reminded Mrs. Quest that there was a committee meeting tomorrow night to consider the problems arising from Peace, and she did so hope Mrs. Quest could attend. Mrs. Quest's being again sprang into hopeful delight at the idea of going to the meeting. She had managed to attend two of them: the atmosphere of appropriately dressed ladies, all devoted to their fellow human beings, "the right kind of" lady, banded together against—but there was no need to go into what right-minded people were against—was just what she needed. But on the other evenings she had been invited, her husband had been ill, and she could not go.

Mrs. Maynard now said, "And how's that girl of yours, what's her name again?"

"You mean Martha?" said Mrs. Quest, as if there might be other daughters.

"Yes, Martha. Martha Knowell, Hesse, whatever she calls herself now—would she like to join us, what do you think?"

This was casual, thrown away. And Mrs. Quest did not at once reply. That *her* daughter was noticed, singled out, by the great Mrs. Maynard, well that was pleasant, it was a compliment to herself. But that her daughter should be invited to work on *this* committee, with "the right sort of people"—well, it was cruel. It was crueler than ever Mrs. Maynard could guess. For one thing, it was likely Matty would treat this invitation with the sort of ribald scorn that— well, which Mr. Quest, in the days when he was more *himself*, would have used to greet invitations to Remembrance Days. But Mrs. Quest did not wish to make this comparison. And for another thing, Mrs. Quest felt with every instinct that the committee in Mrs. Maynard's silken drawing room was a bastion against everything that Martha represented. She could not say this, of course, to Mrs. Maynard, but she might perhaps *hint* . . .

She said, half-laughing, on a rueful note, one mother commiserating with another about the charming peccadilloes of the young: "Of course Matty's awfully scatterbrained, awfully wrong-headed."

Mrs. Maynard said briskly, "All the more reason she should be given something useful to do, don't you think? Well, I hope to see one or another of you, if not both, tomorrow." She rang off, leaving Mrs. Quest with the most improbable suspicion which she really could not make head or tail of—that Mrs. Maynard would be even happier to see Martha than to see herself. It was unfair. It was brutal. Yes, it was really cruel—like the dream. It had the gratuitous, unnecessary cruelty of her dream. Mrs. Quest, who had decided that the cigarette would be the last until Jonathan's safe homecoming, now lit another, and sat by the radio patting the little white dog. On the flowered rug, which slipped about crookedly over polished green linoleum, lay the fragment of white bone. The little dog lay with his nose to it, in wistful remembrance of better bones, juicier morsels.

"Disgusting," said Mrs. Quest, in real revulsion from the clean, bleached, fragment of skeleton. She said in a softer "humorous" voice, "Really, Kaiser, you don't bring bones into drawing rooms!" She flipped it out of the window with a look of disgust. The little dog rushed after it and brought it back, playfully, to lie at his mistress's feet. But she, in a rush of anger, threw it right out of the window and over the verandah wall. This time the animal sensed that he, or at least his precious bone, was not wanted, and he vanished with it behind a shrub. Mrs. Quest sat alone, listening to the radio. It seemed to her that for years, for all her life, she had sat, forced to be quiet, listening to history being made. She, whose every instinct was for warm participation, was never allowed to be present. Somewhere else people danced all night, revolving in a great flower-decked room, watching the Dancer revolve, her cruel smile concealed behind the mask of a beautiful young woman. Somewhere else, unreachably far away, a great chestnut horse rose like an arrow over the dangerous fences of half a dozen leafy English counties, and on the horse's back was the masked Rider. Three red roses, three perfect red roses, with the dew fresh on them . . . Mrs. Quest went to the bedroom to see if her husband was awake. He lay in a dead sleep, although he had had no drug since last night. Just as well he had not gone to the Victory Parade. The servants were cleaning silver, scrubbing potatoes, sweeping steps, snipping dead blooms off rose bushes. The big house, with its many rooms, was all ready for people, for the business of life; and yet in it was a dying man, his nurse, and the two black men and the black child who looked after them. Well, soon Jonathan would come home, and then he would get married, and his children could come and stay and fill these rooms. Or perhaps Martha would have another baby and *she* would need . . . *Mrs. Maynard wanted her on the committee.*

On the radio, the first stirrings of the Victory occasion could be heard. Horses' hooves. Drums—real drums, not a tom-tom. The commentator spoke of the brilliant day, and of the slow approach of the Governor and his wife.

Mrs. Quest heard this, saw it even, with a smile that already had the softness of nostalgia. This little town, this shallow little town, that was set so stark and direct on the African soil—it could not feed her, nourish her . . . an occasion where the representatives of Majesty were only "the Governor and the Governor's wife"—no, it wouldn't do. And the troops would have black faces or, at least, some of them would be black, and the dust clouds that eddied about the marching feet of the bands would be red. . . . Mrs. Quest was no longer in Africa, she was in Whitehall, by the Cenotaph, and beside her stood the handsome man who was her husband, and the personage who bent to lay the wreath was Royal.

The short hour of ritual was too short. Mrs. Quest came back to herself, to this country she could never feel to be her own, empty and afraid. Now she must go and wake her husband—because he couldn't be allowed to sleep *all* the time, he must be kept awake for an hour or so. He must be washed, and fed again and soon the doctor would come. And for the rest of that day, so it would be, and the day after, and the day after—she would not get to Mrs. Maynard's committee tomorrow night, and in any case, Mrs. Maynard did not want her, she wanted Martha.

Mrs. Quest went to the telephone and told Martha that Mr. Quest had been asking after his daughter, and why didn't she care enough for her father to come and visit him?

"But I was there last night."

"Well, if you haven't got time for your own father, that's another thing," said Mrs. Quest, and heard her own rough voice with dismay. She had not meant to be impatient with Martha. She reached for the box of cigarettes with one hand. The box was empty. She had smoked twenty or more that morning. If Jonathan's arm did not heal well, or if he was sunk coming home, then it would be her fault.

"I had a letter from Jonathan," said Mrs. Quest. "I think we might very well go and live in England now that the war is over. He's talking of settling in Essex."

Nothing, not a sound from Martha. But Mrs. Quest could hear her breathing.

The servant came into the room to say that it was time to cook lunch, what would she like? Mrs. Quest gestured to the empty box and pushed some silver towards him, with a pantomime that he must go and buy some cigarettes. Now, the nearest shop was half a mile away, and she was being unreasonable, and she knew it. She had never done this before.

She said loudly to Martha, "I said, did you hear me, we might go and settle in England?"

"Well, that's nice," said Martha at last, and Mrs. Quest, furious with the girl, looked at the servant, who was standing, holding the silver in his palm.

"See you tonight without fail," said Mrs. Quest, putting down the telephone. "What is it?" she said sharply to the man.

"Perhaps missus telephone the shop, I want to clean the veran-dah," said the servant.

"No missus will not telephone the shop, don't be so damned lazy, do as I tell you," said Mrs. Quest.

She could not bear to wait for the hour, two hours, three hours, before the shop could deliver. She had smoked not at all for five years, except for the few days when Jonathan was wounded, but now she would not wait an hour for a cigarette. "Take the young master's bicycle and go quickly," she ordered.

"Yes, missus."

That evening, Martha arrived to find her mother sitting on the verandah, hunched inside a jersey with a rug around her knees, smoking. Mrs. Quest had spent the afternoon in a long fantasy about how Martha joined Mrs. Maynard's ladies, but had to be ex-pelled. Martha cycled up the garden at that moment when in her mother's mind she was leaving the Maynard drawing room in dis-grace.

Mrs. Quest's mind ground to a stop. Actually faced with Martha she yearned for her affection. It was not that she forgot the nature of her thoughts; it was rather that it had never occurred to her that thoughts "counted."

In short, Mrs. Quest was like ninety-nine per cent of humanity: if she spent an afternoon jam-making, while her mind was filled with thoughts envious, spiteful, lustful—violent; then she had spent the afternoon making jam.

She smiled now, rather painfully, and thought: Perhaps we can have a nice talk, if *he* doesn't want me for anything.

She saw a rather pale young woman who seemed worried. But there was something else: Martha was wearing a white woollen suit, and it disturbed Mrs. Quest. It's too tight, she thought. She did not think of Martha having a body. What she saw was "a white suit," as if in a fashion advertisement. And there were disturbing curves and shapes from which her mind shrank because of a curiosity she could not own.

Martha thought that the old woman who sat in the dusk on the verandah looked tired. Feeling guilty about something, from the look of her.

Mrs. Quest said, "You look tired."

"I am tired."

"And you're much too thin."

"It's one of my thin phases," said Martha vaguely. Flames of rage leaped unexpectedly in Mrs. Quest . . . "one of my thin phases" . . . so like her, cold, unfeeling, just like her!

"Then why don't you eat more?" said Mrs. Quest with an angry titter.

"Oh, don't worry, I'll just get fat again by myself."

Martha sat down and lit a cigarette. Light from the door fell over her mother. Martha saw, under the rug, a brownish skirt, and a pink woollen jersey. Martha looked incredulously at the jersey. How was it possible for a woman, for any woman at all, to wear such a hideous salmon-coloured thing? Why, to touch it must be positively painful.

"I had a letter from Jonathan."

"Oh good. You said so actually."

"He's getting better. Of course his arm will never be what it was."

"Of course not," said Martha, with an unpleasant intention Mrs. Quest was sure of but chose not to analyze.

"I've been talking things over with your father. He *quite* agrees with me that it would be wise to go and live in England near Jonathan. If he decides to live there."

"Oh, then my father's better?" Martha got up, ready to go in. But at her mother's gesture, she sat down again.

"The doctor was here, he said perhaps your father has turned the corner. He wasn't feeling up to the Victory Parade this morning, but he's been quite rested all day, and in fact he slept all afternoon without drugs."

"Good."

Again Martha got up, ready to go in.

"I've gone back to smoking," said Mrs. Quest pathetically, almost demanding that her daughter should congratulate her on her long self-sacrifice.

"Well you were quite marvellous to give it up," said Martha politely. "I simply can't think how you do it." She had turned herself away, mostly from the salmon-pink sweater. It seemed to her that everything impossible about her mother was summed up by the insensitivity, the hideousness, of that thick rough pink object.

"Mrs. Maynard was very disappointed we could not go to the Victory thing. She's starting a committee for the problems of Peace, and she says she wants you on it. I can't imagine why, when you're such a flibberty-gibbet." Mrs. Quest brought out this last sentence with a nervous titter, simultaneously looking at her daughter in appeal. She knew quite well that Martha was far from being a flibberty-gibbet, but the phrase had come, because of Mrs. Quest's nervousness, her unhappiness on the point of Mrs. Maynard, from battles in Martha's childhood.

Martha stared at the pink jersey. She was quite white, raging inside with the need to say a thousand wounding things. With an unbelievable effort, she managed to stay silent, smiling painfully, thinking: I hope she has the sense to shut up now, because otherwise . . .

Mrs. Quest went on, "Well, surely you can say something; it's quite an honour to be asked to Mrs. Maynard's things!"

Martha began, "Mrs. Maynard wants me on the committee because of . . . " She stopped herself just in time from saying: Because of Maisie.

"What were you going to say?" said Mrs. Quest, wanting to know so badly that her casualness about it grated. Suspicion was flaming through her: there was something odd about Mrs. Maynard's wanting Martha in the first place; and now there was something odd about Martha's manner.

"It doesn't matter," said Martha. "Don't worry. She doesn't really want me, you know."

The words "don't worry" made Mrs. Quest sit straight up saying, "What do you mean, why should I care if Mrs. Maynard wants you!"

Martha escaped, saying with a vague bright smile, "I'll just go and see if . . ." On the way to the bedroom Martha was muttering, "They'll do for me yet, between them, they'll get me yet if I don't watch out." The smells of medicine and stool filled her nostrils. Her father had just had an enema and the whole house knew it. Martha allowed herself to think, for a few short moments, of her mother's life, the brutal painfulness of it—but could not afford to think for long. It made her want to run away now, this minute—out of this house and away, before "it" could get her, destroy her.

In the bedroom, a small grey man was asleep, against pillows.

"Father," said Martha, in a low voice, bending down.

"Is that you, old chap?" said Mr. Quest, in the voice which meant that he didn't want to wake up.

"How are you?"

"Oh, much the same I suppose."

She stayed there a few moments, but he kept his eyes shut. Anguish, the enemy, appeared: but no, she was not going to weep, feel pain, suffer. If she did, *they* would get her, drag her down into this nightmare house like a maze where there could be only one end, no matter how hard one ran this way, that way, like a scared rabbit.

"Did you get to that Victory thing?" asked the old man in a normal voice, as she straightened herself to leave.

"No. Well, is it likely?"

"She wanted me to go."

"So I hear."

Mr. Quest's lips moved: he planned a humorous remark. Martha waited. But he lost interest and said, "Well, good night, old chap."

"Good night."

"He's asleep," said Martha to her mother on the verandah, just as she had done the night before. She went to the bicycle and slid herself on the seat.

"I don't know how you can bicycle decently in a skirt as tight as that."

"I wasn't thinking about bicycling *decently*," said Martha, sullenly. Then she smiled. Mrs. Quest smiled too. "And where are you gallivanting off to now?"

Martha sat on her bicycle, with one foot on the wall of the steps. She smiled steadily. She was thinking she might say: Well, as it happens, I've got to meet Athen—he's a Communist newspaper-seller from Greece. Maisie's on the thorny path to hell, he thinks. Maisie? Well, she's the mother of Binkie Maynard's by-blow. Yes, I did say

Binkie Maynard. And the reason why Mrs. Maynard wants me in
her gang is so she can get her hooks into Maisie. And that's why
she's being nice to you—if that's the word for it. Yes, and Athen
wants me to give Maisie a helpful lecture of a moral nature . . . The
sheer imbecility of this caused Martha to smile even more brightly.
She said, "See you soon," and bicycled off. At the foot of the garden
she turned briefly to take a last look at the pink jersey, which from
here seemed a small pathetic blob which said: Help me help me
help me.

Mrs. Quest went in to her supper, alone. She had ordered enough
for two, had even cooked some jam tart. Martha is so fond of it,
she had thought. Though she knew quite well Martha never ate
sweets of any kind. Imagining the scene, where she put a slice of
tart, with its trickles of sweet cream, before Martha, but she shook
her head, Mrs. Quest's eyes filled with rejected tears.

She ate a good deal, though she was not hungry, and smoked several cigarettes. Then she listened to the nine o'clock news. All over
Europe people danced among ruins, danced in a frenzy of joy because of the end of the war. Mrs. Quest sat imagining the scenes in
London. As a small girl she had been taken by her father to join the
rioting crowds on Mafeking night. She recreated those memories
and filled London with them in her mind. Then, the radio ceased to
talk of victory, the day was over. Mrs. Quest "settled her husband
for the night"—which meant, this evening, since he was half-asleep
and did not want to be awakened, giving him an injection and another sedative, in case he woke in the early dawn, which is what he
dreaded more than anything. Mrs. Quest patted her little white dog,
went to the kitchen to find him a tit-bit from the refrigerator, then
she went to bed herself. Her powerful unused energies surged
through her, and soon she was again lying wakeful, thinking in
hatred of her daughter. The fantasy of expulsion from Mrs. Maynard's drawing room had gone a stage further. Mrs. Maynard had
arranged for Martha's arrest for "Communist activities." Martha
was in front of judge and jury. Mrs. Quest, chief witness, was testi-
fying that Martha had always been difficult: "she's as stubborn as a
mule, Your Honour!" But with careful handling, she would become a sensible person. Martha was let off, by the judge, on condition that she lived in her mother's house, in her mother's custody.

Mrs. Quest drifted towards sleep. The scent of roses came in
through the window, and she smiled. This time they remained in her
hand—three crimson roses. That brutal woman, her beautiful mother,
remained invisible in her dangerous Heaven. The painful girl,

Martha, was locked in her bedroom, under orders from Court and Judge. Mrs. Quest had become her own comforter, her own solace. Having given birth to herself, she cradled Mrs. Quest, a small frightened girl, who lay in tender arms against a breast covered in the comfort of bright salmon-pink, home-knitted wool.

Martha bicycled through streets which tried to create Victory night. Knots of people walked about with feather blowers and balloons. In the hotels they were dancing. Sometimes a car went past with its hooter screeching. But it was no good. Hard enough for most of these people to feel the war; how then were they to feel the peace? Besides, the Colony's men were still up North, or in Burma, in England, or in prison camps.

In the office were evidences of a just-concluded political meeting. The ash trays were filled with mess, and the air was foul. Whose meeting? Probably one of the African groups. There were two or three now. But there was a new African leader, so it was rumoured, called Mr. Zlentli, and he had nothing to do with the white sympathizers, so he would not have been here.

Martha sat down, doing nothing about tidying the place, simply submitting to the fug and the mess. She was waiting to argue with Athen. It was Athen's contention that she, Martha, should make Maisie leave her job as barmaid, and take what he called "a job for a nice girl." It was Martha's contention that if Athen did not want to take on Maisie himself, then he should not interfere. Last time he had raised the question, Martha said, "Athen, if you're so concerned, then why don't you save Maisie by marrying her?"

To which he had replied by nodding and saying, "Yes, I had thought of it. She is a good girl and she needs a man to look after her. But I think it would not be a good thing for Maisie to be made a widow again."

When the door opened, it was Thomas Stern who came in. He wore the uniform of the medical corps, and carried in his hand a bundle of civilian clothes. He smiled at Martha and said, "You'll excuse me, but I'm going to change." He proceeded to do so, while she turned her back and looked out over the dark town. The National Anthem seemed to be oozing from a dozen different sources, played at different rates and in different manners.

"Tonight is more than I can take," said Thomas Stern. "Otherwise I would offer to escort you around the celebrations." He arrived beside her, on the bench.

He now wore a thick brown sweater. His broad face was scarcely less brown. He smiled at Martha from six inches distance and she smiled back. There was a total lack of haste, of urgency, in this exchange. They regarded each other steadily, then he took her hand and held it against his cheek.

"What a pity I have to go back to the farm tonight."

"And that I have to see Athen!"

"Are you having an affair with Athen?"

"Good heavens, no!"

He now held her hand pressed down with his on his warm knee. "Why shouldn't you?"

"Have you seen Athen's new suit?"

"Of course."

"Has he talked to you about it?"

"Martha, I tell you, there are some things spoiled people like you don't understand."

"Rubbish. But I believe that Athen has sentenced himself to death because he is ashamed of liking nice wine and looking beautiful in his new suit."

Thomas regarded her steadily. Her hand, between his hot knee and his large hand, seemed to be melting into his flesh. He was waiting for her to stop being childish.

"Just imagine all the people today who are secretly sorry the war is over because now they have to start living."

"Yes, but Athen is not one of them. Why are you so angry with him? I agree with him. There's nothing wrong with being a barmaid, but it's not for Maisie. It's not good for her. I went into the bar to see her. Athen is right."

"What she needs is a husband, so what's the use of . . . " Martha's voice grew steadily more angry. "She's in love with Athen."

"When it comes to women and love, then I have nothing to say. Yes, she needs a husband. If I wasn't married, I'd offer myself, if it would make you happy."

"Well, I'm not going to tell Maisie that she should be a shop assistant or something. Why don't you or Athen tell her, instead of getting at me about it?"

Thomas regarded her very seriously for some moments. Then he smiled. "I know what you're thinking, Martha."

"What?"

"You're thinking: This Thomas, what a damned peasant."

"Yes, I was."

"Well, I am. I'm a peasant. I'm a Polish peasant. I'm a Jewish Polish peasant."

"Well, then?"

"You're looking even thinner and sicker than before. What's wrong with you?"

"Everything, everything, everything. And besides, it has only just recently occurred to me that I'm neurotic, and I don't like the idea."

"Well, of course, all women in the West are neurotic."

Now Martha started to laugh. She loved Thomas because with him, there was nothing for it but to laugh.

"And you find me attractive because I'm all thin and tense and difficult?"

"Of course. When I was a boy in our village, all us clever young men, we used to go to town to see American films and look at the women. We knew what was wrong with them. We understood Western women absolutely. We used to make jokes."

"I can imagine."

"Yes. Just like Africans now. They look at white women in exactly the same way we used to look at women in the films or in the magazines. So of course I'm delighted to see you all tensed up and decadent, Comrade Martha. It's the fulfilment of my favourite fantasy."

Martha laughed again. All the same, part of her was saying: But this isn't what I want. For one thing, I'll be going to England soon.

"And your wife?" she said.

Thomas' hands dropped like stones. "Yes, Martha," he said looking dejected. "You're right to ask but there's nothing I can say. I don't know." He got up, went across the room, fiddled with the door of the pamphlet cupboard, then turned back to face her.

"The thing is, Martha, I have affairs all the time, you know that."

She waited, merely looking at him curiously. She thought: I didn't want to have an affair with Solly because he's so childish. He's an idiot. Now I'm afraid to have an affair with Thomas because he's not childish.

But, in any case, what's the point, if I'm leaving.

Thomas came back, sat close to her, and put his two large hands on her shoulders, where they spread slow calm areas of warmth.

"This evening I said to myself: I'll find Martha, then I'll take her for a drive or something. Then I thought: No, that's not for us, we don't need that kind of thing. But in any case, I have to go back to the farm because my little girl isn't well."

They sat looking at each other, with a soft curiosity.

"Listen, Martha. I've got a week's leave, so I'm going to the farm for a week. Then I'll be back in town."

He spoke as if everything was settled. They had never even

kissed, but it was as if they had already loved each other. He did not kiss her now. He got up and said, "Well, Martha . . . "

She smiled, she supposed, but could not say anything. She had understood that to be with Thomas would be more serious than anything yet in her life, yet she did not know how she knew this, and she was not sure it was what she wanted. A few weeks ago she had thought: Thomas, or Joss—a man. Now here was Thomas and he was sucking her in to an intensity of feeling simply by standing there and claiming her.

From the door he smiled and nodded, "I'll ring you when I get back into town."

He went out. Athen did not come, so Martha cycled home through streets full of drunks where the National Anthem still sounded from every other building. Anton and Millicent, both dressed up, were just about to go out to one of the hotels. They all greeted each other with smiling amiability: they had agreed they were to be "civilized" and even, if possible, friends. Martha was invited to join them at McGrath's; as Millicent said a war doesn't end every day. But on the whole she thought not; they went out, and she went to bed.

4

"Public opinion changes."

A couple of decades, a decade, in these rapid days even a year, demonstrate how suddenly the season of a belief can turn. Into its own opposite, the rule seems to be—or at least, often enough to make it safe to ignore the exceptions.

This was Martha's first experience of it. Last time there had been a change, she had changed with it. Four years before, the present "politically conscious" Martha had been born, out of—that's what it amounted to—the Battle of Stalingrad. How odd that "a busybody who ran around all the time" (Anton had said it again only last night) could be born out of a great battle thousands of miles away. Which was a ridiculous thought: Martha found herself sitting with a smile on her face, when the speaker on the platform was in the middle of a sentence about people starving to death in Europe.

But the hall was half full, and the audience were restless, not because they were bored, far from it, but because they were angry with the speaker. Martha ought to be making up with her appreciation for their lack of it. The chair she sat in had a hard edge which cut across the back of her thighs. It was very hot. When she stood up, her pink dress would be marked by a wet line, unless she . . . She wriggled forward on her seat, and Anton gave her a look—do be still!

This winter, Professor Dickinson was saying, millions of people in Europe would be without enough to eat; the children would be marked for life by what happened to them; thousands would die. Yet international capitalism was quite prepared to . . .

A man shouted, "Cut out the gramophone record and let's have facts."

"Yes, yes," shouted several people.

It was the most extraordinary thing, being part of this audience. Everything was suddenly different. At the beginning of this same year, 1945, the war still gripped half the world, and when people said: It will soon be over, they did not really believe it. One had only to mention the Soviet Union to create a feeling of warm participation with a mighty strength used for the good and the true. Germany was a subhuman nation so brutalized, so sadistic in its very essence, that it could only expect "to work its passage back to membership of the civilized world" by long slow degrees. Japan was not far behind in villainy. All these were major axioms. A minor change: six months ago the Tories had governed Britain and, it seemed, always would. But Labour had won the election after all. As for this country, this enormous tract of land nevertheless made unimportant by the fewness of the people it supported—well, its long prosperity, because of the war, was threatened. Its own soldiers returned from various battlefronts, mostly in small numbers, while the R.A.F. left daily in thousands. But if to be in this country was to feel like being churned in a whirlpool, it was no more than what happened everywhere; all over the world human beings were shifting in great masses from one country, one continent, to another: myriads of tiny black seeds trickled from side to side of a piece of paper shifted about in a casually curious hand.

As for "the group," that ridiculous little organism, it did not exist —which was proved by the fact that most of its former members were here tonight, friendly enough, if wary, towards each other.

This was "a big meeting" and therefore everyone had turned out, responsible to the end towards something they had begun and which now was ending. They sat along the back of the Brazen Hall,

which was even scruffier and dingier than before, a dozen or so
people. There were present Anton Hesse and his wife, Piet du
Preez and Marie, Athen from Greece, Thomas Stern from Poland,
Solly Cohen, Marjorie and Colin Black, Boris Krueger and his wife,
young Tommy Brown, and Johnny Lindsay, who looked very ill,
but was being supported by Flora.

As for the dozens of others, comrades, friends, lovers, who everyone thought about tonight, because of their sense of an occasion
which marked an end, they were all over the world—in England,
and Scotland, in America and in Israel. Nearer home, Joss had
settled "up North;" and Jasmine was living "down South" in Johannesburg.

Coming into the hall Marjorie had said, "Isn't it *awful*, when you
think . . . " And big Piet had said, "Man, it gives me the skriks, I
can tell you that!" And Solly had said, "O.K., so I'm a traitor—but
how about closing the ranks just for tonight!"

What could more sharply epitomize the general change than that
"a big meeting" should be taking place here, in this dirty little hall,
even though the speaker was the famous Professor Dickinson from
Johannesburg? Only six months before, it would have been enough
to ask the authorities for the big State Hall, to be given it. But permission had been mysteriously delayed until Mrs. Van, asking for
the reason in person, had been given the verbal explanation that
"it was not considered desirable that the State Hall should be used
for such purposes." The letter of refusal had of course been bland:
the hall was booked for all the nights they had asked for it. Acting
on the sound old principle that "they should never be allowed to
get away with anything," Marjorie Black had written in offering the
authorities twenty more dates supplied by the obliging Professor.
But this letter had earned an exact repetition of the first; the hall
was booked for all the mentioned dates. Again Mrs. Van, respected
town councillor, enquired "off the record." And off the record she
was told that "the Reds" need not think they would ever get the
State Hall again—a decision had been taken and was written into the
minutes. And how, Mrs. Van had demanded to know, was "a Red"
defined these days? Anyone who was a member of the following
organizations, she was told.

And what, she asked, had happened to make these organizations
unsafe which for at least four years had been respectable? A decision had been taken by whom?

At this tempers had been lost, and voices raised. A chill wind blew—that was all. The atmosphere had changed. "Public opinion had changed." What people were afraid of—*that* is what had changed. Fear had shifted its quarters.

Another difference: Mrs. Van had said that obviously Thomas Stern could not be chairman. Now during the war, or at least since the end of "the phoney war," the atmosphere had been such that of course a corporal from the Health Corps could chair a public meeting, of course a twenty-year-old aircraftsman could address five hundred solid citizens on revolutionary poetry—one needed no other credentials than one's enthusiasm.

But Mrs. Van had put Mr. Playfair into the chair—he who had once been reserved for the most tricky of "respectable" meetings. She had said to Marjorie Black, "Really, dear, now that everything's changed, you must have more sense."

The hall was less than half full. The faces were all familiar, of course. These were the public who had made so many activities possible, had raised money, given it, bought pamphlets, and applauded every variety of Left-wing sentiment. And here they sat, their faces for the most part stiff and hostile. And where were the others?

Well, public opinion had changed, that was all.

Professor Dickinson was a lively handsome little man, even more vigorous than usual tonight because he thrived on opposition. What he was saying was no more than what had been said up and down these platforms for four years. The Soviet Union had been allowed a truce by the capitalist powers for the duration of the war, since it was taking the brunt of the war against Hitler (who of course had been if not created, at least supported by, the said capitalist powers as an anti-Communist insurance) but that now the Soviet Union was exhausted, bled white, had lost its usefulness, the capitalist powers would revert to type and do everything to destroy the socialist country, taking up where they had left off in 1940. The war need never have taken place if Britain had responded to the Soviet Union's invitation to make a pact against Hitler; the war had suited certain financial interests extremely well, millions of people had died because finance capital was more interested in making profits than in ...

This thesis—which until a few months ago would have been greeted by everybody with the overloud, overquick laugh of public approval which greets sentiments that have been, or might again be, dangerous, and then with storms of clapping and cries of Yes! Yes!—was now being listened to in sullen silence.

The Professor was saying that within two or three years, Germany the outcast, Germany the fascist beast, Germany the murderer would be the bastion of the capitalist defences in Europe against the Soviet Union, just as Hitler had been during the thirties. The proof? Already the capitalists, particularly America, poured money into German industry. Why? Out of compassion for the starving Germans? No, because it was necessary for Germany to be the strongest country in Europe, divided or not, and he would even go so far as to predict that within five years German troops and American troops and British troops would be marching under the same banners . . . but he could get no further. The whole audience had risen and were shouting at him: "Red! Communist! Go back to Moscow!" Mrs. Van der Bylt rose from her place beside Mr. Play-fair and, since he was not doing more than smile earnestly at the angry audience he was supposed to be controlling, she banged authoritatively on the table with an empty glass.

But no one took any notice.

"Just like the good old days," said Solly, with a loud laugh, and people turned sharply to stare at the group of "Reds" who looked back, with incredulous half-embarrassed smiles. In spite of every-thing, they could not believe that these people, who had been to all their meetings, who were positively old friends, could now be standing there gazing at them with such uneasy, hostile, frightened faces.

But they had to believe it.

They were beginning to understand what they were in for.

It was during those few minutes while the hall seethed with angry shouting people that "the group" finally realized how little they had achieved during their years of hard work.

For one thing, where were the Africans? There was not a black face in the hall—not even a brown one. The Africans, the Coloured people, the Indians—none was here. Yet when "the group" started work, it was axiomatic that it was on behalf of the Africans above all that they would run their study groups and their meetings.

Tonight the mysterious Mr. Zlentli, the nationalist leader about whom the white people fearfully gossiped, was running a study group for his associates. So Clive de Wet had told Athen earlier in the afternoon, when Athen had suggested that since the white audi-ence was likely to be unappreciative of the famous Professor from Johannesburg, it might be a good thing if the other groups came. But Clive de Wet had said he did not see the point of their risking their jobs and homes for the sake of Communism and the Russians.

So in fact their work had been done for the white people; hundreds of white citizens had been pleased to play with "the left" while the war lasted, and now it was all over. And what had happened? The *Zambesia News* had changed the tone and style of its editorials, that was all. Or, at least, there were no other influences ostensibly at work.

The meeting was breaking up. People streamed from both exits, not looking at the platform, where the Professor and Mrs. Van der Bylt and Mr. Playfair sat smiling philosophically.

Solly shouted, "That's right, go quickly, got to be careful now, haven't you?"

"That's right," said Marjorie fiercely. "The heat's turned on so back they scuttle to their little holes, out of harm's way."

Athen said seriously, "But, comrades, this means a new policy must be made—I suggest we go to the office to discuss it."

For a moment silence; then people laughed, uncomfortably, for who were "the comrades" now?

"Yes," said Athen, "but that is not good, it is not enough that we just go home. We have a responsibility."

They stood, looking at the fierce little man who was gazing into their faces one after another, insisting that they should agree, become welded together, forget all their old differences. But of course it was not possible.

Piet said, "Oh, no, thanks, I couldn't face all that all over again." He went off, and his wife followed him, having sent back a friendly, no-hard-feelings smile. Tommy Brown went after the du Preez couple. Marjorie, who was grasping Athen's hands, in passionate approval of what he said, found her husband Colin at her side. "Yes, dear," said Colin, "I'm sure you're right, but don't forget we've got a baby-sitter waiting." "Isn't it just typical!" exclaimed Marjorie— but she went off with her husband. Johnny Lindsay was taken home by Flora and by Mrs. Van and by the Professor, an old friend.

The lights went out in the hall, and by the time they reached the pavement, there remained Anton, Martha, Thomas Stern, and Athen.

Athen stood smiling bitterly as the others went into the Old Vienna Tea Room. Then he turned and said to the three friends, "Well, shall I make a speech just for us here?"

"Why not?" said Anton.

"Ah," said Athen, in a low passionate tone, his face twisted with self-dislike, or so it seemed, pale with what he felt. "It is time I was at home. Every morning I wake up and I find myself here, and I ask myself, how long must I be away from my people?"

"And how do you think I feel?" said Anton. He sounded gruff, brusque, with how he felt. Yet such was the Greek's power to impose an idea of pure, burning emotion that Anton seemed feeble beside him. Meanwhile Thomas from Poland stood quietly by, watching. There they stood on the dark pavement. It was a hot night. A blue gum moved its long leaves drily together over their heads. The air was scented with dust and with eucalyptus.

"Look, Athen," said Martha, "why don't you just come back and —I'll make everyone bacon and eggs." She felt she had earned Athen's reply, "Thank you, Martha, but no, I will not. Suddenly tonight I feel far from you all. And what will you all do now? You will sit and watch how the poor people of this country suffer, and you will do nothing? No, it is not possible."

Thomas observed, "Athen, we'll just have to cut our losses. That's all there is to it."

And now it was Thomas's turn to appear inadequate—even ridiculous. Athen looked quietly at them all, one after another. Then he shrugged and walked off.

They stood, silent. Then Thomas said, "I'll fix him, don't worry." He ran after Athen. The two men stood in low-voiced gesticulating argument a few paces off, then Thomas led Athen back.

"Athen has something to say," Thomas announced. He then stood back beside Martha and Anton, leaving Athen to face them. An audience of three waited for the speaker to begin. Presumably this is what Thomas intended to convey? Was he trying to make fun of Athen? Martha could not make out from Thomas's serious listening face what he meant, then he nodded at her, feeling her inspection of him, that she must listen to Athen, who stood, his eyes burning, his fists raised, his dark face darker for the pale gleam of his elegant suit.

He was reminding them of the evening the Labour Party won the elections. The little office in Founders' Street had been stocked with beer, and for hours people, mainly R.A.F., had streamed in, to sit on the floor, and outside in the corridor, and down the stairs. They were drinking beer, singing the Red Flag, finally dancing in the street. Athen had been there. Towards morning he had got up from where he had been sitting, very quiet, observing them all—the Communists were celebrating with the others—from the bench under the window. He had said, "Good night, comrades. I hope that by the time the sun rises you will have remembered that you are Marxists."

"Is it possible that we are so far from each other—yet we all call ourselves Communists? I do not understand you. Is it that you have forgotten what it means to be a socialist now? Yet when your Labour Party got into power, you were all as pleased as little children that night. I sometimes think of you all—just like little children. Such thoughts, they are understandable from the men in the R.A.F. and the army. They are poor men without real politics. When they are happy their Labour Party gets into power, then I am happy for them. But we know, as Marxists that . . . "

It was grotesque, of course. This was a speech, they understood, that Athen had thought over, worked out, made part of himself. He had planned to deliver it—when and where? Certainly not on a dusty pavement after a public meeting that was almost a riot. Certainly not to Anton and Martha and Thomas. It was one of the statements or manifestoes that we all work out, or rather are written for us on the urgent pressure of our heart's blood, or so it feels, and always at three o'clock in the morning. When we finally deliver these burning, correct, true, *just* words, how differently will people feel our situation—and of course theirs. But, alas, it is just these statements that never get made. Or if they do . . .

The three of them looked at Athen, embarrassed rather than not, and all of them wished to stop him.

" . . . is it true that you really believe that Britain will now be socialist and all men free? And tonight, do we have to be told by a Professor from Johannesburg that, now the war is over, America and Britain will again try to harm the Soviet Union? Is not America now, as we stand here, pouring out her millions to destroy the Communist armies in China? Yes, it has been easy for you to say, in the last years, that you are socialists. But we have been allowed to say it only because the Soviet Union has been crippling herself to kill Fascism. And now it will be death and imprisonment again, just as it was before. . . . "

At last he stopped, though they had not moved, or coughed, or made any sign of restlessness. He said, "Forgive me, comrades, I see that you are listening out of kindness. You would rather be in the Old Vienna Tea Room with the others." Again he walked off. This time no one stopped him. A few paces away he turned to say in a different voice—low, trembling, ashamed, "Perhaps I feel these things because of something I must be ashamed of. I hate you, comrades, because for you it is already peace. Your countries are at peace. But mine is war—full, full of war, still. Good night. Forgive me." He went.

Anton, Martha, Thomas.

Martha wished that Anton would now say, "Let us go and have a cup of coffee together." She would have preferred to be alone with Thomas, but this was not possible at the moment, it seemed.

She had hardly seen Thomas since the scene, months ago now, in the office. A few days after it, Thomas had been transferred abruptly to another city. The transfer was not only unexpected—there was more to it, because Thomas was morose, bitter. It was rumoured Thomas had had a fight in the camp, had beaten some-one up. He had not said anything about the fight to her, though. Then off he had gone, a couple of hundred miles away. From the new camp he had written a humorous regretful letter—the fortunes of war, etc. As for Martha, she felt that she might have foreseen it. Since the war had started—friends, lovers, comrades, they appeared and vanished unpredictably. Of course Thomas was bound to be transferred that moment they agreed to love each other.

Once or twice he had come up for short visits. On one, she had taken the afternoon off, and he had come to the flat. But they had been unable to make love: the bedroom was hers and Anton's. They felt constrained, and sat and talked instead. Besides, a quick hour snatched where they could was not what either of them had engaged for.

Thomas had set himself to amuse her by making a short speech in parody of the solemn group style: an "analysis" of sex in war-time.

"It is popularly supposed that the moment the guns start firing sex drives everyone into bed. But what war fosters, comrades, is not sex, but the frustrations of romance. What will we all remember of the war? I will tell you: the fact that one was never in one place long enough to make love with the same person twice. Partings and broken hearts, comrades—the war has given us back the pure essence of romance. What are the ideal economic and social circumstances for sexual activity, comrades? I will tell you. It is a stable bourgeois society where the woman has servants to take the children off her hands. The husband goes to work or to visit his mistress, and the wife entertains her lover. No society has yet developed anything like this for satisfaction because not only do we get the comforts of—comfort, but just enough frustration to keep love alive. No comrades, I tell you, when I was still a poor boy in my village, I understand perfectly well, from novels, just how things ought to be, and war—nonsense, it's no use to us—but trust me, Matty. I'll be discharged soon, and I've got a place in town that I'll open up again for us."

Meanwhile he wrote sometimes. His erratic love life continued—so she heard. Knowing that she must hear he wrote, "I'm in an impossible position with you, Matty. Do you imagine that I don't know what a woman feels when she is told she is too special for casual affairs? Do you imagine I'd be such a fool as to say this to you? But if I'm careful not to say it, circumstances are saying it for me. But they tell me that this camp is being closed next month, and that means I'll be with you soon."

This afternoon Thomas had said that the camp was not being closed—not for another two or three months.

There was nothing for it but to go on writing love letters.

"I'd like to have a cup of coffee with you both," said Thomas. "But I've got to be off. I'm driving out to the farm tonight—I've got two days' leave."

"Oh, do come and have a cup of coffee," Anton said. Both Martha and Thomas looked at him to see if the drawling emphasis he put into it meant anything special, but it seemed not.

"Or perhaps you'd like to make a speech too?" said Anton.

"Why not?" said Thomas, sounding abrupt. Martha could see that he longed, as she did, for Anton to be somewhere else. This not being possible, he was talking on, saying anything, so as not to go away at once.

"Perhaps we could have a competition about whose country has suffered most?" said Anton.

"It's as useful as most of the things we do now, certainly," said Thomas.

"I don't agree," said Anton, suddenly angry—it was evident that he had been restraining himself with Athen, but was quite ready now to have a real argument. Even perhaps, an "analysis of the situation."

Thomas smiled, recognizing this. He said again, "I haven't time—I must go." But he still didn't go, stood in front of them, hands in his pockets, in his characteristic pose, frowning.

"Then you haven't time," said Anton.

"It's been quite a year, hasn't it?" remarked Thomas.

"That is certainly true," said Anton, on a questioning note: if you have anything to say, do say it?

Thomas remarked, "Today I read that the war damage in Germany is 400 milliard marks." He smiled. "Well, then. Thirty-two milliard pounds. Does that make it any easier? I kept looking at the figures like a madman."

Anton stood looking at Thomas. On his face was a small cold smile.

"Oh, all right, I won't press that point then. How about the mass bombing of Germany then? We didn't know what that involved did we?"

He came a step nearer and stood looking close into their faces—first Anton, then Martha. Now they understood that he was saying what he had been feeling, or thinking, while Athen made his speech.

"There's very little work to do in the camp now. That's a bad thing—I have nothing to do but read. It's like living in a bad nightmare—a thousand empty huts, because all the men are demobbed, but someone's made a slip-up somewhere, and the camp's being kept open. All the machinery is running—the mess is open, all the Health people like me operating away at full efficiency, all the blacks standing at attention waiting to take orders. No one to give orders, no one to eat in the mess, no one in the hospital, no one using my fine efficient latrines—it's a ghost camp. And I sit in my fine well-ventilated hut reading . . . for instance, I've got the latest about the concentration camps. We haven't heard the truth about them, that's obvious, it's too terrible to tell, so we'll get the truth in bits."

Again he looked at them, waiting.

"No comment? Well, I have the advantage over you, because you don't sit all day on a bed in a ghost camp full of food that's rotting in its cases because there's no one to eat it. Well, then, how about dropping the atom bombs on Japan, how about that?"

"We discussed that at the time," Anton said. To begin with the socialists had supported the bombs being dropped. Or rather, the thing had been accepted. It seemed that nothing much worse had happened than had been happening for years. Certainly Hiroshima and Nagasaki were not the words they later became—symbols for the beginning of a new frightful age. Nor had there been a special meeting or even a private discussion since about the atom bombs. Yet people's minds had changed, were changing. Without anything formal being said, or decisions being taken, the incident of the atom bombs was isolating itself, growing in meaning and intensity. But some people still agreed that it was right the atom bomb should have been used—Anton for one.

"What's your point?" said Anton. "That war isn't the prettiest of human activities?"

Thomas looked steadily at Anton, then smiled at Martha. "Oh, I haven't any point. That is the point. Anyway I've got thirty miles to drive. And it has been storming over the mountains, my wife said, so the rivers will be up if I don't get a move on."

"Well, then," said Anton.

"Yes. And there's India. How about the famine in India? It's all right, isn't it—I say, how about the famine in India? But the famine in Germany—that's not the same thing at all is it?"

"What are you getting at?" said Anton, his pale blue eyes like ice. "Are you telling me that I'm a German?"

"No. Of course not. Well, I seem to be talking to myself." Off he went, walking fast. At the corner of the street he turned and half-shouted, "Did you read, they're going to transfer one million people from East to West Germany?"

"Come on," said Anton to Martha, impatiently. "Let's get home."

Thomas was saying, or shouting, "They walk. They put their belongings in handcarts and walk hundreds of miles guarded by soldiers. Like cattle." Now he did go off finally, and they saw him lift his hand and wave it, in a sort of mock salute.

"Yes," said Anton. "So now we all discover that the war has made a lot of mess everywhere. What is the use of such discoveries?"

He took Martha's elbow to steer her safely through the people who were coming out of the Old Vienna Tea Room. "Good night, good night," they all said to each other.

Martha and Anton walked in silence to find the car. Amiably they drove back to their flat.

Their relations were admirable since Anton had a mistress. He believed that Martha had a lover.

Or apparently he did. Yet there was something odd about this, because while he would say to her, "I'm meeting Millicent after work," and she replied, "Oh, good, I'll see you later then," she never said who she would be meeting or what she would be doing. It was assumed that she would be meeting somebody. Who? Once or twice Anton had joked it must be Solly, and he had never mentioned Thomas.

It occurred to Martha that this curious man both believed that she had a lover, because it was easy if they both had someone else, and yet knew she had not. She would never understand him.

They lay side by side in their twin beds in the little bedroom.

Anton remarked that in his opinion Professor Dickinson by no means exaggerated the future.

Martha agreed with him.

Anton said that he had again written letters to his family in Germany. Soon, surely, there must be some news. It wasn't possible that everyone could have been killed.

Martha suggested it might be the moment to get their member of Parliament to make enquiries.

"Yes," said Anton. "If I don't hear soon, I shall have to approach the authorities. It will be a strange thing," he added, "living in Germany again. Sometimes I feel almost British." This last was in a "humorous" tone and Martha laughed with him.

Recently he had taken to saying humorously that he and Martha were having to stay together so long, that they were getting into the habit of it—perhaps Martha would like to come with him back to Germany?

Martha laughed, appropriately, at such times. But she knew quite well that Anton would not at all mind being married to her. It was taking her a long time to understand that some people don't really mind who they are married to—marriage is not, really, important to them. Martha, Millicent, Grete—it doesn't matter, not really.

Martha thought, incredulously: We have nothing in common, we have never touched each other, not really, where it matters; we cannot make love with each other, yet it would suit Anton if I stayed with him and we called it a marriage. And that other marriage with Douglas—he thought it was a marriage. As far as he was concerned, that was a marriage!

What an extraordinary thing—people calling this a marriage. But they do. Now they've got used to it, they can't see anything wrong with this marriage—not even my parents. They'll be awfully upset when we get divorced.

She thought, as she went to sleep: When I get to England, I'll find a man I can really be married to.

part two

Don't make any mistake about this. Real love is a question of compromise, tolerance, shared views and tastes, preferably a common background of experience, the small comforts of day to day living. Anything else is just illusion and blind sex.

From an officially inspired handbook for young people on Sex, Love, Marriage.

1

Six inches of marred glass in a warped frame reflected beams of orange light into the loft, laid quivering green from the jacaranda outside over wooden planks and over the naked arm of a young woman who lay face down on a rough bed, dipping her arm in and out of the greenish sun-lanced light below her as if into water. At the same time she watched Thomas's head a few feet below her through cracks in the floor: a roughly glinting brown head recently clutched by fingers which now trailed through idling light, bent politely beside a large navy-blue straw hat. Thomas's voice, warm from love-making, answered questions about roses put in a voice that said it was going to get as much attention from the expert as her visit warranted. The two heads moved out of her range of vision into the garden.

Martha turned on her back to stretch her body's happiness in cool, leaf-smelling warmth. Through the minute window the tree blazed out its green against violent sun-soaked blue, against black thunderous clouds which at any moment would break and empty themselves.

A deep forest silence. This shed had been built at the bottom of a large garden to hold tools and seedlings. The house (it was in the avenues, a couple of hundred yards from the Quests' house) now belonged to Thomas's brother and his wife. During the war Thomas had appropriated the shed and had built a loft across one half of it, half-inch boards on gum poles, as flimsy a construction as a child makes for himself in a tree. But it was strong enough, for it held a bed and even books and could be locked. The brick floor of the shed below was covered with divided petrol tins full of seedlings. Thomas, based on the farm where his wife lived, was also a nurseryman in the city. During the war he had kept an eye on the farm while he moved about the Colony from one camp to another. Now he moved back and forth from the farm to the town, bringing in lorry loads of shrubs, flowers, young trees grown on the farm to sell here. "Thomas Stern's Nursery" it said on a board on the gate, which was the back gate of Mr. and Mrs. Joseph Stern's garden.

Here Martha came most afternoons and some evenings to make love, or simply to turn a key on herself and be alone.

She had complained that her life had consisted of a dozen rooms, each self-contained, that she was wearing into a frazzle of shrill nerves in the effort of carrying herself, each time a whole, from one "room" to the other. But adding a new room to her house had ended the division. From this centre she now lived—a loft of aromatic wood from whose crooked window could be seen only sky and the boughs of trees, above a brick floor hissing sweetly from the slow drippings and wellings from a hundred growing plants, in a shed whose wooden walls grew from lawns where the swinging arc of a water sprayer flung rainbows all day long, although, being January, it rained most afternoons.

Once upon a time, so it is said, people listened to their dreams as if bending to a door beyond which great figures moved; half-human, speaking half-divine truths. But now we wake from sleep as if our fingers have been on a pulse: "So that's it! That's how matters stand!" Martha's dreams registered a calmly beating pulse although she knew that loving Thomas must hold its own risks, and that this was as true for him as for her.

When he came back into the shed below, Martha turned over again on her stomach to watch him. He did not at once come up the ladder, but bent over green leaves to adjust a label. His face was thoughtful, held the moment's stillness that accompanies wonder—which in itself is not far off fear. "No joke, love," as he had said, in joke, more than once; for these two had not said they loved each other, nor did it seem likely now that they would. But what Martha saw now, on Thomas's face, as he bent, one hand at work on a twist of rusty wire, was what she felt in the few moments each time before she was actually in his presence. No, it was too strong, it was not what she wanted, it was too much of a wrench away from what was easy; much easier to live deprived, to be resigned, *to be self-contained*. No, she did not want to be dissolved. And neither did he. Smiling, Martha, her teeth lightly clenching the flesh of her forearm, her nose accepting the delicious odours of her skin, watched Thomas straighten to come up the ladder, his broad brown face, his blue eyes serious, serious—then slowly warming with smiles. Up the ladder slowly mounted a brown sturdy man, with a brown broad face and blue eyes that seemed full of sunlight. He wore his working khaki from the farm, and his limbs emerged from it no differently than they had from the khaki of his uniform during the war. Slowly he came up the ladder, and Martha's stomach shrank, turned liquid, and her shoulders, breasts, thighs (apparently on orders from Thomas, since her body no longer owned allegiance to her) shrank and waited for his touch.

Thomas sat down on the bottom of the bed, or pallet. It was made of strips of hide over a wooden frame. It had on it a thin mattress and a rough blanket. He looked, smiling, at the naked woman lying face downwards, who then, because his gaze at her was apparently unbearable, turned over on her back. But her hand, obeying this other creature in Martha who was Thomas's, covered up the centre of her body, while her mind thought: Look at that, how very extraordinary! For now that her body had become a newly discovered country with laws of its own, she studied it with passionate curiosity.

Thomas sat quiet, looking at the naked woman whose right hand was held in the gesture of modesty celebrated in art (and at which both were by temperament likely to smile) and she lay looking back at him. They forced themselves to remain quiet and look into each other's faces now, having confessed that they could hardly bear it, and that it was something they must learn to do. For while the word "love" was something apparently tabooed, for both of them, and they had confessed that this experience was something unforeseen, and therefore by definition not entirely desired—when they looked at each other, seriousness engulfed them, and questions arose which they both would rather not answer.

For instance, this was a woman twice married (though she had not been *really* married, she knew) and with a lover or so besides.

As for him, he was married to a woman he adored. One could say, in Thomas's voice, apparently in reply to his own thoughts, since Martha did not mention it, "I *have* to love women, Martha, and that's no joke, believe you me." Or, as Thomas answered Martha, "Yes, Martha, of course. God knows what men do with women in this part of the world, but every time I have a woman, well nearly every time, I realize that her old man doesn't know what he's at. God knows what it's all about, but let me tell you, in Poland when I had a woman I had a woman, here I take it for granted I'm going to be faced with a virgin . . . but for all that, Martha, every time a woman likes a man in bed, then he is her first lover. And who am I to dispute the tactful arrangements of nature?"

But for Martha, every other experience with a man had become the stuff of childhood. Poor Anton—well, it was not his fault. And poor Douglas.

But that was not honest either. For by no means easily had she become what Thomas insisted she must be. Of course her real nature had been put into cold storage for precisely this, but when what she had been waiting for happened at last, then she discovered that creature in her self whom she had cherished in patience, fighting and reluctant. To be dissolved so absolutely—yes, but what was going to happen to her when Thomas—she could not say "when Thomas loves someone else," or "if Thomas goes back to his wife," and she said, when Thomas goes away.

"Why do you say that, Martha?"

"Say what?"

"You say, I'm going away?"

"But, Thomas, you are always going away somewhere."

"Yes, but that's not what you mean."

"Well, something like that."

"But it's you who are going away, you're going to England."

"Ah yes, but even if I didn't go to England."

A silence while they looked at each other—serious. "Yes, I know," said Thomas.

"Well then?"

"But in the meantime, I'm here."

A command, this last—for Thomas, or the creature in him who corresponded to the Martha he had created, demanded that she should give herself to him completely and that she must not listen to the warning: What shall I do when Thomas goes away?

And in any case, what was this absolute giving up of herself, and his need for it; what was the prolonged almost unbearable look at each other, as if doors were being opened one after another inside their eyes as they looked—how was it that she was driven by him back and back into regions of herself she had not known existed, when in any case, she had judged him at the time he had first approached her as, "No, he's not the right one." But then, of course, she was not the right one for him either, his wife was that, he said so. Or rather, that he wished she was.

She lay still, looking at his face. Her flesh was both relaxed, because of its contentment, and yet fearful because his large hand lay an inch from her knee, on the blanket. He was calmly looking her over, then into her face; looking at her hand, her knee, her breast, then into her eyes.

She said, unable to bear it after all, "It's a tragedy, you've made me all happy, and so I'm no longer thin and interesting."

She had put on flesh again. She was again a strong young woman. But she searched for and loved every frail or delicate line in herself as he did. She wished herself as fragile as a bird's skeleton for him who loved so much what *he* was not—the qualities of delicacy, grace.

He said, "You're a fine girl." He smiled gently, his face lit again with the almost-wonder of the moment she had surprised through the slits in the floor. "You think I'm nothing but a peasant, Martha?" He laid his hand on her knee; it shrank like a horse's skin, then she felt, through her kneecap, the warm strength of his hand. "You think: there's Thomas, a peasant from Sochaczen. A fine strong healthy fellow, not a sick thought in him—you think that?"

He bent over her. His face was desperate with what he was trying to make her accept from him. "Martha, do you see this line here?" He ran a finger up the inside of her upper arm: the flesh shrank, then waited.

"See that?"

Martha, serious; Thomas, serious; looked at the curve of flesh, a line as mortal as that made by a raindrop sliding down glass; they looked as if their futures depended on looking.

"I tell you, I want to die when I see that." He crushed her upper arm in a great fist, and his face grimaced with the pain he felt for her. "Do you understand? No, you don't understand. But I tell you, Matty, when I see that line, that curve, I want to cut my throat, I couldn't ever be that, don't you see?"

His face lay, desperate, against the warmth of her upper arm; the "line" that tormented him was for Martha merely a surface of sensation. "Ah God, Martha, I can't stand it, I tell you, I'm insane. You think I don't care for you when I say this to you?"

She smiled, her eyes filled with tears. She let her fingertips, sensitized beyond pleasure, rub gently up the rough surface of his turned cheek. His breath sent warmth over her arm.

"I know you do."

"Yes, I do. But, Martha, I don't understand it myself—I'd give the whole of you and everything I am for that line there, and for where your cheek lifts when you smile. That's something I'm not. Do you understand what I mean?"

"But perhaps they aren't what I am either?"

"Yes, yes, maybe. But I can't help it." He was in a rage of despair. Tears ran down her face, she could feel a hot wetness travelling, with edges of chill, down to her chin. What was she to think, to feel—if Thomas loved, to such lengths, the temporary delicacy of a curve of flesh, if he had singled out, with the eye of an insane artist, two, perhaps three "lines" which had purity, had delicacy, the kind of absolute perfection that kept even her, their supposed owner or possessor or creator, in awed appreciation of them—well, why choose a woman who was shaped, as he always said, half groaning, half pleased, "like a healthy peasant?"

She said, "But Thomas, why not get yourself a thin woman then?"

He said, rubbing his head backwards and forwards over her shoulder, as if he was trying to rub out the "line," "But I care for you, I keep telling you."

"Well, then I don't know, I give up."

He turned her towards him like a doll and said, "I once saw a woman, it was in the Cape—she was shaped like a flamingo. She was like a canary, I tell you. I put the energy into getting her that could have won the war two years earlier, but, Matty, I didn't care for her."

Martha laughed and thought: Well, what about his wife? The photograph of her showed a slight fair woman with a delightful smile. Yes, but how could she, Martha, say: Your wife's like a flamingo, she's as fragile as a handful of canaries, and obviously that's why you married her?

"Not to have this here, I can't stand it."

"What do you mean, *have* it."

"That's the point." His face was full of real anguish, the pain of his mind. "Don't humour me, Martha, don't be maternal—I'll kill you, I tell you, if you go maternal on me."

Their love-making was short—he had to go back to his farm, and she had to visit her father and then run errands for Johnny Lindsay. It was short too, because of the violence of this emotion.

"I tell you, Martha, there are times when I'm sorry we started, it's all too much for me, I can tell you."

"I know what you mean."

"So you do!"

They lay smiling at each other from half an inch's distance, eye to eye.

"I've got to go."

"Wait, I'll take you."

Suddenly a noise as if gravel was being flung about everywhere. It was raining in loud splashing drops through a strong orange evening sunlight. The six inches of glass ran in a streaked gold light. Thunder cracked, but a bird safe in a bunch of warm leaves repeated a long, slow liquid phrase over and over again.

A handful of rain blown in by a hard gust of wind scalded them with cold. They leaped out of bed and stood below the tiny window, through which rods of strong wet drove and stung their strong fresh satiated bodies.

They opened their mouths and let the wet run in, and watched the greenish reflections from the deep tree outside, and the orange lights from the window glass run and slide on their polished skins. They laughed and rubbed the freezing water from the sky over each other's shoulders and breasts. They felt as if they might never see each other again after this afternoon, and that while they touched each other, kissed—they held in that moment everything the other was, had been, ever could be. They felt half savage with the pain of loss.

Then a shrill voice from the back verandah of the house. Thomas's brother's wife, Sarah, was shouting at her husband, her servant, or her children, through the din of rain. Which stopped as if she had ordered it to stop, in a crash of thunder. And Martha and Thomas laughed, it was so sad and so comical.

They stood on tiptoe to see through the minute window a plump woman in a too-tight white dress shrilly agitating on a dripping verandah. Five years ago, she had been a pretty girl, and now—
"God!" said Thomas, in a sudden deep sincerity, "she's a good girl, they're all good people, these householders, but when I see them, I want to run and jump into the lake and that's the truth."

And Martha deepened her vow that she would never be the mistress of a household in a bad temper because . . . but they did not know why the plump woman on the verandah was so angry. She was too far off for her actual words to be heard; but her body, the set of her head, the edge on her scolding voice said, "I'm in a rage, I'm beside myself with rage."

The two crept down the ladder and stood on the red, rough, warm-smelling brick, looking out into the garden, seeing the strong brown trunk of the jacaranda whose lacy masses had waved above their naked bodies, which still stung pleasantly with memories of the lashing rain. All around them were soaked sparkling lawns, dripping boughs, a welter of wet flowers. Everything was impossibly brilliant in the clear washed light. And the bird sang on from its invisible perch. Martha was faint with happiness and with sadness, and Thomas's face told her he was in the same condition. The woman in the white dress went inside her house and Thomas said, "All right now, Martha." They ran over squelching grass to his lorry.

Martha asked, "What does she think, your sister-in-law?"

Thomas frowned.

Martha could have left it, but she pressed, "Well, doesn't she say anything?"

"She said something to my brother, he told her it wasn't her business."

Martha thought this over. She could imagine the scene—the uncomfortable husband, guilty because he was supporting his brother's freedom to do as he liked, the insistent woman in a dress that was too tight, the husband finally making a stand with a vehemence (and she knew it) for reasons neither of them could afford to say out loud.

There was an unpleasant taste in Martha's mouth, which she knew she ought to ignore. Thomas had started the lorry and they were moving off.

She said, "I suppose it's the place Thomas brings his girls to, is that it?"

Thomas gave her a discouraged look, and said, "If you want to make it like that, you can."

She nearly said, "But *I* haven't made it like that, have I?" But she didn't. She was sorry she had said anything. Besides, no one but she, Martha, went to the loft these days, and in fact it had been closed while Thomas was in W—— waiting to be demobilized. All the same, she thought of Sarah Stern, watching Thomas emerge from the shed with other girls, and for a moment she could not bear it. They drove a couple of blocks in silence, and both felt they were a long way from the simplicities of their being together in the loft.

"We'd better stop here," said Martha, before they reached her mother's gate.

Thomas stopped, and sat with his hand on the gear lever, while the engine throbbed. The whole lorry shook, and they shook with it. They began to laugh. "I'll be in town the day after tomorrow," Thomas said. "I don't know whether early afternoon or late, but if you want to go to the shed and read or something . . ."

They kissed, smiling, holding themselves steady, with difficulty, against the vibrations of the lorry. Then she said, "See you soon" and went up the path to her mother's verandah, deliberately annulling the time between now and the day after tomorrow.

The other house, from whose garden she had just come, was almost identical with this. Both gardens, large, deeply foliaged, full of flowers and birds, seemed miles from the streets that ran just outside them. One held the young Jewish couple with their children, a unit dedicated to virtues which would make them honoured members of their community and prosper their shop; Thomas's brother sold sports equipment from a smart shop in the centre of the city. In the Quests' house, everything had changed in the last few months: Jonathan had come home. As Martha came up the path she saw him sitting on the verandah reading a magazine—a handsome fair young man, with a small fair moustache and Mrs. Quest's innocent blue eyes.

Two catastrophes, either of which might have killed him—one, a shell exploding beside him, another, a tank going up in flames—had apparently not marked him, except for the arm, which was in plaster, and about which he was attractively diffident.

The arm still gave him a good deal of pain, and he had to attend the local hospital several times a week for treatment. Otherwise he would already be on his farm, which was waiting for him "up North." This time, up North meant a couple of hundred miles beyond the Quests' old farm, near the Zambesi Valley.

His mother was a woman with a new lease of life. She cooked, she entertained, she smiled and made plans.

Mr. Quest was better. No one had expected him ever to leave his bed again, but now he sat long hours in a deep grass chair on the verandah. He was neither altogether drugged, nor quite free of drugs. His waking condition was like a light sleep, Martha thought. He would see what was going on, without seeming to watch his surroundings, and he might comment on something, but usually some time afterwards. He would let out words, phrases, exclamations, that came out of his thoughts, but he did not know when he had done this. Sometimes he talked to people from the past, usually from "the old war." There was a man called Ginger, whom Martha had never heard of. Well, Mr. Quest talked a good deal to Ginger. They were in the trenches, it seemed, and Ginger was having some sort of brain storm or nervous collapse. Mr. Quest would urge Ginger to pull himself together and be a man. Sometimes Mr. Quest would call out in terror—thick, mumbling, protesting phrases: a shell was going to burst near him, something was going to explode. Or the water in the trench was too high up his legs, which were cold, or he was out in no-man's-land and could not see his comrades. Then Martha, or Mrs. Quest, or whoever was near would sit by him, and talk him gently awake, as one does with a child having a bad dream.

Everyone came to congratulate Mr. Quest on his recovery, just as they enquired after Jonathan's arm. Everyone behaved, Martha thought, as if the long illness, the damaged arm, were matters for pride—even for envy. Martha knew she was childish, she disliked the deep useless rage she felt, and yet she could not bring herself to enquire lengthily after the wounded arm and the painful treatments it needed, or after her father's health. She came in every day and sat a little while with "my two war casualties" as Mrs. Quest now called them, with a fond proud little laugh.

This afternoon Jonathan was not alone. Two young men played Ping-pong on a side verandah, while the little white dog snapped at the ball and jumped up and down and generally made a nuisance of himself. In the front room were two girls. These days, the Quests' house was full of young men and young women. The men were all back from the war, and the girls, as Martha noted with complicated feelings, were a new generation of girls aged eighteen, nineteen, who apparently had sprung into existence during the last year. At any rate, they were not at all interested in the war as such, but they regarded these young men, delivered to their bosoms fresh from the world's battlefields, as escorts and future husbands satisfactorily seasoned by experience.

Martha smiled at her brother, waved at the Ping-pong players and at the girls, for all of whom she was "the Quests' married daughter" and "a Red with ideas about the Kaffirs," and went around the corner of the verandah to see if her father was awake. He sat with his back to a screen of morning glory, whose brilliant but fragile blue trumpets were dwindling into limp rags of dirty white. His magazine had slipped to the floor and he was dozing.

Martha sat down to wait. She had not been moved to such thoughts by the presence of her brother and the young men whose little-boy faces had put them out of court in such matters, but now she remembered that half an hour ago she had been lying in the loft with Thomas. She wondered if her father would sense it.

When he opened his eyes with a start, she saw that he was not really there that afternoon.

"How are you?"

"Much as usual. And you're all right?"

"Fine."

"That's good."

She went on to supply a series of vague remarks until he was not listening: that the garden looked beautiful, and the weather was lovely, and the rain that afternoon had been a real monkey's wedding, half storm, half sunshine.

"That's good," he said again, and sat drowsing.

She thought of how often she had sat by this half-conscious man. Where did he go to, her father, while the elderly shrunken grey man sat dozing? She stared at him, stared, as if the pressure of her eyes could suddenly materialize him, her father, Mr. Quest, the vigorous, irascible man who knew, when he chose, so much about her. She felt as if he were there all the time—as if this invalid were an impostor, a mask. But really her father was there and if so she was in communion with him. Where was he? She looked at the old sick head slipping sideways and at the half-open mouth and demanded in silent and futile rage: Well, talk to me, where have you got to? Meanwhile her heart ached. It ached.

Inside her mother was bustling enjoyably about. Soon Martha went in to see her. These days, now her son was home and she was released into vigour, cooking supper for a dozen young people, running the big house, organizing parties and excursions, Mrs. Quest was good-tempered again. Now the nursing of her husband was only one of many things she had to do, not the reason for her existence. These days she did not complain that Martha was a bad daughter. In fact the two women enjoyed seeing each other.

They kissed.

"Well, where are you gadding off to now?" asked Mrs. Quest good-humouredly.

"I'm going to a meeting on current affairs," said Martha, offering the absurd phrase to her mother in an invitation to laugh.

"Well," said Mrs. Quest, energetically folding towels, "I suppose there's no harm in it, but I should have thought we had enough of *them*. And when are you going to see Mrs. Maynard? Bad girl, she keeps asking after you."

"I'm sure she does!"

The ghost of ill-humour appeared, but vanished again, because of the full strong physical well-being of the two women. *Almost,*

Martha was cold and irritable, and Mrs. Quest cold and unjust.

"What's all this about someone called Maisie? She keeps talking about a girl called Maisie something or other."

"You might very well ask!"

"But I'm not supposed to, is that it?"

Martha laughed, so did her mother, and again they kissed, before Martha went off to Johnny Lindsay's.

2

Martha had given up her job with Mr. Robinson. Otherwise she could not have the afternoons with Thomas. The day after Thomas had said to her, "Well then, what are you earning, what's keeping you there?" Martha, on the simplicity of will that was Thomas's gift to her, walked into Mr. Robinson's office and gave notice. By herself it would have taken weeks of thinking, I should do this or that, and then a drift into a decision. But now she lived from this new centre, the room she shared with Thomas, a room that had in it, apparently, a softly running dynamo, to which, through him, she was connected. Everything became easy suddenly.

Or nearly everything, for of course there were new problems. Martha "worked at home," or, as she told everyone, with an apparently firm intention: "I'm using the flat as an office." It was no good; as far as others were concerned, Matty had given up her job, and was free in the daytime.

She had told Mrs. Van she wanted typing work; and now the members of Parliament who were Mrs. Van's friends, and Mrs. Van herself, brought work to Martha. The hours she sat before her typewriter every day were a third as long as before, and she earned twice as much. If the seriousness of "work" is measured by what one earns for it, then Martha was working twice as hard as she did in Mr. Robinson's office. As Thomas pointed out.

It was the same as when she was the wife of Douglas Knowell— the cast had changed, the play was the same. Now came, every morning, Marjorie Black, Maisie McGrew, Betty Krueger, Mrs. Quest—even Mrs. Van.

Every morning, as Martha sat at her typewriter, transforming scribbled sheets into piles of ordered black print, there would come a knock on the half-open door. (Why don't you lock your door then? said Thomas—But it's so hot!) Into the room would come one or several of these women, each exclaiming that they did not wish to waste Martha's time, that they had work to do of their own in any case, but they had just dropped in. (Why don't you tell them to go away, Martha? Just say, you're sorry, you're working.)

And why did Martha not ask them to go away?

Thomas said, "You never go to them, to their houses, do you?"

"No."

"There you are. It never even occurs to you. It's not something you do. So they come to you."

"Well?"

"So you have to become a woman who is not to be disturbed in the daytime, because it's not something you do."

"Ah, but it's not so easy."

"Perfectly easy, if you decide to do it."

To serve tea, to sit talking, being sympathetic, charming (etc., etc., ad nauseam), creating a web of talk which (she knew quite well and so did they) had no relation to the events and people they discussed but which seemed to have a validity of its own—there was the most powerful attraction in it. She could positively see, after the women left, the soft, poisonous, many-coloured web of comment and gossip they had created, hanging there in the smoky air of the little room.

But of course these were "intelligent" people, some of them even "educated," even—though this was a word they used with an increasingly humorous grimness—"progressive" people. Yet what had changed in the talk, since Martha had chafed at the talk at the women's tea parties in the avenues? These women did not complain about their servants; they deplored, instead, that they had servants, wished they could do without them, and often indeed, took decisions to give them up. And they did not complain about their husbands, but about "society," which made marriage unsatisfactory. They did not talk scandal in the sense of have you heard that so and so has left her husband? They discussed people's characters, with all the dispassionate depth offered them by their familiarity with "psychology." Why anybody ever did anything, was immediately obvious to these psychologically educated females, and people's motives were an open book to them, their own included. Recipes they exchanged—to talk about food was not reactionary, though to discuss clothes for too long was frivolous, if not reactionary. As for politics, there were two kinds of politics, neither needing much comment. Local politics, which meant, here, the situation of the black man—well, one can reach a degree of sophistication which means one has only to glance at a newspaper and exclaim bitterly:

Of course, what would one expect!—to have said everything necessary. As for world politics, the manifestations of "the cold war," a recently christened phenomenon, made it impossible for this tiny group of people to communicate easily, since they represented between them every variety of "Left" opinion, each grade of it needing the most incredible tact and forbearance with the others.

And of course there was a horrible fascination, the dark attraction of Martha's secret fears, in the fact that of the younger women there was not one who hadn't sworn, ten years ago: I will *not* get like that! I *won't* be dragged in. They all felt it, acknowledged it. Perhaps this knowledge, that none of them was strong enough to resist the compulsion to create the many-coloured poisonous web of talk, was why they all felt exhausted after such mornings. Just like the frivolous, nonprogressive women of the avenues, they spent their days over cups of tea, and went home in a sort of dragging, rather peevish dissatisfaction, while in their heads still ran on, like a gramophone record that could not be turned off, the currents of their gossip: The trouble with Betty is, she is mother-fixated, her headaches are obviously of psychological origin, and Martha's trouble is she is unstable, and Marjorie's trouble is she is a masochist, why have another baby when she'll only complain at the extra work, and Mrs. Van—well, she's marvellous, but she's awfully conventional really, and Jack Dobie is not doing the progressive cause much good, if he hadn't framed that bill in such an aggressive way, he'd have got it through the House, but he has a father-complex, which makes it necessary for him to challenge authority.

Because she could not work in the mornings, Martha would say to Anton, on the evenings when Thomas was not in town, "I'm sorry, but I've got to work after supper." Most evenings Martha worked, and Anton read or might go out—presumably to see Millicent.

"You don't feel any guilt about telling your husband you want to work, but you do when the women come around to gossip?"

"He's not my husband."

"Of course not. And this work, typing out reports for Jack Dobie about his trade unionists—that's important?"

"It's better than talking about the du Preez' children's psychological problems and Piet du Preez' power complex."

"Is it? Then if you feel it is, it is."

Martha said, "When I'm here and you say it, of course, it's ridiculous. But afterwards it's all very serious."

"Only because you let it be serious."

Martha said, "All these things that drive us crazy, you put them into words, they sound silly. But it *is* important."

"All you have to do is to come here every morning when Anton goes to work and work here."

They sat on the low bed, side by side. It was in the evening, before he had to go back to his farm. A single small bulb laid shadow and light about them. They were enclosed in a small sweet-smelling world of wood and foliage. He was making white marks on her thigh with the pressure of his fingers, lifting them to let the blood flow in, then pressing down again. Both watched, absorbed, this life of the flesh which flourished in its own laws under their eyes.

"You were going to say something about when I go away, Martha. There's a look on your face which means that."

"Yes, that's what I was thinking."

"I know you were. Well, you're right. Look, I'm not disputing it, believe me."

"Disputing what? I haven't said anything."

"You get a look on your face. That means I should shut up. You are claiming your right to make safeguards."

"For when *I* go away?"

"That's below the belt, it really is, Martha. You mean, because I don't marry you, then you have to sit around all morning gossiping and complaining afterwards?"

"Who said anything about marrying?"

"You're in the right to mention it."

"*I* didn't mention it at all."

"Ah, my God, you'll drive me mad. Then we'll discuss your serious problems. Look then. You say you wouldn't have left that office job except for me? Look how easy that was. When Mr. Robinson got in the way of serious things, like a lover, then you changed your life at once. Now you say the women waste your time in the mornings—then come here, so they don't know where you are."

"Ah yes, but it's all very well, you'll go away. And Heaven knows how long I'll have to stay here, years very likely. Anton hasn't heard a word from Germany yet."

"Just leave him!"

"But you know I can't. If I do then it makes him unrespectable and he'll never be made a British citizen."

"But he doesn't want to be a British citizen."

"Perhaps he does—I don't know. Why do we have to talk about Anton?"

"He's your husband, that's why."

"He's *not* my husband."

That rainy season, she spent nearly every afternoon in the loft, and most evenings. Then there were fewer evenings—Thomas's work was suffering, he said. For a while Martha stayed at home when Thomas was not coming—but then returned to the loft. Every evening, after supper, she told Anton she must work, and she went to the loft.

Every afternoon Martha went to the loft, hoping she would see no one, hoping that Thomas's brother's wife would not see her. But the plump watchful woman was nearly always sewing on her verandah. So Martha went openly across the back garden and into the shed. There she waited for Thomas. Sometimes he did not come, and she read, or simply did nothing, watching the green shadows from the tree ripple on the planks of the floor. Here she was "herself," no one put pressure on her. Even when Thomas did not come, she returned happy, and—this was increasingly the point—armed, against Anton. It came to this: she began to go to the shed in the mornings, not because of the idle women, but because of Anton.

For her feelings about Anton had gone beyond anything she could understand. Like "the circle of women," her husband provoked in her only the enemy, feelings so ancient and, it seemed, autonomous, they were beyond her control.

For consider how irrational it was. First there had been the period of months when they, Anton and Martha, decided that they would "live their own lives." During this time, when presumably Anton had pursued his affair with Millicent, and Martha had had nobody, but waited for Thomas, they lived together amicably—without any emotional contact, but certainly without strain.

This ease had ended, but at once, that day when Martha had first made love with Thomas. She had not expected anything to change. After all, had not Anton assumed, all this time, that she had a lover?

Yet the night after she had first made love with Thomas, Anton made love to her, and for the first time in months. Stranger still, although she was claimed by Thomas, absorbed by what she had discovered and knew she would discover, she went through the motions of compliance with Anton. Why? She did not have to. She did not even mean to. Yet she did. She despised herself for it, certainly, but that was hardly the point, compared with the knowledge that if Anton had come into her bed the night before (before making love with Thomas) she would have said no, or implied no —but of course Anton would *not* have come, he only made love to her because of Thomas.

Who, then, was this person in Martha who first of all signalled to her husband, her legal possessor (or some kind of possessor), that she had been unfaithful to him, and who then went on (without Martha knowing about it, let alone sanctioning it) to signal invitations to him, because apparently she had to buy this disliked husband's compliance, forgiveness even? By offering him her sex?

Martha lay awake after Anton's making love to her, not because of Thomas about whom, even after the first time of making love with him, she had no doubts at all, but about Anton, who had suddenly become a frightening unknown country.

She thought: Suppose I said to Anton, "You've made love to me tonight not even because you're jealous, but because certain instincts have been touched, so that you have to re-establish possession of me"—well, what would he say? He'd look at her outraged, even disgusted. What sort of conventional attitudes was she putting on him? And what instincts? Had she not had a lover, with his agreement, for months? And while his body had been aggressive, violent, even painful, his words had been that of a dear old friend or comrade, making love with an old bedfellow out of a playfully freakish impulse! Rather pleasant, really, his wry but jaunty smile said, as he pulled up pyjamas and tied their neat white cord, to make love to a wife with whom one has such civilized friendly arrangements—yes, civilized, that's what his smile said he felt. And he neatly arranged his long handsome limbs in bed, smiling at Martha as he turned out the light and turned a back which signalled in its own language, right across anything he might think he felt: Very well then—but who owns you? I do! And Martha could feel her body wanting to assume a sort of silly sly giggling posture which said: Oh, so that's what you think, is it?

It was all humiliating, ridiculous . . . she could not let it happen again. She had to cut Anton out of her consciousness, had to bring down a curtain in herself and shut him out. Otherwise she would get ill. There she was, sharing a flat with him, cooking his food, going out with him sometimes, lying in a twin bed every night in a shared bedroom. But she was not there: she had knotted her emotions tight with Thomas and shut Anton out.

Even so, she was on the edge all the time of being ill. It was never far off. This was not at all the vague tight tension of before Thomas, which was not so much the threat of illness as the illness itself: a perpetual dry inner trembling, a superbrightness, extra-attention, a lightness of her being—the stage on to which might walk, at any time, the disembodied emotions she could not give soil and roots to within herself.

No, this was something quite different, on a different level—directly physical. If she let her connection with Thomas weaken; if she let her—what?—body (but what part of it?) remember Anton and that he was her husband, well her nerves reacted at once and in the most immediately physical way. She vomited. Her bladder became a being in the flesh of her lower stomach, and told her it was there and on guard. It did not like what she was doing—did not like it at all. Her stomach, her intestines, her bladder complained that she was the wife of one man and they did not like her making love with another.

But, of course, none of this could be told to Anton, or even mentioned to him. They were being civilized, he and she; they made civilized arrangements about marriage when it was not a success, and lived together like brother and sister, sharing single beds in a small bedroom, saying things like, "Did you have a good day, Anton?"

"Yes, very good. I'm reorganizing that whole department. Yes, I may be an enemy alien and a damned German, but I'm organizing their freight department for them."

"And about time too, I'm sure."

"And I went to see Colonel Brodeshaw. After all, he is member of Parliament for this constituency."

"Oh good, can he help you?"

"I think he wants to. I begin to think that Marxist theory underrates the role that the democratic consciousness plays in the British way of life. It is not only a mask for reaction, it is not just hypocrisy."

"Oh, you think not?"

"No. Although he is a proper old Blimp, he is really very decent."

"Well, that's *because* he's an old Blimp, perhaps."

"Yes, that's quite true, Matty, you've put your finger on it. Only a real old Tory like Colonel Brodeshaw, someone who really believes his own propaganda, could afford to be like that."

"Like what?"

"Well, you know . . . " Anton drawled this out, rather patronizing, apparently, though it concealed a deep gratitude, and even the kind of terror a child feels at the unknown. "I said to him, I cannot conceal this from you, I am a Communist."

"But surely he must know you were one, by now."

"No, that isn't the point. It was essential to tell him so that he wouldn't think I was pulling wool across his eyes. They place great importance on this decency of theirs."

"Well, so what did he say he'd do?"

"It's not easy, after all. I told him that I keep writing letters to everyone I knew before the war. It's all the cities in Germany, when you really add it up." A silence. His breathing changed, harshened. The dark room was filled with it—quick and soft breathing, like panting. Martha listened to it—not for the first time. Anton had bad nightmares; most nights he cried out to oppressors and torturers, and thrashed his long body about in bed. But he did not know he had bad dreams, and considered people who did to be neurotic.

"He ought to be able to make enquiries from the military authorities."

"Yes, he said he would write."

"And the East Zone?"

"He can't do anything about that, of course. I've written to the authorities myself."

"It'll all take time then."

"Yes, well, there's been a war on, there's no getting away from that."

Until Anton's future was settled—that is, until he was naturalized so that he and Martha could get divorced; or until he decided he did not want to be naturalized, in which case Martha could leave him without doing him damage, these two were stuck together. Whether they liked it or not. But he could not make any plans until he could get news from Germany. He was writing letters, dozens of letters a week, into the ruins that were Germany.

"One thing Colonel Brodeshaw did say: he thought that a lot more people were killed in the bombing than we know yet."

"I expect he's right."

"Or perhaps they are prisoners of war in the Soviet Union—no joke that, you can't expect the Russians to be softhearted after everything."

Such conversations, held almost nightly, twisted the strings of pity right through Martha, and made it necessary for her to go and put her arms around him. But she could not, because otherwise she would get ill. Besides, presumably Millicent did. But she was continually torn, and continually on the edge of physical discomfort, if not sickness.

Thomas understood it all perfectly.

"Yes of course, Matty, you know nothing at all about these things. A woman has a husband and she is faithful to him. That is the law."

"Whose law?"

"I didn't make it."

"Shall I go home then?"

"No. Provided you're not surprised that sometimes you don't feel well. Your vagina is very close to certain other organs and they dislike your loose behaviour."

"It's all very simple, then."

"Yes, provided we stick to the rules. But they aren't our rules, that's the trouble."

"And your wife?" she could not prevent herself asking.

His face clenched into the torment he always showed when he spoke of his wife. She waited until he looked at her.

"What do you want me to say, Martha?"

"You are never faithful to her. Is she faithful to you?"

"Yes," he said—but with rage, bitterness.

"Why are you angry?"

"You are right to ask," he said after a while. He took her hands and held them either side of his face. He smiled at her, his eyes troubled.

"I don't understand."

"No. Of course you don't. Suppose I don't?" He turned his warm mouth against her palm and she felt how its chill struck up through his lips. "You're cold, Matty. Perhaps I should get a heater up here?" He pulled the heavy army blankets over her. She lay, chilly, under a weight of blankets. Through the minute window, the winter stars shone, brilliant but distorted by the flawed glass.

He, sitting naked on the edge of the bed, a brown strong man with skin milky sweet and white on the loins, his brown hands holding hers, was warm and easy, sending out waves of heat like a hot stone when the sun goes down.

"I'm not really cold."

"Yes, you are. It's because of your immoral behaviour. Well, there's only one thing for women, they have to stay married to one man and stay faithful, no matter what their husbands do."

"I begin to see your point. Do you think it will take long for our nerves to catch up with our new principles?"

"Centuries, very likely. Perhaps there'll be a mutation though. Perhaps that's why we are all so sick. Something new is trying to get born through our thick skins. I tell you, Martha, if I see a sane person, then I know he's mad. You know, the householders. It's we who are nearest to being—what's needed."

She looked at the big peasant, sitting on the edge of the bed in the low light, while the stars dazzled in the cheap glass. She smiled because he called himself sick.

"Ah no, not that smile—I won't have it. I tell you, everything's changed and only a few people really know it. And even we don't really know much. It was once like this: a child was born in a house that had a tree outside it. It was an elm tree. His grandfather had planted it. The child grew up while the tree shed its leaves and grew them again. He quarrelled with his father, but afterwards lay under the elm tree and felt at peace. He slept with his first girl under the elm tree, and their baby was put to sleep under the elm tree, and when his wife died she was buried under the elm tree, and as an old man, he stood at his gate and looked at the tree and thought: That tree has been with me all my life, I'm smaller than that tree."

"And now—you mean it's a building or a street instead of a tree?"

"Not at all, it isn't a building at all—that's not important, the city isn't important, not really. The big city's not been with us long enough to be important, we are already beyond it. Because now we think: that star over there, that star's got a different time scale from us. We are born under that star and make love under it and put our children to sleep under it and are buried under it. The elm tree is out of date, it's had its day. Now we try all the time, day and night, to understand: that star has a different time scale, we are like midges compared to the star. And that's why you're all on edge and why I'm sick although I'm a peasant from Sochaczen."

"Are you going to go early again?"

"In an hour. So we can't make proper love tonight. But next time, all afternoon."

"Tomorrow?"

"No, the day after." A pause. "You are going to say, once you were here nearly every afternoon?"

"No, but I was thinking it."

"Then just go on thinking it and don't say it. Because I can't help it. No, it's not another woman. Were you thinking that?"

"Of course."

"No. It's money. I'm making money. Unlike you, when I work, I think in terms of money. I'm learning that it's terrifyingly easy to make money."

She laughed.

"Ah no, don't laugh. You're making a bad mistake if you laugh. I knew you were thinking: he's found another woman. But no, you're

enough for me, at last one woman's enough. Though I'm not saying
for how long of course."

"On principle."

"Yes, on principle. But I don't want you to laugh about money.
I've got to outwit it. I've got to find a way of not becoming Thomas
Stern, rich merchant of this city."

"Well, I'll be here, anyway."

Now she was spending all day in the loft. She came at about
nine in the morning, walking across the vivid lawns in the garden of Sarah Stern, Thomas's brother's wife. The two women looked
at each other as if they had not seen each other. Sometimes Martha
did not go home until late at night. Anton's affair with Millicent
took new wings as a consequence, and the women who wanted to
drink tea and talk did not know where she was. She was living in
the shed—that's what it amounted to. This had become her home,
and Thomas visited her in it.

3

The African group—or rather, *an* African group—now met weekly at
Johnny Lindsay's house, because he was too often ill to promise
attendance at the office in Founders' Street.

If he had been well, would so many men have gone to the office?
Probably not. For years dark-skinned people had been going in and
out of Johnny's house in trust; for years it had been a house that
Africans visited when in trouble. Any white person dropping in to
visit Johnny for a meal, knew that there would almost certainly be
a black person sitting down too.

The thing is, how did he get away with it? How was it possible,
two decades before isolated "progressives" asked carefully chosen
black people to their houses, that Johnny had virtually abolished the
Colour bar in his house? Why was it that, living in a street known as
"Coloured" (though of course no law said it was) and working as
a militant socialist and preaching equality and brotherhood day and
night—why was he not arrested, or put in some kind of trouble by
the authorities?

Well, there is no answer to this question. It is, after all, a question
of what people are, and about this we know very little. Some people
can do things other people cannot—so much we do know. Johnny,
because of some quality to which we do not know how to give a
name, had been living for twenty years, quite openly, in a way that

contravened every law, written and unwritten, in the Colony. Nothing had happened to him.

Probably the African group would have met at his house even if he had not been ill. Though of course "the African group" which sounds, put like that, so solid an entity was nothing of the sort. Seldom were the same faces seen at successive meetings. Some had gone back home to countries hundreds of miles away, some were ill, or they had to work late, or they were in prison for some past offence, or so-and-so had died. The black population were always on the move, were vulnerable to unkind chance or accident, and anyway consisted of aliens. In short, they were like the white people. Who ran the African group? Johnny Lindsay, old miner from the Rand, born in Cornwall. Jack Dobie, "Red agitator" from the Clyde. Mrs. Van der Bylt, a Dutch woman from a village in the Cape. Martha Hesse, English, but married to a German and the mistress of a Pole. Athen, newspaper seller from Greece.

And the black people came from Nyasaland, Northern Rhodesia, the Portuguese territories, as well as from distant areas of this Colony whose boundaries were arbitrary lines drawn by conquest. Who, sitting in that room could say: This is my country, this is my home? Not one. Perhaps Johnny Lindsay, who had achieved the remarkable feat, for this Colony, of living in one house for fifteen years. Perhaps Mr. Matushi, who was after all a Mashona. But Mr. Matushi did not think of this town as home; he longed for his village, which was five days' walking distance.

The African group was still officially "the African group of the Social Democratic Party," whose existence had split this Party two years before, when it was the official opposition to the Government. It was this group which had made it impossible for Labour ever to get into power. Because of this group, a minority of white people would forever be marked as Reds and Communists, Kaffir-lovers. Because of it, the respectable right wing of the Labour Party, now consisting entirely of white trade unionists, but men who after all had had positions of national importance, would never achieve Cabinet posts, or be—as at least two of them had had good reason to expect—Prime Minister. These cautious people, wanting to save "Labour" from the smear "Kaffir-loving" had cooked their own goose, they had sunk themselves forever, because of the label: white trade unionist.

Meanwhile the conservative party which ran this country and had done for years, after watching, presumably with delight, the party of its formidable opponents destroy itself over a principle, waited till the dust settled and calmly announced that they were forming an African group. No one left that party on account of this revolutionary behaviour. On the contrary, it was hardly noticed.

To repeat, some people can do things other people cannot do.

At any rate, the great battle which had split a major party and ruined half a dozen careers had left this small spoil on the field—an African group.

For some time it had ceased to exist, since the wing of the Party which supported it had practically collapsed.

Then Mrs. Van, surveying a scene on which half a dozen groups came into existence, had short embattled lives, then faded out, while the mysterious Mr. Zlentli still remained invisible, decided that she would make *their* group do something useful.

"What?"

First had to be asked, what did the Africans most lack?

Clearly—it was perfectly clear to Mrs. Van—it was self-confidence. There could be no doubt about it. The Africans of this Colony, physically shattered, their armies destroyed, their tribes scattered, had none of the self-confidence and pride of the countries up North which had never been conquered.

Not only had they been pulverized in battle, fifty, sixty years before, but since then they had been governed by people who reviled them from dawn to dusk. They could not pick up a newspaper without being told how ignorant they were, how stupid, how backward. Clearly the first task of their well-wishers was, as Mrs. Van put it (if only privately), to "cheer them up."

And how to do this? Well, no doubt about that either! Obviously, in order to fill black heads and hearts with confidence, all one had to do was to tell them the history of Europe and America over the last hundred years. No black nation could ever be (Mrs. Van hoped) as stupid, bloodthirsty, murderous, treacherous and shortsighted as any white nation in the world, and therefore did Mrs. Van draft out a course of twenty or so lectures covering "from the Industrial Revolution to the Second World War." She then summoned Mr. Matushi, as spokesman of the group, to ask if he approved.

Mr. Matushi, smiling gently as—it seemed—he always would, pointed out that while he in no way wished to upset their good friend Mrs. Van what the Africans really needed was instruction on how to get rid of the present white Government, by (a) fair means or (b) foul means. Could she not see her way to providing courses in revolutionary methods?

Mrs. Van said, "But if my information is correct, some of you are already receiving such instruction. Is it not the case that Solly Cohen is running a study group on these lines? And how about your Mr. Zlentli?"

"He is not *my* Mr. Zlentli!"

She smiled at him, he smiled at her. Then he politely asked why Mrs. Van was so anxious to teach them history.

Mrs. Van invited him to bring a group of his friends to discuss this.

These men sat listening patiently while she explained, "My dear sirs, you are all suffering from a really fatal political handicap. You believe in your hearts, the propaganda of your enemies. Now, if you knew anything about recent European history (and of course it isn't your fault that you don't, your schools being what they are) then every time a white man told you you weren't fit to govern, you'd simply howl with laughter."

These remarks, having gained the sympathetic smiles she had designed them to earn, she continued, in a different voice, "And besides, my dear friends, you will find it useful to know what your own futures, under independence, will be unless you are very careful indeed. Do we believe that white races, black races, are more or less intelligent than each other? We do not. But I've a suspicion that you think when you get self-government you'll be more intelligent than Europeans? Well, you won't be. I, personally, am fighting for your independence because I believe you have the inalienable right to be as cruel and as stupid as we are."

So Mrs. Van, with a calm nod and a smile. They laughed, of course. But these remarks were repeated. And repeated. Some people didn't laugh. Such views were in advance of their time—as the saying goes. Much more tactful neither to say such things or—better still—not to think them. Mrs. Van, whose career had been ruined—she did not regret it—by the scandal over the African group, perhaps thought she had nothing to lose and could say what she pleased. But it is possible that she was tired, and perhaps sickened by a lifetime's battle with stupidity, and so there was self-indulgence in saying such things. At any rate, words which at the time made her friends smile, later had repercussions.

Meanwhile the twenty or so lectures on white history were not given. The Africans conferred, said they agreed it would be a help to know more history, but what about their own? Mrs. Van searched around, made enquiries, wrote to universities, but had to confess that the Africans (officially) had no history yet. It was all there, but scattered over the world in old records and archives and bills of sale. There was no single book, or even pamphlet in existence in 1946 which Mrs. Van might order and make the basis of a study group on the "History of Africa before the coming of the white man."

The Africans conferred again and suggested it might be a help to know the history of South Africa. Was it possible, for instance, that the Nationalists could take power? Of course everyone said it was impossible, they knew that. The world would not tolerate such extremist views—1946 this was, and the sort of people who wrote leaders for newspapers were saying that the world would never again stand for extremist governments. Yes, they understood, the Africans said, that they had nothing to fear, for one thing that liberal country Britain would not allow it, but suppose the Nationalists *did* take power, what might happen to this country, which was so close to South Africa in spirit, not to mention history?

This demand was met much more easily than at first seemed likely. Here was Johnny Lindsay, who had been first in South Africa at the age of eighteen. He had fought in the Boer War (which fact now filled him with shame and remorse) and had taken part in every industrial battle in South Africa until the Great Strike of 1922. He undertook to give lectures. The trouble was he did not have enough breath to talk. For the first lecture, on the stupid brutality of the Boer War, he had sat up in bed, an old coat flung around his shoulders, the oxygen tank standing close to him, and he had wheezed out sentence after sentence while his eyes filled with humiliated tears and his audience of half a hundred black people— sitting on the floor, the bed, anywhere they could find a place—listened in sympathetic silence. It occurred, first to Mrs. Van, but then to Johnny, who pointed it out himself, that when he died, he would take with him day-to-day memories of a history still unwritten. What could be more extraordinary, more paradoxical, more violent, than the history of the Rand? They called in a shorthand writer, but Johnny could not talk; it was too late, he did not have enough breath for more than half a sentence at a time.

He had to write it—a pity, since his way of writing had none of the lively quality of his speech. When he had finished an episode, he gave it to Martha. She typed it, and was paid for doing so by some Foundation alerted by Mrs. Van.

So it was Martha who, every week, sat by the old man's side and read out what he had written during the week. He would amend, alter, add, as she read—or as far as his breath would allow.

On a certain Wednesday evening in winter, the tiny room in the Coloured Quarter was filled with men, mostly Africans. There was a lot of coughing, for people were not warmly enough dressed, nor did they eat enough. Behind them, children of the Quarter hung about on the verandah, listening. As a backdrop stood the winter's sky, in a solid cold glitter.

Johnny was propped up on pillows. He was very ill that night. Martha brought out one sentence after another, more and more slowly, because she had to raise her voice against the harsh irregular breathing. But no one liked to suggest that he should clip the oxygen tube to his face before them all.

Flora was not in the room. Mrs. Van had said, "I think Flora's glad of an evening off nursing sometimes." But it had become known that Flora had said, "I don't see why everyone should work a sick man to his grave."

Mrs. Van had explained that Johnny was probably only still alive in order to give up, week by week, the precious accumulation of his memories, before it was too late. At least, that is certainly how she, Mrs. Van, would feel. "It takes all sorts to make a world," said Flora, and took herself off.

For the first time people were looking at Flora, and seeing a pretty middle-aged woman of conventional South African upbringing who had been living for years with the old agitator from the Rand—presumably for love, since they were not married; and who had accepted, among other things, that she should cook for, act hostess to, sit down at table with, black men, black women. What had she thought of it all? She did not say, but went to the pictures on Wednesdays.

She was a widow and had met Johnny when he was a vigorous man with lungs that "played him up sometimes."

Behind the bed sat Mrs. Van, knitting a garment for a grandchild. Across the bed from Martha sat Athen, attentive to every movement, every breath of Johnny Lindsay, whom he revered, although as he said, "In my country he would be a class enemy, he's a social democrat—but, Matty, he's a good man and he has given his life for the workers, according to his lights."

Athen wore his elegant pale suit, and was suffering with the suffering of the old man, who sat half suffocated, his chest heaving.

Martha read, "The strike committee shifted its headquarters from Benoni to Johannesburg. At the same time the Government was arming the terrified bourgeoisie into bands of special constables. Troops were still arriving armed to the teeth, with their horses ready saddled in open trucks. Guns were unlimbered in the open spaces. A few of the strikers began coming into the central part of Johannesburg, and along with them crowds of sightseers. All business came to a stop, and armed patrols rode through the streets dispersing groups of people. The general mood of the public was one of anger and bitterness. The mere presence of the troops was sullenly resented, and understood as a move to overawe the town."

The old man lifted his thin hand. Martha stopped. "There was no need for the troops, no need at all, it was a provocation," he said.

She waited, but he gulped in air and sat, eyes closed. Then he lowered his hand. She went on:

"Outside the Rand Club, which symbolized the luxury and callousness of the capitalists, small crowds gathered. A number of the more stupid club members stood on the balcony and jeered at the people, snapping their fingers at them. The situation became ugly. A few stones were thrown, and an attack was made on the Club entrance. The street was cleared by dragoons. The crowd raided a bread cart and pelted the troopers with loaves. . . . "

The deep hoarse breathing changed—Johnny's mouth stretched—Mrs. Van began laughing in sympathy, and the roomful of people laughed with her. One or two people sat with demonstratively serious faces however.

"It was the funniest thing . . . " said Johnny. Mrs. Van laughing, leaned over to wipe the water that soaked down papery cheeks, and Martha waited, smiling. Then Johnny's face fell back into the strained lines of his fight for breath, and they were all able to stop laughing.

"After patrolling the streets for some time, the dragoons were ordered to dismount. They formed a square on the corner of Loveday and Commissioner Street and began to pour volleys into the crowd. Scores fell, killed or wounded. From the windows and roof of the Rand Club, a number of unscrupulous members joined in the firing and accounted for a number of casualties."

A young man sitting on the floor raised his hand like a child in class. He was one of the men who had refused to laugh in sympathy with Johnny.

"What year was this, Mr. Lindsay?" Martha looked at Johnny, who shook his head and pointed at Martha.

"1913," said Martha for him.

"July," said Johnny, in a difficult whisper. "If there had not been a war next year, we'd have beaten them; we'd have had socialism in South Africa."

No one commented. They all looked at the questioner, but it seemed he had nothing more to say. Martha went on:

"The fury and dismay of the crowd knew no bounds. Only a few carried hip-pocket pistols, as was common on the Rand at the time, and they tried to fire back ineffectually. But the great majority were peacefully inclined and unarmed, and many had nothing to do with the industrial struggle. A dramatic . . . "

Again the young man raised his hand. "Excuse me please. But I am not clear. This was a white crowd you say?"

For a moment no one answered. It was becoming clear that this youth was trying to make difficulties.

Johnny heaved in breath, "Chamber of Mines against the white workers. Chamber of Mines instructed by Smuts and Botha."

Martha waited, looked at Johnny, looked at the young man, who, having made his point, sat in frowning silence.

"A dramatic and tragic interlude which recoiled heavily on the heads of the Government was the death of the young Afrikaaner miner Labuschagne. Stepping from the pavement into the middle of the street, Labuschagne shouted, 'Stop shooting women and children, you bastards. Shoot a man!' At the same time he tore open his shirt to bare his chest. From point blank range, a trooper deliberately shot him through the heart."

All over the room the men shook their heads and clicked their tongues. There were murmurs of "Shame."

Johnny suddenly sat straight up, and leaned forward, sucking in air, supporting himself on two trembling arms. Mrs. Van leaned over him.

No one moved, though. After a few minutes, Johnny lay back again, very white.

"I think," said Mr. Matushi, who sat at the foot of the bed, "that we should let our friend rest."

But Johnny agitatedly lifted his hand. "Go on," came his hoarse whisper.

Mr. Matushi remarked, "It is important for us all that we should know these things, even though it was a battle between white men."

The way he said this, delivered to some neutral point in the crowd—not to the young man who had raised his hand, which made it even worse, caused Mrs. Van, Martha, and Athen to look at each other.

Now the young man did again raise his hand. He said, "And where were the black miners during this struggle? I understand that every year at that time 8,000 Africans were killed in accidents?"

Tongues clicked again, but it was being understood that this was some kind of deliberately provoked showdown.

Mr. Matushi said, "Gentlemen, we agreed we should hear a history of South Africa in recent times. But we all know that the big fights on the Rand were white miners against their government."

"And when do we enter the picture, Mrs. Van?" asked a young man who had not spoken yet.

"Well, here you are," said Mrs. Van with a firm nod. "And what are you going to do about it?"

Some people laughed. But most were silent. There was a strong tension in the room. Meanwhile Johnny lay back on his pillows, quite still.

The second young man said to Mrs. Van, "Is it true that you expect us, the Africans, should behave like the bad things we have just heard? I must say this, Mrs. Van der Bylt, I do not have it in my heart that one of us should kill a man like this Labuschagne."

Mrs. Van observed him carefully, to find out if he meant to be provocative. But his face expressed only earnest sorrow. She asked, "What is your name?"

"And what has my name got to do with it?"

"You know mine," she observed.

Now that there was a situation, an unmistakable atmosphere, Mrs. Van had put down her knitting, had folded her hands in her lap, and sat looking alertly around, missing nothing. Thus, she was formidable.

Mr. Matushi sat very upright, his hands on his knees. He suddenly said, "Gentlemen, I am ashamed, I am truly ashamed."

Athen said, "I think we should stop the meeting. Our friend is too ill for such things."

Johnny seemed asleep; he certainly was not with them.

People got up from all over the room, unfolding their legs from under them, stretching, coughing, shivering. Mr. Matushi went to Mrs. Van, held her hand in both of his and said, "I must say this to you—we are truly grateful for this series of instructive lectures."

"Yes, yes," said various voices. But not many.

"I take it," said Mrs. Van pleasantly, "that some of you consider these talks not useful?"

"No." And "That is not true," from voices on the verandah.

Another voice from the verandah said loudly, "People who call themselves our friends. But they can only talk of the white people."

"Shame!" said Mr. Matushi firmly, to the verandah.

Athen said, "Comrades, when the guns of the capitalists point at strikers, it is the same whether the strikers have black skins or white skins."

For a moment, silence. Then the voice said from the verandah, "Oh, quite the same! And also when the white men earn many times as much money as the black men." A loud laugh, in which a great many people joined. Then the sounds of feet departing across hardened dust.

A few men came to shake Mrs. Van's hand, and Mr. Matushi said, "I can promise you that some of us at least find these talks useful and I for one will be here next week."

He leaned over Johnny to say goodbye. Johnny's eyes were now open. Mr. Matushi laid his hand on the sick man's shoulder, pulled a fold of blanket up to mark his desire to help, then went, nodding and smiling.

"It would seem," observed Mrs. Van, "that our study group is in difficulties." Then she bent over Johnny. Athen touched Martha's arm, and they said good night, quietly, and went out into the street. It was about seven in the evening. All the buildings were lit, every window, every doorway filled with faces. Men stood in groups on the dusky verandahs. A strong smell of sour water mingled with gusts of fresh grass from a corner lot.

"We're late," said Martha. They were off to a party, which had been arranged because Athen had suggested that Maisie should be invited one evening. "Something gay, Martha, not boring. To show her a decent life is not boring."

Asked what he had in mind, he suggested dancing.

"But, Athen, I am sure Maisie is asked to dance a dozen times a week."

"But not with people like you, Martha. Ask her. I want you to do this."

Martha saw that Athen wanted this, not for Maisie's sake, but for his own.

Eventually it was decided that a party of Athen and Maisie, Anton and Millicent, Martha and Thomas, should go dancing, in order, ostensibly, to give Maisie a lesson in wholesome enjoyment. They were all going to a hotel several miles out of town. Athen already had on his beautiful suit. But Martha wasn't dressed yet.

"Well," said Martha, " if we all stayed here much longer we'd find ourselves arranging meetings so that they didn't upset our sundowner parties."

Athen walked beside her, silent.

"What's the matter?"

"Did you say that because of something in my character?"

Martha understood that he was still tormented about his suit. They had joked that Athen was a dandy, saying that they imagined him as an austere monk, solitary, but emerging from his cell to tend the vices of other people as gently as if they were wounds. Then he would return to a small white room where he would turn the pages of an old book and very slowly sip the monastery liqueur. This joke had reached Athen, and he had suffered over it. He recognized his character in it, he said. Yes, he accepted it as real comradely criticism.

"Look, Athen," she said, hurried and even offhand because of her affection for him, and because she was conscious of futility, brother to incongruity, the pleasures of which she could not prevent herself from looking forward to—the six that evening!—what a collection of people, how ridiculous, how absurd! And how enjoyable. "Look, Athen, you're taking it all much too seriously. Every time you start, I think you can't really mean it." The face he raised to her, sombre with feeling, made her words ridiculous, but she said, with an uncomfortable laugh, "Can't you see how absurd it is to be so unhappy because you've spent a few pounds on a suit?"

He said nothing so they continued up the pavement side by side. So now of course he was thinking about it—and probably would for days. She was filled with irritation, also with remorse—he was going any day now, and that would be that. Athen and Martha—they had known each other three years; they were friends; she trusted him; she could not think of him without warmth. That was love, wasn't it?

Last night she had dreamed badly. She was on a high dry rocky place and around it washed long shoreless seas. Across this sea, which she could not reach, no matter how much she leaned and stretched out her hands, sailed people she had known. All the people she knew. Among them was Athen. And, as she noted when she woke up, Thomas.

Martha and Athen had arrived at Maisie's bar, which had groups of young men lounging outside it, waiting for something to interest them. They held glasses in their hands, and some of them were tight.

"Pick Maisie up and come to our place, right?" said Martha. But he said, "No wait, Martha, I must say something."

"Oh no, no, Athen," she protested. "No!"

He looked at her seriously.

"Athen, you've demanded a lighthearted evening. For the Lord's sake then, let's have one."

He remained serious. She began to laugh—but with discomfort. The lounging youths were all absorbed in this scene and making comments on it.

"Martha, why are you laughing?"

"Because I simply will *not* be serious, just for once."

"When you said that, Martha, I was thinking: Well she's right, what does it matter if for a few months in his life a poor man from Greece lives like a rich man? Of course it does not. But, Martha . . ." He took her hand, and one of the young men let out a shrill whistle. "I tell you, for the last few months everything has been wrong with me. When the war ended, I told myself, now comrade, you must have a wide view. Your country is still at war. But it is a small country and not important. But if they would only send me home, that's what's wrong with me."

"Well I'm glad they are keeping you here."

"Then you are not a real friend, Martha, because with every day I get further from myself."

"Better than being killed," said Martha, obstinate.

"No, Martha, it is not."

Apparently the little man's intensity had the power to subdue anyone: the group of young men watched, probably even listened, in silence. He had dropped her hand, now he took it again and came a step nearer. "Tell me, Martha, have you thought at all—have you thought about this war?"

"Obviously not, when you ask like that!"

"No, I can see you do not think. That is the most terrible thing of all—people are not thinking any longer. The newspapers, books— everything. And now you say the same."

She said nothing. He held her hand and looked close into her face. "The last five years, Martha, I tell you I can't grasp it. I lie awake at night and I repeat just small things. I say, 'There are two million people in Europe now without homes.' People like you and me, Martha. I keep trying to imagine it."

One of the young men said, or rather suggested, in an amiable interested way, "That's right, give it stick, Romeo!"

"We are corrupted people, Martha."

A window above the bar shot up, light spilled over the pavement, over Athen and Martha, who were lit as if on a stage.

Martha moved out of the light, pulling Athen by the hand, and the group of youths said, "Ai, ai, ai!" and made raspberries. Athen, of course, was quite oblivious of the bar and the men outside it.

"It's not possible for us to understand," he said. "I tell you, if one dead person lay here on the pavement, well, we could not take that in, not what it meant. But suddenly human beings have to understand—in the last five years millions and millions of people have been killed. I read yesterday, it's forty-four millions. The human race killed forty millions of its own people—you hear me, Martha? I leave four millions and what difference does it make?"

Maisie's head appeared in the lighted window. "Hey, Matty, is that you? Athen—both of you come up. I'm not dressed."

One of the young men said, "Some people have it laid on."

Athen said, "You must think about it, you must think. We do not think enough about what these things mean."

He went in to the building; Martha waved to Maisie. A plump dark little girl appeared in the lit window and cried, "Aunty Matty, Aunty Matty!" and was hauled in again, protesting. Martha cycled home. In the front room, Anton, in a suit, was talking to Millicent, who wore a white evening dress. Here was a problem already: Maisie had been told they were not wearing evening dress. She was not allowed telephone calls when the bar was open. She would come in an ordinary dress. Who was Martha to support, so to speak? Well, obviously, Maisie. Martha put on a short dress in black crepe. When Martha came out of the bedroom, Thomas had arrived. Millicent was saying she could not possibly be odd-woman-out. Anton took her home to change.

Thomas and Martha sat in the front room of the flat, waiting for the others. Thomas wore a suit. She did not like him in it. And he did not like her black dress either, it seemed.

They sat several feet from each other, and smiled. Yesterday afternoon they had been in the loft for several hours. They were embarrassed because they had forgotten what it was like to be in company.

"You see what an ivory tower we've made ourselves, Matty? Now I don't like being with you when other people are around." He picked up books, looked at their spines, put them down, fidgeted.

"What's wrong?"

"Ah yes, you see, you sleep with a woman and she knows what you are thinking, that's the price you pay." He smiled, but he was serious. "You're right. I've been quarrelling with my brother. He thinks I'm not serious enough about the business of making money. And of course he's right. If one doesn't make money in this paradise for businessmen, one is a fool. He wants me to set up a real gardening shop in the Main Street. He would sell there. I'd grow the things. And his wife's brother would run the sports shop. So there would be two businesses run by the Stern family. So you see how hard it is to escape one's fate, Martha? In Poland, middlemen, money-makers—the Stern Brothers. And here? My brother's a rich man already, and we left Poland with what we had on our backs, eight years ago."

"Let's have a drink, let's both have drinks, let's get tight."

He went on, without responding, or apparently even hearing, "And there's my wife. The farm—it was given to her by her old aunt. Now that was a woman who understood the times she lives in. *She* left Poland before the First World War. Very intelligent, that was. She married a man who's rich as Rothschild out of property in Johannesburg. The farm in this country—well, it was just a little item in a parcel of land her husband picked up. Imagine the scene. Aunt Rosa from Sochaczen hears that her favourite sister's daughter has arrived in Africa, the continent of opportunity. She goes to her husband, 'Boris,' she says, 'give me a little plot of land for my favourite sister's child.' So my wife, who had forgotten even the existence of her Aunty Rosa, suddenly got two thousand acres of fine tobacco-growing land in the Machopi district."

"Why don't you want a drink?"

"If you offer me one I'll have one."

She got him one. He sat watching her, frowning. "My sister-in-law's getting restive," he said. "It's time Thomas was caught and punished for his fornications. She wants the shed as a playroom for her children, she says. Oh she hates you, Martha, you'd never believe it."

"Oh yes, I would."

"But for the time being we are safe, because my brother doesn't want me in a bad mood, he wants me to become half of the Stern Brothers, merchants. So he tells his wife to be quiet, it will be time to take the shed for her children when Thomas has signed his name to all the documents."

He came over to her, took her in his arms, and let her go again. "No, I can't do anything here, it is Anton's territory."

"Well, I live here too."

"No, that's no good, Martha. You talk nonsense. And tonight is all no good. You are looking at me, suddenly you see Thomas as he is, and you don't like him."

"Well then, what is Thomas?"

"If I'd stayed in Poland, I'd look like I do this evening. I'd wear a respectable brown suit. But my nose would be more red, I think. I'd be drinking quite a bit of vodka. I'd be neither a peasant nor would I be a tradesman. Something in between. A middleman. I told you, you can't escape your fate. Perhaps I'd have been a corn merchant, supported to begin with on loans from my brother peasants, who trusted me to be one per cent more honest than the other corn merchants. That's how my Uncle Caleb started."

She waited, while he frowned, moved about the little room, picked up books, set them down again, took large swallows of his beer, looked steadily more unhappy.

"You're a gardener," she said at last.

"There you are, something in between. Neither town nor country. If I were of the soil, I'd be running my wife's farm. But I don't live there and I don't live in town. I bring things in to the towns to sell. And I meet a woman in my brother's wife's garden shed."

She remained silent, sitting in the corner of the sofa. She thought: Well, so he dislikes me tonight. I'll simply have to get through tonight somehow.

After a while he looked at her, smiling tightly. His blue eyes were not kind. "All this is because I can't stand the way you look, Matty. In that dress you are recognizably the same genus as my brother's wife."

"It's only a formal dress, that's all."

"Why can't you wear a dance dress—I saw you in one once. I was looking forward to seeing you all evening in a real dance dress . . . yes, yes, of course, dance dresses were no part of my life, so I take them seriously. But apart from that, in that black thing you look like one of my sisters dressed up for a funeral. . . . " Suddenly his face closed up, and he sat down, and he said, "Well, serves her right for wanting to be respectable, and Uncle Caleb too." This referred to most of his family dying in the Warsaw Ghetto; he had recently got letters telling him so. "Do I have to go to this damned dance?"

"You said you would. It was Athen's idea."

"Well, can't you put a dance dress on then?"

"Millicent's gone off to change out of her dance dress."

"Oh then, you mustn't upset Millicent."

"Seriously, I don't think I should."

"Right. Then that's settled!"

She remained where she was. But then, feeling the distance between them, she quietly got up and went to the bedroom. Her evening dresses were neglected: when did they ever have time to dance? At the back of the cupboard she remembered was a dress of dark blue material she had pushed there and never worn. A couple of years ago, she had seen a romantic dark blue dance dress, with bare neck and shoulders, and full skirts glinting with sequins. She had bought it on an impulse. It was too formal for tonight's dance, but she decided she would wear it, because Thomas would like it.

She came out to him smiling. His face warmed to a smile and he lifted her hand and held it against his cheek, "Thank you," he said, "thank you."

Soon Athen arrived with Maisie, who wore a tight cornflower blue crepe dress. An evening dress. She had misunderstood. And then Anton returned with Millicent in the short dress she had changed into. A great crisis, a real scene, with Millicent almost in tears, but putting a good face on it, Maisie apologizing, as if everything were her fault, and Martha sitting tight, determined only that she would keep this dress on for Thomas.

At last they all got into Anton's car and drove to Millicent's, so that she could change again. Millicent did not have as much time as she needed for changing, and she was flustered and resentful, and she too kept apologizing all round although she was the only one in the right. Particularly did she apologize to Martha; her guilt at sleeping with Martha's husband showed thus: that she was positively weeping with guilt because she had to change her dress twice, Martha being at fault. And she would not sit in the front near Anton, where Martha wanted her to sit, and where she wanted to sit.

So Martha had to sit by Anton, wife by husband, on the front seat, while the others crowded in behind. Maisie fitted her large hips to one corner, Thomas sat in the other. Athen was in the middle, and Millicent was neither on Thomas's lap nor on Athen's, but disposed across both, with many flutters and cries of how much she hoped she was not heavy.

Martha sat in silence, listening to all the fuss. Anton's last woman (apart from herself) was just such another flutterer and exclaimer. And both had pretty vivacious faces and both had sombre eyes in dry meshes of tired skin. Toni Mandel, the Austrian refugee had blue eyes. Millicent had green eyes. Both tended to flutter their lashes and peer up into men's faces with alluring sideways glances. Martha let these thoughts slip through her mind, disliking herself for their uncharitableness, their dryness—but she was listening to her old enemy, the hound Repetition, snapping at her heels. Toni Mandel had announced the entrance of her, Martha, on to the scene. Whom did Millicent herald? Because while Anton seemed to have been genuinely fond (his word) of Toni, was "fond," he said, of Millicent, apparently it had never occurred to him to marry either. Would Anton always fall in love with desperate women being gay girls at all costs, but then leave them for—whatever quality it was he had married Martha for? Presumably he even made love with Toni and with Millicent. Why would a perfectly presentable young woman of thirty or thirty-five choose to have an affair with a married exile from Germany without a penny and with no future until he could return to—of all dubious places from her point of view—East or West Germany? After all, this was a country where women could pick and choose. Millicent had chosen Anton. Because she enjoyed being lectured on politics? (Martha had come on a scene of Anton lecturing Millicent on world politics.) Well, Martha doubted it.

Meanwhile they drove fast through the bush in the direction of Portuguese East Africa and the Indian Ocean. For a while suburbs, then nothing, just bush and kopjes. Sometimes as the car lights swung over dark scrub, green eyes stared low towards this hurtling bit of black machinery—a beast had raised its eyes from where it grazed. It might be, even now, wild—a buck, or wild pig, a jackal. Even, not impossibly, a lion—a lion had been shot on these hills last season. But more likely it was a domestic cow, for this was good grazing land under tall branchy trees, and milk and butter came from these acres to feed the city.

The road curved, shot up hill, curved down, drove across low misted valleys. The moon was away somewhere, but stars stood solid in a glitter of cold. In the car, the windows steamed, the women covered bare shoulders with wool or fur, and the men were glad of the women's warmth.

It was twelve miles fast driving, and when the lights of the hotel appeared in a brilliant cluster on a rise, they were the only lights for miles and miles of dark bush spread over rising and falling ground. Over this country, fifty, sixty years ago, had been fought the last fearful battles of the Mashona Rebellion. Not long before that, here the desperate Mashona had fought the raiding Matabele. All this earth had been piled with the corpses of black warriors and a few of the corpses had been white, with names that appeared in history books and on monuments.

So heavy with memories was this land that people building houses here had been known to run away from them. They were unable to forget the painted warriors who walked for all to see with assegais and shields through the dark hours. The hotel, Parkland Hotel, had been such a house, a fine spreading homestead deserted by its first builders, sold and sold and sold again, and finally bought by the hotel company. For ghosts would not walk, so it was felt, where casual company dined and danced. But another house, across the valley, was being sold now, at this very moment, because its lady could no longer stand being awakened nightly to see the impis march across her verandahs.

As usual there was a long line of about fifty cars, although it was midweek. It was just as well the six had booked a table.

The hotel was halfway up a sharp hill. In front the ground fell away to a small river from which rose a wraith of white mist and a smell of stagnant water. The building was long and low, across the hill. All its front was glassed in to make dining space. Behind this, was a long low-ceilinged room with a platform for an orchestra. Very different, this place, from those where Martha had danced, in another epoch, five years before. Then, the city's young people moved from place to place, as if they owned them all; everybody knew each other, and the managers knew them and greeted them by name. Now, as the six went through the dining tables, and then stood waiting for a moment to cross the dance room, there was no face they knew. The men's clothes were again civilian, save for a few R.A.F. officers who were here to supervize the final closing of the training camps. One or two of the men with wives looked familiar: they were probably the old wolves of the sports club bewitched into good husbands and neighbours. But, strangers, they looked at this party of six, and, as strangers, the six looked back. Meanwhile the band, once mostly made up of amateurs playing for the fun of the thing as much as for the money, were now professionals allowing just so much music, to the minute, in return for just so much money.

It was quite early. Most people were still eating. The big dance room had a few couples in it. Anton gallantly bowed to Millicent and danced across it with her, his elbows stiff, back straight, as he would have danced in a hall in the poor district of Berlin where he had been a boy. And Millicent, clutching her fur piece to her shoulder with a hand that already had a beaded evening bag in it, smiled up at him as he whirled her, in a flurry of white skirts, around and out the other door. Athen walked across, with Maisie on his arm—a small dark dapper man, holding himself upright beside a big fair lazily moving woman. Then came Martha and Thomas, not touching; it was enough to walk beside each other across the sprung wooden floor that sent up a smell of wood and fresh beeswax. As they emerged on to the far verandah, Thomas put out a hand and just touched her bare shoulder and said softly, "I'm happy, Martha, do you hear me? I'm happy tonight with you."

Behind the hotel the ground lifted steeply to the hilltop. It was bare rocky ground, with a few msasa trees standing poised there like birds ready to take wing, so light and airy were they in the greenish starlight.

The back verandah had a dozen tables and four or five big braziers sending up roaring red flames from beds of crimson coal. The flames hissed slightly, and swayed as the waiters hurried back and forth, making currents of air. There was a light dry scent of fire, and the smell of chilled winter leafage, and, stronger than these, as strong as the smell of food, the cold heavy smell of half-frozen metal. The tables were of green metal but there was a cloud of cold on the green, and the women exclaimed and wrapped up their arms—the cold had stung bare flesh, and Maisie held out a big white arm into the light of the flames to show—what of course they could not see in the shifting light—gooseflesh because of the frosty table. They sat exclaiming and enjoying the cold—one of the sharpest pleasures of living in hot countries is this—to savour the vivifying degrees of cold on a winter's night. Wine came and soon they were all a little tight; they knew they had to be a little drunk to float over the reefs of the evening. When the food came, they ate for the most part in silence, wrapped up, and holding out their hands in between mouthfuls to the brazier nearest to them, whose flames forked dangerously, swaying as the air poured in down the hillside past rocks and tree trunks. And besides, they were three couples, and they had come to dance. Martha longed to go inside and dance with Thomas. She saw how Maisie's eyes returned again and again to Athen, and how Millicent played with her food and watched Anton—she was waiting to dance with him.

The food was not very good. They made up with the wine. Martha saw Athen sitting a little back from the table, examining a globule of pale straw-coloured wine enclosed in frosted glass. The grave dark face had a small bitter smile as he lifted the cool pale gold globe to taste the wine. He sat with the glass in his thin brown hand, turning it, feeling the chill of the wine coming through the glass on to his skin—then lifting to taste again. It was quite a good wine; good wine still came in, through Portuguese East Africa, in spite of the war. Athen sniffed the wine and lingered over it, and Martha saw a small scrambling soldier in sweaty khaki rinsing out his mouth with dark wine and spitting; then putting back his head to let the thick heavy wine run down his throat—she saw him, this roughened fighting man, head back, his white strong teeth bubbling with thick red, his eyes closed under a pouring yellow sunlight; she saw glossy dark lashes lying close to the worn skin of the tired fighting man as he shut his eyes momentarily, standing in the sunshine on the hillside, while the wine, strong and purple, ran down his gullet and, where he had spat it from a dry mouth into the dust, made a bubbling dark stain.

There he sat, across the table, Athen Gouliamis from Greece, small, pale, troubled, his cap of black hair glinting in the starlight, his pale suit flickering red where the flamelight ran over it, and he looked at the fine globule of glass in his hand and at the pale golden wine with its minute bursting bubbles and its cloud of frost.

Athen felt her looking, lifted his dark eyes, and smiled at her.

"Well, Comrade Martha," he said simply, in a way which continued the conversation from outside Maisie's bar. "Well, comrade? It's all too hard for us—that's the truth. And now I shall drink to you." He drank, and then, as he did so, turned his face so that when he let his glass lower, he was looking at Maisie. He smiled, a simple tender smile straight into her face.

"I can't dance these dances, Maisie. I've only done village dancing."

"Like me," said Thomas at once. "Before I came to this promising continent, I'd never done anything but village dancing. But now I can do this." He stood up, held out his right arm in a stiff half-circle, half shut his eyes, and circled across the flagstones between the fires, his face smirking in a parody of—well, it was like Anton's stiff correct dance across the dance floor.

But as he came back and saw Anton's smile, he bent and put his arm around him in a bear's hug. "Ah, Anton," he said, "Anton, there's no hard feelings, you understand."

Anton looked sarcastic for a moment—since after all, it was he who might be expected to have the hard feelings—and had not Thomas just been making fun of his dancing?

Instead of being angry he got up slowly, stiffly, as if he were going to be angry, his face clenched in a mask that threatened, while his lips maintained a small humorous smile which insisted: I'm not really serious! Then, having confronted Thomas as if he were going to run a bayonet through him, he extended his arms with a deliberate self-conscious smirk. Thomas frowned: for a moment he did not like it. Martha certainly did not like it. In that second when the tall handsome man shifted his pose from aggression to a simpering invitation which was meant to be a woman ready to dance, there was a painful reality in it. Then Thomas bowed, put his hand correctly on Anton's back, and the two men circled among the braziers, Thomas with a look of stiff self-conscious pride modelled on Anton's look when he held Millicent, and Anton smiled foolishly, which is how Martha had seen Millicent look at Anton. But there was nothing in Anton's parody which showed Millicent's anxiety.

People at near tables laughed. One or two clapped. Then, when the two men were down the other end of the building, they abruptly fell apart. There was a sudden loud noise of raised voices and Martha saw that Thomas faced a man in loud argument, while Anton stood to one side, watching. Then Anton and Thomas strolled back. Anton smiled still, with a look of pleasure because he had unbent, he had been able to play the fool. But Thomas looked black and scowled.

"Silly fool," growled Anton, without heat, about the man Thomas had quarrelled with.

"I'll kill him," said Thomas briefly. There was a look on his face she had never seen—there was a simplicity of hatred on it, and she felt she did not know him. She put out her hand to touch his sleeve. He felt the touch, jerked away his hand, which clenched into a weapon, then, seeing it was Martha, his mind told his hand to go loose. But it trembled in the effort of losing its tension of hate. He sat down, or rather collapsed, his legs shooting out in front of him, and he sat staring before him, breathing heavily, up the dark hillside with its airy illuminated trees.

Anton did not want to lose the ease his moment's clowning had earned him. He said to Millicent, "Gnädige Frau!" and made her a small smiling bow. He held out his arm. Millicent smiled with devotion, put her hand with its scarlet nails on his sleeve, and stepped across the paving stones, through the tables where people were again absorbed in their own affairs, into the dance room. The rose-coloured lights from the braziers flickered in Millicent's white skirts and melted her hair into a mass of gleaming copper.

At the table, they listened to Thomas's heavy breathing. Maisie said, "Ah hell, Thomas man, if someone says something to upset you, then you forget it."

Thomas looked at her without replying.

Athen rose, indicating with his eyes that Maisie must go with him. As he went past Thomas he laid his hand on Thomas's shoulder, which tensed in rejection of sympathy.

Athen followed Maisie into the dancing room. Maisie's broad blue hips, held in corsets, swayed regally like a matron's up and down. Her bare neck where it merged into her back was a deep fair smooth expanse, and her hair fell down over it in a gleaming coil, the same colour as the dry-scented pale gold wine. As they reached the dance floor, the small dark Greek put out his hand and swung her around to face him—"like a warrior-king," thought Martha, so simple and commanding was that gesture. But then, as the big woman turned, smiling, the two fell apart, and Athen stood ready for instruction, and their faces concentrated in the effort of learning and teaching the mysteries of the dance as suitable for the Parkland Hotel. The dim light of the big room, lit by the flowering colours of the women's dresses and white patches which were people's faces, received Athen and Maisie, who circled slowly off past Anton and Millicent.

"What's the matter?" said Martha.

"Nothing."

"But of course it's something."

"Why do you want to know?" He looked at her as if he did not like her.

"I've never seen you like this before."

"No. But supposing this is what I am and you don't like it?" He held the back of his hand to his mouth and took a piece of flesh between his teeth. His eyes stared, the flames made red lights in the whites.

"Why do you say that? Why is it so important?"

"Ah, forget it."

"All right then, we'll forget it."

She sat inside her beautiful dress, shut out, cold, wanting to cry. More, she was afraid. She had not imagined Thomas's face like this —black, clenched, hurtful.

"Well, all right then," he said at last. "If you're going to sit there, like that, I'll tell you." He sat for a while looking at the end of the space full of people and flaming braziers. At the table where there had been the quarrel. But Martha could only see two men, two women—a party out for the evening. "See that crowd down there— see that bastard there—well, it doesn't matter. You'll never meet him, he's not in your orbit. He wouldn't have been in mine, except for the war. His name is Tressell." He stopped.

"Tressell?" she prompted.

"Yes, I tell you, it's so bad even saying the name makes my head start throbbing! Sergeant Tressell. Yes. He was in charge of the Africans in the last camp and I was under him. He was supposed to be supervising their welfare and my job was to carry out his orders. Food and sanitation—that sort of thing." He sat silent, looking up the hill. The music came very loud from inside. Martha saw the four people get up from the end table and come closer on their way inside to dance. A man, presumably Tressell, turned his head to stare long and deliberately at Thomas, who stared back, his eyes narrowed.

A rather heavy man in a badly cut dinner jacket, escorting a woman with yellow hair and freckled shoulders.

"Thomas," said Martha.

"Yes. Well, all right. What does it matter? I'm surprised at it all myself. I knew I hated him for the rest of my life, but when the war was over, I thought it wouldn't matter so much. I thought: Right, the Tressells can go back to their pigsties now and you can just shut up and forget it. But I didn't forget it."

"Obviously not."

"How can I tell you when you are so disturbed about it?"

"Yes, I am, I don't know why." She was. She felt as if she had never really known Thomas and as if loving him were a mistake if not worse. His face frightened her.

"Then how do you expect me to tell you—oh, all right then. I was under Sergeant Tressell in No. Four Camp for months. He was just a bastard. But that wasn't it—he was a bastard out of carelessness, out of sheer indifference—that was what killed me. How can I explain it? Well, he'd go to the stores to issue rations. It was a sort of weekly thing, we all went to the stores with forms and orders and a lot of fuss. There'd be three thousand African soldiers let's say, and the rations should be so and so. But the rations would be four hundred men short. He'd stand there and the clerk from Centre D'd say, 'So many men.' And Tressell would say, 'So and so many pounds of meal, so and so many pounds of beans'—always short. Sometimes not much, sometimes badly short. Just because he couldn't be bothered—that was the point. Do you understand? That was the point. Or I'd go to him and I'd say, clicking to attention and saluting"—here Thomas's body stiffened as it remembered how he had saluted—"I'd say, 'reporting the latrines for D Block.' And he'd say, all injured and peevish because I was disturbing him, 'Ah, Christ man, forget it, will you? The latrines have been up the pole for weeks.' 'Yes, sir, that's why I'm reporting them.' 'Oh, forget it, go away. Go and read a nice book.' That was his idea of a really funny joke. He'd say, 'Go and read a nice book,' and kill himself laughing. Then there was a day a man collapsed in a stroke at drill. I knew enough medicine to know he was in danger. I reported it, and Tressell said, 'Send the bastard back to his hut, he is scrim-shanking.'"

Martha said, "But, Thomas, it goes on all the time."

"Yes, I know that. But Sergeant Tressell was too much for me. I couldn't stand it. I went to the C.O. and I said, 'Sir, I understand why we nationals of countries who were actually invaded by Germany are too dangerous to fight Germans, you have to keep us cleaning latrines for the safety of Zambesia—okay, as a principle I understand it. But speaking personally,' I said, 'send me to the war somewhere, I'll guarantee I'll kill Germans for you.'"

"That wasn't exactly accurate, anyway!"

"That's what the C.O. said. He said, 'Stern, you've let your feelings distort the facts.' He was a decent fellow that commanding officer. That's the word for it. He told me to sit down and have a drink. We had a drink. Then we played some chess. Then next day I went back to taking orders from Sergeant Tressell."

It seemed for a time as if this was all. The waiter brought a couple more bottles of wine. The music stopped inside for a moment, and then started again. While it was quiet, they could hear the small night noises from the wild hillside.

"What happened to the man who was scrim-shanking?"

"Ah forget it, forget it, you sit there listening. It's driving me mad."

"Let's go and dance then!"

"Christ, Martha, at the moment you look just like my wife. She does that too. I can see her thinking: Thomas always makes so much trouble for himself."

"I wasn't thinking that at all."

Behind Thomas, through the dance room door, came the man in a badly fitting dinner suit. He looked steadily,with hard narrowed eyes, at Thomas. Who seemed to feel it. He slowly turned his head. The two men looked at each other. Then the man walked off to his table.

"He came out hoping to catch me alone."

"No, he didn't!"

"You mean, you hope he didn't. You think I'm inventing Sergeant Tressell." Twenty yards away, the man sat, by himself, drinking Scotch and looking steadily across at Thomas. "I tell you, it was Sergeant bloody Tressell that finally made me understand the world."

Now the woman with the bare freckled shoulders came out and went to sit by, presumably, her husband.

"There you are," said Martha. "He was just waiting for his wife."

"We are being saved from violence by our women," said Thomas. "Think of it!"

"What happened to the man who was shamming sick?"

"He died. He had bilharzia and hookworm and malaria and should never have been a soldier at all. Well, if we were going to use such criteria as good health to choose black soldiers, there wouldn't have been any. Three weeks later the same thing happened: I said to Tressell, 'Sir, do you remember the man who died—it's going to happen again, unless you give orders for so and so to be discharged.' He couldn't remember the man who died. He couldn't see the point at all. He said, 'Ah man, you kikes kill me.'"

"Ah," said Martha involuntarily.

"No, it's not that. I thought so for a time. You anti-Semitic bastard I thought. But he wasn't even anti-Semitic, that's the point."

At the other table, the man was telling his wife something. Presumably about Thomas. His gestures, his face, expressed moral indignation. She was listening sympathetically to a tale of outrage.

"It's like this, Martha. That husband of yours—oh, all right then, not him, it's in bad taste to say things about one's mistress's husband. There are men who if you order them to shoot fifty men they lie awake all night worrying if there's a man short—the indent would show a man short. Well, that's what we understand now, that's the clerk's attitude to murder. The little clerks in power are dangerous. That's the German contribution to human knowledge. But we don't begin to understand murder through good humour, murder through sheer bloody good-humoured carelessness. I'd say to Tressell, 'Sir . . . ' 'Ah hell, it's the kike again, what's eating you this time, kike?' I'd say, 'Sir, the rations are fifty men short.' 'Oh for crying out aloud man, what's eating you?'

" 'But there's not enough food to go around, Sir.'

" 'Oh, bugger off. Go and read a good book!'

"Do you imagine he was selling the stuff? I thought for a while, now this is interesting, the rich white herrenvolk, they have inherited traits from their impoverished ancestors—they pinch food and sell it, just like us poor swine from the European heartland. They're human after all, I thought. But not on your life. He couldn't be bothered. When another man died and I said to him, 'So and so is dead;' he said, 'Good Kaffir that, I liked him.' I tell you, these people are capable of killing off an entire black population out of stupidity—it's my dog, my dog likes it when I hit him. Well, perhaps we'll have another world war in order to learn about murder by good-natured stupidity—that's the South African style. There are national styles in murder. I used to look at Tressell and think, if I was black I'd have to live every day of my life under that swine. I got to hate Tressell so much that—I used to look at him and try and work out ways to kill him. I thought, I'll fix you you bastard. I went to him and I said, 'Sir! I think it would be a good idea if the lazy ignorant filthy savages were taught some lessons. Speaking as the Medical Corps, that's what I think. I suggest you authorize me to give them some lectures.' He looked suspicious. 'They're a danger to all civilized people, the filthy swine,' I said. Then he cheered up. 'Ja,' he said. 'Bright idea that—now we've got all the stinkers in one place in uniform, might as well use our opportunities, eh, kike?'"

At the other table, the woman had shifted her chair so that she sat alongside her husband, and was able to stare across at the man about whom she was hearing such shocking things. Her large over-fed good-natured face was sorrowful, troubled, because of what she was hearing.

"It was arranged I'd lecture the men one afternoon a week. The point was, I had learned Shona, but Tressell didn't know a word. Imagine the scene—I had two thousand men marched out from their quarters and on to the parade ground. I stood them at ease and addressed them in Shona. First, I called Sergeant Tressell every name I could think of. There they stood, they all hated him, but not a muscle of their faces moved. Then I explained to them they were going short of food and their latrines always broke down because of Sergeant Tressell. Then I told them that if they wanted to be free of the Tressells, they needed some basic education, and I proposed to give it to them. I lectured them for half an hour on their wrongs —Lenin, so to speak, using a class on hygiene to address revolutionaries. There were two thousand men, and me explaining politics to them, and Sergeant Tressell, looking benevolent. So then I marched them off, and Sergeant Tressell said, 'Hey, Stern, you didn't say you were going to address these monkeys in Shona.' 'But, sir, it's all they understand,' I said. Now he was supposed to learn Shona, but he was too lazy. 'I hope you agreed with what I was saying,' I said. 'Did you think I was on the right lines, sir?'

"'Seemed all right to me,' he said. So three Wednesdays went by. All the Africans lined up in companies on the square, at ease, in the sun, while I gave them lessons in elementary revolutionary tactics, and Sergeant Tressell stood listening.

"Then one afternoon the C.O. came out. He'd heard of the lectures on hygiene. But he knew Shona. I had to give the lecture as promised on keeping water clean and washing behind the ears. The C.O. smelled rats by the dozen. He had me over to chess that evening. He said, 'Stern, I've told you before, you're letting your emotions override your common sense. Can't have that, you know.' 'No, sir,' I said. I was never left alone with the men again, and then I was transferred. Just before I left Tressell came into my hut. He said, 'You think you're clever, don't you? Well, I'll show you.' One of the Africans must have given me away. So we fought. Neither of us won. He'd land a blow on my chest and say, 'That's for you, Jew.' And I'd land my fist in his face and say, 'That's for my sister in the Ghetto.'

"At one point he actually stopped and said, 'We're going to leave the ladies out of this, Stern!' 'That's right,' I said, 'That's for my mother,' and I landed a kick on his groin. We nearly killed each other. It was just after that I was posted and our beautiful relationship had to be postponed for so long."

The woman with Tressell had stood up, and was urging him into some course of action. He shook his head, she insisted. Finally he did what she wanted, and the two went into the room to dance, she giving Thomas as she went past a long look of sheer incredulity: Imagine that such men were allowed to walk the earth, she was thinking.

"Were you going to fight again?" she asked. "I mean, when you were near his table?"

"No. I just saw his stupid red face. He was looking at Anton and me playing the fool. I remembered the fight. I remembered how every time he landed a blow, he said, 'That's for you, kike. That's for you, Jew.' Only two words in his vocabulary—very ill-educated. I suppose he thought I was going to attack him. He picked up the wine bottle by the neck and held it—I swear, Martha, it would be the greatest pleasure I could imagine, to kill that man."

After a few moments he turned towards her, trying to smile. "Well, you made me tell you. But I shouldn't have."

"Why not?"

"There are things we should sit on, shut up about."

She shrugged.

"That's right, that's the only thing to do."

"If you can't forget him, we'd better give up this evening."

"I can't forget him and I don't want to give up the evening. All right, all right, give me time—I'll drink."

He seized a glass, filled it, drained it. He sat fidgeting and frowning in his chair, glancing at the door so as not to miss the reappearance of his enemy.

They were alone under the trees that seemed to stand above the music and the movements of people like plants growing out of water. The tops of the trees seemed infinitely remote. They stood in quiet starlight, moving their leaves in a small wind.

Martha waited. Slowly, the heat went out of Thomas and he sat back, relaxed. "Ah," he said, "you're right." He drank some more wine. "Now," he said, "you must sit there and let me look at you."

For hours, it seemed, Martha had been waiting for this: to be conscious of herself as a pretty young woman in a romantic dark blue dress. She had wanted to sit, close to Thomas, feeling her firm white breasts just under the defining dark folds of the dress, and her strong white body upright in soft drifts of dark transparent stuff. She would have thought: these arms, my strong thighs—they hold this strong man close in love. And this is what Thomas had wanted, when he made her change into this dress. But it had all gone wrong, spoiled by Sergeant Tressell.

She smiled at Thomas, sitting, so to speak, for the portrait: pretty young woman in a lovely dress. She tried to be only that, nothing more, not to think of the rage that she knew quite well was pounding through Thomas even now. She tried not to remember Sergeant Tressell.

But her heart felt large and tender, it felt painful.

He smiled at her and said, "Ah, Martha, you don't like me at all, not really."

"Stop it, Thomas, stop it, just for this evening."

"When I say that what I want more than anything else in the world is a dark night and a chance to murder Tressell, you don't like it."

"No, I don't." She sat, her heart painful, looking at the broad brown face, at his eyes, so direct and clear and blue.

"You're so pretty tonight."

"I'm not pretty!"

"Then I'm not a nice man who grows plants and gives housewives advice about their gardens. Martha, I was looking forward all day to sitting by you and thinking: This is a pretty woman, and not, this is the female I love. It's easier."

"Am I the female you love?"

"What do you think?"

"Well, we run true to form," she said at last. "It's at the Parkland Hotel that we use the word love. And you came all the way from Poland for it."

He slowly poured long streams of pale wine into her glass and then into his. Past his shoulder, she saw the enemy come out of the dance room and sit down. She hardly noticed him, from which she understood she was tight. And Thomas did not turn his head.

"Come and sit by me," he said.

Martha and Thomas sat side by side, hardly breathing—breathing, as it were, through each other. They did not look at each other, but felt Thomas, Martha, through their arms, their thighs, their stomachs. They sat side by side, a pretty young woman in a dark blue dress that showed white arms and shoulders, and a man with rough brown hair and a broad brown face, blue-eyed—a strong man, a peasant. They sat in these guises and felt life running through them. In front stood the fine, airy, balanced trees, silvered with starlight, and the rocky shapes of the rising hill. Behind them the dance music throbbed, and the flames hissed in the braziers. Martha felt the low long swooping movement of the flames, from the flamelight running warm on the rough tree trunks; she felt the firelight she sat in, a warm low element far from the thin cold light of the stars on the treetops. Drunkenness made her alive, alert. She simultaneously felt each beat of the music, the texture of the pockets of shadow in the tree trunks, the dull scratched metal of the table and the sharp cold coming from it, the light splintering in the matrix of a drop of spilled wine. She had twenty senses and a heart so filled with delight it held all the night and everything about her. She could even feel the minute delightful exasperating sting from the individual hairs on the back of Thomas's hand against her own. She sighed with pleasure and turned to smile at him as if waking from a sleep in his arms.

He felt it and turned to her smiling, and her heart fell into sorrow, remembering what had been beating at the edges of her consciousness for days now—a long time; that of course all this was going to end, and soon. Tonight, she and Thomas together, the six of them together—it was like the lift of a wave towards the sky before it breaks into a fragmented crest of flying white foam. She and Thomas would soon part, and soon this love (she could use the word, presumably, once it had been used at the Parkland Hotel), this love, which had taught her what loving a man was, would have gone, been blown apart. Like a town in Europe, dark under a sky bursting with bits of flying flame and steel. And the Tressells, now sitting in a group of noisy friends at their table: their appearance this evening could have been foreseen. Martha felt as if she had known all her life that on this evening, this starry winter's evening, she would sit by a man she loved with her whole heart, and look past flaring braziers at a red-faced fattish man in a badly cut dinner suit, and know that he was an enemy too strong for her.

She said, "Please give me some more wine."

He poured more wine, and for himself. Again for a long time they sat quiet, side by side. The others came back to the table, in an interval when the music was silent, but then they were no longer there. Her forearm rested in Thomas's big hand. She could feel, through his hand, that he was restless, disturbed. He said, "I've got to move off for a bit. I can't stand it, it's more than I can stand, sitting beside you like a stuffed horse at a fair."

He went off down the side of the building towards where the mists came off the river. She let herself go into a condition of pure delicious drunkenness. She was a space of knowledge inside a shell of swaying drunkenness, and she swung from dark to light, from light to dark—then she felt a dry warmth on the back of her neck and turned her head to see why the dank secretive smell of river water seemed so close. Thomas's hand lay on her neck. In front of her eyes brown cloth beaded with a minute dew. She brushed it off and now her hand smelled of the river. Thomas said, "Martha's drunk."

The others were there, and sat around her like many-coloured ghosts of people she had known a thousand years ago, under the cool light trees over which the stars stood—but differently, they had moved across the sky. Trunks rose into remote starlight from pools of music, firelight, faces.

They sat in silence. Martha could not have said anything, nor did she want to, and she knew that they were in the same state. She rested her head against Thomas's cheek, feeling the warmth of his face against the cool slippery surface of her hair. From this position she smiled at a tall fair man called Anton Hesse, from Germany, and at a fat anxious woman with big white breasts that bulged out of cornflower blue crepe.

Maisie said, "Funny, isn't it, think of all the times you and I have been with the boys at parties. What I mean is it's funny."

Her shining pink lips were parted in a smile asking Martha to express what, as usual, she could not. But Martha smiled and smiled. She had forgotten how to use her tongue. Meanwhile, from outside this scene, she watched a pretty young woman with bare shoulders smiling at a smiling fat woman. Then she saw this pretty girl look down at her hand, curiously. She was Martha, looking at her hand—extraordinary; it moved by itself, not on her will, but on its own—extraordinary, extraordinary, her hand, and very ugly, with its fingers like tools or talons.

Anton said, or had said recently, "Well, it's not every night that we are going dancing." Martha heard these words and after a time looked around to connect the voice, if possible, with Anton. She saw a blond youth with a frighteningly direct concentrated stare say these words—saw him, in a crowded beer hall lean forward to say (to some young edition of Millicent perhaps), "Well, comrade, it's not every evening we have the time for going dancing." She loved this correct, stiff boy, proudly taking out a girl (Grete perhaps—he was showing the rich girl the poor district he lived in?) and she smiled maternally at him where he sat disguised as Anton. And when Anton smiled at her, it was this boy who smiled. They, at least, liked each other, the stiff dedicated boy and a Martha who understood his need for her and forgave it.

Then Anton and the red-headed woman had vanished and in their places sat Maisie and Athen.

Where was Thomas? Martha tried to turn her head to find him but he had gone off somewhere.

Maisie was saying, "What do you think, Matty, tell Athen." Martha could not make out what she was supposed to tell Athen.

A small dark Greek sat smiling, while light from the braziers flowed over him as if he sat in a red river.

Athen said, "Maisie, you must change your life."

Martha saw how Maisie sat in her chair and laughed. Maisie shook with laughter, but Martha could not laugh outwardly, she could not even make her lips smile. But she laughed inwardly, she laughed and loved everything. She thought: I am good now. At this moment I *am* good. When I'm sober I must remember how I was good tonight. Meanwhile she watched Maisie yell with laughter: a fat yellow-haired woman with a red face, a wet red-cheeked face, with minute broken veins in the skin, stretched her mouth laughing, and her inflamed blue eyes blinked tears. Her great fat breasts shuddered with laughter. Martha looked at this gross Maisie and thought of the sweet-fleshed girl in the office of before the war: she thought of Maisie when she was a pregnant girl.

"He keeps saying I should live differently," said Maisie, yelling with laughter.

"I feel very sick," observed Martha.

"Well, sit still dear and it will pass," said Maisie, transformed in a trice into a sensible ministrant behind a bar. Martha could see her breast resting in a reassuring white bulge on a slope of brown wood. Martha took a bite or two out of white sweet flesh. Like blancmange. Insipid it was. Boring. She smiled at Maisie and thought: If I said to Maisie, I've just taken a good bite out of your left breast, she'd say: That's right, dear, well have a drink of water, you'll feel better. And Athen would say: But, Martha, you must live differently.

She said, with difficulty, to Athen, "I've just taken a great bite out of Maisie's breast." Concerned, he leaned forward, and his face came white out of the running red flamelight.

Then Maisie stood up, and she stood up. They took each other's hands, and thus supported, they went unsteadily around the side of the building where a flower bed stood in a circle of raised stones around a tree. Here they were sick, and instantly they were both sober, resting side by side in cool starlight. Below them the valley, where an invisible stream sent up coiling white mist, a cold weight of dank water smell, a smell of weedy, secretive dark river.

"What am I going to do, Matty, what shall I do with my life?" Martha heard these words, and wild sobs, and saw Maisie's face, refined by starlight, with tears running down it. "What shall I do about my Rita? Binkie's driving me mad and I don't know what to do?"

Martha said nothing. The roots of her tongue were stunned by sorrow and everything she might say would be ridiculous.

"Binkie says to me he's got a woman he wants to marry but he loves me best of all and I say I don't love him and he says he will marry the woman she's a widow with two children of her own from the war and I say, well, marry her and good luck that's all I can say."

"I'll come and see you tomorrow, Maisie."

"Yes, come and see me tomorrow, you are my good pal, Matty, I don't care what anyone says. Pals are the best thing in life."

Then they carefully went back to the table. They all sat around the table. In front of them tall slender greenish bottles, clouded with cold, a flicker of orange fire in their glass depths. Inside the building the saxophone lamented and the drums beat for war.

Martha saw Athen lean forward towards Maisie.

He was earnest, serious, his dark burning eyes holding her tired sweet blue eyes, which were fastened on him in the simple statement, I love you, Athen. And her mouth was held in a foolish patient smile.

Across from Martha sat Thomas, his elbows on spread knees, his head bent to rest on his fists, swaying a little. He was a strong man in a brown suit, and Martha looked at him like a stranger and wondered what he was remembering. He swayed, and looked at the paving stones under his feet while the red light moved on his rough brown head.

Maisie said in a loud childish voice, "Isn't it funny, this time next year, where will we be? Athen will be in Greece . . . " she was ticking them all off on fat white fingers " . . . and Anton will be in Germany, and Matty will be . . . " She smiled, hesitating, because she did not know whether to say aloud that Martha would not be with Anton. "And here we'll be left, me and Thomas and Millicent."

"Not me," said Thomas.

"What?" said Anton.

"Not me," said Thomas, lifting his head off his fists to look at them and then past them at the tree trunks, at rocks, at the lifting line of the hill. His eyes encountered the glitter of the stars, and he fell back in his chair and gazed up at the sky. "Not me," he said, or muttered, and then Martha was in Thomas's arms, dancing. They whirled around and around the low-ceilinged white room, which was swept with currents of air from the women's dresses, that flung out their skirts around the tall pillars who were the men holding them. She rested in Thomas's arms and whirled around. She was tired and she rested in Thomas's arms. She might very well go to sleep then and there, on his broad chest, as it whirled her round and round on the shifting coloured lights, on the steady pulse of the drums. They passed, and passed, and passed again, the open doors to the verandah where the flames flickered low in the braziers and the trees lifted airy crowns of silvered leaf to the stars.

"Martha," said Thomas, "I'll tell you something, because I feel like saying it. It isn't true but if I was struck dead now I wouldn't care."

"Of course," said Martha, laughing in her stomach, though her face was too stiff with sorrow to laugh. "Of course."

Then it was very late and there was no music. People sat around the tables in a cold late starlight. Now a small moon was half risen behind the hill. The braziers revealed themselves to be cylinders of rusted iron punched with jagged holes; full of grey ash where a rosy gold glowed and dimmed as the wind came eddying down the hill past rocks and tree trunks.

The waiters stood yawning against the pillars of the verandahs, tired black men in dinner jackets and white aprons. The trees, like white birds tinted by dawn light or starlight, lifted their shadowed branches.

Millicent was lying with her wild loosened hair spread over Anton's chest. Martha watched, friendly and compassionate, how her husband gently, tenderly, lifted this half-drunk woman into a more comfortable position and looked down into her face. They all watched Anton, unconscious of himself and of them, as he smiled protectively at the woman sleeping against him. They all smiled at each other. No one wanted to go home. The tables were still full of people. The waiters stood and yawned in vain.

Martha had again discovered her hand. She sat opening and shutting her hand. It was monstrously, unbelievably ugly, like a weapon. Maisie had been crying. Her face was stretched with woe. It was a mask of dragging pain. One side of her mouth was pulled down, as if with pain or because it was paralyzed. Her eyes were inflamed, they looked like little pig's eyes. Then it seemed as if one eye was a great red scarred socket. Martha shook her head to clear her sight, and saw Maisie, a tired woman with a sad smiling face looking at Athen. Martha's hand provided fresh revelations. The shape made by her forefinger and thumb, touching each other—it was like a revelation of brutality. Her hand was like a pair of pincers, the claw of a lobster, something cold and predatory. She looked at her left hand, astounded by its cruelty. Meanwhile her right was in the depths of Thomas's hand, through which she received simple messages of warm health.

Her left hand, her hand—never had there been such an extraordinary thing as that circle of bone, lightly laid with flesh, like the beak of a bird, like a mouth opening and shutting, like . . .

Athen sat smiling. He said, "I'll never forget tonight." Maisie turned her face towards him. Martha could only see the back of a coil of fair loosened hair, a helpless-looking fat neck. Athen smiled gravely, from a distance, into the supplicating woman's face.

Martha was full of pain for Maisie. She wanted to say to Athen—but what? Some kind of demand, a protest. Her mind worked fast, registered everything with miles—she felt everything together, the starlight thinning overhead, the charred smell of chilling iron from the braziers, stale sour wine, cold metal from the table top, Thomas's warm hand, the dark smell from the river. She was fused together and what she felt made it impossible that Athen should at last gravely bow to Maisie and go away from her to Greece.

She fought with her tongue, and at last said, "What about you?" Incredible aggression had forced that question out, she had put behind it the energy of pure resentment. But it came out blurred; in spite of everything she felt her face set in a smile.

Athen looked at her courteously, distant.

He said, "Did you say something to me, Martha?"

"Matty's tight," said Anton.

"Of course I'm tight," she said, clearly, smiling, proving that her tongue was not paralyzed after all.

They went to the car. In a group of people behind them were Mr. Tressell and Mrs. Tressell—Sergeant Tressell and his wife. But Thomas did not look, he did not turn to look, it seemed he had forgotten his enemy Sergeant Tressell. Behind them the hotel, apparently deserted, burned a hundred lights which went out, all at once. The stars had been absorbed into the thin grey of an early morning sky. But over the Indian Ocean the sun was rising, for a dark line of trees in the east marked a low horizon behind which a faint glow of rose pulsed strongly into pearl grey cloud.

Before they started the car a bird had woken, tried its voice, and gone silent again.

Martha wanted to get into the back seat with Thomas, but order again prevailed, and she was in the front seat with Anton. Behind her Millicent slept on Thomas's shoulder, and Maisie sat bolt upright, her pale cheeks shaking with the movements of the car. In the centre of each cheek was a wild spot of pink, and her eyes were red with tears. Athen dozed. His head fell sideways on to Maisie's shoulder. Martha saw the girl push her coat away from the bare skin of her shoulder, so that Athen's head could lie on it.

So Maisie sat, hardly breathing, while Athen's head lay shaking defenceless on her shoulder.

The others were all aware of Maisie and what she felt, and the car sped in silence across the hillsides under a reddening sky.

4

Jack Dobie and Martha sat opposite each other in Dirty Dick's. Jack, to please Martha, had asked Johnny Capetenakis to cook special food, and they were eating it; although Jack did not like this food, kebabs on saffron rice, and would rather have been eating eggs and chips with the other customers.

Jack had been appointed member of a Select Committee on the condition of urban Africans. There were few suitable statistics. He was engaged in collecting facts and figures, at his own expense, in his home town of Gotwe, and he wanted Martha to go down for a few days, to help him. Besides, he wanted to have an affair with her.

Martha was refusing to go because she did not want to leave this town, which meant, now, the loft among the trees, or to miss any chance of seeing Thomas.

Jack sat with his scarcely touched plate in front of him, his chin aggressively stuck out, his eyes focused on his point, which was that he insisted on sensible explanations from Martha.

Martha ate Jack's food as well as her own and laughed and said

no, said no, said no, said she was sorry, but of course she would if
only insuperable obstacles did not intervene. ·

This scene, occurring as often as it does in life, is too often overlooked in fiction in favour of the more explosive moments: Yes, I
will go to Gotwe with you, but I am risking my marriage, yes, I will
leave my husband if you will leave your wife, do you love me? I
might have loved you if only . . .

Jack found Martha attractive; a man married to a woman who
increasingly disapproved of everything he was and did (she was a
socially ambitious girl who had never imagined herself as the wife
of a crusading member of Parliament); a man who would have, and
probably already had, invited Marjorie or Betty or any other attractive woman to Gotwe, Jack did not really care whether Martha said
yes or not.

For her part she liked him, would do anything not to hurt his feelings short of going to bed, and would do that if not otherwise engaged; hoped he was not the sort of man to let vanity disrupt a pleasant working relationship; Martha found this scene irritating on the
whole because she was so involved with Thomas.

Meanwhile one part of her mind was thinking, while she smiled
and shrugged her shoulders at Jack: so, you think if I *did* go to bed
with you, it would be just another charming experience to you?
Hmmm, well *what* a pity I can't show you . . . And he was thinking:
If only I could get her there, I'd show her a thing or two. In short,
this scene of modern gallantry was running its usual course.

Meanwhile Martha moved salt cellars and sauce bottles about, and
thought that she and Thomas, their feelings for each other, the relationship—whatever was the right word for it—was in an altogether
new dimension. They were in deep waters, both of them. And neither
understood it, could not speak about it.

Together in the loft, they spoke less. They were in the loft less
often. To be together was like—she could not say. It was true for
Thomas, too, because when they looked at each other, the sensation of sinking deeper and deeper into light was stronger. Being together was, for both of them, a good deal more than Martha being
with Thomas. Sometimes it was so intense, they could not stand it,
and separated. Or the loft seemed too high, too fragile, too small, and
they left it and walked very fast through the streets. But this could
only happen at night, because of the danger of being seen. Sometimes when they made love it was so powerful they felt afraid, as if
enormous forces were waiting to invade them. But they did not
know what this meant.

"What it amounts to," Jack was saying, "is that you are going to make the only progressive member of Parliament apart from Mrs. Van miss two days of the Parliamentary sessions because you won't give up two days love-making with Thomas?"

"That's right."

"Well, when my turn comes, I shall insist on the same treatment."

"But that goes without saying!"

She told Anton she was going to Gotwe for a few days to do some work for Jack Dobie.

She had realized this could not be a casual announcement. Remarks dropped by Anton recently had told her that he was convinced her affair with Thomas was over and that she had a new lover. But why should he think this? Because, she realized, his affair with Millicent was ending or over. She thought: How extraordinary, Anton does not know, except with that part of himself that makes love to me on a compulsion of rivalry, though of course he would put other names to it, whether I'm with another man or not. His *mind* would not be able to say. But I know what kind of an evening he's had with Millicent by looking at him.

They were in the little bedroom. It was cold. He wore thick dark-blue flannel pyjamas, and she wore a white frilled nightdress she had bought thinking of Thomas. She wore a quilted red jacket over it. There they were, Anton and Martha, Mr. and Mrs. Hesse, side by side in their twin-bedded room.

She knew there was tension between them because muscles tightened in her lower stomach. She picked up a nail file and began work on her nails.

His long white hands lay on his knees. She watched his hands sideways over the flying bit of glinting metal that shaped her nails, and thought: If I look at Thomas's hands, it is as if they were holding me, but Anton's hands, they might belong to someone I'd just met.

But if that were true—why was her stomach tightening? Somewhere at the back of her consciousness the knowledge began to hammer, just how terrible a crime she had committed by marrying Anton, by marrying Douglas . . . against herself and against them. But how was she to have foreseen the world she would enter when she loved Thomas? Why had no one told her it existed in a way that she could believe it? How strange it was—marriage and love; one would think, the way newspapers, films, literature, the people who are supposed to express us talk, that we believe marriage, love, to be the desperate important deep experiences they say they are. But

of course they don't believe any such thing. Hardly anyone believes
it. We want them to believe it. We want to believe it. Perhaps people
will believe it again.

The way things are, for the second time Martha looked at a
stranger across a bedroom and thought, how was it that no one made
me feel that it could matter, marrying someone.

"Matty?" said Anton suddenly in a low voice.

She said, "Look, Anton, what's the point?"

He came over, sat by her, put a long arm through which she
could feel a lank flat bone around the cage of her ribs, put his cheek
against hers. She could feel the papery dryness of his lips moving
against her cheek.

Her body, wrenched out of its loyalty to Thomas, instantly began
to ache.

She said, "No, Anton, please not, it's so silly."

"When we've both finished playing around, Matty."

She said, "Anton, you know you and I are no good together. . . .
Don't be angry," she added weakly.

"Angry. Well, that's a funny way of putting it." He went off to the
bathroom, angry, miserable. When he came back he got straight
into bed, turned his back, switched off the light. Left sitting upright
in the dark, she put aside her nail file and lay down.

He said, "Well, if you're going to play the fool like this, I'm going
off for a few days myself."

"But, Anton, believe me, I'm not having an affair with Jack."

He was silent, waiting for her to go on.

She nearly said, "What's happened with Millicent?" But she
waited, just as he waited.

At last he said, "Well don't imagine I'm going to be left on the
shelf."

She said, placating, soft, humorously, "But Anton, we did agree,
didn't we, that we'd leave each other free while we waited for a
divorce." Even saying this made her muscles ache, so she knew it
was all terrible nonsense. However, on this level they "got along,"
so on this level they must continue.

He said, "Very well then, I know what to do."

Next day he told her he was going to spend a few days with the
Forsters, a rich businessman and his family. He had met Mr. Forster
one day when lunching with his superior in the railways. "He's not
a bad sort of type," he had said of him afterwards.

Meanwhile she rang Thomas to make sure she would not miss one
of his visits to town, and he said that since his farm was on the way
to Gotwe, why didn't she and Jack drop in for lunch?

"You want me to come to the farm?"—meaning, You want me and your wife to meet?

"Yes, yes. Why not? It means I'll see you. Yes, I'd like you to come."

Jack was pleased. He liked nothing more than visiting farms. His great-grandparents had been small farmers, and when he retired he proposed to farm fruit himself. In his youth he was a shipworker on the Clyde. In this country he had been for decades a railway worker and a member of Parliament concerned with industrial matters. But how he really saw himself, he said, was as a farmer; his real life would begin when at fifty-five he tended pears and peaches on a plot which he had already bought, in the mountains.

This was how Martha visited Thomas's farm, how she saw Thomas's wife and the little girl. She never forgot that day. It was a heightened, painful day—not one she would have missed, far from it. But afterwards, when she had only to shut her eyes to see the picture of Thomas with his little girl, the day shifted its emphasis. The rest became blurred, a scene of magnificent mountains and somewhere off among the shrubs the sound of Thomas's wife, laughing. But she kept seeing Thomas, stretching out his hands to the little girl.

Jack picked her up about ten in the morning, in his old lorry. He drove very fast. This long journey across two hundred miles of veld was something he had to do three, four times a week, when Parliament was sitting. Almost at once they were in open country. It was a cold clear day, with white clouds driving fast overhead. In all directions swept the flattening dry-cold grass of winter, it was all miles of pale gold, then blue-green kopjes, then pale blue sky where the clouds swept. Everything was high, austere and in movement. Across empty miles poured the wind which battered against the lorry, so that it tugged and swerved to leave the road. She was exhilarated, and looked at Jack to share it. He felt her looking and smiled and said, "Here I am, mad with love for you, driving you to meet your lover."

"Not all that mad, I hope."

"And how long has it been?"

"Has what been?"

"You with Thomas?"

She had to think—"Some months. A year. Something like that."

"I thought you and Athen were having a thing together."

"Well, give us all time, and I suppose we'd all have affairs with each other."

"He's a fine laddie, that one."

"He's going back to Greece next month."

"Is he now?" Jack clicked his tongue. Never had so many hearts—in their political aspect—been broken so fast and so thoroughly as in the first few months of that Labour Government. Jack's was the one worst hit. An old socialist, lifetime Labour Party supporter, when the Labour Party got in in 1945, his oldest dream came true.

Now he was bitter. "Well," he said at last, "if I were in Greece now I'd become a Communist, just to show what I think of Labour —I couldn't say fairer than that, could I?"

"Athen had a letter saying he mustn't go home, he'll be arrested as he arrives. Last week they let all the collaborators out of prison, and they're arresting the Left. And a lot more of Athen's friends have gone to the mountains."

"We've had some fine people through this country, with the war."

Quite so: this country, her life, Jack's life—everybody's life that was the point—empty spaces through which people blew like bits of paper.

She said, "Maisie's in love with Athen. But I mean, really in love."

He said at once in the bluff no-nonsense voice which shouts disapproval, "Well, that young woman's been in love often enough."

She said, not by any means for the first time, "You forget, she's been widowed twice."

He was silent, but his mouth twisted in a small knowledgeable smile.

She persisted, "Maisie's the sort of girl who'd have stayed married to her first husband. But he was killed."

"Well, it's not my affair."

"It's funny though. We still talk about people, we make judgements just as if there hadn't been five years of war. What sort of sense does it make, saying about Maisie—she's been in love too often, when you think of what's happened to her?"

Again the small knowledgeable smile—an ugly smile, horrid, on whoever's face it comes.

"Don't you see, it comes out of a different sort of thing altogether —talking like that. It really is funny how we've gone back to talking as if the war didn't happen."

"I haven't noticed we don't talk about it!"

"I don't mean saying things about it—like the war has done a lot of damage, or it will take ten years to restore agriculture in the Ukraine or something, I mean, really feeling things are different."

She saw she was repeating herself—yet as she spoke, she felt as if she were in the grip of a new kind of knowledge, a new insight.

She understood what Athen had been trying to say outside Maisie's bar. She had not understood Athen—she had merely made an assent to his words with her mind. It was the difference between hearing a phrase and thinking: Yes, that's true, and forgetting it; and letting the real meaning of the words sink into one, become part of one—as if one had eaten them, swallowed them, "digested" them, in short. She knew Jack had heard what she had said and had assented: Yes, there have been five years of war, there's been a lot of damage. But just as she had been irritated with Athen, impatient, because she wanted to enjoy the evening, so now Jack was annoyed, or at least impatient, because he was a man who worked very hard, and he had wanted to enjoy today.

After a mile or so of the fast swerving journey through swaying grass, trees, he said, "I didn't mean to run down Maisie, I didn't know she was so much a friend of yours."

She said, "It's all right," but she was absorbed by the swooping movement through the high sparkling air. The empty space was opening inside her, and she was gazing into it with passionate curiosity. Martha and Jack, two minute fragments of humanity, rattling in the machine across immensities of empty country, they were only two of the figures that moved, small and brightly lit, against the backdrop, while she watched. She saw Maisie, if there had not been a war: married to her first husband, producing a child, two children; the in-laws would very soon have said, Well, she's a nice enough girl really. Soon she would have been a fat middle-aged woman with reserves of lazy good nature, and spoiled children and a husband she protected and ordered about. Instead—well, Thomas said she was sleeping with men from the bar, and probably for money.

But what did it matter? The two pictures of Maisie stood side by side on the empty space—and cancelled each other out. Both were true. Both were untrue. Yesterday someone had written from England: one of the young men who had visited the Hesses in their old flat was badly wounded and in hospital. He had been in hospital for nearly a year. His leg had been cut off. He was the fair young man who used to sleep on the floor when he was too late to catch a camp bus. Much to Anton's annoyance. But how could the two things fit together: a man in hospital with a leg cut off, and the boy asleep on the floor with the sun on him. Why, she had only to shut her eyes to see him there, rather flushed, his hair untidy—a flushed defenceless-looking boy asleep in the morning sun. She could see him clearer than she had in life. And Athen—Athen was going back to Greece any day now. If he wasn't arrested first, he would be with the partisans in the mountains very soon. "Mine is the only country in Europe that still destroys itself." But it was as if someone flicked a scene off a cinema screen and put on a new one. "Greece is still at war." "Greece is at peace." Turn the scene back two years: Europe was crawling with tiny ants, murdering each other. Turn it forwards: Europe was at peace, bandaging wounds, clearing away rubble. Asia was "at peace" again, though in China great armies still fought. But in Europe the armies were quiet, though millions of people were hungry, the newspaper had said that morning; and next winter would be famine again. Turn the scene forward—how many years? No ruins left, no hungry people?

The empty space swelled up to the great wind-scoured skies: it was the size of the great landscape, this enormous stretch of country lifted high, high, under a high pale-blue cloud-swept sky.

And soon the car would come to Thomas's farm. She and Thomas loved each other. Whatever that meant. And whatever it meant, it was the most sure, the most real thing that happened to her. But blur the scene slightly, and Thomas did not exist—*almost* he had not left Poland at all. If he had not—well, none of his family was left alive, several dozen brothers, sisters, cousins, relatives were all dead, they had died in the gas ovens, on the gallows, in the prisons, and the concentration camps in those years of our Lord, 1939–1945. But here Thomas was alive. And all her life Martha would say to herself—whatever else had been untrue, whatever else had not existed, *this* had been true: this was true, she must hold on to it, even though, when she touched Thomas, it was with an anxiety that related not to Thomas now and here, but to the scene which she could create by a slight dislocation in her mind: Thomas very nearly had not left Poland.

Up hillsides that hissed and tossed with the long movement of wind, and down again; it was a world floored with immensities of tossing pale gold grass, roofed with depths of pale blue—turn her upside down, she would be floating on pale blue depths where white foam flowers hissed and died, looking up at a great bubble of pale gold, where the movements of wind showed in mile-long currents of whitening light.

Perhaps, when Thomas and she touched each other, in the touch cried out the murdered flesh of the millions of Europe—the squandered flesh was having its revenge, it cried out through the two little creatures who were fitted for much smaller loves, the touch only of a hand on a shoulder, simple hungers, and the kindness of sleep. Instead—it was all much too painful, and they had to separate.

Last week Thomas had said, "Why should I stay in this country? I'll tell you something, I've just understood it—when you've left one country, then you've left all countries, forever. I'm a wandering Jew, like my fathers were. So why should I stay here?"

"Where will you go?"

"I don't know."

Meanwhile Jack and she were going to "drop in" to Thomas's farm for lunch. Though dropping in here meant a ten-mile drive off the main road, and then ten miles back on to it. And she, Martha, would meet Thomas's wife Rachel, and his little girl Esther. And then she, Martha, would be driven on to Gotwe by Jack Dobie, expert on the wrongs of India, ex-agitator from the Clyde, the Colony's most energetic Kaffir-lover, who wished to have an affair with her; leaving behind Thomas, whom she loved, and who this week was occupied, he said, with preparing new seed beds. Nothing fitted, ridiculous facts jostled with important ones, if one only knew which was which, and the empty space dazzled with its growing distances—she wished very much she had not said they would drop in for lunch; suddenly everything was unbearable and she wished she was back in the refuge of the loft, reading, or already in Gotwe with Jack, working. But here they already were, Jack and she, half-way along the rough farm road to the house. And the empty space not only contained her and Jack, two tiny antlike figures, she contained the space—she was the great bell of space, and through it crawled little creatures, among them, herself.

There was Thomas's house. It was nothing special: like a thousand others, it was a brick bungalow under corrugated iron. But it spread attractively, and the pillars and the verandahs of warm brick supported flowers and foliage. All around were gardens; they had driven through maize fields that surrounded the homestead, bare fields now, light red earth where the plough had turned furrows of darker red and everywhere patches of glinting gold leafage marked where the mealie stooks had been. Then there were banks of shrubs to break the winds which swept across leagues of country from the circling mountains, then roses, it seemed acres of roses, gold and scarlet and white, drenching the sharp winter air with their scent. Then lawns, studded with poinsettias, and beyond the house the working beds where Thomas grew plants for selling in town.

On the verandah stood a fair young woman holding a blonde little girl by the hand. Behind them a dark bearded man of middle age who nodded and smiled, indicating that his English was poor.

And Thomas came in from the garden, wearing his khaki shorts rolled up to the top of his thighs. He was brown and polished by wind and sun. And he was shy, nodding awkwardly at Martha, but putting the warmth he felt for her into his greeting for Jack.

They went into lunch. There was a long room, windowed at either end, showing descending hillsides covered with roses and flowering shrubs and, a long way off, blue mountains. In the middle of the room, a long trestle table made by Thomas, with salads and fruit and pickled fish, prepared by Rachel.

They were Thomas and Rachel, Esther, who was about two or three, and Jack and Martha and the silent bearded man who was a professor of something or other.

Martha eyed Thomas's wife, who examined her.

Rachel at first sight was not pretty at all, but then, extremely pretty, though that was too banal a word.

She was slender, but strong; she was white-skinned, with the solid white skin that browns well. Her hair was a curling light brown—almost gold. She was all clear colours: healthy brown cheeks, very white teeth, blue eyes with clear whites to them, and warm golden hair curling around her face. She had the combination of a fine robustness and delicacy of a Leonardo woman, which is what Martha was reminded of, as Rachel smiled and talked like a hostess, protesting that they did not often have company. But soon she fell silent, leaving the business of entertaining to her husband, while she sat beside her little girl, quietly directing her in Polish about spoons and forks. Esther was newly admitted to the grown-up table, it seemed, and was watching her mother to learn how she should behave. Meanwhile Thomas and Jack argued about Zionism, and Martha thought of Caroline, now seven years old, and watched the delightful little girl who sat beside her mother and glanced up continually to see how she must handle a spoon or convey a piece of bread to her mouth. The two, mother and daughter, had the most marvellous freshness and delicacy; they glowed in the dark cool depths of the dining room as they sat together at the end of the table.

Meanwhile Jack was indignantly reproaching Thomas for being a Zionist, for how could a Marxist be a Zionist? Not that he, Jack, was a Marxist, he was just concerned that the proper categories of thought should be maintained. And Thomas was saying, "Logically you are right. A Marxist is not a Zionist. But I am a Marxist. And with every day I become more of a Zionist. I see British soldiers allowing refugees from Europe to drown rather than land in Israel, and I am a Zionist."

Meanwhile they ate stuffed aubergine and sour black bread, baked on the farm; and Thomas, interrupting a sentence about the Labour Party and its policy in Europe, said something to his wife in Polish, and she instantly clapped her hands. A servant came in, and took away the plates. He brought in clear soup. It was to be a real feast, and there would be no moving away from the table for hours yet. Not once had Thomas looked at Martha—or not *really*, as she put it. Then, briefly, he did look at her, and Martha felt the touch of his warm blue eyes on her face, so strongly, that she understood why he did not look at her. She felt that Rachel must have sensed the look and what it meant. But if so, she made no sign, and went on chattering to the little girl in Polish and Yiddish, and to the servant when he came in in Shona, and to her guests in charming broken English.

The long meal went on. The sunlight sparkled on the cold windowpanes; the petals of the poinsettias, scarlet and pink and yellow, fluttered in the wind; the roses scattered their petals on the brown earth. How many times had Martha sat, at lunch in a farm house on the veld, looking through windows at mountains? And how many hours had she heard discussed, the colour bar, war, politics, the "native problem," Communism, oh my God, forever, it seemed, she had sat talking or listening, and here she was again and now it was Zionism.

Zionism in the middle of the veld, in the middle of mealie fields scooped out of the bush, and beautiful Rachel from Cracow, and Thomas from Sochaczen, and herself, and the dark silent Professor, and Jack from the Clyde. Jack was positively sending out sparks of rage in all directions, he was almost dancing in his seat with exasperation, because of the total inconsistency of Thomas.

Now they ate cold chicken. It was very good, and they watched white and black and golden-brown chickens run scratching among the shrubs outside.

Martha felt a current running strongly between herself and Thomas. He had hardly glanced at her again. Several times he got up and went abruptly out of the room and Martha thought of how he had said at the dance: I can't sit beside you like a stuffed horse at a fair.

They ate apple cake and then nuts and fruit and drank strong Turkish coffee. It was four in the afternoon. Then Rachel laughed and said that Martha and Jack must not leave before having tea. Thomas said, "But they have to get to Gotwe before it's dark." And she said, laughing, "Then they must drive in the dark, it won't hurt them!" Suddenly Thomas walked off, by himself, around the side

of the house, crushing a handful of leaves between his fingers. All
the air was pungent with the smell of the crushed leaves. Jack, oblivious of all these currents, said he wanted to see the gardens. He had
no time these days for gardens, but he wanted to pick up tips for
when he started to grow fruit. They went off to see the gardens, in
a group. Coming around the side of the house, they saw a long bed
in which were clumps of shining green leaves and by it Thomas,
squatting on his heels, his bare knees brown and shining. But in
front of him stood Esther, the tiny child, and these two were looking at each other, in silence. Thomas did not know the others were
there, but Esther did; she glanced, very serious, as if apologizing
or explaining, past her father's shoulder at her mother and the Professor and the guests, and then she looked back at her father, in the
way someone waits out of politeness.

Rachel said, "Come on, we must go this way." Rachel and Jack
and the Professor went on, and Martha stood still a moment, watching Thomas, twelve paces off. She could see he had been crying. His
cheeks had red stains on them. He was half turned away, his shoulder was presented to her, as he stared into the face of his child.

There Esther stood, as light and airy as if she could blow away,
in a minute yellow dress that fluttered around her thin knees, her
fair wisps of hair blowing about her head. She looked steadily at
her father. Thomas held out his hands to her, but the child did not
respond.

"Esther," he said, coaxing, then said something in Yiddish. But
she would not. She stood frowning, the sun dazzling in her moving
wisps of hair.

Thomas let his hands drop—in a rough despairing gesture. Then
gently, gently, he lifted his right hand and held it out to the child.
It was this gesture that did for Martha, made her understand—but
what? Here, she felt was something she should know, should have
known, about Thomas. She sensed that the real being of Thomas
spoke out in that gesture—the big strong hand going out so gently,
delicately, to the child. Thomas squatted there, holding out his
strong brown arm where the hairs glinted gold, but held it as if it
cost him very heavily to plead so. He did not touch Esther, he was
giving her the opportunity to accept him. It was the way one offers
a hand to a cat to sniff, to accept or reject as it wants. Esther looked
doubtfully at the big brown arm held out to her, at the pleading
hand at the end of it—and then, slowly, she backed away. She was
not coquetting, she simply backed herself away, and her face
frowned. She looked in a kind of distaste at her father's hand, held

out to her. It trembled, very slightly. Then she lifted her serious blue eyes at her father and the little face showed a puzzled disapproval, even a dislike. Certainly a "go away, don't touch me." Then she stood still for a moment, the yellow cotton blowing about the ridiculously small brown legs, her hair whipping in the wind— then she turned and ran off towards her mother. And in her movement, the way she ran off, was a wild relief, as if she had been released from an oppression. She was running away from what was too heavy. Her father was a weight on her.

Martha watched Thomas lower his hand. He let it rest on its knuckles on the earth, among the clumps of glistening leaves. His cheek, half turned to her, was wet. The others were out of sight. Rachel's voice, light and laughing, chattered in Polish to her child. The Professor's voice said something in Yiddish. Rachel's laugh came ringing across the sunlight.

Thomas had turned his head and seen Martha. He nodded at her. "Hello, Martha," he said. He wiped tears off his face with the back of his hand, unconcerned that she saw him.

He said, "You'd better get to the others." Then, as she obediently went, she heard him say, low and fierce, "Don't forget, you must be in our house the day after tomorrow, you *must*, please."

This comforted her, and she held the thought of his needing her as she went with the others around bushes and across lawns, and admired vistas of veld and river and mountains. It was a beautiful place, and the gardens were superb. Thomas lived in a beautiful place surrounded by gardens which he had made. But he would not stay there. Soon he would go away.

They all had tea on the verandah, while the little girl chattered to the dark bearded man, who now had a white panama hat on his head, tilted forward because of the glare. The Professor was called Michel Pevsner, and he was free to touch Esther, to stroke her hair, and to hold her on his knee. But her own father was not. Thomas watched Esther with Michel, and addressed remarks to the two of them, as if they were a unit. He did not say anything more to Esther. Esther prattled with her mother, flirted with the Professor, and looked at her father as if he were an unpleasant fact in her life which she had to accept.

Soon Jack and Martha had to leave. There were another 150 miles to cover before they reached Gotwe.

Martha found a hotel in Gotwe, and Jack and she were very efficient about collecting figures. Meanwhile she kept seeing Thomas and the tiny girl together. She would not think about it, however.

She saw it, saw the scene, against her lids—every time she shut her eyes, or so it seemed. But she would *not* think about it. And she kept hearing Rachel's light laughter; she heard it, but she would not think about her either.

The afternoon she got back into the city from Gotwe she slowly climbed the ladder to the loft, above the rising odours of damp foliage from the tins of seedlings on the floor.

Thomas's brother's wife, Sarah, had been standing on the verandah, hands on her solid young-married-woman's hips, watching, as Martha came in at the gate. That gesture, the finality of disapproval in the hands on the large hips, told Martha that soon Sarah would see to it that this shed would be needed for something else. Perhaps Sarah was so angry that she would simply come into the shed and up the ladder and make a scene? Why not?

Martha did not care. She stripped off her clothes, flung them on to the floor, and got under heavy blankets. The dry sunlight came in, the foliage from the tall trees showed light and dry through the pane, the scents from the garden all had a tang of brisk chill and dryness.

Soon she heard a lorry stop, then Thomas's voice calling across the lawns to his sister-in-law, "How are you, Sarah? That's fine. Good."

Then she heard his voice beneath, "Martha?"

"Yes."

"Are you undressed?"

"Yes."

"Good."

She waited. He came up, serious, leaned over her, kissed her, serious, sat looking at her—serious, serious.

"Thomas, what's the matter?"

"First, we make love."

"Oh goodness, Thomas, you look so desperate."

"Yes, and *you're* thinking: I came here to be with my lover, and not with this madman!"

"So that's what I'm thinking?"

"Yes. More and more often I look at you and you are thinking: How did I land myself with this maniac?"

He was making love as if she were a blanket to pull over his head, or a dream he wanted to lose himself in.

Later he lay beside her, quiet, holding her hand over his eyes with his own. She could feel his lashes moving against her fingers as he stared up into the darkness her hand made.

"First, I must say something, Matty."

"Oh, Thomas, can't we *not* say anything!"

"No."

He took her hand off his eyes and lay holding it against his neck.

"I'm sorry I asked you to come to the farm. But you should have said no."

"Yes, I know I should."

"And what did your wife say?"

They were silent for a time.

Then he said, "Martha, have you ever been in a situation—no, that's the wrong word." Again he lay thinking.

"What, then?"

"You see, I can't even describe it. It's as bad as that. Have you ever felt at the end of something—I don't mean just unhappy or somebody going away, not that." She could not help reacting to his "somebody going away" but he did not notice it. "I would never have believed once, if someone had told me, there are things you can't do something about, you come to the end of things in yourself. Once I believed that one had only to make up one's mind to do anything."

"You mean," said Martha, "you feel something for your—family, and they don't return it, is that it?"

"I suppose something like that."

Now he did not say anything for a long time, and when Martha looked, his eyes were shut, and she thought he had gone to sleep.

At last he said, "My wife was the daughter of a university professor. We only met because I was a Communist and she was wondering if she should be one. She came to a lecture a friend of mine was giving."

"And then you fell in love?"

"I like the way you say that, fall in love—so simple. Well, that's how we saw it then, simple. And I knew the war was coming. She and her circles did not think there would be war. We Marxists have many advantages—for instance, we knew the war was coming." In this last sentence was the mechanical irony that goes with failure; and her laugh was as mechanical.

"I made all arrangements to get her out of the country with me. But her father and her sister would not believe me. She believed me but they didn't. So we married and left Poland. They were left behind. So they're dead."

He was trying so hard to explain something to her, but she had no idea what.

"If there wasn't a war, I'd never have met her—a professor's daughter. And as for me, Martha, as far as they were concerned, I was just a peasant."

"But she did marry you."

"Yes."

Against Martha's closed lids she saw descending miles of sun-lit country, the blue mountains beyond, and, in the foreground, the big man squatting, holding out a pleading hand to the little girl.

She kept her eyes shut and looked at this picture: it explained what he was not able to say.

"And Michel?" she said.

"The joke of it is, I used to despise Michel. I thought he was nothing, just a word-spinner, a schoolteacher with good manners. You know, Martha, I tell you—it's something when you look **at** something, your whole self gives way, and you want just to give yourself up. And it's not that she doesn't accept it, or she hates you, or anything like that. It's just that there's something like seventy per cent of you she leaves out of account."

"Seventy-five per cent," said Martha, trying to make him laugh.

"No, Martha. No, you must listen to me—you love her so much, and she says Yes, Thomas, you're a nice man, and thank you for being kind, but you're too rough and clumsy and—so seventy per cent of you doesn't exist. Not hatred, or she doesn't love me, but I don't exist. Because she never really liked what I am. Once I tried to change myself. That was a joke, Martha—believe me, now when I remember it I laugh. But at the time I was too serious. I told myself I'd forget the village, the dried herring and the sour milk and the potatoes. I forgot how to haggle over a horse or choose a bit of cheese. I was stupid. I didn't understand a damned thing. I really imagined that—because the point was, she was quite prepared to like me, but she had to forget me to do it, you understand, Martha? Well, so that's it. I used to think: Well, I'll make her like me. After all, I'm not a bad man. I'm kind. I don't beat women. And I'm a good gardener. And I know how to study."

"How to what?" she said, surprised.

"How to study," he said, seriously. Then he turned and looked at her. "That's the point. It took me years to understand why you said that, in that tone. I used to say to myself, 'I can learn anything, if I set my mind to it.' I learned French in one month because she knew French and I thought she'd love me for it. There was a time when every day I said I'll learn something new today, for her."

Martha kept her cheek pressed to his and said nothing.

"And then there was the child. It's the same with her. Well, you saw how it was."

Martha did not know what to say. She wanted to comfort him. She said at last, "Well, now it's peace perhaps things will be better."

"What do you mean?"

She had not meant anything much, and she already felt foolish, but she said, trying to laugh, "Well, in peacetime professor's daughters don't marry handsome peasants and run off to Africa with them."

He said, fierce, lonely, disappointed, "You didn't think when you said that. Sometimes I forget—you're very young. I mean, you are young in your self, because your experience has been to keep you safe."

"Is that what matters, being safe?"

"There are two kinds of people—those who know how easy it is to be dead, and those who think death can't happen to me. . . . I told you, everything's changed. I'm the norm now. I told you, the elm tree and safety's finished. Who is the freak, the unusual person? The man who is born in X, who goes to school in X, who marries a person from X, or perhaps from Y, and who dies in his bed in X. All that's over. My mother's first husband was killed in the first World War. Her second husband was an old man, and she didn't love him, but she was right to marry him—a woman needs a husband and all the young men were dead in our village. And she had seven children. And her whole life was a struggle to feed us. But it was all a waste of effort, because all her children are dead, except me and my brother. That's what normal is now. My family's all dead and I'm in exile. And my wife's family are dead and she's an exile. . . ." He was going to say something more, but he stopped.

Martha said, "You were going to say something about going away?"

"Was I?"

"Yes."

For a time he lay still. stroking her arm. Then he turned over and held her near to him. "Well, Martha, never mind, let's not think of it now."

"You are seriously asking me not to think about it?"

"Yes. I am. Seriously."

"All right," she said, after a time. "I'll try not to."

But soon they talked about it. He wanted to go to Palestine. "No, for my sake, Israel, Martha, not Palestine." He wanted to go to Israel. Not necessarily for good, no. Perhaps for a visit. He did not know why he wanted so much to go, but he did.

part three

My God, in what a century have you caused me to live!

SAINT POLYCARP: AD 156

1

A year had gone round and it was winter again. In Europe the worst winter in decades was over, and their Northern summer was healing, it was to be hoped, some of the scars of cold and hunger. But at that moment there was famine in Greece, famine in China—in both countries accompanying civil war; famine in India, in Yugoslavia, in . . . Martha had just come from Mrs. Van's office where the old woman was engaged in bringing her news cuttings up to date. She was surrounded by great piles of newspapers from countries all over the world, and the heaps of cuttings in front of her destined to go into the drawer marked "Food Shortage" was higher than any other.

Martha and Thomas sat in the Piccadilly. There was a letter from Joss lying on the stained tablecloth near a cruet which looked like the Albert Memorial and had seven different kinds of vinegar and pickle, apart from the usual salt, pepper, mustard. Joss wrote that the economic conditions in Northern Rhodesia were so and so, the political situation such and such, and that he had had a letter from his brother Solly: it looks to me as if someone politically mature ought to be keeping an eye on him, what are you people up to? With comradely greetings.

This letter, having passed from Marjorie—the energetic one these days, but she was having another baby—to Betty, to Marie, had arrived at Martha with the query: how had it come about we have to hear about Solly from Joss, who isn't even in the country?

Well, they could make what explanations they liked, but the truth was . . . Martha's word for what had happened during the past year was that everyone had become silent.

There was Anton, who, three, even two years ago, was certain to greet any situation with a speech or the demand for one; now he and Martha did not exchange more than half a dozen phrases a day. Did he "make analyses of the situation" for anyone? Not with Millicent, whom he no longer saw. Perhaps for the Forsters, where he now visited most evenings. Mr. Forster was employed by a large oil company, as a kind of technical adviser. They lived in the newly-built West suburb, surrounded by tennis courts, swimming pools, servants. There were three sons and two daughters—one a war widow. So much Martha had discovered from Anton's reticences. But he was embarrassed by his liking the Forsters; he enjoyed playing chess with Mr. Forster, he said. Two or three times a week Anton went to the government office where his papers were manipulated, in a process which would eventually lead to his being a British citizen. He said he proposed to go back to Germany the moment he had his passport. Suppose he wanted to leave Germany again for a holiday or a visit? Who knew how long Germany would be occupied by foreign armies—not that Germany didn't deserve it, he said. But living in a British country had given him a taste of freedom. He hoped Martha would understand that he was using the word in its relative or bourgeois sense.

Martha and he sat at meals together—silent. They went a great deal to the pictures.

Athen was silent because he had gone back to Greece. Shortly after the evening at the Parkland Hotel, he had arrived in the Hesses' flat, but not alone. Five other Greeks came with him. They had all been eating their hearts out to get back to their real allegiances. The six men had fitted themselves somehow into the little room. Martha had understood how partially she had seen Athen. Two or three times a week he had come to visit her, or Maisie. But for all those years of waiting, what had his real life been? Certainly not the evenings in town. No, it had been with these men who, affable but silent, had come with Athen to say goodbye to his friends. It was agreed that if no word came from Athen, either by post (within three months) or by word of mouth through friends (within six) then he must be considered dead. And this was true for all of them, they agreed, smiling and nodding. Things could not be worse, in Greece, for their side. The anti-Royalist armies still fought from the mountains, but the Royalists were in power, put there by Britain and America. Over 4,000 Resistance men were in exile in the islands, in spite of a hundred promises that the old fighters would not be arrested at all. These six men all planned to make their way to the mountains. They joked that they expected to be very hungry soon: there was a new policy, deliberately not to cultivate certain areas so as to starve the guerrillas out. But after so much good eating in this country, they said—smiling, smiling, to show that they were joking, it would not hurt them, they all needed to lose weight. They gave Martha a list of ruled writing paper on which were their six names and the addresses of people who could be trusted. Then they shook her by the hand, one after another, and departed. Athen held her hand a moment as he left, and said, "Martha, I will think of you all, all my good friends, for all of my life." That had been nearly a year ago.

Thomas above all was silent. The change between them was partly because Thomas's brother's wife had got her way over the shed, which was now a playroom for Thomas's nephews and nieces. Four of them; a new baby had been born at Christmas—as a result, Thomas claimed, of the quarrelling between husband and wife over taking the shed away from Thomas. Thomas's lorry was easily adapted for love-making, but it was not the same, although they saw each other often. Thomas would ring Martha to say, "I've got a couple of hours free." They would meet at the Old Vienna, or at Dirty Dick's, and sit together for the most part in silence. Or, the nights being very cold, since it was winter, they went to the pictures and sat in the back row like schoolchildren, their cheeks pressed together, holding hands.

Thomas said, "We always make a great mistake, Martha. We always make our calculations based on the fact that Sarah will not take away our shed, because she has enough rooms already and because it would be spiteful of her. But the truth is, she always does. Because she is too stupid to know that she is spiteful."

Thomas had agreed to his brother's plans. There was a shop in the Main Street called Stern Bros. Everything for Your Garden.

Thomas was a sort of consultant there. He did not sell things, his brother did that, but he advised people about their gardens and how to lay them out. He had not yet gone to Israel—his wife had decided to go first, with the little girl, to visit relations. The farm was being run by Michel.

So Thomas was in town a good deal. Thomas, waiting to go to Israel, Martha, waiting to go to England—they felt like people filling in time before trains on a station platform.

Martha was no longer "running around and about." What was the point, when she was going away at any moment? She would not organize things, she would not go to meetings—not that there were many, these days. So what good was it to give her the letter about Solly?

Besides, it had been decided they would do more harm than good, working with the Africans. Individually and collectively, they were Reds, Communists, traitors, spies—the atmosphere was such that people they had known for years looked embarrassed when they met, or hostile, or made a point of coming over to greet them.

"The Africans have got enough problems, without being called Communist," Marjorie had said.

"But they're called Communist anyway!"

"Yes, but no one can prove anything."

"Since when did they need to prove anything? And besides, look at Solly, running around down there, he doesn't worry about the Africans being called Reds."

"But he's a Trotskyist!"

"Yes, but *they* don't know the difference."

This conversation, at Marjorie's house, had the force of hours of discussion at one of the old meetings, because its effect had been that they did not approach the Africans.

Who in any case were not, it seemed, keen on being approached. Mrs. Van's weekly meetings had dwindled from fifty, sixty people, to five or six. It had happened suddenly. One week, the men had simply not come, or only a few. Marjorie had heard that in Solly's group it was said that Mrs. Van despised the Africans. She thought they were brutal savages who would kill the opposition when they came to power. Attempts had been made to find out the exact words which Mrs. Van was supposed to have used, but they were irrelevant. Mrs. Van der Bylt had congealed, and she knew it herself, into a figure, a set of words: she was a "reactionary paternalist, who meant well." This might be temporary, it might be permanent, but

Mrs. Van said that there were times when there was no point in trying to do anything, the tide ran too strongly; the only thing was to sit tight and wait.

So much for Mrs. Van. So much too for Johnny Lindsay, who was still slowly dying but who received African friends every Wednesday. But since Africans came to his house every day, in the natural course of events, why were the Wednesdays special? They had become a symbol of some kind, that was clear, for Mr. Matushi came to sit by the old man every Wednesday, talking himself, tactfully, because Johnny did not have enough breath to talk. Mr. Matushi said that Solly's group—no, it was not the same as Mr. Zlentli's group, he had been told—was too extreme. All those groups, they were extreme. They were nationalists, not socialists, and they talked of throwing all the whites into the sea. So Mr. Matushi heard, but he had not been at the meetings, so perhaps all that was just malicious gossip.

What was Martha supposed to do or say when she had contacted Solly—or his group, or Mr. Zlentli? She did not even know how to contact Solly, who was not living at home.

Thomas said, "Well, tell them they can get help from us if they want it."

"But surely they must know that already?"

"It sounds to me as if Joss knows that Solly's causing trouble."

"You say that exactly like a leader in the *Zambesia News*—certain agitators are causing trouble among the blacks."

She spoke without heat—casually almost. As indifferent as he sounded.

Then Thomas said, "I can't imagine Joss writing a letter without a good reason for it."

"I suppose not."

"*I* wouldn't want to get mixed up with anything Solly has anything to do with."

"Well, perhaps someone ought to just see what's going on?"

He did not reply to this. He had made a heap of white glittering salt on the cloth and was stirring it with a match. At last he said, "Why don't you ask Anton to find out?"

"Anton won't do anything political these days. He say he thinks his naturalization's being held up because of his politics."

Thomas shrugged. "If this was Poland, that would be the case."

"He goes to the office practically every day, and the man keeps saying: Next month, next month."

Thomas shrugged again. There was irritation in it, as in all his movements these days. "I don't understand the unwritten rules of this country. In Poland next month means in ten years or never. If you say that in this country next month means next month—then I can only say that . . ." He frowned.

"Say what?"

"Perhaps Sergeant Tressell's the price you have to pay for next month meaning next month."

She felt shock—she had forgotten about Sergeant Tressell.

He was scowling and digging about in his pile of white salt with his match.

"It means next year," she said.

"And then you'll be off to England."

"I hope so."

"Have you noticed, all the progressive people are slowly going? It's like Poland before the war. Suddenly one morning you looked around and your friends had all gone. Only Sergeant Tressell was left."

"Why are you talking about Sergeant Tressell?"

"It doesn't matter. I tell you, I know this atmosphere. I had a letter from a friend—my rich aunt's cousin, in Johannesburg. I know the smell. The Nationalists are going to get in, I can smell it."

"Oh, they can't get in, we'd never get them out again, it would be too terrible!"

"Then of course it can't happen. Terrible things don't happen."

She put her hand on his sleeve, and felt the warm flesh of his arm coming through. He said, "Ah, Martha, I know how I must sound to you, believe me. But I feel as if I were under the sea, or dead—or something. I can't say anything I want to say. I hate myself all the time."

She looked at this healthy strong man with the direct blue eyes; he sat with his fists clenched up, and she felt the muscle of his arm tight under her hand. "Why do you keep saying you hate yourself, what do you mean?"

He tried to smile at her, frowned, glanced quickly around the restaurant, with an irritable absent look.

"I've got to get back to the farm tonight. Michel telephoned to say there's going to be an official visit from the police. Michel's English is not good enough for the police, he says."

Martha remembered the casual visits from the local police, on the farm. "But is it a special visit? Did they say there's something wrong?"

"I don't know. How do I know?"

He went off, promising to telephone her after the police had been.

Martha tried in vain to find Solly. She left messages for him to ring her. She sent messages through Mr. Matushi that "certain representatives wanted to meet Mr. Zlentli." Representatives of what, that was the question.

"Communism," said Colin Black. "Whether you like it or not, that's what you represent."

"But that's nonsense," said Martha.

"What people think you are, that's the effect you have," said Colin.

"Oh nonsense, dear, you're getting so reactionary these days!" said Marjorie, smiling. She sat at the supper table's head, a small child on either knee, and a baby in the pram. She was pregnant. Her stolid husband calmly ate his way through a large supper, praising or criticizing the dishes, while she said, "Yes, dear, good," or "Well, don't eat it then, dear."

"If I didn't think I'd some link with all that, there'd be no point in living," Marjorie went on. The child on her knee reached for some cake, and Marjorie pushed away her hand, "No, Jill, I said no more cake, it's bad for your teeth. If I thought this life, if you can call it that, was everything, then . . ."

She sat smiling. She was a woman who could never let herself be angry, or say something sharp, without smiling. Now she was flushed, flustered, irritable—but she smiled.

"I've got to get to a Civil Service meeting," said Colin, and left, having kissed his wife affectionately as he did so.

"Goodbye, dear," she said warmly.

"Well, what am I to say to Mr. Zlentli—if it is Mr. Zlentli?" asked Martha.

"Oh dear, I wish I wasn't pregnant, I'd love to come with you."

"You're welcome to it, believe me," said Martha.

"Oh dear, don't say that you're losing interest too, Matty?"

Martha left; she had to go home to wait for a call from Thomas. When he rang, it was to say that the police had been and it was bad news. He would tell her when he came into town. No, it wouldn't be in the next day or two, he had things to do.

He sounded—not like himself, Martha had been on the point of describing his voice, his manner; when she realized that on the contrary, he sounded exactly like the Thomas of this year, of these last few months. He sounded utterly unlike the Thomas she had first known . . . the Thomas of the loft, as she put it to herself. She took her bicycle and went off to meet Mr. Zlentli, heavy with worry about

Thomas, and feeling that this business of seeing Mr. Zlentli was ridiculous, badly prepared, and bound to come to no good.

And so it proved.

In the street parallel to Johnny's, in a minute house similar to his, where she, Martha, had often enough sold *Watchdogs* in the old days, three Africans were waiting for her. One was the young man she recognized from Johnny Lindsay's—he had raised his hand like a boy in class to ask provocative questions. An older man, bearded, with a majestic composed air, sat in the background and never opened his mouth, not once. At once Martha assumed this was Mr. Zlentli and directed everything she said to him.

A third man, rather young, probably about twenty, brusquely welcomed her; he was going to be spokesman.

She had leaned her bicycle against the wall, and left it there.

"Do you not lock your bicycle?" said the spokesman, with affected concern. He was of a type like Solly's, Martha decided: dramatic, self-conscious—childish, in short. His eyes were wide with pretended concern. Normally Martha would have enjoyed it—the young man playing his part with such relish. But instead she found herself irritated.

"No, I don't."

"But surely in such rough parts of the town, it is wise to lock your bicycle?"

Martha again said briefly, "No," with the intention of showing she had not come to waste her time. She looked at the majestic man who was smoking in silence, watching her. The question-asker sat by him, quietly. Although it was he who had decided what was going to happen now, he looked quite unconcerned, as if nothing of this was to do with him. The lively sarcastic young man now introduced himself as Mr. Simon, and pushed a chair towards her. She sat. It was still warm from somebody's body. Mr. Simon's? The chairs in the little room were several, and arranged in a rough circle, and by each were ash trays full of stubs. Martha recognized the atmosphere of the political meeting. A door stood half open into an inner room. Behind that door, Martha suddenly knew, sat, or stood, one, or two or more people, who had been at a meeting when interrupted by Martha's arrival. Among them, perhaps Mr. Zlentli? Or even Solly? How was one to know?

And now she knew she ought not to be here, or at least not like this. She thought: Two or three years ago, if we met Africans, or they met us, we *knew* we could help each other. And now I haven't the faintest idea what to say.

She said, "I expect you want to know why I am here?"

They did not reply. She was sitting, trying to think of the right words to use, when Mr. Simon said something unexpected, "And how *is* our good friend Mrs. Van?"

"But I didn't come here to discuss Mrs. Van der Bylt," said Martha.

"But there is no doubt she will be interested in the results of our discussions."

Martha had no idea what to say. She had understood that Mrs. Van was a villain of some kind, in these circles. Not just someone "misguided—a misguided paternalist"—but somebody assumed to be intriguing against them.

Martha looked towards Mr. Zlentli—if it was Mr. Zlentli, and hoped he would say something. After all, she thought, if he had not expected something from her coming, he would not be here at all. And he will probably have made his mind up by now—but his face said nothing, so she said to Mr. Simon, looking at Mr. Zlentli, "You've made a mistake; my visit has nothing to do with Mrs. Van."

"But we are always so interested to meet our white sympathizers," said Mr. Simon, drawling.

"I am sure you are. Now, all I really have to say is this: If you want help of any kind, there are people who are prepared to help."

This sounded lame; she thought that in a different atmosphere these same lame words might be the beginning of something really useful. So she sat, making herself smile, refusing to feel annoyed when Mr. Simon said, immensely sarcastic, "And what kind of help could you possibly have in mind?"

"That would depend, wouldn't it? For instance, there are books we could order for you. Information—all kinds of things."

Now Mr. Zlentli glanced at the young man next at him and at Mr. Simon. The three pairs of eyes communicated—but unintelligibly as far as Martha was concerned.

"Thank you," said Mr. Simon. "We will remember your kind offer."

"Also we know people who have contacts—for instance, if you have students who need training, we could help perhaps."

"Trained for what?" said Mr. Simon.

Martha could not help smiling—there was an unmistakable air of interest suddenly.

"For instance, there might be scholarships to learn engineering—or medicine or teaching. Things like that. Through trade unions and that kind of body."

They did not look at each other. The atmosphere announced that an opportunity had been missed, or an expectation failed. She knew she might just as well go.

She said, "When so few of your people are trained for anything at all, then surely it's worth while even to get one or two some education." No response. "How does one know what help one can give without knowing each other?"

She did not expect an answer to this, and she got up. Mr. Simon said, "Very many thanks, Mrs. Hesse, we are grateful for the interest shown by certain white people in our affairs."

Suddenly, without knowing she had been going to say this, she remarked, "Mr. Solly Cohen—he's not the only help there is, you know."

And now at last real response, a sudden agitation. Eyes met, and separated.

"Solly Cohen?" said Mr. Simon quickly.

"I understand you are friends of his."

"No, that's not the truth, we have never heard of any Solly Cohen."

"Never have been in his organization," said the youth near Mr. Zlentli—speaking carefully and just this once.

"That is so, we have never been associated with Mr. Solly Cohen at all," said Mr. Simon.

"Ah," said Martha. "Well, it's a misunderstanding. It was understood that Mr. Zlentli and Solly Cohen were working together. I am so sorry."

"This is too bad," said Mr. Simon, putting on an air of fierce resentment. "And here is Mr. Zlentli implicated as well!"

Martha looked at the mysterious man against the wall, who looked back at her. The large controlled serious face, with its trim beard, the straight lively eyes—if they belonged to Mr. Zlentli, then she was disposed to approve of Mr. Zlentli. But while he allowed his face to look as if it *nearly* smiled, while his eyes showed he was not angry, that was his lieutenant's function, he made no further sign, merely put his cigarette in his mouth, drew in smoke, and sent it out through flaring nostrils.

"Look," said Martha, to the three men generally. "Let's get this straight. I'm not here to spy on you." As she said this, it occurred to her that in a way she was. "I'm not here to find out anything—or to tell tales about you afterwards."

"Tell tales?" said Mr. Simon, with hostility. "How do you mean, tell tales?"

"As far as we are concerned—we wish you luck, and if you need help, come and ask. If we can, we'll help."

With which she smiled all round and went down a short flight of cement steps on which a dog sat licking its fleas. Getting on her bicycle, she looked up to see Mr. Simon watching her over the verandah wall.

"And you must give our kindest regards to Mrs. Van," said Mr. Simon, with a social amiability as false, as "put on," as enjoyably theatrical, as his hostility.

"When I see her, I shall," said Martha. And she bicycled away, while the dog ran beside her, yapping at the back wheel, and Mr. Simon shouted, "Come back here, sir, come back here at *once!*"

2

It was a couple of days later. Again Martha sat in the Founders' Street restaurant with Thomas. He had telephoned Martha to say there was something urgent he had to tell her. But Jasmine was there too, and there had been no chance for him and Martha to talk.

Jasmine was on a week's visit to her parents, after over three years in Johannesburg. They had heard suddenly that she was married. A frightful family crisis!—and here she was, to take part in it.

"You'd never believe the fuss," said Jasmine, smiling composedly, drinking tea. "You know how it is—when you're working for the Party day and night, and you haven't time for personal matters, you forget about how things are in ordinary life."

It was early evening. Soon Thomas had to leave. On the telephone he had said, "If you can get an hour free, we can go to the park and talk." Now he sat with a plate of fried meat and chips in front of him, silent. It looked as if he were not listening to Jasmine. They were all waiting for Solly, who had promised to come. Jasmine had said to him, "I'm your cousin, for one thing, and for another I'm from the Party."

"And why should a dirty Trotskyist listen to the Party?"

"It's in your own interests. You'll hear something to your advantage, as they say in the lawyers' advertisements."

"It's funny being back home," said Jasmine, staring around the bare restaurant, which as they looked at it with her eyes became the ugly sordid place it was. "When I think I spent years of my life in this dorp and I ever took it seriously . . ." she looked at Martha, remembered Martha's situation and said, "When are you going to England, Matty?"

"When Anton's got his nationality and then we can get divorced."

"Luckily getting divorced, there's nothing to it these days."

The sophistications of the big city had not changed Jasmine's appearance at all. She was still a tiny slender dark girl, with black curls all over her head, and enormous dark brown eyes—the picture of a protected Jewish girl destined for a secure marriage. A great white wool sweater added to her delicate look. She was telling the story of her marriage.

It appeared that a year ago the police asked her to leave the Union of South Africa. She was not a national and they were getting rid, as Jasmine said, of any spare Reds. She investigated her status; it turned out she did not have one at all, was not even Zambesian. For reasons no sensible person would be able to understand, although she had lived all her life in this country, she was not its national. The police suggested she might like to go back to Lithuania, where her parents came from.

There was nothing for it, she would have to marry a South African. The Party was able to help her. An ex-serviceman who had been wounded in such a way as to make marriage irrelevant to him said he was willing. "I said to him, 'Are you sure, comrade, because you've got quite enough problems, it seems to me.' He said, 'Help yourself to what's left, comrade.' "

They married and had lunch together. "We had quite a few interests in common, it turned out, but he was off to organize a branch in Ramsdorp, so we kissed and said goodbye. We cried, too, wasn't it ridiculous? We sat at the table and shed a few tears about life in general." Six months later came the divorce, on grounds of desertion. Jasmine had turned up at the Court, properly dressed, as she said, but she had not known women were supposed to wear hats for the purpose of being divorced. She had no hat. Five minutes before she was due to stand up and "speak up for myself," her lawyer said, Where's your hat? "So I got a duster from the cleaning woman and tied it over my head. Suddenly, there was my cousin Haimi. 'What are you doing here?' he said. 'I'm getting divorced,' I said." Here Jasmine rolled her eyes demurely, in the old way, which seemed to disassociate her forever from anything even remotely irregular. "He said, 'What have you got that filthy doek on your head for?' I said, 'Well whose fault is it, if you must make such silly laws?'—because he's a lawyer you see. He borrowed a hat from a woman in the audience—so to speak. It was black straw—very smart. So I got divorced in the black straw and I handed it back to Haimi and said, 'Thanks for all your trouble.' Then I suddenly understood I was out of touch with reality—this was my cousin Haimi. 'Don't tell my parents,' I said, but it was no good. There was a telegram that night. When I got home I said to them, 'Keep your hair on, I only got married to give myself a South African nationality. He's a good type,' I said, 'and he was doing me a favour.' But my mother went to bed and cried all night, and said she would never forgive me, so then I said, 'All right then, if that's what you want—he was a filthy beast who made me pregnant and then when I had a miscarriage he deserted me and he beat me too. I divorced him for cruelty and I will carry the scars until I die.' Then my mother felt fine and kissed me and said she would always be my mother, and my pop gave me £100. And now everybody's happy and for Pete's sake, thank God I can go back to Johannesburg now, because how anyone can stick this dorp I really can't imagine," said Jasmine, rolling her eyes again.

"We *can't* stick it," said Martha.

"I suppose it's all right for the Africans," said Jasmine. "They're persecuted day and night, it gives them an interest in life. But I swear, all my parents' friends, they might just as well have been dead and buried these last fifty years. And you're not far off, Matty, I'm warning you."

"Well thanks," said Martha.

At which point Solly came in. He smiled at them generally, and said, "Up the Reds!"

Then he sat down, and, seated, directed a mock obsequious bow towards Jasmine. "I hear you have orders for me, cousin comrade?"

"Not orders."

"That's a good thing, in the circumstances."

Johnny Capetenakis stood by his old customer Solly, offering him a plate of stuffed vine leaves.

"And how goes it, Johnny?"

"Fine, Mr. Cohen. I'm going back home soon."

"You'll get a bullet in your back."

The Greek shook his head. "No, in my village things are quiet—the rebels are chased out."

"*You* are the rebels, Johnny."

"I do not have politics in this restaurant."

"And have you heard from Athen?" asked Jasmine.

The Greek tactfully averted his eyes at Athen's name, but listened.

"No," said Martha. "I suppose he must be dead."

A moment's silence, then Johnny said, in a hard angry sorrow, "He was a brave man. He was a brave man, but he was crazy." And he walked away, shaking his head.

"So let's have it, Cousin Jasmine, because I'm on my way."

"The Party has decided your activities are all Right-wing deviations," announced Jasmine.

"How can I deviate from something I'm not a member of?"

"It's an objective truth," said Thomas, speaking for the first time, and bitterly. The note he struck was so sombre, so harsh, that for a moment they were silent, looking at him.

Then Jasmine turned back to Solly, "That's not really what I wanted to say, though. After all, no one can stop you if you want to play Napoleon, all by yourself."

"Why don't you make enquiries of Comrade Matty here? She's an old friend of Mr. Zlentli, aren't you, Matty?"

"I went to see Mr. Zlentli, if it was Mr. Zlentli, because Joss wrote and told me his little brother was up to no good," said Martha.

"And what is my big brother doing up North? *He's* playing Napoleon too, but I suppose that's all right," said Solly.

"At any rate he accepts discipline," said Jasmine.

"And how *was* Mr. Zlentli?" said Solly to Martha.

"If it was Mr. Zlentli, then he's fine. But surely you should know?"

"I don't know, why should I know?"

"Do stop it, children," said Jasmine. "I'm not surprised that everything goes from bad to worse here, if you go on like this."

"I haven't been going on at all," said Martha. "You must apply to Solly for information."

Here Solly grinned, made another mock bow, stood up, and with his hands folded together meekly on the table, in a pose of willing patience, looked at Jasmine.

"Okay," said Jasmine. "It's this. The people in the Party who know this kind of thing . . ." Here she rolled her eyes again. ". . . they've got a contact in the Special Branch, and they have found out that *they* are hand in glove with the police here."

"Well, of course," said Solly.

"Of course," said Martha.

"It's one thing to say of course—that's theory. But it's different finding out it's really true. What I have to tell you is this: there is some kind of demonstration being organized, a national demonstration, with a man called Zlentli running it. Well, the authorities here know all about it. They're just waiting. The South African authorities tipped them off, they intercepted some letters. So the Zambesian authorities just sit here, waiting to scoop up the leaders. So I'm detailed to tell you, since I was coming up here anyway, that if you are in contact with Zlentli, that you must warn him *they* know everything and he'd better lose himself for a time till things blow over."

She was eating a stuffed vine leaf, as she talked, and now she wiped her fingers carefully on a scrap of handkerchief. She frowned as she discovered traces of yellow oil on a small pink fingernail. She said to Solly, "That's all. So if you are in a position to do anything about it, it's all yours."

Solly had absorbed this, as one could see from the quick darting movements of his eyes while he tucked away the information and made plans. Now he redirected an intent black stare at his cousin—but in fact he was pleased and this was merely routine aggression, "How am I to know it's the truth and not some kind of trap?" said he, widening his eyes and putting his face close to Jasmine's, in a fierce scowl.

"Please yourself," said Jasmine, picking up another stuffed vine leaf between thumb and forefinger. "I've done what I said I'd do and now it's up to you."

"But what if Mr. Zlentli doesn't trust Solly?" enquired Martha.

"Then Solly had better see that Mr. Zlentli gets the information from some source he does trust," said Jasmine.

They all smiled at each other, sweet and knowledgeable.

Then Solly smiled, said, "Will do," and departed. As he passed the Greek, who was serving a table a few paces off, he laid his hand on the man's shoulders and said, "See you on the barricades."

"Everything goes on as usual, I see," said Jasmine. "When I think the fate of a big national thing is in the hands of Cousin Solly, then . . ." She rolled up her eyes and began collecting herself to leave.

"What you don't realize," said Thomas, again in the overintense, harsh voice, "is that that's how things are everywhere. Everywhere in the world Cousin Jasmine sits licking her pretty fingers and thinking: No wonder everything's in such a mess if they are in the hands of Cousin Solly. And of course that's the point, they *are* in the hands of Cousin Solly."

Martha and Jasmine looked at him—it was from a distance, a distance he was putting between him and them. What he said was meant for a light tone, and should have been followed by a laugh. But he spoke in a dark angry voice, and everything was discordant and disconnected.

"And you're all getting very defeatist," said Jasmine; and her words, fitted for a half joke, were suddenly harsh and sorrowful. She looked surprised herself. She got up. "I'm going to pack now. Goodbye, Matty. If you get fed up waiting for Anton to sort himself out, then drop down South and see me some time." She hesitated before saying to Thomas, in a tentative gentle voice, "Goodbye, Thomas." He nodded.

Jasmine bent over to kiss Martha and said softly into her other ear, "Do leave, Matty. You've no idea how nice it is to get out—you're human when you get out. People have no idea how awful this place is until they leave it."

She stood up, raised her gloved hand towards Thomas and said, "Barricades!"—which abbreviated farewell was the fashion, apparently, that year in "the Party down South."

She departed lazily, wrapped in her thick white wool. As she went past Johnny, she said to him, "Good luck in Greece—but I'm only speaking personally, if you get what I mean."

"Well," said Thomas, "if that had gone on another five minutes I'd have shot myself."

"You mean, anything that happens here is too unimportant to take seriously," said Martha. Hearing what she had said, she realized Thomas was about to announce his departure.

"What were you thinking about—while that went on?" enquired Thomas.

"Went on—I suppose it is of some importance?"

"What was Jasmine saying to you?"

"That I should leave."

"Of course. You're mad to stay."

After a moment she said quietly, very hurt, "One of the things I was thinking, while Solly was here, was that I can't be all that mad—because instead of having an affair with Solly I stuck around for you."

"Well, of course," said Thomas. Again, it should have been light—humorous. But it sounded irritated. Seeing Martha's face, he sighed, and shut his eyes a moment. Then he said, "I'm angry with you because I'm trying not to care about you. I'm leaving."

"So I thought."

"When I got home that night the police were there. I'm afraid even to tell you—it's so impossible. But they had worked it all out: my wife's third cousin is in the Stern Gang, or so it seems. Not that I knew it, or my wife knew it. But they know it. And I'm a Red. And my name is Stern. Put these facts together—and I'm responsible for the atrocities in Israel."

His face was swollen with anger, with hatred.

"I nearly laughed at first. You can imagine how it was; my friend Michel sitting there stroking his pretty black beard and smiling: All this has nothing to do with me, I'm just a man of peace. And two nice Zambesian boys with their raw red thighs and their stupid faces. Tell me, Mr. Stern, are you responsible for the murder of our fellow national the poor British Tommy in Haifa last week? Do have a drink, Sergeant, sit down, Trooper Jones. No, I must explain things to you—the fact that my wife happens to be visiting her aunt in Tel Aviv does not automatically make me responsible for the murders of your British boys in Haifa. They smiled—embarrassed at putting me to such trouble. But excuse me, just for the records, your name is Stern, sir, isn't it?"

Martha waited. Then, as Thomas didn't say any more, she said, "Well, I know it's—ridiculous. But that's all it is. That's what this country's like, isn't it . . ." She realized she was apologizing for it, as if she were responsible for it.

After a time Thomas said, "I found out recently that Tressell is in the C.I.D. these days."

Martha, absorbing this, discovered that she had not taken a breath for some time. She set her breathing going again, unknotted tensed muscles, drank a mouthful of muddy coffee, sat back. Here it was . . . there was always a point at which anything—loving someone, a friendship, politics—one went over the edge into . . . but she did not understand into what. Neither the nature of the gulf nor what caused it, did she understand. But a note was struck—and that it *would* strike could be counted on. After that . . .

When they occurred, these sharp improbable moments, one felt as if they had nothing in common with what had gone before; that they were of a consistency, a substance, that were foreign. Yet later, looking back, it was always precisely these turning points, or moments, which seemed to contain or announce a truth—harshly and improbably, because up till that time one had refused to acknowledge their possibility. And afterwards, it was not the moments like these, whose common quality was a suddenness, a dislocation, that were wrong, faulty; but one's way of looking at what had led up to them. There had been a failure of imagination. A failure of sympathy. Her way of seeing Thomas, his life—it was that which had been wrong, at fault.

Thomas said, "You're thinking: Thomas is paranoiac."

She said, "Something like that. But what does it matter?"

"Except for one thing, Tressell *is* in the C.I.D."

She was watching his hand. It was a fist, and he was pressing down on the stained cloth with the weight of his powerful body behind it. It trembled with the force he was putting into it.

She wanted to stroke the hand, or to lift it and hold it against her cheek. But there was nothing to be done.

"And what now?" she said.

"Martha, are you suggesting that Tressell would be incapable of it?"

"Look," she said carefully. "A fool, an idiot—something reminds him of a man who irritated him when he was in the army. He thinks: How can I get my own back? He has an idea, and he rings up a country office from his town desk and he says: Drop over to the Black Ox Farm and find out if the man who owns it has anything to do with anti-British activities in Palestine. The local man says, Oh hell, just when I said I'd take my girl out swimming. But I suppose orders are orders. So he takes one of the troopers and out they go to the Black Ox Farm. The people on the farm obviously know nothing about it. The Sergeant thinks, Oh Christ, those fools in the town office, what do they think they're doing? He rings up the town office and tells Tressell he's been out to the Black Ox Farm. Tressell thinks, Well, I've given that bastard Thomas Stern an uncomfortable afternoon, that's something. And off he goes to play golf."

While Martha brought this out, in a voice which she tried to keep "humorous," she watched his frowning face. He was hardly listening to her.

"I'm going to Israel the day after tomorrow."

"For good?"

"I don't know. I've got a cousin in Haifa. And my wife's got relatives everywhere."

He beckoned to Johnny Capetenakis, who came over with his little pencil and his little pad, and made out the bill. Thomas handed him a note, and said, getting up, "Keep the change—for the Royalist cause."

He walked out of the restaurant. The Greek looked at Martha—bitter, reproachful. He pushed across the change at her. After a moment she picked it up and said, "Everybody's upset today." Her voice sounded weak and false.

She went out after Thomas. The lorry stood in a filthy smelling side street that was full of old paper, bits of vegetables, and stacked bicycles.

Thomas stood by the door to the driver's seat. Martha went up to him and said, "Well, goodbye."

"Goodbye," he said. He looked at her, severe. Then he smiled. She saw that his eyes were full of tears, and she felt her cheeks were cold and wet.

He said, "I'm not going to kiss you, because what's the point? I'll write to you, Martha."

Then he got into the lorry and Martha stood on the pavement and watched him manoeuvre the machine back out of a mess of bicycles and a handcart. Some small black boys came running out to shout, "Ticky, baas, sixpence, baas, sixpence, baas, baas, baas!"

It appeared he did not see them. Martha gave the largest child the change Johnny had pushed back at her. He gaped at the sight of so much money. The other children came clustering around, their faces stunned into immobility by awe. Then they rushed off with their haul screaming like birds.

Thomas, shaking with the shaking of the machine, sat frowning at Martha. A car hooted behind him. The lorry shot forward and disappeared into the stream of traffic in Founders' Street.

3

A large tree stood in the middle of the avenue, in an island of earth and grass around which the Tarmac flowed in two streams that were almost as wide as the street itself. A hundred yards up, a fine clump of indigenous trees spared by the road engineers grew so near the street that a close look showed it made a slight bend South to accommodate them. On the map, though, and even in people's minds, North Avenue ran as straight and as measured as all the other streets in this grid of streets.

Standing under the tree, looking west, the street arranged itself as a double line of trees which, since many of them were jacarandas and it was October again, looked as if bouquets of airy blossom had taken root beside garden fences. From the sky, the town would announce itself as much by trees as by buildings, and at night, from the air, transparent-seeming shells of building rose from dark or illuminated foliage. Night or day, it was trees, then buildings, that showed where man had staked his claim on the grass-covered high veld. Buildings and trees covered the veld for a mile north, though not so long ago this street marked the extreme boundary of the city, and in five years would have spread another five, and in ten years ... But now, the city was a few-miles-wide patch of trees and buildings in a landscape mostly grass. Looking from the air, or from a tall hill, even now, in moonlight, it would seem as if for leagues the wind raised and flattened grasses which whitened or moved into dark under racing cloud shadows. (Although it was October, the clouds were not yet rain clouds, they were unstable and fled in illuminated shreds and streamers from horizon to horizon.) Just so, looking from the hill on the farm, the hundred-acres field beneath it reflected the movements of wind or cloud on a surface of rippling foliage. Just so a patch of lawn in a suburban garden shimmers a vivid liquid green, currents of air violently agitating each individual blade exactly as the minute hairs on the back of a leaf flatten and shine when it is held into a draught or when you blow across it.

Nearly a hundred miles away, in the red earth district, the old house had sunk to its knees under the blows of the first wet seʻson after the Quests had left it, as if the shambling structure had been held upright only by the spirit of the family in it. Already it had been absorbed into a welter of damp growth and it was hard to tell, so Marnie Van Rensberg said her father said (he had bought the Quests' farm to run his cattle on) where the old house had stood. But morning glory and golden shower creeper festooned the trees in blue and gold all over the hill. It was wet and sultry on that hill, because of the heavy growth, although a thousand winds poured over it, and so walls and roof had rotted years ago in a fierce compost. The wet heat spawned, and the undersides of rafters sprouted fungus, and mosquitos bred in old shoes.

But here, if this city were to be emptied, nothing would happen for a long time, except that dust would slowly film the roofs which now stood glistening in the changeable October moonlight. Then dust would fill the corners of verandahs and pile up around the trunks of trees. This city, if emptied, would be conquered at last by dust, not by wet; its enemy would be dryness, the spirit of the high veld where tall dry grasses have grown since—well, long before man first stood upright here, that's certain. For how many millions of years has the central plateau stood high and dry, dry above all, lifting upwards to the drought-giving skies? Where Martha stood on dry dust beneath the great tree, bones of drought-bred creatures had lain for—but what use was it to say words like *millions,* if she couldn't imagine, really feel them, longer (say) than twenty thousand? Dryness, dryness—the air snapped with it, she could feel the pressure of dryness shaping her substance, the dust was its creature and the air of October gritted on her tongue. Yes, this city could be like the minute brittle transparent cases that have held insects and now lie blowing about on the sand. It would be like the carcass of a stick insect, so light it can be lifted into an eddy of air and up into the empty sky in columns of glistening trash to drift until the rains come to wash the air clean. Standing waist-deep in long dry grass, a small rivulet of white sand appears beneath gold-brown stems that grow as clean as if from water. On the white sand minute faint-brown stains move—the shadows of leaves of grass, tiny dry fragments of leaf that flutter on long powerful stems. They lie on the sand, small shadows so faint that the sunlight *almost* is stronger than they, grains of sand sparkle in the shadow as if the shadow itself were of a specially thin texture, a kind of light rather than a depth of shade. But it is not a leaf shadow, no: the carcass of a grasshopper lies on the sand, lifting, moving slightly as the wind breathes among the grass stems. It looks like a minute insect modelled in Perspex, all complete, with even its big eyes staring, but empty.

Yes, emptied, this town would stand slowly desiccating, filling with drifts of dust, white, pink, yellow, until . . .

In Europe, it was more than two years since the war ended, and cities still stood in ruins and people in the cities expected a hungry winter. Last winter had been disastrously cold and now the world grain harvests were one-fourth less than had been expected.

Chance, luck, had kept this city whole and peopled, and now allowed its citizens to sleep at night with full stomachs. Chance might just as easily . . . forty-four million people had died in the last war. (But what was the use of saying forty-four million, as Athen—presumably now dead—had pointed out, when one could not *feel* more than, let's say, half a million, and even that with difficulty, after long strain.) During five years of Martha's time, of days when for the most part she had been bored, waiting for life to start, forty-four million humans had died, had been murdered by their kind. The world was peopled by a race of murderers who had done their best to annihilate each other—but Martha, by chance, had not been where the fighting was; she had been in this city where lived a couple of hundred thousand, the sort of figure one would not bother to tack on to a figure like a *million*—though a million were not enough to bother about, "about" forty million people had been killed in the years 1939 to 1945.

Suppose that in the newspapers tomorrow headlines said that two hundred thousand people in a city on the central plateau of Africa had suddenly vanished into the earth. They'd say, how awful. If in this city, white and black began murdering each other, then it would be another city in the grip of war, that's all, just as these mornings one read that in Israel another British soldier had been shot in ambush by men presumed to be members of the Irgun or Stern gangs.

Since Thomas had left a few weeks ago, Martha's life had been turned inside out. Once her life was a daytime life, she woke to a

day in which she would probably see Thomas. But now the days had
lost their meaning, and it was at night that she came awake and
lived. She walked through the streets of the little town, watching it
empty. First, a hurrying and emptying before the curfew hour of
nine, when black people must be behind their own doors. Then,
again at eleven, cars sped home in streams of moving light from
the cinemas. After eleven, most windows were dark. But the town
was all light—reflected from roofs, from glittering masses of foliage,
and now, in October, from the jacaranda trees whose masses of
blossom looked like crystallized light—the sober trunks lifted millions of tiny bells of hard cool light. Above, starlight and moonlight,
great spaces of remote light; below squatted the town with its
windows low and square and yellow, and the street lamps shedding
a thick low yellow where Martha walked as if wading through stale
water. Martha walked, walked, down one street, up another, into
the avenues, down one avenue, up another—one could hop from intersection to intersection like a child playing hopscotch, one could
walk from the centre of the city to its edge in a slow hour and see
no one but an occasional patrolling black policeman. A quiet city
this, here, in its white reaches, a city without violence, where an
occasional policeman was enough to impose order on straight, regu-
larly crossing streets.

Thomas had not written after a first letter in which he had said
he was no writer and, in any case, what was there to say she did
not know. He thought of her, he said. He knew she thought of him.
"Last week I nearly wrote. I was visiting my teacher. I told you
about him. He is a clerk in Tel Aviv now, but he was the Rabbi in
Sochaczen. I wanted to be educated. The local school was not
enough. He was supposed to teach me religion. I wanted him to
teach me Latin and science. He said to me, what do you want with
Latin and science? All the idiots in Europe have been learning
Latin for hundreds of years. And science—do you know how e'ec-
tricity works yet? Can you mend a fuse? Every day I sat on his
doorstep and said, Teach me. He said, so you want science? For
most people, Copernicus is not yet born. I tell you, you want to
learn science? Then every morning you wake and think: The sun is
a great mass of white light, and in the sun's light a dozen small
particles of substance spin around. You live in a small bit of sun-
substance and you spin around the sun. Now *feel* it. I said to him:
Teach me about Einstein. He said: Every time in the day you come
to yourself, think where you are—imagine the earth and the plants
and you on a planet spinning around. When you wake in the dark

at night, think how your half of the earth is turned away from the sun and how the slopes of the Hindu Kush are just coming into the light. He said: Think how in the dark sea, the fishes sink to the depths of the sea, and as the light comes, they rise to the surface to the light. Think of the birds moving all over the earth, backwards and forwards, summer and winter. That's science. He said: Think of the trees breathing in at night, out at day. Feel it. Feel the earth turning under you and the planets moving around together. When you feel this, feel it with every bit of you, so that every minute this is how you feel life, then come to me and we will talk about Einstein. I said all right then, teach me Latin. He taught me Latin, and he said I was a child of pre-Copernicus. He said it was evolution, that the next thing for man was to feel the stars and their times and their spaces. Otherwise he was a maggot in dirt. When the war started, he was first in a Russian prison camp, and then he walked hundreds of miles in snow, and his feet rotted under him. At last he got to Israel. I said to him, And how's evolution with you, my teacher? And he said to me: Is that you, Thomas Stern? Are you still working hard at your Latin? Well, Martha?"

A person who has gone away is still here as long as one can hear what he says; Martha could hear what Thomas said. She argued with him. Ten times a day she caught herself in discussion with Thomas.

When he went away, it was, he said, to visit his wife (who had now returned) and his wife's relations in Israel. Presumably he would in due course come back after that most ordinary occurrence, a visit to relatives.

But what Martha was saying to Thomas was, "Thomas, you shouldn't do it, it won't achieve anything."

Thomas said, "After a war in which six million Jews were murdered by Europeans—that is, murdered by the most civilized and advanced section of the human race, or so we believe we are, British policemen with guns prevent Jews from reaching safe soil in Israel. Yes—do you agree?—do you think that is an unfair way of putting it? Am I being a propagandist when I say that? But Martha says to me, don't be violent, Thomas, it won't achieve anything."

She said to him, "Thomas, if you do this, you'll put yourself outside everything you believe."

"Are you telling me what I believe, Martha? What difference does it make what I believe. In the last decade forty million human beings were murdered and so many millions crippled, wounded, starved, stunted and driven mad that we'll never count them. You're following me, Martha? Right. Tell me, what difference did it make, Thomas Stern learning Latin and my teacher telling me about the stars?"

"But, Thomas, you know what I'm saying is true—violence does not achieve anything."

"Two years ago the British and the Americans dropped an atom bomb on the Japanese out of military curiosity, so it turns out, because the war could have been brought to an end without that, our enemies were suing for peace, though of course our rulers did not tell us that at the time. We dropped two atom bombs on them just to see how this brave new weapon would work. You're with me, Martha? But Martha doesn't believe in violence."

"No, and neither do you."

"There's a civil war in China, at this moment millions of people are involved in a civil war in China, but Martha does not believe in violence."

"It doesn't matter how much you give me lectures, Thomas—the fact that I'm right is proved because all I can say is this—you know yourself you shouldn't do it."

"And there's the Soviet Union too—but I'm not going to criticize my own side. That's a joke, Martha—that's the kind of joke non-violent idealistic people make."

"You shouldn't do it, Thomas."

"Martha doesn't believe in violence—go on, tell me about it, I'm listening, Martha doesn't believe in violence."

Where the tree stood in the middle of the street lay thick shadow. A street lamp a few paces off intensified the shade, lacing the tree's leaves with black and gold. Under it, one stood in dark, looking up into mixed lights and thicknesses of dark, one looked out along a street that ran light like a river. Insects crawled around invisibly on the bark, sometimes a night bird arrived on the tree and, sensing the human, lifted its wings and went off down the street to the safer, thicker clump. The tense fighting smell of October, like cordite; a tension like the invisible balances of electricity; a smell of dry leaves where the sap rose fast towards the rains which lay surely ahead, even though the skies were dry still and the clouds as fast and skittish as running horses. A few days after Thomas had left, Martha heard herself arguing with him, and knew why he had gone. She knew suddenly; though of course she had known perfectly well all the time, but had not wanted to know. Thomas had gone to Israel to get his own back on Sergeant Tressell.

Sergeant Tressell would live out his own life in this city (unless it was suddenly bombed, perhaps by accident?—or engulfed by an earthquake) working in a well-ventilated office from eight until four, dying at the age of sixty with thrombosis, leaving behind him a well-insured widow and two children. In Israel a British soldier would fall dead (if he had not already done so) in Sergeant Tressell's place. Martha could see Thomas with a gun in his hand. When she understood how she argued with him, all day, half the night, she listened again to what he said, to what she said, and then she saw him holding a gun. She could see him, being just as careful as was necessary, no more, standing behind a window with the sun on its panes, waiting to shoot at soldiers who would soon pass in an open truck. Or perhaps he would stand, was standing, gun in hand, behind a rock by a road where a patrol would soon come.

"But, Thomas, what's the point of it?"

"So, Martha," she heard him say, conversational rather than aggressive, as if he were conducting a discussion in the current affairs group, "So, you don't believe in violence, is that it?"

Suppose one has loved a man or (however one wants to put it) been influenced by him, or (if you like) touched by him, but certainly in one's deepest self, and this man then picks up a gun and murders another man out of revenge, what does it mean, saying: I don't believe in violence?

Having lived through a war when half the human race was engaged in murdering the other half, murdering more vilely, savagely, cruelly, than ever in human history, what does it mean to say: I don't believe that violence achieves anything?

Every fibre of Martha's body, everything she thought, every movement she made, everything she was, was because she had been born at the end of one world war, and had spent all her adolescence in the atmosphere of preparations for another which had lasted five years and had inflicted such wounds on the human race that no one had any idea of what the results would be.

Martha did not believe in violence.

Martha was the essence of violence, she had been conceived, bred, fed and reared on violence.

Martha argued with Thomas: What use is it, Thomas, what use is violence?

She watched the light shift glittering in the leaves overhead, watched the Tarmac throw off tiny gleams of salty light, saw the roofs shift and balance whitely under the turning sky, felt her mind fill with emptiness. If Thomas were here, standing with her under this tree, what would she say? Nothing. She would put her arms around him. She would put her hand in his and feel the life running through it under her palm. That was all.

The soul of the human race, that part of the mind which has no name, is not called Thomas and Martha, which holds the human race as frogspawn is held in jelly—that part of Martha and of Thomas was twisted and warped, was part of a twist and a damage—she could no more disassociate herself from the violence done her, than a tadpole can live out of water. Forty-odd million human beings had been murdered, deliberately or from carelessness, from lack of imagination; these people had been killed yesterday, in the last dozen years, they were dying now, as she stood under the tree, and these deaths were marked on her soul, and when Johnny Capetenakis from the Piccadilly restaurant (as it might very well have been) lifted Athen's head on a bayonet and stuck it up in a row of other heads in the market squares of the cities of Greece (so the newspaper had announced, casually almost, a week ago—Government troops with the connivance of America and Britain were displaying the heads of traitors, Athen's, and his friends' quite likely, in the market towns of Greece) well, when that happened, it happened in Martha's soul and in Thomas's and in . . . But standing silent under the tree, knowing this was true, her mind could not stand it, it became numbed, a dry painful sorrow like a useless remorse began running in her blood and she felt her pulses beat like warnings of time passing, the blood flowed as if ebbing out into dry sand, and she wished that Thomas were here, for if he were she could put her hand into his hand and not have to be alone. He would stand here, close, and he would say simply, "Well, Martha? So I'm back."

From the big tree it was half a mile to the flat she shared with Anton, half a mile to her parents' house near the park. Instead of walking straight home, she walked right around the big trees of the park and stood outside the Quests' garden. Her father's bedroom would be dark—it was dark, these days, by eight in the evening. Sometimes Martha stood outside the fence and looked at the dark window and thought: That couple in there, that man and that woman, when they conceived me, one was in shellshock from the war, and the other in a breakdown from nursing its wounded. She, Martha, was as much a child of the 1914–1918 war as she was of Alfred Quest, May Quest.

Sometimes the light came on, and Martha could see her mother's shadow move across the curtains, back and forth, and then the shadow went away and the light went out. Martha heard what they said to each other, could see their gestures and the expressions on their faces without being in the room. Once, very quietly, she crept like a burglar into the big garden towards the lit window. She held the yapping little white dog's jaws closed with one hand and stood in a flower bed under the window, the cold scent of violets rising from where her shoes sank into a damp soil. She could see over the sill and past the edge of the curtains. Her father sat up in bed, a pink wool bedjacket of her mother's around his shoulders. He was staring around him, wide-eyed, not blinking at all—the way a child stares when suddenly awakened. His mouth was half open and had fallen in, because his teeth were in the glass by the bed. Her mother, nearly asleep, wearing an old brown dressing gown that had been her husband's, bent to put a spoon of liquid into the old man's mouth When Mrs. Quest straightened and turned to the window, Martha saw her face: under wisps of white hair that stuck out wildly, her eyes glared desperately, reddened by sleep, in a red swollen face. She looked a half-savage old woman, a wild sorrowful old female, trapped, caged, standing there holding a little silver teaspoon in one hand and a sticky medicine bottle in the other. Over the odour of crushed violets came the sour smell of the medicine.

Martha dropped the twisting little dog and ran to the gate through shrubs and flowers. The dog yapped, yapped; and Mrs. Quest came out on to the verandah and said in a sad rough voice, "Kaiser, Kaiser, come here at once!"

Cruelty: Martha hated that dog so much she wanted to strangle it. The dog aroused in her waves of pure red hate. Martha could not easily visit her father because of her cruelty. She wished him dead, which was bad enough; but she watched her mother satirically when the exhausted old woman announced two, three times in a month that her husband could not last another week. The young man Jonathan had been waiting to get married until a time when the sadness of that house would not lie over his love like a sickness, but they could not wait forever, and so soon there would be a hurried, almost apologetic wedding. It was no longer a house of young people, they were all sorted out into couples, married or engaged, and Mrs. Quest once again spent her energies nursing. In that house people sat around, waiting for an old man to die. Martha was afraid to visit her father, because she wished to wipe that house and everything in it out of existence, it was so terrible and so ugly. But she went nearly every day. Before she set out to see her father she took herself in hand, held herself quiet: the house was more than ever like a nightmare, all her most private nightmares were made tangible there, and that is why she stood outside it at night, looking at it like a stranger. In this way she focused it, targeted it, held it safe so that later, when she got home and went to bed, she would not actually dream of it because she had forced the dream into her consciousness: she had already experienced, awake, the quicksand which swallowed so easily love and the living.

When she got home, the light was on, very often, though it might be one, two, three in the morning. Anton would be reading. He would look up to smile as she came in:

"And how are you, Matty?"

"Fine. And you?"

They smiled. She began to undress. Sometimes he put down his book and that meant they would talk.

"It's a marvellous night, Anton," she said, casually, a little childishly—as if she walked because of the marvellous night.

"They certainly know how to have fine nights in this country."

"Yes, we'll miss them when we leave."

"I thought of walking home too, but Mr. Forster was kind enough to give me a lift."

"It's not going to rain yet, the clouds aren't heavy enough."

"The farmers will start their grumbling soon if the rains don't break. On Mr. Forster's farm he says the seed beds are all ready."

"Oh he has a farm too, has he?"

"He doesn't stint himself for much, I can promise you that."

Most evenings Anton spent at his new friends, the Forsters, who entertained a great deal. Most weekends there were swimming parties and tennis parties. Anton had learned to play tennis.

"I would not have thought," he said, with his new almost diffident smile, "that the sports were in my line."

But sport was, it turned out; and so were dinner parties and tea parties and sundowner parties.

"Heard anything about your naturalization?" she might enquire as she got into bed.

"I dropped into the office after work today. They say it might be another four or five months."

Recently, Anton's going back to Germany had not been much talked about. At last, after persistent enquiries and dozens of letters most of which were returned marked, Addressee unknown, a letter had arrived from an aunt in Hamburg—a refugee from the Russian zone. She had previously lived in Dresden. She had survived, she said, the bombing of Dresden, but it looked as if the bombing of Hamburg had been as bad. Her sons had been killed on the Russian front but her daughter was alive and her daughter's husband was alive and not much wounded. They had a new baby.

She was living in a basement shared by three families, under the rubble of the flats which had stood over it, but the flats would be rebuilt soon. If he, Anton, wanted to come home to Germany, then she had no suggestions to make. She was an old woman now, and she was sorry but she had no suggestions.

Martha's sleep was thin and shallow; often she woke believing she had not slept at all, for her dreams had been so vivid. She dreamed, of course, of war, of her father, and of Thomas with a gun in his hand. She dreamed, when she dreamed of herself, as standing on the high dry place while ships sailed away in all directions, leaving her behind. On this high dry plateau where Martha was imprisoned, forever, it seemed, everything was dry and brittle, its quality was drought. Far away, a long way below, was water. She dreamed, night after night, of water, of the sea. She dreamed of swift waves like horses racing. She woke, again and again, with the smell of the sea in her nostrils, and a tang of salt on her tongue. Then she sank back to sleep to hear waves crashing on rocks, to hear the slap and the suck of waves on distant shores. The sea was her sleep now, she went off to sleep returning to her old nurse, the sea. She was becoming obsessed with the sea, which she had not seen, did not remember. She had only to shut her eyes and waves lifted and crashed across her eyelids and an enormous longing joy took possession of her. She no longer thought: I'm going to England soon; she thought: I'm going to the sea, I'm going to get off this high dry place where my skin burns and where I can never lose the feeling of tension and I shall sit by a long grey sea and listen to the waves break, I shall hear the waves break and sink in a small hiss of foam.

In that ugly city bedroom where Anton and Martha lay side by side in twin beds, the sound of wind moving in dry leaves came into her sleep and she sat up in bed, incredulous that she was still here—the sea had been running in her sleep so strongly that it filled the air around her, and she could not hear the dry wind in the trees, she heard waves hissing on a grey chalky shore.

4

The rains had come and would soon be over. Thomas was back, but Martha had ceased to hear what he said some time ago, and her argument with him was a monologue: she talked in *his* voice as if believing what he believed.

When he came she heard of it from Jack Dobie.

"Thomas is back."

"Oh, I didn't know."

These days Martha worked mostly for Jack. And Thomas, so Jack said, was thinking of working with him too. "We've got schemes afoot—*I'll* show those bastards yet, even if they have chucked me out of Parliament!"

Eventually Martha and Thomas met by chance in the Piccadilly. Martha was with Jack, who sensing the situation went off to talk to the new owner, Johnny's successor.

"Well, Martha?"

"Well, Thomas?"

He was considerably thinner, and much browner. Martha realized that meeting him in the street she wouldn't have known him. She thought, if I had just met him I'd think, what a tense suspicious man—what's wrong with him? He was eating fried eggs and chips, not looking at what was on his plate. His eyes, now sharply, startlingly blue against his burnt skin, examined her from a distance.

And herself—she was in a phase least likely to appeal to him, though she hadn't thought about it until feeling his inspection of her—she had not, so to speak, looked into the mirror recently. She was heavy again, almost lumpish. She was a heavy pale young woman with a mass of thick hair. That night she was wearing an orange linen dress she did not much like, but she had not known she was going to meet Thomas.

She thought: He probably wouldn't have known me either, and it's only a few months.

"We've both changed," she said.

He nodded, after a bit: he was abstracted. Then, feeling she wanted more from him, he attempted to joke, "You look like one of the kibbutz girls."

"What, I'm not to your taste!"

Already he had gone away, but he made an effort to come back, "You looked prettier when *I* had you."

She was not going to say that now she had no one. She sat smiling, feeling the change in him: but she did not know how to define it.

"Yes, girls like you need a lot of serious love-making to keep you in shape."

This, the sort of jest lovers make, offered to her out of—well, courtesy, politeness, made her understand that she must let the personal lapse, and immediately.

It had jarred—badly. They both looked uncomfortable.

She said, "Are you a Zionist now?" meaning it as a serious query. She understood that had jarred too, it rang false; perhaps anything either of them said now would sound false.

His eyes fastened hard on her face, abrupt, surprised. She said, "I'm sorry, I was just making conversation, I suppose."

After a moment, he shifted his legs under the table, let his eyes move away from her face, and began playing with the magnificent cruet in the table's centre.

"Seeing this art work, it makes me feel I'm at home," he remarked, apologetically.

That was better, it was suddenly easier to be together.

He took out a glass stopper and sniffed, amused, at the raw vinegar. "Somewhere in the world there must be a factory to make this horrible vinegar especially for Dirty Dick's," he said.

"And for Black Ally's."

"Before my time."

He sat holding the glass stopper in his hand. Across the room Jack was talking to the new owner, a handsome fat Greek who was a cousin of Johnny's from Johannesburg. He looked across at Martha and Thomas to see if they were ready for him to join them. He went on talking to the Greek, keeping an eye on them.

"You see, Martha," said Thomas conversationally, suddenly coming back to be with her—as she felt it—"we were wrong all the time, things aren't how we thought."

"Why?" she asked, after waiting for him to explain.

A moment's immobility. Then a rough dismissing movement, an irritated movement. "That's all!" Then he looked up, saw her face, and said, shrugging, "If you don't feel it, then I can't tell you."

"All right," she said carefully, after a pause.

He sat frowning, playing with the little glass bottles. Then Jack came back, seeing that the two sat there, not speaking. Having first tried to sense whether it was safe to say it, he joked, "Well, I'm glad you're back home, Thomas, now there's a chance for me."

Thomas laughed, in relief, so did Martha, Jack joined in. Then they began talking about Jack's plans for work with Thomas, and how Martha could help; they were all relieved to get away from the personal.

A night or so later, Martha had this dream: It was a small town somewhere, but she did not know where; and there was an atmosphere of impending events: a great stir and a bustle in the town, something was going to happen.

Then Martha knew: someone was going to be hanged.

She thought: I must try and save this person, but first, who is it? Me, perhaps? But she was talking to a group of people she recognized to be officials of some kind, and presumably she would not be doing that if she were a criminal, or at fault with them.

Then she was inside a big barn or shed where the execution would take place. There was a wooden scaffold already erected there. It was rough, there was something informal, or at least makeshift, about it all because it was wartime. And there was a feeling about the dream older than the present—or rather, the recent war, World War II. Was it a war in the past? Or the last war, but a village or a town that had an older feel to it, an atmosphere almost, of the Middle Ages?

Suddenly Martha knew it was Thomas who would be hanged—she had known it all the time. She knew, too, that she must not save him, because he had extracted a promise from her not to come near him, she must not interfere. "I must work out my own destiny," he had said, at some point.

She stood a few paces behind Thomas, and thought: If he turns and sees me here he will be furious, I'm breaking my promise. But it's all right: he will *not* turn and see me, it's not part of the play, the order of events, that he should turn and see me. Her hands kept stretching out towards him, palms up, to help him, but they fell again, empty.

Then, through the door of the big barn, she saw, coming up a hill on a country road with a backdrop of solemn blue mountains, a small procession of people in black: first came a large black-robed man with a silver cross swinging on his breast—he was the Mayor of this town, and he was followed by various officials, one of them holding up a silver cross and another swinging a censer and another reading aloud from a small black book.

Thomas went out of the door towards them. He was not driven out, he went. He walked through the great open doors of the barn and the people outside fell away on either side as he appeared. He was not bound in any way, and his hands were free.

He stood, while the party headed by the Mayor came forward, but he was not looking at them. Martha was just behind him, she was wringing her hands, and her heart was aching with a dry useless anguish.

Thomas looked different. He looked more Semitic, or Eastern. He was darker, thinner, and his brown hair had darkened and was curly. Chips of wood and straw were tangled in his hair. His eyes searched this way, that way, moving all the time up at the sky, down at the earth. But not for escape, no, they were movements of eyes in deep thought. Thomas was dishevelled, his clothes were torn, there was dust on his head as well as straw, and wood chips. He was isolated from this crowd of people, but he was not aware of them or of Martha or of anything; his red-eyed stare was introspective. He stood, waiting, with the heavy sunlight on him, in a sombre, savage . . . but what? What was this mood, or way of thinking, or mode of being, she could not name? The look on his face—that was the point of this dream, that was why she was dreaming it; she had to discover the meaning of this sombre dark look. Why did Thomas stand there, looking at the sky, looking—almost abstractedly—at the group of officials who were coming to hang him, as if he did not care about them? Surely he ought to be running away, or protesting, or struggling?

She was weeping, *she* was protesting, *she* was anguished. But Thomas turned red-rimmed sombre eyes around him, as if he—as if . . . *as if what?* What was the look on his face?

The necessity to understand that look woke Martha up. Awake, she stared at Thomas's face, needing as badly to understand it as she had asleep.

Then the dream faded . . . and came back, sharply, at odd moments. The look on Thomas's face would return before her eyes, as she worked, or talked to people, or when she woke up in the morning. She got no closer to understanding it. The dream went further away, she forgot it, finally she forgot it altogether, except that when she thought of Thomas, or saw him, the question the dream had left with her stood in her mind, unanswered.

Thomas worked now with Jack Dobie.

Thomas knew a certain amount about medicine, or at least, public hygiene, because of his war experience. Returning from Israel, he told his wife that she must not expect his help on the farm, that she must rely on Michel Pevsner. He told his brother that someone else must grow plants and shrubs for the shop in town. It appeared that Rachel Stern accepted it, or at least, made no protest. The brother was angry, but made no impression on Thomas, who was intent on his own path, whatever that was.

Jack Dobie was no longer in Parliament because of the cold war. Or rather, the cold war had given Jack's unpopularity a final turn of the screw.

His white trade unionist constituents had put up with him during the war, when his brand of socialism was fashionable; they had been pleased to have him, to give their own reaction a gloss of socialism, as long as socialism did not cost them anything. They had tolerated, too, but only just, his campaigns over India.

A few months ago, India got independence, and Jack tried to organize a meeting to celebrate. None of the big official halls was available to him, even though at that time he had still been in Parliament. Finally the independence of the continent of India had been celebrated in a dingy little hall near the Coloured area, by Jack Dobie, Mrs. Van, Johnny Lindsay in his wheel chair, and a few Indian tradesmen, some schoolteachers and the children from the Indian school. Then the whispering campaigns and the poison letters began again. There were two criticisms of him. One: Jack Dobie was not interested in his own constituents, only in a lot of blacks thousands of miles away in India—why didn't Jack do something for his own blacks, weren't there enough blacks in Zambesia, if he wanted to nurse blacks? The other: Jack was only interested in blacks, he hated his own kind, the white people, why should white people elect a Kaffir-lover anyway? So Jack was out of Parliament. He was very hurt, but he pretended not to be.

Now he was a fitter on the railways again. He used his position as ex-member of Parliament (after all, he might be elected again, next time, he said, though he knew it was unlikely) to raise money, rouse public opinion. He and Thomas went around the Reserves, often behind the authorities' backs, reported on conditions, agitated, wrote letters to officials and to newspapers, and generally made nuisances of themselves. Jack did all this briskly, almost gaily. But Thomas worked with a grim concentration, seven days a week, nothing seemed to exist for him now, except this work. He drove to distant Reserves where few white people ever went, he spent time there, advised on wells, polluted rivers, food supplies, hygiene. Then he came out with files full of facts and figures that it was Martha's task to put into shape. The Native Affairs Departments, the Native Commissioners, knew about Thomas, and hated him. But he was quick and wily, he made friends with the Africans, who trusted him and who did not give him away. He was always a step ahead of furious officials, who in any case were in a bad position, because of the amount of information he was able to make public.

Martha did not see Thomas. He sent material to her by post. "Dear Martha, This is the Ndosi Reserve. This stuff speaks for itself. Sort it out. As ever, Thomas."

At first she thought he was avoiding her. Then she understood he was avoiding people.

Martha was being paid by some Foundation founded by Mrs. Van, and worked at home again. There was no longer the protection of the shed in the garden, so she tried to work in the afternoon, when most of the unoccupied women slept.

Betty Krueger, Marie du Preez, Marjorie Black.

Marie was now the wife of a very successful builder, and she enjoyed her new wealth. But Piet had new friends, all rich ex-artisans, and Marie was bored. "Say what you like, Matty, but those were good days, weren't they, when we actually did things?"—as if those days were decades, instead of three, four years before.

Betty Krueger's delicate charm had all vanished into an obsessed maternity. She had two small boys, and she might just as well have had a dozen. No one could go near that house with pleasure, certainly not Boris Krueger, who had escaped into money-making; he now made a great deal of money and worked hard for it—out of the house from eight in the morning until eleven at night.

Marjorie Black, whose humorous grumblings had sounded almost tentative, as if about a temporary condition; her lively earnestness licensed by herself to express a smiling defiance, an amused self-criticism—Marjorie was silent, almost grim. She snapped out at her husband, her children, and then smiled, sighed, apologized. She said to Martha she was ashamed—she slept badly, and was ashamed of that; she slept in the afternoons and she despised women who did; she found her husband intolerably conservative and dull—but she hated women who married men for their solidity and then complained.

In short they were all, already, in their late twenties, early thirties, middle-aged women neurotic with dissatisfaction, just as if they had never made resolutions not to succumb to the colonial small-town atmosphere.

And the terrible thing was, they could never forget it: they watched their own deterioration like merciless onlookers. These days, all over the world, there are people like these, mostly women: the states of mind that once only afflicted people on deathbeds or at moments of acute crisis are their permanent condition. Lives that appear to them meaningless, wasted, hang around their necks like decaying carcasses. They are hypnotized into futility by self-observation. It is as if self-consciousness itself has speeded up the process, a curve of destruction. At thirty-five they drink too much, or are in nervous breakdown, or are many times divorced. And it is these people who are at twenty the liveliest, the most intelligent, the most promising.

All these women envied Martha: you're all right, you're going to England! You're going to get out of here.

Even Mrs. Van had said to Martha, "I envy you, going to England."

But people Martha's age don't like to be told that the old envy them, it is too frightening.

Martha saw a good deal of Mrs. Van, whose career had also been brought to a stop by the cold war. She was out of Parliament and had not easily retained her seat on the Council. She was getting old, and she was tired. The young women ran errands for her.

This often meant that she wanted someone to talk to. Her house was full all the time, but mostly of children. Her husband was busy with one big court case after another. Her old crony Johnny Lindsay was out of bed, though the doctor said he should not be, but his energies were spent on keeping upright and, as he said himself, on not being a nuisance. He sat in a grass easy chair by the doorway on to the street, and the children of the street came in and out. When his breath allowed it, he talked to the children about the high old days of industrial battle on the Rand, while Flora sat knitting.

Mrs. Van talked a great deal about Johnny.

A few weeks ago, Flora had come in late from the pictures, having left him in the care of one of his African friends.

Flora had taken the old man a cup of hot milk.

He sat up in bed, holding the hot milk, looking at her—a thin old man with the battling blue eyes of his youth. Flora had faced this look steadily.

"Johnny, is there something you want to say to me?" she had asked at last.

Johnny, smiling, patted Flora's hand, then, without a word, had shut his eyes and sat quietly in the dark, ready for sleep.

Flora had gone next day to tell Mrs. Van this incident. Mrs. Van had told Martha. Or rather, Mrs. Van had asked Martha to come up and keep her company while she watched an assortment of her grandchildren at play.

"I felt terrible, Mrs. Van," Flora had said to Mrs. Van. "I felt as if he should kill me right away and be done with it, Mrs. Van."

"But Flora, my dear, surely you can't talk of someone like Johnny killing?"

"Oh, Mrs. Van, that's how I felt when he looked at me—I'd rather he killed me."

Martha and Mrs. Van sat on the verandah. On the lawn outside a small black boy pushed a lawn mower up and down, shouting some song of his own over the clatter of the machine. The cut grass fell aside behind him in fringes of bright green.

Under trees at the far end of the garden a group of small children sat on grass having a tea party, while three black nannies watched them.

"Yes, Matty, Flora's an honest woman, but I can't help feeling: surely she could have waited for his death to start love-making? There's that man from the store at McGrath's, you know."

"Perhaps she feels he'll never die," said Martha, insisting on her right to say it, looking Mrs. Van straight in the face.

"I daresay she sometimes feels that, Matty, but we all feel discreditable things sometimes, and it doesn't mean we have a right to feel them, does it?"

"Mrs. Van, Mrs. Van, oh, then he said, 'come over to the bed, Flora.' So I went over. I was trembling so I could hardly stand, I promise you. Then he opened his eyes and took my hand and he looked at me and he said, 'Flora my dear, you are a young woman still.' 'Oh no,' I said, 'don't say that, Johnny, I'm getting on you know, I'm over forty!' But he smiled and he said, 'You're a pretty woman, my dearest—' oh, Mrs. Van, then I started to cry, I can't stand him, he's so good, do you know what I mean? And he said, 'when you did me the honour to share my life with me,' oh yes, that's what he said, did me the honour, Mrs. Van . . ."

"Because of course, Matty, he couldn't marry her, he had a wife living and children—the children won't speak to him, or at least, they didn't for a long time. But he adores Flora. Isn't it strange, Matty, that grand old man, he adores her, and when you come down to it, she's a girl he picked up in some dance hall. I see you're smiling, Matty?"

"That's so like you, Mrs. Van."

"Is it? You mean, I'm a snob?"

"No, you're not a snob. It would have been all right if she'd sold books in a book store!"

Mrs. Van sat pleating her blue silk skirt with one fat ringed hand —the other now rose in an irritable gesture to her ear. She shouted across the noise of the lawn mower, "Please, Silas, can you mow at the back of the house, I can't hear myself think."

The child Silas grinned, and pushed the machine away around the house, across lawns, paths, gravel, in a fearful din. Silence. The small children, in their pink, white, yellow dresses, sat scattered on bright green.

Martha was secretly playing a game. She shut her eyes: the noises of the afternoon, children's voices, insects in the grass, wind in leaves, made waves, made sea; against her dark lids rose and crashed thundering salt waves. She opened them: a calm hot afternoon in Mrs. Van's garden.

Mrs. Van said, "Well, that's how I *do* feel I suppose. I can't help it. Recently I've been feeling there *is* something limited about my judgements, I *have* been feeling that, but I can't help it, it's too late to teach an old dog new tricks."

From the back of the house came the now distant sound of the lawn mower. Martha shut her eyes and heard seas running on distant beaches.

"About Flora, Mrs. Van? What else did she say?"

"And we're gossiping I suppose. I don't like gossip!"

Outside Mrs. Van's gate rose a large tree whose leaves fell in regular bright fronds. As the wind shook them, the whole tree surged in an untidy mass of shiny gold spangles. A deep dark glossy green, glistening light, a ripple of white . . .

"Jack said Johnny knew she had a lover, he could tell from how she walked, and her eyes, and he was happy for her. He hoped that when he was dead, she would be happy with this man. He said she needed a man her age and not an old man like him."

In the wrinkles under Mrs. Van's little blue eyes lay webs of wet.

"It's no good, Matty. I think about it and I think—Johnny's a great man. Yes, he is." She nodded emphatically, in her old way. "How many people like him have I met? Well, Matty, I tell you this, once or twice in a lifetime you meet someone like Johnny—he's *naturally* good."

"Yes, he is."

"He literally does not understand—evil, if I can use such a word."

"I don't see why you shouldn't."

"It's not one of my words. I'm surprised that—but I'm surprised about less and less these days. But Johnny, we were talking about him."

A small boy, as fat and brown as toffee, in bright yellow, came staggering towards the verandah. "Gran, Gran, Gran . . ." he called. A large black girl rose off the grass, took two long steps, picked him up, tossed him in the air in a great curve and caught him as he descended where he had started from. He laughed. She laughed. Laughter and cries of "See me, Gran, see me?" Over them the tree's branches shook and pranced.

"Are you stupid, my old friend, I was thinking—recently I've been sitting there thinking, are you stupid, Johnny?—No, I mean it, there's something stupid about someone who never expects people to behave badly. Well, do you know what I mean?"

"The thing is, people don't behave badly with Johnny."

"Don't they?"

Martha shifted her chair a couple of feet. Now she could see Mrs. Van's flower garden which seemed to be growing, this hot afternoon, swarms of greenish-white butterflies. The air was full of variegated scents.

That morning Martha had sat by Johnny Lindsay while he cut out small paper figures for a little black child who stood by the old man's knee, one hand on the knee, watching the flashing scissors shape birds and cats, which fell into his other hand in long unfolding white patterns.

Flora had been in the back room cooking something. She was now as much Johnny's nurse as Mrs. Quest was her husband's. She cooked, and sometimes sent Martha a troubled, anxious smile, and said, "Are you warm enough, Johnny? Are you sure you're warm?"

"He held my hand, Mrs. Van, and said, 'Flora, my love you're the love of my life, you're the loveliest thing in my life, my love, I fell in love with you when I saw you that night when you were dancing, remember? But now be happy.' Well, I didn't know what to say, Mrs. Van. Did he want me to go away? I was crying so hard I didn't know what to say—did he want me to go away? I wouldn't know what to do without Johnny, that's the truth! Then I got cross. What did he mean by saying, Now be happy! He's dying, isn't he? What does he think I am? How can he say, Be happy? I was so angry, Mrs. Van, God forgive me, but I wanted to shake him. I said, 'But Johnny, have a heart, what do you mean? Do you want me to go away and leave you? Because you're making up something too much of me and Dennis'—his name is Dennis, Mrs. Van. He's got a job at Mc-Grath's, he looks after the stores and the labour. But he's married—well, sort of. I don't know how Johnny wants to see it, but it's not as he thinks. I said to him, 'But man, Johnny, have a heart.' If I said to Dennis, Johnny's thrown me out, I don't know what he'd say. That's Johnny's trouble, Mrs. Van—he always thinks things are better than they are."

Martha looked at Mrs. Van's severe face, and waited. Mrs. Van glanced up. Slowly she smiled.

"Yes, all right, Matty, I *was* thinking, if he didn't see things better than they are, how could he love a woman like Flora."

"I know you were, Mrs. Van!"

"But haven't I admitted it? I'm censorious! But now be honest, Martha. what *is* Flora?"

"A red-headed floozie from a dance hall?"

"She's a blonde this week, she's dyed her hair. She looks horrible." Martha laughed.

"No, it's no good, it's no good, Matty, when I think of him and I think of her . . ."

"But Mrs. Van, he loves her."

"Yes, yes, he does. And imagine, to be loved like that—Matty? Well, I can understand why she was so angry." Mrs. Van's eyes were sparkling in a change of mood—she was flushed, and she smiled. "Flora was so angry, she was angry for hours afterwards, she said. He kept saying to her, 'Be happy, my darling Flora. I shall die happy if I can think of you happy'—almost as if he wanted her to go off, she said, and—'well, I don't know what really, because all that happens is that Dennis and I meet in the cocktail bar at McGrath's twice a week when his wife visits her mother. Then he drives me home in the car—well, it's not *much* more than that, Mrs. Van. Of course I'm not pretending I wouldn't like there to be more . . .' She's honest, at least, Martha."

The flock of brightly coloured children had run to the central lawn and stood throwing up the newly cut fronds of jade-green grass all around them. The nurse-girls joined the babies. They all stood throwing up handfuls of strongly smelling grass, the tall strong black girls, the tiny white children.

"She said to me, 'I swear if I told him that was all there was to it, he'd be disappointed. Because after all, a man like Johnny, it's not every day you meet a man like Johnny, although I don't mind telling you, it's gone against my grain often enough, all these black Africans all the time, I mean, I'd never dare tell my mother or my friends what I've done with Johnny, like sitting down day after day to eat with black people in my own house.'"

"So what's going to happen, Mrs. Van?" said Martha.

"That I don't know. Because Flora's really upset, she really is. Because if you think about it, Matty, it *is* strange of him—everyone knows, particularly Johnny, he might die any moment, and Flora says she cooks him his supper and is all ready to sit by him for the evening, then he says, 'Now run along and enjoy yourself, my darling.'"

In spite of herself, Martha laughed.

Mrs. Van raised a severe head, then smiled. For a moment she was a mischievous girl.

"Yes, yes, Matty, the thing is, it's quite natural for him to behave like that, but he can't see it isn't for others. And he's been like that all his life. It's not only since I've known him. I know people who knew him when he was a young man." Mrs. Van sat smiling, pleating her blue skirt.

"He was handsome, I should imagine?"

"Oh yes, Matty, he must have been handsome, mustn't he? He's handsome now, isn't he? He's as straight as a die even now? But people I've met say that even then, when he was young, he was . . . well, he's never been like ordinary unregenerate mortals like you and I, Matty, he's spent all his life like this, and it's never even occurred to him there was another way to live."

When Martha went to visit Johnny, she would look for Flora in the kitchen at the back. Flora would come out, taking off her apron, and look enquiringly, half ashamed, behind her old husband's back. Martha nodded. Then Flora making beseeching, guilty signs not to be betrayed, would creep out the back way to go to the pictures. Martha had to say Flora had gone shopping. Flora could not have endured the smiles, the blessings, the goodwill that Johnny would have certainly sent after her if she had actually said, "I want to go to the pictures, I want to meet a friend in McGrath's cocktail bar."

part four

The Mulla was thinking aloud.

"How do I know whether I am dead or alive?"

"Don't be such a fool," his wife said. "If you were dead, your limbs would be cold."

Shortly afterwards Nasrudin was in the forest cutting wood. It was midwinter. Suddenly he realised that his hands and feet were cold.

"I am undoubtedly dead," he thought; "so I must stop working, because corpses do not work."

And because corpses do not walk about, he lay down on the grass.

Soon a pack of wolves appeared and attacked Nasrudin's donkey, which was tethered to a tree.

"Yes, carry on, take advantage of a dead man," said Nasrudin from his abject position; "but if I had been alive I would not have allowed you to take liberties with my donkey."

THE SUFIS; Idries Shah

1

So many jokes had been made about the "little bit of paper" it was as if the bit of paper, when it arrived, was the product of the jokes. There it lay, a thrice-folded sheet of foolscap in which was stated, in five and a half lines of print, that Anton Hesse and his wife Martha were both British citizens.

The two stood examining the paper, each holding it by a corner, each waiting for the other to speak; so many decisions had been postponed until this bit of paper arrived. At last Anton spoke, "So, here it is. And now you have decisions to make." With which he went off to the bathroom.

The fact that Anton had chosen *not* to announce decisions—this was in itself a decision or an announcement.

Martha began to tremble with anger, not only because of Anton's walking off, literally washing his hands of the thing, but (to her surprise—she thought she was long over that childishness) because she, born of so-British parents, had been deemed not-British and then as arbitrarily allowed to be British. Though the emotion itself was infuriating, since "what did it matter what nationality one was?" And what could be more ridiculous than being angry, just as if a button had been pushed, about something one had been living with and making jokes about for four, five years?

And what sort of a monster was she to be angry about Anton's saying, "And now you have decisions to make," when this was his way of covering deep hurt? For, apart from the aunt in Hamburg, Anton had not yet discovered any relatives alive in Germany. When he got information, it was of death. The Hesse family ranged from a pure Jewishness that merited (Anton's grim joke—it was for some months a joke he made continuously in various forms) a pure death in the gas chambers to branches apparently not Jewish at all whose members (like all the other good Germans) were killed by bombing, or as soldiers on the Russian front, or by starvation. Anton Hesse was linked with the fate of his country so deeply and by so many fibres that the cataclysm which had engulfed Germany had also engulfed him who had fled from it and had been living so many thousands of miles away. And now the Communist Party in East Germany did not reply to his letters, to his demands to come home. They simply did not answer. Nothing. Silence. The old Germany, which would have killed him, was dead; and the new Germany would not answer his letters.

A traveller from Europe who had visited Berlin which stood divided and in ruins said, "What do you expect? As far as they are concerned, you are a spy, anyone from the West is."

At which Anton had, after a pause, nodded, and said, very dry, very cold, "Of course. They are entirely in the right. I would take the same attitude myself."

If he wished to live in East Germany, they told him, he must travel there and take his chances. From all over the world, refugees travelled back to East and West Germany and he must do the same.

"They are in the right," he said.

Now he stood in the bathroom, bent over the wash basin, a man absorbed in the business of washing his hands. Martha stood in the front room watching him. She watched him shake the drops of water off his hands into the basin. A few drops scattered on the wall. He carefully took a cloth to wipe the wall dry, then he bent close to peer at the wall—yes, it was dry. He took a small towel and dried his hands. Then he examined his fingernails, then he looked into the shaving glass and ran a long white hand over his right cheek. Finally he returned to the front room, smiling. He sat down, flinging one leg across the other, and began examining his hands, back and front, with a calm smile.

"The divorce is nothing but a formality," said Martha. "I asked Mr. Robinson."

It cost Martha a good deal to say this—though of course the decisions had been made a long time ago.

Now Anton nodded, smiled, and said, "Yes, my researches into this subject confirm Mr. Robinson's view."

The drawling tone he used for this, a kind of formal superciliousness, was not aimed at Martha, or at Mr. Robinson, but at the processes of bureaucracy. Thus he had joked, drawling, about the little bits of paper.

"If we start proceedings now, it will take about six months. Because there's a long waiting list for divorces."

"Naturally. The war has held up civilized life long enough. Serious matters like divorce have had to wait."

Martha laughed, quickly. This judicious humour of Anton's, a creaking into irony, was new in him, a result apparently of his social life at the Forsters'; and she was grateful because of this Anton who could smile, laugh, even if with difficulty. There was a look of pride on his face at such moments, and he would glance at her as if to say: And you call me pompous!

"One of us has to divorce the other," said Martha, continuing this conversation which they had had before. But not for some months—the arrival of the piece of paper, after years of waiting, had been a shock.

"That's logical enough."

"We can go on living in this flat because of the housing shortage, but one of us has to deny our bed to the other. I mean, we have to swear it in Court."

And now Anton scrutinized his long hand, back and front, and a smile almost arranged itself on his face. And Martha thought: No, please don't make a joke now, because I couldn't laugh at it.

The point was, to use the language of the courts—conjugal relations had been resumed. A phrase which, as far as Martha was concerned, would do to sum it up. But for Anton it was not so simple—which was why this conversation was taking place. When Anton had gone into the bathroom, leaving her alone, she had known perfectly well that even now if she had put her arms around him, and murmured *Anton, suppose we*—then there would be no divorce.

As far as Martha was concerned, when they occasionally lay side by side in the narrow single bed, it was from good nature, from courtesy. But not long ago Anton had said, "We don't do so badly, do we, Matty?"

And Martha could see that he really thought so.

She did not understand any of this, but it was because of Thomas. As far as she was able to sum it up, or even to think about it—which she tried not to do, because of the grief which accompanied thoughts of Thomas—her experience with Thomas had been so deep, in every way, that she was changed to the point that . . . but here it was that she was unable to go further.

Was she saying that because of the relationship she had had with Thomas, she was spoiled for anyone else? Surely not, it should be the other way around! But she did not know what had taken place between her and Thomas. Some force, some power, had taken hold of them both, and had made such changes in her—what, soul? (but she did not even know what words she must use) psyche? being?— that now she was changed and did not understand herself.

Surely she ought to have some inkling, be able to answer some of the questions? Here she was Martha Quest—well, if you like, Martha Knowell, Martha Hesse (but she did not feel herself to be connected with any of these names) but here she was, a woman living now, many thousands of years after the human race had begun to think, to make statements about its condition, and surely she ought to be able to say: Such and such a thing has happened to me because I and Thomas loved each other.

But she could not use the word Love, for she did not know what it meant.

What did it mean that she had been married to Anton, when she knew quite well that when they parted, which would be soon, they would not even be able to hear what the other said, even for a short time.

So how could she say she had been married to Anton, and "in love" with Thomas? Though of course she had never been "in love" with Thomas; that particular fever, in its aspect either of sickness or of magic had had nothing to do with it. But what had been the essential quality of being with Thomas?

Well, she did not know. Something rather ordinary, perhaps? As if she had been eating superlatively good bread for some months, taking it for granted that of course one had good bread, and then, this marvellously simple good thing vanishing, she had looked around and found that after all there wasn't much around. Yes, the best thing about being with Thomas (and this had been the essence of her self-deception and precisely what had prevented her from understanding the rarity of the combination Thomas, Martha) was that to be with Thomas was as natural as breathing. And even the long process of breaking-down—as they both learned to put it—for the other; of learning to expose oneself, was something they did together, acknowledging they had to do it. And to admit it had been easy, because they were only putting into words each other's thoughts. There had never been anything they could not say aloud, as soon as they thought it.

Last week she had walked into the office in Founders' Street and there was Thomas. He was on the point of leaving for some village miles away. He had said to her, "Martha, do you ever think about when we loved each other?"

"Well, what do you suppose?"

"Yes, I know." He looked at her, frowning. Not at her—the frown was because he was having difficulty with finding thoughts. "You and I together—that wasn't really what either of us expected, Martha."

"No. And all the time I was actually thinking—well, after all I'm waiting to go to England, so this doesn't really count."

"Yes. I know. And I used to think: this woman, she suits me better than any of the others—no, you're smiling, you're offended, you didn't understand what I said!"

"Yes, I did. Yes, that just about sums it up."

"I've been trying to think about it—something happened between us—I mean, not just loving each other."

"Yes, I know.

"No one knows anything about that sort of thing, that's what I've been thinking. We haven't any idea about it really."

"Or about anything else, if it comes to that."

"Ah, well, now—but I can't afford to admit that, Martha, no, I can't. I spend all my time shouting at poor bloody half-savages plant this, plant that, dig boreholes, clean your teeth, wash your children. I wouldn't be able to do that if I was thinking, I don't know anything."

A few days ago Martha had visited Maisie. "Isn't it funny, Matty? Now I go to bed with people and you know, I don't really care? I mean, I like it, don't get me wrong. I like enjoying myself for them, but it's quite different. I feel quite different, as if I'm in another room. Do you know what I mean, Matty? I mean, perhaps it's because of my husbands being killed and then Andrew turning against me like that?"

Well, Martha knew what she meant, or thought she did—for how could one be sure if one knew what other people meant? It was the phrase, in another room. Yes, that was it. A couple of weeks ago, being alone in a small town with Jack Dobie, she had spent the night with him. Now, as far as he was concerned, they were having an affair and he was madly in love. His phrase. But Martha, "enjoying herself" well enough, and even thinking Good Lord, what sort of a fool is it who does without sex, even for a day, had been, was, in another room.

"Do you know, Matty, I've discovered something. The reason why they like me, they like sleeping with me—" Maisie, offering these intimate facts to Martha, would not use the words that went with them; she could say, they like me, but not, like sleeping with me, without a quick frowning look at Martha to see how she was taking it. "The reason they like sleeping with me, if you know what I mean, it's because I can do it so well because I feel as if I was somewhere else. I mean, when I think of Andrew, before he turned against me, I mean to say!"

It is likely, Martha said to herself, drawling it, as Anton drawled out the words he found so hard, "There is evidence to suggest that Thomas, when he went off to Israel, took a good part of me with him." A cliché. How many other clichés are there that I've been using all my life and never thought they meant something, after all? Because it *is* as if some part of me has died. What part? Or it is in another room, looking on. Yes. And the joke is I'm going off to England (I am going to the sea, oh soon, soon, because I shall go crazy soon if I can't reach the sea), I'm going off to "begin life" all over again, but how can one begin life, begin anything, when a part of oneself is Thomas's prisoner and saying, with him, that no one knows anything about anything?

"The point is," said Martha, "Mr. Robinson says the judges are all quite sensible and human these days. Because where could we desert each other *to,* if we decided to move out? One of us has to swear on oath that we have dramatically moved our bed into another room. We're lucky to *have* another room, the way things are. . . . We don't actually have to move our bed, we just have to swear to it."

A long silence. Martha and Anton sat on either side of the tiny room—so small their legs almost met in the middle. They looked at each other. They were both of them embarrassed at this sudden intrusion of the law (long expected though it was) into their precarious balances. They had not expected this embarrassment, this pain for the other's situation.

After all, they had been married for four years. According to their lights they had nothing to reproach themselves with. It had almost been an arranged marriage, could almost be described as a marriage of convenience. Here they sat after four years of it, and at least they had given each other space to find consolation, they had not quarrelled—not destructively, at least; had not done each other damage. Martha had behaved well by waiting until Anton was naturalized; Anton had behaved well by taking it for granted that she *would* behave well. They had both of them behaved in what both would describe as a civilized way. So while they were not married, nor ever had been, there was nothing to be ashamed of. And they felt for each other a kind of dry, patient compassion—well, that was something.

"Let's toss for it," said Martha.

She expected Anton to say she was frivolous. Instead he smiled, took out a coin and said, "Heads or tails?"

"Tails."

He won. And would therefore next day instruct his lawyer to sue Martha for divorce unless she immediately restored conjugal rights.

Meanwhile they separated to attend to other business; Martha to find out how soon she could get a passage to England, and he to visit the Forsters, who expected him to lunch. He had not said anything at all about going to Germany.

Her life was again full of runnings about and around—it was not only a question of being divorced and going to England.

Marjorie, who had taken over Martha's role as general dog's-body was run down—the doctor said, and needed to take things easy. Marjorie came to Martha, "Of course if you don't believe in anything any more, then you must just say so!"

"But I'm not going to be here for long."

"But, Matty, you've said that for years!"

"Look, Marjorie, I'll help you, of course."

"I can see you don't want to—nobody cares, nobody cares about anything. I suppose it's because of that book. Well, I think the book should have the opposite effect, not making everybody destructive and lazy!"

It was "the book" which was the reason for the new (though brief) period of activity. What was "the book"?—they all referred to it like this, not by the title or by the author's name, as if it did not matter what it was. And in a way it did not, there were so many of them by now. This one had been written by a Russian peasant who had been caught up in the 1917 Revolution and become a minor official. He had come under the eyes of the authorities as early as the late twenties, and for some years had suffered imprisonment, persecution, etc. Having escaped, he was in America, writing books like this one, which was the first to reach the group—or what remained of it. Marjorie read it first—in tears. She had given it to Colin, but he said he was too busy. Being pressed by Marjorie, "This is really important, dear," he had read a chapter and said it was badly written. Marjorie took it to Betty Krueger, who said she was sure it had been written by the FBI and that Timofy Gangin did not exist. Boris said he did not have time for bad journalism. Besides, where had Marjorie got this book? It had been sent to her through the post, she suspected it had come from Solly—well, of course, then, what else did one expect? That dirty . . .

Martha read it. If this was true, then everything she had been saying for the last seven years was a lie. But perhaps it was exaggerated?—after all, a man imprisoned unjustly was bound to be bitter and to exaggerate? That word exaggerate . . . it rang false, it belonged to a different scale of truth. Reading this book, these books, it was her first experience, though a clumsy, unsure one, of using a capacity she had not known existed. She thought: I *feel* the book is true—although it is badly written, crude, sensational. Well, what does that mean, to *feel* something is true, as if I'm not even reading the words of the book, but responding to something else. She thought, vaguely, If this book were not on this subject, but about something else, well, the yardsticks I use would say: Yes, this is true. One has an instinct one trusts, yes . . .

Martha gave the book to Anton. At first he said, "I'm not going to read this trash." But he read it, dropping, as he did so, sarcastic remarks about the author's character—an unpleasant one, he said. Then he became silent. Well, nothing new about that. Martha waited, while the book lay on the table, apparently discarded. Then Anton said, "After all, they aren't saints, they were bound to make mistakes." And off he went to the Forsters, just as if he were not aware of the enormity of this remark. He did not mention the book again—and was not talking at all about Germany.

The book, in fact, most sharply raised the question of Anton. In what role, then, did Anton, bitter and experienced old-guard Communist from the heyday of the Communist Party in Germany, present himself to the Forsters, who were, after all, rich capitalists— to describe them, as Anton did himself.

Martha had met people who were visitors at the Forster home. Apparently Anton was a great success. "Treated just like a son," one woman had said, with the intention of annoying Martha. "Or like a son-in-law?" Martha had replied.

Granted that Anton's efficiency had transformed a whole department administered by a friend of Mr. Forster—granted that it appeared no decisions could be made without him; but how did Mr. Forster deal with the fact that Anton was a German, and a well-known Red? Well, the fact that he was a German was no problem at all. Anton in the Forster house was, or had been, "the good Ger-

man" for as long as being German had been a difficulty. It was no
longer. After all, our gallant ally Russia had been transformed again
into a nation of serfs groaning under the tyrant Stalin, just as if the
war had not occurred; and Mr. Forster had done business with Germany before the war and was making arrangements to do business
again. He found the Germans reliable, efficient, and good company,
and the German cities were clean—it was the only country in
Europe whose water he had been prepared to drink straight from
the tap. Many a pleasant evening he had had with German businessmen in their beer cellars before that unfortunate business, the war,
had taken place. He thought the sooner Germany was again united
as a bastion against Communism the better; he was most interested
to hear about Anton's political experiences in the thirties . . . and
the fact that he had been a Communist? Well, what more natural, if
he had had a hard time as a child? Mr. Forster had been a socialist
himself, at university. And the fact that Anton was working class by
origin? It turned out this was a point in Anton's favour too. Mr.
Forster's father had been a poor boy in Scotland, and he was disposed to approve of people getting to the top by their own ability,
which was why he, Richard Forster, was in Zambesia: he was impatient of the class system of his own country.

So what it amounted to was: Anton was almost a son of the house,
because, not in spite, of the fact of his past. Everything that had
made him, everything that had been his deepest experience, had
become salt to the Forsters' pie.

And Bettina Forster, the daughter who (as Martha was naturally
predisposed to see it) was likely to have something in common with
Martha? How did she see Anton, this man who was after all a clerk
in the railways, even if her father's closest friend did say that he
couldn't run the department without him? In what way was this
woman (described as pretty, intelligent, neurotic) the successor
to Grete and to Martha? It seemed she was a liberal of some kind,
she thought something ought to be done about the natives, and she
might even go into Parliament or the Town Council. So Anton Hesse
was going to be the son-in-law of a big businessman whose rebellion
against society had been exhausted after he had said he would not
submit himself to the class nonsense in the old country, whose wife
said he was a poor dear brave boy, and whose daughter would find
his political experience absolutely invaluable in getting a seat on the
Council or in Parliament.

And he refused to attend a meeting summoned by, or at least
caused by, Solly Cohen, on the grounds that "he didn't want to have
anything to do with Trotskyist traitors, thanks very much!"

Solly had sent verbal invitations through Marjorie, to anyone who was still interested, to meet him and an African contact. Which African? Oh no, they must wait and see!

But Marjorie had become for all of them the source, or at least the spreading point of the disquiet caused by "the book."

She was demanding that "it was only fair" that they all should get together and discuss Timofy Gangin's book. "After all," she had said earnestly to Martha, "if we have been spreading lies all over the town, then it's only right we should say so."

Martha agreed to a discussion, so did Colin, "if he had time." The Kruegers could see no useful purpose in it. Anton refused. Therefore there would be no meeting. Meanwhile everyone had read the book, and discussions had taken place between pairs of people. It had been read, conclusions had been come to because of it, things would change—but there had been no formal meeting. But Marjorie rang people up and wrote letters: they all lacked responsibility, she said, she would never have believed that people could be so frivolous and casual.

So everyone was irritated by her. Yet it was she who was summoning them to a new meeting which, if what Solly promised came true, would inaugurate a new era of cooperation with the Africans. They might, at last, after all these years, actually achieve their goal of "working with the Africans."

What it amounted to was: because of Marjorie's quality of earnest readiness for anything, she was the focal point of both new possibilities—serious criticism of Russia and serious political work with the Africans.

Like all good organizers, Marjorie was not going to hold a meeting at all, unless she could be sure people would come. She was not well, so Martha ran around trying to find out who might come.

An extraordinary collection of people: Marjorie, of course, and Colin—but probably only because he was after all Marjorie's husband. Solly, and his mysterious contact. Mrs. Van der Bylt. Johnny Lindsay—but this was a token interest only, for he was confined to his bed now. Jack Dobie, if he were in town, but he was too poor these days to make journeys without very good reason. Thomas, if he was in town. And Maisie, of all people, who said she often thought of the old days: it would be nice to see everyone again.

A meeting was convened in the office in Founders' Street for a Thursday afternoon. It had to be changed to a Wednesday because of a last minute message from Solly; was cancelled because it appeared Mr. Zlentli (though what role he was playing Solly would not say) had vetoed the whole thing; was uncancelled because of a change of policy of some sort; was arranged for two weeks later in the evening, but at two days' notice was changed for the afternoon of that day because of Mrs. Van, who in any event did not come at all: Flora had sent a message that Johnny was very ill and asking for her.

That the thing was ill-starred was clear by now to everyone, but it all dragged on, on a momentum of muddle and inefficiency. For instance, on one of the cancelled occasions, a whole lot of people had turned up from the old long-dead discussion groups, under the impression that this was a resurgence of Communist activity: they had come to disassociate themselves not only from the present but from the past. But no one was in the office when they arrived. One man, a most active attender at the old meetings, wrote a letter to the *News* warning "everyone concerned" that Communist spies were planning an uprising. As a result of this, Colin was warned by his superior in the Department that he must be careful; Anton made many deprecating and explanatory remarks to Mr. Forster, and Mrs. Van got a new batch of poison-pen letters.

On the afternoon of the meeting, Martha saw a stranger looking out of the window into Founders' Street. When he turned, it was Thomas; a lean, burned man examined her with his bright, bright blue eyes. His hair, coloured by the fierce suns of the Zambesi Valley, was pale, greenish almost—like a wig over the dark austere face.

He did not smile. She busied herself with the state of the literature cupboard. Then he said, "You've no idea how strange it is, coming into town again after being in the bush so long."

"Do we seem unreal?"

"The town seems unreal." After a few moments he added, "Well at any rate come and stand by me."

She was going to finish what she had started, but he said, "No, don't do that. Please come."

They stood side by side looking out into the street. On the waste lot opposite the Piccadilly a new block of offices rose like a rocket away from Founders' Street.

"Well, Martha?"

"Well, Thomas?"

She was thinking: It's the look on his face—I simply *cannot* understand it. Where have I seen it before? And what is happening to Thomas? It was difficult to remember what he had been a couple of years ago. Once there was Thomas, a large, even stout, open-faced blond man, whose immediately obvious quality was the energy that seemed to explode from him. All his movements, his gestures, had been restless, energetic; once everything about him had gone out, had included, had warmed. Now here he stood beside her, shut in himself. His face, burned to a dark glistening bronze from the hot sun of the valley was—not refined, but sharpened, made wary. Solitary. She kept glancing at him, at the dark proud face whose expression she could not read.

"Thomas?"

"What is it, Martha?"

But she did not know what question it was she should ask.

Soon Jack Dobie came in. He had been on the point of coming to Martha. But seeing her with her former lover he gave them both a shrewd look, then a smile, then sat on a bench by himself. But Thomas, oblivious of this small episode, nodded at Jack almost absently.

"Jack Dobie!" said Jack humorously.

Thomas looked at him, from a distance, then understood he was being criticized. He shrugged.

Maisie came in, followed by Tommy Brown. Not that Martha at once recognized Tommy. She saw the young man, thought how like Maisie it was to bring along just anybody she happened to be with, was prompted by his friendship-claiming smile (an aggressive, not a pleasant one) into a closer look ... and stood silent, searching for the earnest enquiring boy Tommy who had been in the common-place you-can't-catch-me-out Zambesian who sat with his raw red thighs spread out on the bench.

"Move up and give me space," said Maisie. Tommy moved up, having first grinned at the others as if to say: I don't have to do what she says!

Then Maisie sat on a bench, lazily smiling at them. They all watched her, even Thomas. She kept, had perfected, if such a thing was possible, the physical assurance which had always been her gift, so that to watch this large, rather blowzy woman sit down was to be made part of the experience of sitting. She sat, and her two large but beautiful legs in their very high-heeled shoes arranged themselves in a socially correct pose, side by side, as if they had been reminded by Maisie: we are in company. Obeying her, they glistened with their own satisfaction. Her fat thighs reposed under a glistening mauve-flowered silk. Her great breasts presented the ugliness of the silk to everyone with indifference: look, what does it matter what we wear! Her face, which now had a look, painful to those who had known her earlier, of decorum; a simpering watch-fulness, yet retained, in its fat, reddening surfaces, an innocence that was still her deepest quality. Her lazy blue gaze offered itself, in spite of the defensiveness of her face, to them with complete open-ness: take me or leave me, I don't care! And her hands—but it was her hands that they all watched. Those hands had a life which went on quite apart from her mind, her heart. These two white capable hands, they stroked her thighs, lifted to touch the white organdie flower (slightly grubby) at her throat, placed themselves around the cheap white handbag on her lap, or folded themselves together in a gesture of absolutely open, calm knowledge, quiet assurance. The hands knew that they were in the right, that they were good, that there was no need for them to listen to criticism.

Maisie looked at them over her hands and her face said: This is young Tommy Brown, well what of it! And his foolish embarrassed grin said: I know what you're thinking, but Maisie's an old comrade from the old days, isn't she (not that anyone is a comrade these days of course) and am I the sort of man to sleep with prostitutes? Meanwhile they almost expected to see the tuft on the crown of his head stand up and signal to them his desire to improve himself, his awe at being here at all.

"Maisie said it was a sort of get-together from the old days," said Tommy.

"Well, it's not exactly a get-together," said Martha.

"I understood you to mean that, Matty," said Maisie.

"No, it's a meeting about whether we can do anything to help the Africans."

But before she had even finished, Tommy let out a loud young man's knowledgeable guffaw which said: I'm not likely to be taken in by that kind of thing any longer. "I thought it was just a get-together." He had already stood up, saying with all of himself, "I'm here under false pretences."

"I must have got it wrong," said Maisie, "but it's nice to see old friends."

"Well, it won't hurt to *talk* about the Africans, will it?" said Jack.

"Oh no, you don't catch me again," said Tommy, roaring with laughter, "I mean, things have changed, haven't they?" He was already at the door.

"What's got into you? Afraid of losing your job? You're working for Piet du Preez, aren't you? Well he's not going to give you the sack for *talking*."

"I wouldn't be too sure," said Marjorie, bitterly. She had just come in. She was flushed up with the heat, and with guilt because she was late. She had her youngest child in her arms, and there were fingermarks on her white linen dress.

"Anyway, I'll see you," said Tommy, and went, saying with a special half-proprietary, half-embarrassed smile at Maisie, "I'll see you Maisie."

"Don't mind Tommy," said Maisie. "He's not a bad boy really."

"Yes, he is," said Marjorie, fierce. "He's changed out of recognition."

"Well," said Maisie summing up, as it were, "time's not stood still, well has it?"

The telephone rang. It was Mrs. Quest, asking Martha to come. She was apologetic—anxious. Martha knew she must go, her mother really wanted her.

"I must go," she said.

"But, Matty, if you're going," said Marjorie, "there's hardly any one here as it is."

"But Solly's not here anyway."

Thomas said, "What is all this about Solly? I don't like meetings in aid of Solly anyway." It was quite extraordinary how an old Thomas came to life, briefly as he said this—a blunt, aggressive, obstinate man, very different from the solitary silent person he almost at once became again.

"Well, all that does seem irrelevant now," said Marjorie, belligerent, because she had found herself unable to say, "the book."

"Why?" said Thomas. But after a small interval, as if he had reminded himself he should show interest.

"Well," said Marjorie again, this time apologetically, because she could hear, before she said them, how flat her words would be, "we've just read a book, you see—yes, I know we've always said . . . but it does look as if—we've been wrong about Russia."

She blushed as he stared at her. Then he looked at Jack who, out of this argument, sat grinning, watching; at Martha, who nodded; at Maisie, who was looking out of the window.

"Then I don't know," said Thomas, abruptly. "I haven't anything to say." He stood, for that moment every inch the old Thomas, bristling with energy, his blue eyes close and hard on their faces. Then he lost interest, and turned away.

"That's not good enough, you *must* have something to say," said Marjorie.

Thomas said, almost absently, "The Soviet Union's always been the same—it's we who change."

This remark, preposterous compared with what they expected of him, caused Jack to laugh and Martha to say, "Thomas has been in the bush so long, no wonder everything here looks a bit ridiculous!"

"I don't agree," said Marjorie fiercely, "that's no attitude at all!"

"What do you want me to do? Read a book that says the Soviet Union's no good?"

"I really don't understand your attitude," said Marjorie, bitter, as if it were she who were being betrayed.

"It's a question of which side you are on, that's all."

"Oh-ho," said Jack, "that's frank at least!"

"Yes," said Thomas. "If the Soviet Union is rotten, then that's what she's been from the start. If she's a paradise, then ditto. What difference does a book make to that? But as far as we are concerned —we're just like America then? The cold war starts, and the Soviet Union's not fit to associate with. That's not what her enemies said when she was doing most of the fighting in the war."

"You sound like an editorial in *Pravda*," said Marjorie.

"I don't see why people shouldn't have their own opinions," said Maisie, in an effort to preserve peace.

"I would never have expected it of you, Thomas," said Marjorie. "I mean, you were never just one of the dogmatic hundred per cent Communists. It almost sounds as if you think we shouldn't have read this book."

"Of course you shouldn't," said Thomas. He stood gazing out into Founders' Street, hands in his pockets. It was perfectly clear to Martha that it was not so much that he was bored by this exchange, or that he was not really taking part in it. One part, a small part, of his mind exchanged words with Marjorie—but as the price he had to pay for being left in peace. He was preoccupied with something different: again his eyes had the dark brooding look of his introspection.

"It's absolutely ridiculous," said Marjorie. "Just as if one can't read books dispassionately, like sensible people."

"That's ridiculous," said Thomas after a pause. That phrase was automatic, mechanical. Then he turned from the window, and Martha saw that he was "coming back" as she put it. It was extraordinary to see the attention coming back into his eyes. his face, "How can you talk such nonsense," he said irritably. "That's real intellectual nonsense. Of course if you read a book you're influenced by it."

"I don't agree," said Marjorie.

"You haven't any right to agree or not agree," said Thomas.

"Well!" said Marjorie, affronted, smiling brightly, looking at them all in turn, for support.

"What do you know about books?" said Thomas. "You're brought up to take them for granted. To understand books you have to talk to someone who had to fight for them. I had to fight to learn to read and to write. Every book I read until I left Poland I had to fight for. I had no time to read books that were no use to me. I knew very well that if you read a book for relaxation, as they say, it fills one's mind with rubbish. And if you don't have reference books and libraries, you remember what you read. You people never remember anything you read because you know you can always look up anything in a dictionary or go to a library. You know nothing about books. And the Communist Party and the Roman Catholic Church are right—if you want to stop people being contaminated, you have to lock up books."

"Well!" said Marjorie, when he had finished. "I think that's absolutely terrible!"

"You want it both ways," said Thomas. "You want to be nice liberals, everything free and *laissez faire,* and at the same time you want to run a state on strict organized lines. In a time of war."

"In what?" said Marjorie, surprised.

"In a time of war. In wartime."

"But the war's over."

"Oh, but I don't think it is, I don't agree." This was let out, dropped out, in the tone of his self-absorbed indifference. His back to them, he gazed sombrely away over the roofs of the lower town. His profile showed against the sunlit sky. Of course, thought Martha, of course, "It was my dream, that's what I keep remembering. Lord, yes—that's just how he walked out, alone, solitary, into the crowd of people who fell away on either side, to give him room, and because they did not want to touch him. And that is how we all treat Thomas, almost without knowing it; we treat him in a special way, as if . . . as if *what?*"

"I've never been more surprised in my life," announced Marjorie. The child on her lap strove to reach over for a toy that had fallen on the floor. Marjorie automatically bent down to get the toy for the child. "Really, Thomas, you could knock me down with a feather."

He did not answer.

"I've got to go," said Martha, looking towards Thomas, hoping he would turn and say goodbye, or walk down the stairs with her.

Maisie said, "I'll come with you, Matty."

Now Thomas nodded briefly at both of them, "So long then!"

Martha and Maisie went downstairs together.

"It's living in the bush so long," said Maisie. "You were right when you said that. I've got a brother, He's a surveyor. When he comes out of the bush sometimes he's funny for more than a day."

"How's things with you?" asked Martha.

"Oh," said Maisie, "it's just the same. Binkie's marriage isn't too good, that's what's driving me mad. He keeps coming down and coming down to get away from his home. But I say to him: Look, Binkie, you've made your bed, why keep driving me crazy?"

"I'll come and see you soon. Have you heard from Athen?"

"No. The trouble with Binkie is his new wife doesn't want any more kids, she said when she married him, she had two kids from the war, you know her husband was killed, and she wanted to stop at that. But Binkie didn't believe her, he hoped love would change her feelings. But now he's hankering after Rita. Oh dear, Matty, but I suppose we all have our troubles."

They lifted their bicycles out of the bicycle rack, and pointed them in opposite directions.

"I'm going to get married one of these days," said Maisie bitterly. "Yes, I will, I'm being driven to it, it's the only way I'll ever get any peace and quiet."

She cycled off, her great lazy body shifting from side to side on the saddle, the mauve silk glittering hotly in the sunlight.

2

Martha sat in her mother's living room, her attention being demanded from at least three directions. In front of her, on a low round table, was a great pile of keys, just deposited there by her mother with a small laugh saying, "There, bad girl, only of course you'll lose everything anyway, being what you are." She had gone out to the kitchen, blushing.

Martha sat looking at the keys. They'd be appropriate for—but she had never seen such keys, enormous black keys such as no one used these days. They were keys fit for a dungeon. Meanwhile the radio was on, much too loud, outside on the verandah, and every time Martha turned it off, her mother turned it on again. Meanwhile the little white dog yapped as he ran in a frenzy of activity in at the door, up on to a settee, out of the low window, on to the verandah, in at the door, around and around, snapping at the noise from the radio, at a bee on the golden shower, at Martha's ankles. And meanwhile Martha thought that her daughter was with Mr. Quest, and had been alone with him for some time, and that this, which made her uneasy, was something which apparently she could not prevent.

The room was full of light reflected from the glittering foliage in the garden. This room, so unlike the living room of the house on the farm with its windows opening on to a landscape that showed ranges of mountains East, West, South, yet resembled it—why? Because through the windows one saw the shrubs and trees of the garden, the waving tops of trees in the park; because the light changed here all day, so that one could say: It is full sunlight, it is a clouded day, by one glance at the air in the room—which tended to be a bit stale this afternoon, or seemed so, perhaps because of the jigging radio, the smelly little dog.

The radio must be on because Mrs. Quest had said: It's nice for your father. But of course he could scarcely hear it from where he was. Where he was with the small girl Caroline.

Martha sat, looking at the keys. When Martha said it looked as if she would really be going to England at last, Mrs. Quest looked out all the keys she had ever had in her life, put them together on a new key ring, and presented them to Martha. "I suppose some of the boxes may have got lost, but it's always a good idea to have plenty of nice keys."

She was now making scones in the kitchen. She could not really hear the music from the radio. Martha got up and leaned through the window and first turned the sound low, then off. Silence. Blessed silence. Martha, straining her ears, could *just* hear a small girl's voice, three rooms away. It sounded normally cheerful, that was something.

Again Martha sat down, by the table on which were the keys. Yes, this room *was* like that other room—although one was of mud-plastered walls and thatch, the other of brick and plaster; one almost part of the bush which surrounded it, the other set in a big lush town garden. Why were they alike? Because some of the pictures were the same? For instance, a picture of a comical small boy who sat fishing on the side of a stream; but he had gone to sleep, and on the end of his line was a great fish the size of a whale who peered up out of the water with an expression which said: *Who* is this monstrously impertinent imp who has dared . . .

This picture, probably given to the Quests as a wedding present by some person who had said: What on *earth* shall we give dear Alfred and May, had hung on Mrs. Quest's walls wherever she had moved for nearly thirty years. The little dog, yap yap yap, bounded around in another circle, and Martha lost her temper, and swept him up roughly as a flame of rage licked through her blood and caused her to drop him out of the window. She slammed the door. He jumped back in, wagging his tail. She picked him up and threw him into the dining room, and with two doors shut between herself and him sat with her head in her hands, listening to the silence. Real silence now. She could not hear Caroline's voice at all, though.

There were the keys still, black, rusty, jutting, awkward, all by themselves on the table. Mrs. Quest, so she had informed Martha, had lain awake all night worrying, because of Martha's going to England. She had got up at five in the morning to ferret out the keys, and assemble them, and she had been at a shop when it opened to buy the key ring. Yet the date for Martha's leaving was not yet fixed, the ships were so full of people deprived of pleasure-tripping for the duration of the war. Nor was the divorce fixed, for there were long waiting lists for that amenity as well. Yet Mrs. Quest already lay awake. She had lain awake all last night, afraid that Martha would not accept the keys, it would be just like her, she said, handing the jangling, rusty, appalling object to Martha looking as guilty as if she had just stolen something.

The thing was unbelievable, preposterous—it had the same quality of preposterousness as that awful coy picture which had been part of the Quests' lives for no reason at all for thirty years; as that frightful smelly little dog who was whining two rooms away; as the fact that Caroline was with her grandfather, Mr. Quest—described by Mrs. Quest as: It's nice for the poor little girl to get to know her grandfather while she has the chance; as the fact that Caroline was here, in the same house as Martha at all.

Yet at the same time this horror was absolutely natural and indeed inevitable: Mrs. Quest, whose life was so narrowed, so deprived (her son had married and gone off to farm in the mountains three hundred miles away), was right to want to have her granddaughter in the house as often as she could.

Of course.

Just as: why not collect half-a-century's keys on a key ring to present to one's getting-on-to-thirty daughter? Why not treat a little dog as if he were a loved baby and call him, "in joke" Kaiser? Why not leave a child of eight alone for hours with a sick old man who scarcely knew what he was doing?

And above all, could Mrs. Quest be blamed, as busy as she was, if she forgot to tell Martha the child was there, if she forgot to tell the child's father and her stepmother that Martha would be there—if she, faced with his situation, which was entirely Martha's fault, behaved as if there was no situation?

After all, it *was* a situation for which there were no precedents, Martha could see that. She could remember no novels about it, no plays, no poems—though it was the sort of thing that occurred in Victorian melodrama. There wasn't even any mention of it in the books on "child guidance" which presumably the child's new step-mother used, as Martha had done.

Anyway, for some months now Martha had been coming to her mother's, and finding the little girl there. Elaine Talbot was having a baby of her own at last, and it was natural that Caroline should spend time with her grandparents. All absolutely natural, in order, and indeed, bound to happen.

Meanwhile Martha inwardly howled with sheer rage, with pain—and saw everybody's point of view, and above all, saw no point in feeling anything at all, since what good would it do? She came to the house, greeted the little girl, her daughter, like a stranger, and then, as the child became used to her, like a friendly grownup—an "auntie." Caroline called her Auntie, and Mrs. Quest never lost an opportunity—Let Auntie Matty tell you a story dear, Auntie Matty will take you to wash your hands.

So Martha was neither "seeing" the child, nor "not seeing" her. "You know you aren't allowed to see her, it's not fair on her," said Mrs. Quest, at least once a week, even now. "Seeing" apparently meant Caroline's knowing that Martha was her mother. Well, of course, Caroline should not know, if that meant knowing so casually, that Martha was her mother. But surely she should not either meet a woman who was her mother, as if there were no situation at all.

But who was to be censored for all this? Martha, of course. Mrs. Quest? Of course not, for the essence of Mrs. Quest was that she could never be censored for anything, she was so much of a victim. Victims cannot be blamed. The weak cannot be blamed. The defeated are in the right. The old, the exploited, the miserable, are to be pardoned.

So this, the situation of the child, like the business of the keys—and like everything else, Martha could not help muttering—had this quality of sheer, brutal farcical impossibility. There was a surface of sense, of civilized life: Well, it's nice for Caroline to get to know her grandfather while she can. But underneath there was such horror that . . . if a young woman commits the crime of leaving a child, without the wailing, the weeping, the wringing of the hands that make it, almost, an act within nature (as the writers of Victorian melodrama understood very well) then everything will be unnatural, horror will remain unreleased, and of course Martha "behaving sensibly," as it was *her* nature to do, must run into a pretty little girl of three, five, six, seven years old at her mother's house and hear, "There's Auntie Matty!"

"Are you my auntie?"

"Yes."

A week ago, Martha was cycling past the Quests' on her way to take Jack Dobie a letter from Thomas, which described the sufferings of a village of Africans in the Zambesi Valley. Their crops had failed through drought. "No one would ever have heard of it if I hadn't been here by chance. They are dying, they say, because Nyaminyami, the River God of the Zambesi is angry with them." She had dropped in to see how her father was. On the verandah was her brother and his wife. They were already a family. A handsome fair young farmer, with a crippled hand; his plump, freckled little wife; two tiny children, one a baby. It was about five in the afternoon. "Yes, your father is awake," Mrs. Quest had said.

Martha had gone to the door of her father's room. It was half open. Silence. He was asleep? Martha had stood hesitating, on the point of not going in after all. Then she heard the old man's voice, "It's my hand, it's my hand, it's my hand." It was a fierce hungry whisper. Then, while Martha chilled to the rapaciousness of the old man's voice, a child's voice said, polite and firm, "No, Granddad, it's my hand. It's mine."

Martha had taken a step forward, already disgusted—no, that was not the word, appalled, though she did not know why the scene she was going to see would be terrible. Perhaps it was that the child's voice, the cold correctness of it, the politeness, was the voice of common sense—which was the mask for all this horror. "It's nice for the little girl to get to know her grandfather." "Are you my auntie?" "No, it's not your hand, Granddad, it's mine."

Martha saw the old man, not only sitting up in bed, which he had not had strength to do for weeks, but sitting up and forward away from the pillows. His shoulders slumped with weakness, but the sick white face was clenched with purpose. The hand, bone merely, a skeleton's hand with thin folds of flesh loose on it, was gripped around the plump fresh arm of the little girl.

Caroline wore a pretty pink dress. She was a charming little creature, with her black eyes, her black curls, and she sat perched high on the bed, one brown leg under her, the other down, so that a bare brown foot was propped on the fat neck of the little white dog, who devotedly crouched by the bed, waiting for her to come and play. She sat like a little queen, her delicious brown foot on the fat white dog, and Martha saw how she teased the dog, rubbing the folds of fat back and forth over his neck with her toes. She had kept the dog by her, by tantalizing him with her foot, while she had sat politely on the bed "getting to know" her grandfather. Meanwhile the old dog rolled up its eyes in ecstasy, shivering and groaning. Caroline was very pale. She sat up straight. Her mouth was slightly open. She breathed irregularly, staring at six inches' distance into the face of the old sick man. She tried to bend her head back as far as it would go, without seeming to. There was a look of disgust on the fresh little face. The room smelled of sickness, a thick sweet cloying smell, the smell of death.

Mr. Quest had hold of the child's arm and was saying fiercely, "It's my hand, it's my hand."

"No, it isn't, Grandfather, I've told you already, it's mine."

"It's my hand, it's my hand."

And he clumsily slid his hand towards him along the plump forearm of the little girl, afraid she might wrench it away from him. Now he was gripping the wrist tight with his right hand. Then, balancing himself upright with difficulty, he laid his left hand on the crumpled sheet beside the imprisoned hand, which Martha could see was beginning to redden and swell. He stared at the white bony hand, which was damp with sweat, and at the little girl's hand.

"It's my hand," he muttered, "yes it is."

"Oh no, Grandfather," said Caroline decidedly, in the high clear tones of a well-brought-up little girl. But there was "charm" in that voice, too—Martha could hear, behind the cool self-sufficiency of this voice, the murmuring self-effacement of the two women, the Talbots, mother and daughter. "Oh no, really, Grandpa, it's my hand, of course it is."

Martha stepped forward. Mr. Quest and Caroline heard her. Mr. Quest raised his eyes, from which water flowed weakly down his cheeks. His mouth was open, his lips trembled. And Caroline's face was sharp with relief.

"Here's Auntie Matty!" she exclaimed.

But the old man had forgotten he still held the child's wrist in a circle of bone. She tugged, hard, and he swayed back and forth, then she said, "Granddad! You're hurting!" "Oh, dear," he muttered, and let go. Caroline leaped off the bed, rubbing her wrist, her face a mask of fear and revulsion. In a moment the little girl and her attendant dog had whirled from the room in a din of yapping and cries of "Down Kaiser, down Kaiser, down!"

Martha gently laid the old man back on his pillows. Tears ran down his face. "I don't want to die, I don't want to die," he muttered. He held up that hideous object, his hand, and looked at it, his lips trembling. He let it drop with a grimace of shame and pain. "I don't want to die, I haven't lived yet, I don't want to die."

Martha sat by the bed, thinking not of her father, but of the child: how would she remember that scene?

"Shhh, Father," she murmured mechanically, her mind on Caroline, who at that moment rushed past the windows with the leaping, yapping little dog—"pretty little girl in a sunlit garden," yes, she could be described like that, felt like that. The child's face was concentrated on the business of holding up a stick for the dog to leap up at. But she raised her eyes and encountered Martha's eyes. Martha dreaded this look, which they exchanged, often. There was knowledge in it, a sharp almost cynical knowledge. There was a sharp knowledgeable quality in the little face, and even now, as she ran away among the flowering bushes, there was a look on it of fear, Martha was certain of it.

Mr. Quest whimpered, with shut eyes.

Then he said, in an effort which clenched the muscles of his face and neck, "It's so shameful, it's so humiliating . . ." His head fell sideways, his mouth fell open. He was, apparently, asleep. Martha sat by him in silence. The smell in the room was so strong, she felt it cling to her clothes, damp and thick, like a fog.

Soon Mrs. Quest came in.

"May, May, May . . ."

"What is it, dear?"

"I don't want to die."

"But we all have to die some time, dear." Mrs. Quest sounded brisk, efficient. She was bustling around the room, tidying it up. The dog had brought in a bit of stick, and Caroline's jersey lay on a chair.

"Yes, but I don't want, I don't want."

"We'll meet again in Heaven, I keep telling you that."

Mrs. Quest, revived by the presence of her son, stood smiling by the window, looking into the garden where Caroline stood holding up the stick for the dog to jump at.

"Yes, but how do we know?" said Mr. Quest fretfully.

Mrs. Quest turned from the window and hastily tucked in the bedclothes. "Never mind," she said. "I think it's time for your medicine."

The old man whimpered, turning his head from side to side on the pillow.

"Why don't you give me an injection, put me out of my misery? You'd do it for a dog," he said.

"We can't do that," said Mrs. Quest.

Briefly, Martha and Mrs. Quest looked at each other, with guilt. Every one of the family, Martha knew, had gone to the doctor, after scenes like this, asking openly or disguisedly, as their natures dictated, if Mr. Quest could not be "given an injection." From the way the doctor took it, it was clear it was not the first time he had been asked. He had said to Martha, "If your father wants to die, all he has to do is take all the pills in one of the bottles by his bed, he knows that."

The doctor, a good man whose attendance at this interminable deathbed was more for support to the family than for the sake of the patient, showed his goodness by not being shocked, and by discussing at great length the ethics of the thing. "Putting people out of their misery," as Mrs. Quest put it. "Murder," as Martha put it.

"How do you know," said he, "that there's not a part of your father looking on all the time, watching? How would you feel, killing him?"

"That's just the point," said Martha. "If there wasn't a part of him conscious, it wouldn't matter. I sit by him and I'm afraid a part of him is awake, is conscious—and that's so terrible. . . ."

"I don't want to die, I don't want to die," muttered the old man, clinging with his hard bony fingers to his wife's hand.

"But we all have to go," she said again, looking tired and distressed now. "I'll make you a nice cup of Benger's," she added, and went off to the kitchen.

Suddenly Mr. Quest returned to himself. "I don't think I want to see any of you again," he said as crossly as his weakness would allow. "Bad enough having you day in, day out, without having to put up with you beyond the Pearly Gates as well!" Martha laughed with relief. "Laugh," he said, "laugh. Funny thing, laughing. It makes a funny noise. I never thought about it before. What's laughing *for*? Well, I don't want to hurt your feelings, but I can tell you, I could do without any of you for a hundred years or so, two hundred, if it comes to that."

And now Caroline was with her grandfather again—had been with him a couple of hours. And what disturbed Martha was this: a little girl with such a will, such self-confidence, she would not have gone in to visit the dying man unless she had wanted to. "Caroline's very fond of her grandfather," Mrs. Quest had said, in a chuckling sort of voice, that went with the normal situation: small child, grandfather.

Martha stayed in front of the keys, refusing to go in. Suppose he sat there again, gripping the child's wrist and saying: It's mine, it's mine, clinging on to the last breath of life, even at the cost of any dignity or pride? And, worse: suppose Caroline sat there willingly, suppose she teased the old man with her freshness, her self-confidence, just as she teased the little dog? Or sat there out of curiosity, or wished the nearness of death?

Outside was a steady spattering sound of falling water: the sprinkler was on, and water flung out in great arching sprays. Martha shut her eyes and listened—water, water falling, water. Somewhere was water, was rescue, was the sea. In this nightmare she was caught in, in which they all were caught, they must remember that outside, somewhere else, was light, was the sound of water breaking on rocks. Somewhere lay shores where waves ran in all day with a jostling rush like horses racing. Somewhere long fresh blue horizons absorbed ships whose decks smelled of hot salt.

Martha opened her eyes. Under a deep blue sky, a flowering white bush glittered with fresh water. There were blue gulfs where white foam fell and dissolved in a hissing toss of water. Somewhere, outside this tall plateau where sudden hot rains, skies of brass, dry scents, dry wastes of grass imprisoned its creatures in a watchful tension like sleeplessness, somewhere hundreds of miles away, the ground fell, it slid to the sea. And one day (only a few months away, incredibly) Martha would quite simply, just as if this were a natural act, natural to her, that is, who had never done it, stand on a shore and watch a line of waves gather strength and run inwards, piling and gathering high before falling over into a burst of white foam. Soon. White flowers tossing against a blue sky. White foam dying in a hissing gulf of blue. White birds spreading their wings against blue, blue depths.

Meanwhile, Martha could not sleep. Meanwhile, Mrs. Quest's face had increasingly the reddened sullen look of a creature driven so far beyond its strength she had forgotten what strength was. Meanwhile, the old man lay, whimpering in his cage of decaying swelling flesh. Meanwhile, the little girl came into the room where Martha sat and said, "Is Granddad your father?"

"Yes, he is."

"Then how can you be my auntie?"

Caroline did not sit down, but skipped about the room, and stood on one foot while she swung the other foot, and clapped her hands back and forth, first behind her, then in front of her—did everything but actually look at Martha, who sat still and said nothing. Of course, "the situation" demanded she should tell some suitable lie. If Mrs. Quest had been here, the lie would have been forthcoming. As it was, Martha said nothing, watched Caroline hopping on one foot carefully along the edge of the rug, and thought how extraordinary it was that six years before, when she had left this child, she had actually said, and believed it, meant it, felt it to be true: One day she'll thank me for setting her free. What on earth had she meant by it? How could she have said it, thought it, felt it? Yet, leaving the child, it had been her strongest emotion: I'm setting Caroline free.

Here was Caroline, her face sharp with tension, *not* looking at Martha, having as good as asked, "Are you my mother?"

As Martha said nothing, Caroline dropped into a chair, drew her two brown knees up under her chin, and looked long and steadily at Martha, who looked back, steadily. Then Caroline put out her tongue at Martha, and ran out of the room shouting, "Kaiser, Kaiser, Kaiser, where is my pooh-dog?"

Martha left the keys on the table, and went to find her mother, who was sorting great piles of linen in the bathroom. Mr. Quest's sheets had to be changed several times a day.

"I don't think Caroline ought to be allowed in Father's room."

Mrs. Quest did not hear, or so it seemed, so Martha repeated it.

"Well anyway, it can't be long now, the doctor said it was a matter of days."

"But, Mother, it's been like this for years."

"No, not really—anyway, that's what he says." And at Martha's look: "What do you know about it! You aren't nursing him all the time."

"Well, I must run along."

"Can't you stay for supper?"

"No."

"Well, you never can, can you?"

"I've been here all afternoon."

"It's quite natural young people haven't got time for their parents, these days," said Mrs. Quest, almost automatically, as she folded a sheet together by holding its middle down to her upper chest with her chin, and bringing its two sides in from outstretched hands to meet at arm's length in front.

"Can I help you do that?"

"I've done it by myself long enough, haven't I?"

Martha went off. She had to visit Solly. The situation there was, if possible, even more ridiculous than before.

On the afternoon three months before when he had asked Marjorie to get everyone together, he had turned up with an African no one had ever seen. But it was after everyone had gone—there was only Marjorie, locking up.

Who was this new African, where was Mr. Zlentli?—Marjorie had demanded—fierce, much too aggressive, because she was annoyed at Solly's being late. Solly had been evasive, then abusive, about Mr. Zlentli. Mr. Zlentli was nothing but a power-loving politician, said Solly; and the silent African with him had nodded his head.

Marjorie had gone running around to Jack Dobie, Martha, Mrs. Van, Johnny Lindsay. They felt something was very wrong—"even more wrong than usual," as Mrs. Van said. They had temporized and made excuses when the new African, Mr. James, had said he was the head of a new and powerful political party and that Mr. Zlentli was a back number.

Wisely, as it turned out. For since then, things had been pieced together as follows: Solly had quarrelled with Mr. Zlentli, long before Martha's meeting with him. Solly had begun another "study group" of his own. But the shifts of power and politics among the rival African groups had brought Solly and Mr. Zlentli together again, about a year ago. A great strike or demonstration had been planned, not once, but several times, and each time, something had happened to prevent it—once the message from "down South," through Jasmine Cohen.

Mr. Zlentli had been, for a time, acknowledged leader of all the submovements and groupings among the Africans.

But a new leáder had recently appeared (not Mr. James) in another city. Solly had written to this man, and offered to work with him. Mr. Zlentli, regarding this as betrayal, had quarrelled with Solly. Then Mr. Zlentli became allied with the new man, and Solly found himself suddenly out in the cold, because Mr. Zlentli said he was unreliable.

The man who came with Solly to the office, Mr. James, was a small merchant of some kind, and as far as they were able to make out had no following. He was Solly's man, Solly's creation.

What it amounted to was this: Solly had mishandled things so that he had lost all credit he had ever had with the real African movements, and now he was falling back on what remained of the white Left group to help him. Meanwhile Martha had written to Joss, who was still "up North," to find out what he knew of his brother, and Joss had written a mysterious letter back to the effect that great things were being planned for a few months ahead, but he was not in a position to tell them more. This letter had been brought by a silent smiling African who had handed it to Marjorie and gone away.

Solly had been pestering Marjorie and Martha with letters and telephone calls: why wouldn't they and Jack Dobie and Mrs. Van —above all, Mrs. Van, support Mr. James (this was just a pseudonym, of course they must realize that, his real name was Noah Kitinga), who was at that moment organizing a strike. This letter had come by ordinary mail, and Martha was going to see Solly and tell him not to be so foolish.

Martha cycled towards him reluctantly. She could imagine every word of the interview that would take place—imagine his anger, her placatory remarks, her warnings about the mail, his accusations of her, of them all. She would almost certainly lose her temper—she looked forward to losing it. They would quarrel.

But she had to do it, because Marjorie was in bed with flu—if it was indeed flu, and not, as Marjorie herself said it was, a neurotic protest against her way of life. Whatever it was, running around of any sort had been forbidden by the doctor. She was worn out, he said, and she had quite enough to do with the four children and her husband. Martha had promised Marjorie to do any running around for her. There was no escape for Martha until she could go to England, that's what it amounted to.

3

One evening the radio remarked in the unemphatic, almost affable voice which unfolds history in our bloody times, that there was going to be a national strike for a period not yet determined, but probably for some weeks; organized by a strike committee in (the authorities thought) not this city but another one; and that the identities of the strike leaders were not known. This news was received in a silence reverberating with what had not been said. After all, for how many years had these people talked of the Kaffirs rising and throwing the whites into the sea; of murders, blood baths, throat slittings, rape and arson. The discrepancy between fantasy and the tone of the announcer was an insult in itself. The hostility towards their own authorities which characterized the white people during that strike started from the moment they heard the bland voice of the announcer. He was white, yes, but he was part of the government, because everyone near authority was; and Government "as usual" was not handling things right.

The note of farce, of grotesque improbability—the characteristic of every event in that unfortunate country—was struck from the very first moment.

On this evening Martha was talking to Mrs. Van, who had telephoned immediately after the news, when sounds of anger came from the next verandah, where Mrs. Huxtable berated her servant.

"Well, Jack," Martha heard, as Mrs. Van said, "Matty, have you heard the news?"—"and what have you got to say for yourself, that's what I want to know!"

Martha had not seen any of her friends for some time because of her father's death, and her grief over Thomas's death. She was out of touch and prepared to accept the admonishing note in Mrs. Van's voice: "I hope you're not busy with anything important, I'm going to need help."

"Of course, Mrs. Van."

"What's your dear friend Solly up to?"

"But why Solly? He's just an idiot."

From the verandah: "Missus? What are you saying, missus?"

"Yes, but that brother of his, Joss, is up to all sorts of things. I had a man from Northern Province in last week, and he was telling me about a white man called Cohen. A good clever baas, he said. Well, that couldn't possibly be Solly, so it must be Joss."

"After all we've done for you," came Mrs. Huxtable's aggrieved voice from the verandah.

"I think the citizens are all likely to be very hysterical," observed Martha. "They've started already."

"Quite so. And that's why we must find out what's going on soon. Get hold of Solly, find out from him what his brother's doing, and let me know."

Before telephoning Solly, Martha went to her verandah. Mrs. Huxtable, a plump female in a cocktail dress of black crepe that showed a fat creased neck and the backs of fat red arms, was standing on her verandah, and in front of her stood her cook, arms down by his sides, looking puzzled.

"I would never have believed it," went on Mrs. Huxtable. As one time-honoured phrase followed another, each as predictable as those used in the parent-child confrontation scene which this so much resembled, her voice rose, sharpened, was weighted with the consciousness of her betrayal.

As for him, he was beginning to understand this was not a question of dust on the furniture.

"But, missus, what have I done?"

"You stand there, butter wouldn't melt, but all the time you are planning to cut our throats, yes, I can see it in your eyes, don't think I don't know what you're thinking."

"Hau!" protested the man, suddenly angry, his anger carrying the scene into dignity at a stroke. "What is this? Have I not done your work? Why do you say such things to me?"

Small hedges separated the garden of this house from the gardens on either side. People came out on to verandahs, or went down on their lawns to get a better view. The angry housewife and the angry servant were like people on a stage.

"I have always known that one day this is how you would repay us. Always!" said Mrs. Huxtable, her eyes raised to the sky.

"Here I stand," said the man. "You say these things to me and my heart feels sorrow because of your words. But not once have you told me what it is you hold in your heart against me."

"It's not only you, you cheeky thing," said Mrs. Huxtable, sinking back to the ridiculous, "it's the whole lot of you. Well, I'll promise you something, the Government'll have the troops out any minute, then watch out, that'll teach you."

"That's right," came a violent voice from across the street. "They all need a good hiding to make them come to their senses."

The man glanced quickly around: across the street, women with their arms akimbo, glaring at him—people glaring through hedges. He understood, because of the word troops, that something was happening he knew nothing about. He turned and walked away, fast. He was frightened.

"Ever hear such a thing, strike," said one of the women. "Who do they think they are?"

"They can't keep a house clean, and they think they know how to run a strike."

"Enough to make a cat laugh, I don't think."

"I'm going to get out my old man's revolver—they'll get what's coming to them."

And so on. As usual.

Meanwhile, Martha rang Solly. He was, as he pointed out, roaring with laughter.

"Well, enjoy yourself. But what's happening?"

"Search me. Why don't you ask Joss?"

"How can we? Has he got anything to do with this?"

"Why should I tell you, Comrade Matty?"

"For past services. What's happened to that man—your protégé?"

"He's in jail. Pass offences."

"And Mr. Zlentli—working away, I suppose?"

"No, they deported him last week. He was from Nyasaland."

"Ah." Martha waited. Nothing. "You really don't know?"

"All I know is about a dozen men were taken to various borders by lorry and dumped over, a couple of weeks ago—including all my contacts."

"Luckily they haven't dumped the right ones, from the look of it."

"That is a matter of opinion."

"Well, thanks for all your help."

"Any time."

Martha telephoned Mrs. Van, and went to stand on her verandah. In a few moments, the target drew arrows. Mrs. Huxtable, then another woman, then several, came to accuse Martha, the "Red," of personally and collectively fomenting the strike. "This is what comes of putting ideas into their heads, etc., etc."

"If it's not the Reds, it's the Communists," said one woman.

"And why aren't the troops here yet?" asked another.

"But what do you want troops for?" said Martha.

"My boy has run away," said Mrs. Huxtable.

"So has mine. His blankets are gone from his room."

The women agitatedly went off to see after their servants. Shrill voices up and down the street. Groups of white youths were observed gathering on the street corners. A white man came striding down the street shouting: "Vigilantes. Vigilantes. Anyone interested, come to the Sports Club, five o'clock." The white youths drifted after him, some of them shouting: "Vigilantes! Vigilantes!"

The women came back and stood about on their verandahs and lawns complaining that their servants had mostly run away. Later it was discovered that in the first few hours, many Africans had simply run off into the veld and prepared themselves to sit out any trouble there. Very sensibly as it turned out.

Soon Anton came in. His news was that the Africans on the railways were not coming to work next day. An announcement had been made to this effect. Everything was being done correctly, except that it was illegal to strike, illegal to belong to trade unions or to form them. The strike leaders remained invisible. It was rumoured among the white railway workers that the strike was well prepared, that the black workers had been warned against agents provocateurs; that the air of the Africans going off work this evening had been reassuringly calm. The white workers, in their roles as whites, had been alarmed and indignant. In their roles as workers, they had been impressed, and had even wished their black colleagues good luck as they went off.

Nothing like this had been seen in the Colony's seventy years of "history"—that is, of white occupation.

Before Anton had even sat down for a drink, the telephone rang. It was the Forsters, who were perturbed about the news, and needed Anton's presence. They suggested that Martha should come too, which could only mean they felt everyone was in the grip of a frightful emergency. "Getting all the women and children together under one roof," said Martha, bad-tempered. Anton said, "They mean to be kind, Matty," and departed to the Forsters.

The telephone rang again: the exchange at Dilingwe, in the Yani Valley. Mrs. Quest had booked a call to Mrs. Hesse, but the lines were jammed with calls, would Mrs. Hesse hold on? Martha held on, and waited for her mother's voice.

Mrs. Quest was now an old lady living in her son's house on a remote farm among mountains a hundred miles or so south of the Zambesi escarpment. Living on the Quest farm she had thought this must be the furthest possible point of the journey away from her beginnings in the tall Victorian house in South London. But she had been wrong. The mountains she now lived among were those glimpsed sometimes from the Quests' old house after rain had washed the skies clean. Far mountains moved nearer in a pure air; they opened, and between them appeared distant hilly valleys usually invisible; and beyond them again, rose faint blue sunlit peaks. No one lived up *there*, it wasn't settled yet. But it was settled now by, among others, young Jonathan Quest and his family.

Mrs. Quest came back from the funeral to the big house which now had in it herself, a cook, a house servant, a gardener, and a small boy for the odd jobs. And the little white dog. For years Mrs. Quest had run things, managed things, arranged and planned and organized. She had kept her husband alive long after anyone else could—so the doctor had told her, over and over again. Now here she sat, an old lady on a verandah with a little dog on her lap. It had happened from one day to the next.

It seemed she had not foreseen it. She had not really understood, when she talked year after year of "in my old age" just what that would mean.

For years and years now, Mrs. Quest had not been allowed to be more than a physical being. And now, suddenly, there was nothing for her to do. No matter how one put it, looked at it, glossed it over, that was the truth. There she sat, a vigorous old woman in the middle of a great garden which she must leave; and Martha watched how her limbs strove and wrestled with enforced inactivity. Mrs. Quest would suddenly *find* herself on her feet—her physical memory had told her legs that it was time for her husband's wash or his medicine—and she would be halfway to the kitchen or the bathroom before she had understood it was years of habit which she must fight, subdue, change. She would return to her chair by Martha, her hands slowly twisting together, her eyes staring sullenly in front of her. Then she said, "This won't do, will it!" Martha and she lit cigarettes. A minute later she would be off down the verandah towards the kitchen on some errand for the dead man. Catching herself out she would stop, and pretend to be attending to a plant on the verandah. Or she called to the servant, "Make tea for two, Jonah!" She came back saying, "He can't really hear me from this end of the verandah." She sat, slowly, trying to smile, while her eyes lowered themselves to hide their fear, their distress. What was she going to do with herself? How to use all her knowledge, her energy, her flair, and above all, the sudden explosion of old needs which was bound to make itself felt now when at last the braces were taken off Mrs. Quest's real nature—which was gay, and kind and sociable?

Day after day, and still day after day, the two women sat on the verandah, smoking, while Mrs. Quest looked (not too clear-sightedly yet, the truth was too painful to face) into her future as a guest in

other people's houses. And Martha sat, fearful, because she knew
her mother would now want to share her life. But Martha was going
to England. "Perhaps I'll come to England and live with you," Mrs.
Quest kept saying, with a painful laugh, her eyes not meeting
Martha's. And Martha would say, as uncomfortably and falsely,
"But I'm not there yet!"

Meanwhile, the practical things were being done by Jonathan,
who arranged for the sale of the big useless house and the garden,
that fruit of Mrs. Quest's frustration, which would add, so the agent
said, hundreds on to the sale price. It was suggested that Mrs.
Quest should go and stay a while with the family in the mountains.
The daughter-in-law needed help with her babies. Mrs. Quest
listened to this invitation smiling drily; she knew just how much
the young wife would welcome the arrival of a masterful old woman.
But she packed her things and went. Standing on the verandah of
the house from where, only a few weeks ago, they had taken the
body of Mr. Quest for what she had insisted was his last sleep, looking around the magnificent scented garden with the little white
dog clutched to her chest by one arm, the other holding a parcel
full of toys for her son's children, she had seemed to Martha like
a defiantly brave small girl.

At last Jonathan's voice sounded, not Mrs. Quest's. He said
irritably that if the townspeople wanted to take all this sort of
nonsense seriously, then it was their affair, but all his Kaffirs were
working, and if they weren't still at work tomorrow, then they'd
know what to expect. Anyway, ignorant savages, they had not heard
there was a strike on, and how could they, since there was no radio
for miles, except in the Quests' house, and he, Jonathan would personally see to it that the newspapers never got into the hands of
servants who might spread the news to the compound. But he knew
better than to expect Martha and her ilk to behave as sensibly. Mrs.
Quest then came on to speak. She was worried about the house, not
yet sold, and standing empty. She felt it was in danger of being
looted or burned down. "Not that it's likely," said Mrs. Quest. "They
aren't capable of doing a good day's work, let alone running a
revolution."

"But, Mother," said Martha, hearing the flat, almost jolly sound of
her voice with disquiet at the ineffectiveness of common sense in
time of public emotion, "this isn't a revolution, it's just a strike."

"What? Oh, I see. You know what I mean, dear, and I do want
you to go up and see if everything's all right."

Martha promised she would look at the house, decided she would
do nothing so absurd—but, of course, went.

At the gate she looked into a garden which was already an overgrown solitude claimed by birds. Willing herself to walk up the path, and into the house, she found herself, instead, creeping like a trespasser through the garden and around the outside of the house. On tiptoe in the overgrown flower bed, she looked in at the room where Mrs. Quest had nursed her husband. Now it was an empty room with a forgotten wooden chair lying on the floor. It was a small room. There was a brown stain on the discoloured wall. Well, so it was just an empty room now, and people would soon buy the house and the room would be used as a bedroom again, perhaps even as a nursery—and no one would know the horrors that had gone on here. But supposing, she asked herself, against the surge of angry protest that must accompany any thought of her father—suppose that had been no worse than what went on in any room, long enough built? No, no, no, please God, that was not true, it couldn't be. . . . Martha went nearer, actually clambered on to the windowsill, sat on it. She hoped that a mouse might appear from the floor and run over the boards, or a spider let itself down from the ceiling—something alive. But nothing. All around the silent house the garden rang, shrilled, clamoured with birds. Outside the garden moved hot noisy traffic. Martha had not been with her father when he died. (Well, of course not! said Martha's bitter inner commentator.) Mrs. Quest, telephoning to say that Mr. Quest could not possibly last till morning, had caught Martha undressing for bed. She had dressed again, actually thinking: If I don't of course it will be tonight that he decides to die, it's *exactly* the sort of thing . . . Then Marjorie arrived, with a letter from Thomas's wife saying that Thomas had died of blackwater in the Zambesi Valley. The Africans of the tribe had done their best for the white man who had so inexplicably chosen to live with them—which is what it amounted to: Thomas had been staying in the same village for six months. They had been good to him, but anyway he was dead. (Well, of course! said the uselessly savage commentator—what else had he been wanting but to die, futilely, away from his own people, and among strangers.) Martha had not gone to her mother that night. Instead she sat with Thomas's wife's letter in her hand, not thinking about Thomas—for what was there to think? And not crying over him either. And she certainly was not able to hear what he said.

When Martha went to her mother's house, Mr. Quest had become a grey brushed elderly gentleman lying with closed eyes in a shaded room. His face was very white, and so were his thin, thin hands. At first the room was horribly silent, but then a fly buzzed about, and kept settling on the pillow beside Mr. Quest's head. Mrs. Quest and

Martha chased the fly out, after a good deal of trouble, then it was really quiet, and they stood on either side of the dead man, looking at him. They felt something should be said, for the other's sake; but they could not think of anything. They embraced awkwardly, and a futile irritation entered them both. Soon they went to sit on the verandah.

Mr. Quest had lain after his death only twenty-four hours in this room, before the undertaker had borne him away in a neat coffin with a silver cross on it. They had stood flowering branches about the room and thrown scented water into the air to cool it. At one point a small girl in a pink dress had stood in neat white shoes and white socks beside the dead man and said, "Is that my grandfather?" Her face had a look of polite, disapproving curiosity on it and she had turned and gone willingly away on Mrs. Quest's hand.

Now the room was empty, the house was empty, and the garden was particularly and unbelievably empty, and Martha kept looking for a pink-frocked small girl who might be playing there with a white dog.

She walked back home through the deep avenues where every window and door let shafts of light fall across gardens, where women stood on the verandahs, waiting for something to happen, where the youths hung about on the street corners, their faces sharpened by willing suspicion.

At home Marjorie and Mrs. Van were waiting for her. But first Martha telephoned her mother to say the house had been visited, and everything was all right. Then she added her person to the forces of common sense and reason—Mrs. Van with a look of calm purpose on her face, her hands folded, thinking aloud; Marjorie with a pencil and some paper, ready to take down the results of such thoughts. It was a question, said Mrs. Van, of deciding what was the right thing to do, and doing it quickly. The white people were all quite crazy already; and if the Government did not do something soon, there would be bloodshed . . . at which point Anton telephoned from the West suburb where, he said, there was panic. An African delivering a parcel to an unfamiliar house had been observed standing on the back verandah with "a very funny look on his face." The daughter of the house, a friend of the Forsters' youngest daughter, had lost her head and set her dogs on the man. They had torn open an arm, and the parcel, revealing a newly altered dress. But the man's explanation that he had been looking for the servants to give the parcel to did nothing to mollify. The houseboys had run away, said the girl, she was alone in the house, how did she know he was not part of the plot? She had telephoned the Forsters in tears; they had gone by car to fetch her. They also brought the African. He had his bitten arm bound up in the kitchen, while he was told it was "all his fault anyway, for going on strike." At which he asked, what was a strike? The Forsters' kitchen was full of neighbours who wanted to start Citizens' Protection Committees. "But it's quite all right, there's no need to lose our heads," Anton kept saying loudly, in the avuncular voice which went with his role in the West suburb.

"But perhaps it isn't all right," Martha said. "Mrs. Van says she saw a group of white schoolboys beating up a black man outside her house. Next, someone's going to be killed."

"If the good woman had any sense . . ." (In the Forster household, dislike of the socialist Mrs. Van was expressed thus, and Anton had adopted the phrase.) "If the good woman has any sense, she'll see that the Town Council takes steps."

"Which steps?" said Martha. "The good woman is here. Perhaps you'd like to give her instructions." She was angry because she knew his tone and the words were for the benefit of people listening to Anton.

"Now now now," said Mrs. Van, while Marjorie smiled. "There's a time and a place for matrimonial tiffs," said Mrs. Van, with her emphatic nod.

"If you analyze the situation," said Anton, "you'll see the danger is the whites." His voice had lost the false geniality of the last remark, and Martha said, "Oh, you're alone again, good."

"Precisely so, so listen . . . but not now."

"Damn," said Martha.

"The authorities should see that they are all locked up in the Locations for a few days," he went on, but with a tone that told Martha he meant what he said, even if the words were being chosen for other ears.

"Well," said Martha, "all the same, it's hard to know whether this is brilliant strategy or merely the future son-in-law speaking."

"Matty!" said Mrs. Van, crossly.

"But if the authorities want to take reprisals, how convenient to have them all locked up," said Martha.

He said, "Yes, yes, but there are other factors."

"Or are you saying it is the lesser of the two evils?"

"Taking all the factors into consideration, the sooner they are locked up the better."

"Is there any chance of you being alone in the next few minutes, if so I'll just go on talking."

"No, it doesn't look like it."

"Well, it's very annoying."

"There is information to the effect that there are strike committees in each township. The strike leaders have instructed all the Africans to stay in their houses tomorrow."

"Oh."

"The townships are full of speechmakers and agitators of all sorts."

"Oh, I see."

"Yes, that is the position."

"Well, I'll tell Mrs. Van all this."

"And are you going to spend the night with Mrs. Van der Bylt?" enquired Anton, the sentimental note returning to his voice. "I hope you are looking after yourself."

"Oh, damn it," said Martha. "Do stop. Oh, very well, tell them that I am, if it's going to make a good impression, why should I care!"

Martha transmitted information to Mrs. Van, who received it with the comment that it was a pity personal emotions could not be kept out of politics.

The telephone again: Mr. Van der Bylt, in search of his wife: Mrs. Maynard was "in full cry," he said, and waiting for her in the drawing room. Mrs. Van said to the two young women, "You two had better come with me—if there are any errands to be run, you'll be useful."

They fell in behind Mrs. Van.

Mrs. Maynard was waiting on the verandah. The two formidable matrons did not bother to exchange politenesses. They stood facing each other, Mrs. Maynard, from force of habit, picking dead leaves from a creeper that grew on a verandah similar to her own, Mrs. Van der Bylt twirling the car keys around her forefinger.

"In my opinion," said Mrs. Maynard, "they ought all to be locked up in the townships at once."

"I think I agree with you," said Mrs. Van.

"You do?" said Mrs. Maynard, surprised.

The Van der Bylts' houseboy now arrived on the verandah, agitated out of his usual manners. "Madam," he said to Mrs. Van, "there's a man in the kitchen. He says I've got to go to the Location, madam."

"Oh poor things, isn't it dreadful!" said Mrs. Maynard.

"Then you must go, he is a picket," said the socialist Mrs. Van.

"A picket?" said the servant. "But I do not think he is a good man."

Mrs. Van turned towards him, and opened her mouth—probably about to launch into a history of trade unionism. But she relinquished this pleasure, and instructed Martha and Marjorie to "go into the kitchen and explain why he has the duty to go on strike."

Marjorie and Martha accompanied the bewildered man to the kitchen, and heard Mrs. Van say, "I suggest you and I sit down and have a quiet drink to celebrate the first time in our careers that we have agreed on a course of action without quarrelling about it." She sounded amused, but Mrs. Maynard certainly was not, "Oh, my dear!" the young women heard her exclaim, "I'm glad you can joke. It is at moments like these I remember what a powder keg we live in. And of course everything could be handled so easily if only people would keep their heads. All one needs is to deport a dozen or so of the ringleaders and throw trouble makers into prison. But no, people have to run around shouting about guns and Citizens' Committees. So annoying."

"However that might be, I suggest . . ."

The drawing-room door shut on the two generals.

The young women now confronted Mrs. Van's houseboy and her cook who had been with her, as she claimed proudly like any conventional white mistress, for forty years. There were also two little black boys and an old man who was a gardener. Marjorie began, "Now, it's like this, do you know what a strike is?"

"No, madam."

"Then I'll explain. That man who has just been here is called a picket. I'll tell you what that means."

"Wait a minute, missus." One of the little boys was sent running to the hedge; in a minute the servants from next door had arrived. Soon, twenty or so Africans, with two nurse girls, were in the Van der Bylt kitchen; a sort of informal meeting was in progress. The man from the strike committees had reappeared, and stood morosely vigilant at the back of the room, neither nodding nor disagreeing with what Marjorie, then Martha, said. Finally the servants said, "Thank you," or shook their heads doubtfully, and began drifting off towards the Locations. "You had better take some food with you, just in case," said Marjorie, out of some kind of inspired insight. Mrs. Van's cook, a dignified old man, said, "I go only because my madam tells me to go. I think this is a wicked, wicked thing, and I do not understand it. God will forgive me."

Eventually a group of about thirty men and five women, who were children's nannies, set off down the street with the picket walking behind like a jailer. The dignified cook went first, leading a small boy by the hand, and carrying some bread and fruit tied into a large checked cloth.

Marjorie and Martha found Mrs. Maynard energetically telephoning; while Mrs. Van sat sipping orangeade. Mrs. Van allowed herself a small wink at her two aides. Mrs. Maynard was saying, "Yes, I'm sure of it! There's not a moment to lose!"

It was now getting on towards midnight, and certain orders must be got out: it was a question of getting other people to give certain orders. And tomorrow's newspaper was being held up from the printer's on the suggestion of a friend of Mrs. Van who knew the editor.

Calls had been made by Mrs. Maynard to Government House, to the Prime Minister's wife, to the houses of various Ministers—these calls were, of course, quite informal and could never appear in any log book, minute book, or record. And Mrs. Van had telephoned, on a lower social level, but perhaps more immediately effectively, to all kinds of officials and organizations.

It appeared that, "They are all bone-stupid, but they'll get the point in time," as Mrs. Maynard said.

She sat down again, sweeping out a large hand, palm upwards, in a grateful gesture towards her old rival, "My dear, what a relief it is to have a sensible person like you beside one, at a moment like this."

Marjorie and Martha, exchanging glances, interpreted the situation as one which would be pleased to be rid of the possibility of their ironical comments on it. They said good night, as Mr. Van, palely courteous as always, came into the drawing room saying, "Well, ladies, I gather there's the spirit of unrest abroad?"

"Typical," said Marjorie, as the two young women separated to go to their homes. "When something *does* happen at last, where are we? Running around with Mrs. Van and that awful Maynard female, and giving lectures on trade unionism to house servants."

The avenues were quiet, but the street Martha lived in had groups of people sitting behind darkened windows, looking out. Presumably they had guns. As Martha approached her house, a young man with a gun bulging the khaki of his trousers stepped forward from under a tree where a group of young men had set themselves on guard. He said, "Excuse me, but I'm warning you, it's not safe to walk around alone at night." "Oh, don't be so damned silly," she said, noting that she sounded as dictatorial as Mrs. Van, but they were all too far gone in their fantasies of heroism to understand this was a traitor, not merely a reckless citizen.

"You get indoors quick," he said, "and don't worry, sleep tight, we'll be here standing guard all night. If the Government won't do anything then we'll have to, that's all."

Next morning the newspapers carried exhortations to keep calm and use moderation, under enormous headlines of Strike, Total Strike, National Strike, Threat, Danger, Alarm. And there was not a black face to be seen.

All the Africans were in their townships, because an order had gone forth that any African demanding admittance to a township must be let in, but that no African could be allowed out. The boundaries of the townships were patrolled by police and troops, and it was an offence for any white citizen to go near the townships. The second and third days were the same. People read the violent and exclamatory newspapers feeling expressed by them; while the radio, which continued to announce this national occasion like "a bloody old maid at a bloody tea party," caused nothing but ill-feeling. In a house near Martha's a man smashed his radio to express his emotions.

The telephones were worked overtime, not only with messages of consolation and support (white women did their own housework and looked after their own children for the first time in their lives) but for news. Which, however, tended to be the same, all over the country. When Mrs. Huxtable's cousin from the opposite end of the Colony to Jonathan Quest was telephoned he said, "All my Kaffirs are at work, they don't know what a strike is, and neither would yours if you didn't educate them to read the newspapers." Farmers everywhere were for the most part untouched. For one thing, it was hard for men to strike from farm compounds from which they could be flushed like so many birds—unless they ran away, and many did. For another, the strike committees did not have the resources to travel thousands of miles from farm to farm. No, it was an affair of the towns, and of industry, proving finally those wiseacres to be right who had said that the good Kaffirs were those who had not encountered the three R's.

Martha rang Jack Dobie: he was delighted to be able to say that all his white trade unionists were furious at the efficiencies and discipline of a strike which proved that they, the white unions, could never again refuse membership to Africans because of the black man's backwardness. "But they will, of course."

Martha was telephoned by Solly, who had left the city for a friend's house in a small town, because he was convinced he would be arrested by the authorities on account of his long career of seditious activity. He had sat waiting in his parents' home for three days with everything packed ready for prison, but nothing happened. When he reached Braksdorp, he suddenly remembered it was only thirty miles from one of the largest mines in the Colony, where the strike was total. The authorities would imagine that Solly was responsible for the striking mine workers, he thought. In which case, Martha would find, hidden under a stone urn in the Cohens' garden, a full documented account of his, Solly Cohen's, work over the last seven years for the Africans. Martha was to hand this document to a suitable lawyer. "Very well, I shall. And how's the strike with you?" "Fine. Of course, the objectives are incorrectly formulated." "Oh, how should they be formulated?" "But we can't discuss that kind of thing over the telephone, the wires are probably tapped." "In that case, your document will have been filched from under the garden urn before I can get to it." "It doesn't matter, because I've got copies of it here." "Cheer up, Solly, they'll arrest you yet. I'd do it myself to make you happy."

"*Very* funny, I don't think . . ."

On the fourth night, a telephone call from a friend of Maisie's; Maisie did not have a telephone. Martha was to come at once. Mrs. McGrew was so upset, she didn't know what to do with herself.

Martha bicycled down to Maisie's, which was no longer over the bar, but a few streets away. She had a large room in a house which supplied food. But it was more informal than a boarding house. Maisie and the little girl Rita lived in a large room off a verandah which was as large as a second room. Maisie had many parties, or rather her life was a permanent party, for she never arranged anything, people—men and women—dropped in at all hours. There were a couple of unattached women in the same house who lived the same way. And sometimes Flora came, if there was someone to sit with old Johnny. Maisie had cheap drink from the bar where she worked and the landlady let her use the kitchen as she liked. There were all the ingredients for good times. Few evenings Maisie did not bring home friends from the bar, or find them there, when she got in. Few evenings failed to prolong themselves till dawn. Maisie rose late, dawdled about, made cups of tea, did her nails, washed her hair and invented new hair styles. Meanwhile her little girl watched her. This child, who had a bed on the verandah outside the room, joined in the parties when she was awakened by the noise, got up and went to bed according to the lazy impulses of Maisie, was petted by the innumerable people who came to the house, was fed by the landlady when Maisie had a hangover. Kind gentlemen asked her for kisses and took her for drives. The granddaughter of the Maynards was leading the life of a prostitute's child. But Maisie was not a prostitute. "After all, Matty," she said, looking upset—someone had said something not very nice to her in the bar—"there's no harm in what I do. I like having men around, that's my trouble. But my rent gets paid by my wages from the bar. Sometimes one of my friends gives me a present, but I never take money. No, that's always been my greatest principle, I never take money from people." But according to report, Maisie, the most inefficient barmaid in the history of the trade, was given her high wages and allowed to be late and lazy because she attracted so much custom to the bar.

At any rate, there was Maisie—enjoying life, as she said. And there was Rita. Rita Maynard, as Martha could not help calling her, privately.

When Martha stepped off her bicycle in the big moonlit garden, which was filled with pawpaws, grenadilla vines, moonflowers, from which the verandah, filled with more plants, was separated only by a wooden trellis, the little girl Rita stood on the steps, a lighted room behind her. Rita, now six years old, looked much older. She was unfortunate physically—a great lump of a girl with heavy limbs and a thick neck. "Just like Binkie, drat him," as Maisie said. "Imagine, Matty, when Binkie and I decided to have some fun that time, we didn't even take it so seriously. I mean, it wasn't worth it, because now . . ." But she did not say in so many words Rita was not the child she would have chosen. Black-browed, self-consciously smiling, awkward, more like a ten-year-old than a child of six (Martha could not help comparing her with Caroline) Rita stood outside a door through which Martha could see Mr. and Mrs. Maynard—large, heavy, black-browed, red-faced.

They sat side by side on a sofa, and opposite them sat Maisie, languid and sulky, fanning herself with a frond of leaves. The ceiling light, dim, rather yellow (the garden outside seemed brighter with moonlight than this room) was as much a source of heat as of light.

Maisie's mother, who had been invited to come into town to help with Rita because of the lack of servants, sat smiling nervously in a corner.

Maisie looked fat and hot and distressed, but the slow movement of her white hand with the leaves in it asserted her independence. Her face was irritated, but her body, flagrant in damp blue cotton, knew they would go soon, and then her life could go on.

The room seemed full of hot stuffy shadows.

There was a sweet smell—oversweet, insistent. Unconsciously they all kept looking for the source of the smell—too much, in the airless room.

Mrs. Gale, a run-down heat-drained woman, the widow of a small mine worker in a remote town, sat holding a saucer with a blob of pink pudding in it for Rita. The pudding was melting in red and white streaks and it was this which smelled. Mrs. Gale's face had a look of distaste, while she sat conscientiously holding the saucer trying to nod and smile Rita towards her supper.

But Mrs. Gale's face was not only tired with the heat, it was strained because of her distrust of these two formidable people, the Maynards, and altogether she looked, because of her variety of expressions, as if she might either cackle with laughter, sneeze, or begin to cry. But the way she sat, the ease of it, the way her small feet in neat shoes were placed before her, the relationship between her hand and the saucer it held, came out of a different level of existence from anything in her face. Maisie and she were mother and daughter, the fat blonde woman and the greying old one were, unmistakably, the same flesh. And Maisie's irritation was probably partly due to the fact that inviting her mother here, to "show" the Maynards, very likely, how unnecessary they were to Rita, had made things worse by emphasizing, by pushing down everyone's throat, the extraordinary, fantastic, cruel facts of inheritance. For whose child was Rita? Maisie's? No. Nor was she the grandchild of Mrs. Gale. Perhaps Rita's daughter might inherit this smiling ease of the flesh, but Rita, as she stood on the verandah trying to ignore the sweet smelly pudding, smiling at her mother, examining the lady and the gentleman who were such frequent and such upsetting visitors—she was a Maynard.

What bad luck, now savage! For if the genes had not fallen so, in such a pattern, how much easier to refuse the Maynards, to send them away when they came—so unbearably often, and more and more often, separately and together. And Maisie would have forgotten Binkie, have been able to accept, perhaps, another father for Rita, than the ghost of Athen.

In Maisie's room, full of pictures of dogs, kittens and pretty ladies, there was no sign now of her dead husbands or of Binkie or of divorced Andrew. On a table all by itself, with a perky black ribbon pinned to its corner by a black-headed pin, was a Christmas card from Greece. Printed in the United States, this card had on it the picture of an Evzone, the Greek soldier in his kiltlike skirt and fancy pose. Like something out of a chorus, the Evzone smiled and said in Greek and in English: A Happy Christmas. Inside were the words: Dear Friend, Thank you for your letters to Athen. I am told to instruct you: Athen was arrested the summer he came to his home. He died of an illness in the prison. His friends Themos, Manolis, Christis Melas had illness in prison at the same time as Athen.

There was no signature to this message.

This was all Maisie or Martha or any of them ever heard in reply to their many letters to Greece. Everyone who came to Maisie's room was told about Athen. "Yes," Maisie had been heard to say, "if he hadn't got sick in prison, then I would have gone to Greece to marry him." Sometimes late at night visitors saw Maisie pick up the card: she wept, in a moment of abstraction from the party which went on around her. They looked at each other, and poured her another drink. "Cheer up, Maisie," someone would say, "tears don't bring back the dead." "You're right," she said, as she sat letting the tears dry themselves on her cheeks, "but sometimes when I think of him my sorrow gets too much."

In short, Athen was officially Maisie's dead man and now she need never marry.

When Mr. Maynard had picked up the card to enquire, "And who is this deceased gentleman?" Maisie had held out her hand for it, looking him proudly in the face. "It's nothing you would understand," she said.

The Maynards had descended on Maisie tonight because of the strike; if all the servants were locked in the townships, then Rita was without a nursemaid. "This is Mom," Maisie repeated. "This is my mom, she's here to help with Rita."

"Of course," said Mrs. Maynard, "it's asking for trouble, having the child sleeping on the verandah, and even all through the rainy season."

"I don't agree," said Maisie, and yawned.

After a moment, Maisie's mother remarked, smiling politely, but stirring the melting pink blob around and around and around, "Maisie always slept on the verandah when she was little. She said she liked to see the stars."

Mrs. Maynard let out an explosive breath that sounded like Pah!

"Surely she ought to be in bed, it's after nine," Mr. Maynard said.

"It's her bedtime when I say it is," said Maisie. Her irritation exploded in, "Mom, if Rita's going to eat that jelly, but if not, it's making me nervous."

Mrs. Gale held out the saucer to Rita, who unhappily smiled a refusal. The little girl was on the point of tears. Mrs. Gale got up and took the saucer out of the room. When she came back, she had a piece of iced pink cake, which the child began cramming fast into her mouth, making crumbs everywhere. It was evident she was hungry.

"Doesn't Rita get a proper supper?" said Mrs. Maynard.

"When you've finished that cake, Rita," Maisie said to the child, ignoring Mrs. Maynard, "you must go with Gran and have your bath."

This was not the first time Martha had been a witness of this *impasse* which, as everyone knew, would go on for years yet. She hesitated on the verandah, no one knowing she was there, for some moments. But Rita had seen her; she must go in. She smiled socially at Mrs. Maynard, nodded as coldly as she knew how at Mr. Maynard, kissed Maisie's damp hot cheek, shook Mrs. Gale by the hand. She sat beside Mrs. Gale to make a demonstration of her loyalties.

"Well, I suppose we might as well go?" enquired Mr. Maynard, of his wife, but Maisie said, "Please yourself." She sat fanning, fanning. The air from the moving frond of leaves quivered a tendril of hair on her fat neck under her ear, and shook the surface of a glass of water on the table. Globules of coloured light on the table top shook too. Rita, forgetting the grownups, was slowly drawn towards these patterns of light. She stood by her mother's knees, and put her forefinger into the light, where it dissolved into a watery gold and rose. She took out her finger—behold, there it was! She put it into the light—it was gone. She smiled with pleasure and looked up at her mother. Maisie saw what she was doing, and smiled with her.

"Look, Mommy, my finger goes away."

Rita held her finger in the magical dissolving light, and the two smiled at each other—close.

Mr. Maynard looked at his wife and rose. She slowly got to her feet. Mr. Maynard went out to the verandah, nodding at Maisie and at Mrs. Gale. "He treats Mom like a servant," Maisie complained afterwards—and snubbed him now by yawning as he went out. Mrs. Maynard, with a smile partly wistful and partly peremptory, held out her hand to the little girl with the same impulsive, open-palmed gesture she had used for Mrs. Van with the words, "a sensible person like you!" She was offering the child, so to speak, her own defencelessness. Rita kept one forefinger in the pool of quivering lights, and almost offered her hand to the tall old woman bending over her. But she glanced quickly at her mother, and put her almost friendly hand behind her back. Mr. Maynard, watching this incident from the verandah, let out a sort of bark or grunt, and said to Martha, "Martha, I'd like a word with you."

Martha glanced at Maisie, Maisie shrugged. She went on fanning, fanning. Rita now tried to climb on her mother's lap. "Oh, Rita," said Maisie, irritated; but then made herself smile as the great lump of a child clambered awkwardly up. Maisie smiled sourly at the Maynards past Rita's head; then Rita put her face down against her mother's shoulder so that she, too, could receive the cool streams of air from the waving leaves.

"Well?" said Martha. Her dislike of the Maynards kept her face rigid. But she thought that only three days ago she had been a sort of aide to Mrs. Maynard on the night the strike began. An unwilling sour smile, like Maisie's, came on to her lips; she could feel it there and could not make it go away. She knew she was smiling from fear, as Maisie did. But Maisie was honest, "They scare me so much, Matty . . ." She, Martha, did not find it easy to admit how much these people frightened her. But—Lord! to be in the hands of these people, to be at the mercy of these great charging blundering . . .

Mr. Maynard said to Martha, "It's an absurd situation, impossible!"

"How would *you* feel," demanded Mrs. Maynard.

They were appealing to her, even commanding her, Martha; they, the Maynards, feeling themselves to be in the right, as they always were, stood confronting Martha, side by side, two great, strong, heavy-jowled people in their plated armours of thick stiff cloth.

"But whose fault is it, after all?" Martha said, feebly, because she knew the futility of it.

"But, my dear . . ."

Mrs. Maynard was smiling mistily at Martha, her lips quivered, and it was clear that she felt, and would always feel, that she was the victim of cruel circumstances.

Mr. Maynard gazed past Martha into the room where mother and child sat together in the big chair. His eyes filled with tears and he turned and walked off the verandah. His wife followed, fumbling for the handkerchief which was hoisted, like a white flag, from the cuff of her sleeve.

In a moment they had been swallowed by the great car that stood waiting outside the rooming house.

"They always park it in full view, just so everyone can say: Judge Maynard's visiting Maisie again," Maisie complained continually, in frenzies of resentment and annoyance.

"Oh, my God!" said Maisie, as the Maynards disappeared; and she heaved off Rita in a convulsive movement, as if the child had been smothering her. The heavy child scrambled down, and stood smiling in embarrassment for her uncouthness at her mother.

"Oh, *God!* Christ. Damn them. Blast them. Oh, drat it! What shall I do—*oh!*" Maisie spurted tears, while she patted the child's shoulder with the hand that held the leaves. The frond caught in Rita's black hair, tickled her face and made her sneeze. Then she, too, began to cry; it was a sort of double hysteria, in relief at the Maynards going at last.

Maisie said, "I've just remembered, Matty. Those silly idiots, they made me forget what I asked you for. The thing is, my friend that rang you up got what I said wrong. I didn't want you to come here, I wanted you to telephone Mrs. Van der Bylt with a message from Flora. Flora says, she's got to see Mrs. Van der Bylt on something urgent to do with the Kaffirs and the strike. Johnny said she must tell Mrs. Van der Bylt. But Flora can't leave Johnny, he's not too good today."

"Why don't you ask Mr. Maynard to take Flora up in the car?" suggested Mrs. Gale.

"You couldn't ask the Maynards to go to Johnny's house, they'd die of shock, knowing that sort of house existed," said Maisie.

"Wait," said Martha, and she ran after the Maynards' car, which had just begun to move off. She said to Mrs. Maynard through the window, "Could you ring Mrs. Van der Bylt and tell her that her friend Johnny Lindsay has got urgent news for her? Maisie doesn't have a telephone."

"Of course Maisie doesn't have a telephone. Maisie doesn't have anything an ordinary sensible person would have," said Mrs. Maynard, nodding emphatically. But she had been crying; her great commanding face was all soft and appealing.

When Martha got back, Maisie was lying down on the bed or divan under the window which overlooked the verandah. Rita sat timidly beside her mother, smiling awkwardly, as if she were at fault, or in some way lacking. The poor little girl's size defeated her in this way too; everyone, including her mother, forgot how young she was and expected from her the reactions of a ten-year-old. Now she wanted to do something for her mother, but she did not know what.

"I shall have to get married, Matty," Maisie was saying, twisting her head from side to side. Water sparkled in the creases of her fat neck, water streamed down her red cheeks. Tendrils of her hair were matted on to the pillow. "Perhaps I should marry Jackie. But I don't want to get married."

"But, Maisie, if you did get married, what difference would that make?"

Mrs. Gale, sitting by the head of the divan, leaned over to fan her daughter. Rita sat swinging her large legs. She reached down to scratch inside a soiled white sock. She smiled apologetically, knowing in the fatal helpless pain of a clumsy child, that she was bound to irritate. And sure enough, the energetic scratch of her fingernail on bare skin sounded loudly, and Maisie said, "Oh dear, Rita—don't do that, and don't crowd me, there's a good girl, it's so hot." She hastily smiled, to soften her complaint, and Rita smiled painfully. The grandmother watched, with her sharp kind eyes, saying nothing.

She fanned Maisie, and smiled at Rita. Suddenly Rita let her head droop, under the accumulated miseries of the evening. Tears squeezed under the thick black lashes. Mrs. Gale held out her hand. Rita flung herself at her grandmother, knocking the bed and Maisie's bare arm. Too big to climb on the old woman's lap, she stood pressed against Mrs. Gale's thighs, her thick arms around her neck, blubbering loudly.

Maisie lay, her mouth half open, breathing heavily, listening to the little girl cry, to her mother's quiet, "There, girlie, there, it's so hot, that's what got into all of us." Maisie smiled resignedly at Martha, who said, "Well, I've got to go."

"There, there," said the old woman to the child. "Now don't be upset. Perhaps you'll come and stay with me in my little house in Gotwe, would you like that? Your mom'll let you come and visit your gran, and you'll like that."

"Well, it would keep the Maynards off me for a bit, that'd be something," said Maisie.

"I'll telephone Mrs. Van myself when I get home. Do you know what Flora wants to tell Mrs. Van?"

"I don't know. It seems a Kaffir got out of the Location and came to tell Johnny they were being badly treated inside. But what can Johnny do? He's on his last legs, Flora says."

Martha cycled home, telephoned Mrs. Van, was answered by Mr. Van. Yes, Mrs. Maynard had telephoned, but Mrs. Van had not come in yet. He had put a message for her on the pad.

Martha thought: Perhaps I should go down and see Flora? But because she was tired, she remembered again, "running around and about." How ridiculous, how absurd, this business of always rushing off on someone else's affairs. All over the town were people who automatically said: Ask Marjorie Black, ask Matty Hesse, if they needed anything. But nothing was changed, except that Marjorie and Martha felt important and that they understood life. Martha went to bed, and was dropping off to sleep, when Anton came in—for the first night since the strike began.

"Well?" she said. "And how is it going?"

Anton kissed her cheek, and said, "It's nice to see you, Matty." They smiled, even held hands a minute. Then he began undressing. "They are sensible people, on the whole, when things are explained to them," he said.

"Well, that's a good thing, in the circumstances."

Anton drawled humorously, "Yes, you could say that."

"Well," she said at last, "how very extraordinary everything is!"

"Yes, you could say that too."

The telephone rang. Anton answered it.

He said to Martha, "A friend of Maisie's says I must tell you that Mrs. McGrew says that Flora says she's at Maisie's. I hope that makes sense." He continued undressing.

"I suppose I'd better just make sure. . . ." Again Martha rang the Van der Bylt house, and Mr. Van, elaborately polite, said for the second time that a message was on the pad for Mrs. Van. "Could you please change it to say that Flora's at Mrs. McGrew's?" said Martha.

"My wife is to go to Mrs. McGrew's place when she comes in?"

"So it seems."

Next morning, when Mrs. Van telephoned, it was to say that Johnny was dead.

What had happened was this:

An African had somehow got out of the main township past the troops and made his way to Johnny Lindsay's. The strike was four days old, and there was hardly any food left in the Locations, and none was being brought in. The troops would not allow people out to get food. "All the people had to eat were the fine words of the strike-leaders and the children were all crying," said the African.

Johnny told him that he did not think he could do anything about it, but that he would tell Mrs. Van. Meanwhile the man said he wanted to hide in Johnny's house. Johnny pointed out that he, Johnny, the old socialist, the old trade unionist, was being put in an impossible position—how could he hide strikers who ought by rights to be with their comrades? The man had said that surely ordinary rules could go by the board when troops, not pickets, disciplined strikers. Johnny had agreed, his last recorded words being (in an unfinished memorandum addressed to Mrs. Van), "The damn fools lock up every black man inside the townships: one per cent of the Africans knew what a strike was before, now there isn't an African in the cities who hasn't had a week's course in the theory and practice of trade unionism. And if an African actually tries to run away from this home course in strike tactics, the authorities drag him back and make him listen."

Flora asked this man to stay and watch Johnny while she went off to Maisie's, to get Maisie's friend to ring up Mrs. Van. But when she got there, she and Maisie decided it was too difficult to ring Mrs. Van. For one thing, a message had already been sent once, by the Maynards. For another, they couldn't face telephoning that house because that "old nanny goat Mr. Van" was enough to put anybody off.

So Maisie's friend had gone back to her place, and telephoned Martha and got Anton, who told Martha who rang Mr. Van for the second time.

Normally, of course, a servant would have been sent up to Mrs. Van with a note, and none of this running around and about would have been necessary.

Meanwhile, a patrolling policeman had caught a glimpse of a black man in Johnny's room. When he arrived at the sick man's bedside, there was only Johnny, apparently asleep; the African had run out of the house on seeing the policeman, and had hidden himself. The policeman searched, but did not find him. Half an hour later he came back to lecture Johnny for "harbouring the enemy" as he put it to the coroner. "Didn't Johnny know," he had planned to say, "that there was a strike on?"

But Johnny was asleep.

"And how was I to know he was so ill?"

"Didn't you see the oxygen tanks?"

"But it was my duty to round up any Kaffirs I saw and take them back to the townships. It wasn't my duty to nurse sick people."

At Maisie's place Flora had quite a good bit to drink. Maisie was still upset by the Maynard's visit, and Flora was worn out by nights of sitting up with the sick man. Flora dropped off to sleep, and woke up about 2 A.M. sober. She wanted to go back home, but while it was only a short way from Maisie's place to Johnny's house, it was a rough area of town, and the strike made her nervous. Flora consoled herself by thinking that it was all right, Johnny wasn't alone, he had the black man from the Location with him. And more than likely Mrs. Van would have made her way to him by now. She tried to doze off again in a big armchair, but it was no use—"something kept tugging at me, and I decided to go home." But she was frightened. Mrs. Gale made her coffee and offered to walk with her; she had spent all her life in tough places, she said, what was half a mile's walk even in rough streets compared to what she was used to? But Maisie said she would be nervous without her mother. Then a policeman, seeing the lights on, had appeared and asked if everything was all right. It was three in the morning. Flora asked him to walk with her back to her home. He did, and when they reached it, no one was there. There was no Johnny in the bed, the sheets and blankets were anyhow, and an oxygen tube lay on the pillow, and the oxygen tank was quite empty.

"Oh God, oh God forgive me," sobbed Flora, clutching the policeman.

She tried to console herself by thinking Mrs. Van might have taken

Johnny home with her. But why should she have done? She had often sat a night through with Johnny in this room, and the old man had not been out of bed for weeks. As it happened Mrs. Van knew nothing about all this; coming in late and tired, she had glanced at the messages on the pad, but not thoroughly: the two messages about Johnny or, rather, Maisie were on the back of a sheet.

Flora and the policeman began running through the streets around the house. They had seen some blood on the doorstep. At last they found Johnny face down on the doorstep of an Indian shop a few hundred yards away. He was dead, and had been dead, so the doctor said, for three or four hours.

He had been trying to go for help? To find Mrs. Van to tell her about the situation in the townships? Of course no one would ever really know, but Flora knew. She confided to Mrs. Van that he must have been worried about her, Flora; he had gone to look for her. He had not been able to let Flora out of his sight that last week or so. He kept calling, even if she was out of the room for a few moments, "Where are you, Flora, where are you, my love?"

The strike lasted a few more days. It was not "broken" by hunger, because some food did get into the townships, though not enough. Perhaps it was the absurdity of the situation that ended it. There the Africans all were, up and down the Colony, locked in because the authorities were frightened about what the white people might do.

Things got more ridiculous every day. Car loads of white people went down to the boundaries of the Locations to shout insults in at the Africans, and then began shouting at the white and black guards too. In the townships, many Africans sat waiting gloomily for death, at last, they said, the white people had got them where they wanted them—all locked up, weakened with hunger, and helpless. Soon, they said, the troops would move in and slaughter them. The ghost of Lobengula had been seen, it was claimed, with his impis. A few Africans got out somehow from behind fences and cordons and had run away to join earlier fugitives in the veld.

The strike leaders, still invisible, continued to issue orders for discipline, order, restraint. They claimed their authority was absolute, and probably it was; but how was this to be proved when it was white troops who played the role of pickets?

Meanwhile everyone waited with nerves on edge for something to happen which would spark off real trouble.

The strike came to an end, both sides claiming victory, though the strikers' main demand, namely, that a law should be passed insisting on a minimum wage of three pounds a month, was not gained.

The day after the strike, Johnny was buried. There had been no graves dug for some days because the grave diggers were all locked up in the townships, and the first labourers emerging from the gates of the townships as the strike ended were commandeered by the authorities for that by now most essential service: to dig graves which would be filled as they were completed.

Johnny did not have a religious service, although Flora wanted one. Mrs. Van spoke an address "as a humanist and a socialist." Half a dozen services were in progress that afternoon: all over the cemetery groups of people stood above open graves, with white-robed priests and censer-swinging little boys.

Flora stayed alone in the little house for some days. Then she moved into Maisie's rooming house in the next room along the verandah from Maisie. Rita had gone with her grandmother to Gotwe for a prolonged stay—there was talk of her going to school there.

"They get on very well together," Maisie said. "After all, my mom never knew Binkie, so she doesn't have to get all upset, being reminded about him. And that fixes the Maynards. They can't go running out to Gotwe every time they've got nothing better to do. It's nearly two hundred miles."

4

For some months everything dawdled and delayed. The divorce had to be postponed because an unexpected letter from Poland said that Grete had been heard of, still alive, in a Russian prison camp. If this was true, then Anton and Martha had never been married. The lawyers decided the safest thing was to conclude that Anton was still married to Grete, and to make some suitable formula for a divorce so that he could marry Bettina. Anton did not tell the Forsters about this complication. He discussed it with Martha—or rather, talked, while she listened. "After all, Bettina has had a sheltered life in many respects, and there are many things she does not understand. I don't want her to be upset unnecessarily." Then a further letter, which said the first had been a mistake: the woman heard of as Grete was someone else and, in any case, she had died in Siberia. The divorce with Martha was on again. Anton and Martha continued to live in the minute flat, treated each other with increasing courtesy, and wished only that they could part. But they could not, the lawyers said so. If Anton, living by himself in a room or a flat was caught with Bettina, then Martha could sue on the grounds of adultery. Anton swore she would not. Was it likely?—Martha exclaimed, exasperated, to a legal gentleman who maintained a whimsically detached look. Martha might turn nasty, he told Anton, who apologized, "What can I do? I can't suck a sensible legal system out of my fingers!"

As usual, nobody's fault; but the irritation of it all did nothing to soften the fact that the ship she had booked on was suddenly taken out of commission because of necessary repairs to war damage. She was given another sailing date. These dates, that of her leaving the country and that of the divorce, were within a week of each other. If something happened to upset the divorce again, then it might mean expensive and difficult legal processes from England. Better, perhaps, to postpone the sailing date? In the end, she and Anton decided to take a chance, but the uncertainty of it all made them increasingly prickly, and it was difficult to maintain the tolerance towards each other which was a question of self-respect now for both of them.

Meanwhile she worked on Johnny Lindsay's memoirs. This meant running about to see people who had known Johnny in the old days; and long discussions with Mrs. Van about political difficulties. Mrs. Van said it would be useful to have the two views "Labour" and "Communist" about the book. But it turned out that it was their temperaments, and not their politics, which dictated their differences. Unless these two strands could be considered to have met when Mrs. Van complained that Martha "like all Communists" was getting very reactionary? "You all go on as if the Russians were the whole human race. Just because they've made a mess of things, you behave as if socialism itself has failed."

"Well, but you must admit, it's all very discouraging. That is, if all these books are true."

"Why should you need all these nasty spiteful books at all? All you had to do was to listen to your elders and betters. No, I've been fighting you Communists all my life, and you are romantics, every one. You exaggerate, you have no sense of proportion, you think anything is justified if enough people die for it. No, I've no patience with you."

Thus Mrs. Van, with a queenly nod, to her old enemy: everything that was not sane, disciplined, reasonable. But then, having softened her statement with a maternal smile, she bent her head over the manuscript where she encountered the enemy again. For her old comrade Johnny Lindsay's life had been full of the qualities she distrusted so much, impeccably "Labour" though he had always been.

"Do you really think we ought to leave this in, Matty?"

"Why not, Mrs. Van?"

"It's not exactly the sort of thing it gives one pleasure to read!"

"You mean, he behaved foolishly?"

"No. And if he did, it's no more than one expects from everyone. It's that he describes these terrible things with such gusto—as if he enjoyed it."

"But I think he did."

"I've never been able to tolerate that—the schoolboy's picnic aspect of socialism—children defying authority—*you* know! For instance, when Johnny and his friends were kidnapped by the police, it was a question of hanging, and some of them *were* hanged. But Johnny always told the story roaring with laughter." Remembering the story, Martha smiled. "Oh yes, yes! If something's colourful and bizarre, that's all you ask! And they were all very brave, of course. But if more sensible methods had been used, perhaps none of the derring-do would have been necessary?"

"Well, Mrs. Van, I wasn't there."

"Well, it irritates me, it always has."

Martha said, "Always, Mrs. Van?" So hard was it, even now, to near what this old friend always called "personal matters," that Martha heard her tongue trip, and she went red. Mrs. Van reddened too, and lowered her eyes. She sat wryly smiling: a look often on her face these days, since Flora had moved into Maisie's rooming house. Flora and Maisie were increasingly subjects of scandal, the latest being that Flora was living with—not the man from McGrath's stores—"at least they are the same age, Matty!"—but young Tommy Brown. Malicious people even said that Maisie and Flora shared him.

"It's all so very strange, Matty. The more I think about it all, the more I—I can't stand it, Matty. There's something about life . . . Did you know that Johnny came to this country in the first place because of Flora? Yes, it's true. He left everything he made for himself on the Rand—and he was chairman here, and secretary there, and everyone knew him. But his children hated Flora and she was miserable, and so he came here to make a new life for her—you're going to say, *it happened,* I suppose."

"Well, yes, I was."

Johnny had dedicated his memoirs—not to the Labour Movement, not to Mrs. Van, not to "world socialism," but to Flora. "To the love of my life, Flora, the best and the kindest and the most beautiful of women." He had whispered this to Mrs. Van late one night while Flora was at the pictures. "Write this down for me, my dear . . ." She had done so. "Now read it to me—yes, yes, that's right." She had put it, as he wanted, in front of the memoirs. "Of course," she said to Martha, "I'd be quite within my rights to tear that dedication up! He was not in his right mind that night. He was rambling, earlier."

"But, Mrs. Van, you *didn't* tear it up!"

"All right! *It happened.* But *my* point is made, I think!"

In the event, nothing was suppressed, or even toned down; and reading it was like listening to Johnny's voice: they were the memoirs of a gallant and innocent boy; and Mrs. Van sat smiling as she turned the pages of the history which to her had been a lifetime of a committee work, paper work, research, self-discipline, self-deprivation.

Concurrently with this, Martha did a very different job of editing. Some weeks after Thomas's death, the Native Commissioner in S . . . . had delivered to his office by an African in a loincloth who said he came from Chief so and so, with greetings, a sheaf of stained damp papers which were found in Thomas's hut. These papers were sent to Thomas's wife, who sent them to Jack Dobie, who gave them to Martha, since, he said, they were clearly meant to be part of Thomas's report on conditions in the rural areas. They were in a dreadful state, for the ink had run where rain water had dripped on them, probably from an ill-thatched roof. Ants had left half a hundred sheets looking like red-edged lace paper. And in any case, the pages were not numbered, and apparently had never been put in order. How was Martha, or anybody, to know what Thomas had meant? How much had been destroyed, or lost? Also, there were notes, comments, scribbled over and across and on the margins of the original text, in red pencil. These, hard to decipher, were in themselves a different story or, at least, made of the original a different story.

Every morning as the sun rose, Thomas had risen too, and had sat in the doorway of his hut, a writing pad on his knees and a bottle of ink in the dust beside him. He sat, writing, while the village came to life all around him. People emerged stretching and yawning from their huts into weak sunlight, the women fetched water from the river, and attended to the millet patches, the men sharpened their spears for hunting. Thomas sat there, and wrote; and again at night, in the light from the cooking fires and, more than once, by moonlight.

But what was he trying to write? A paragraph about life in Sochaczen was followed by poetry, in Polish. Translated, it turned out to be a folk song. Then, how his mother cooked potatoes. Then, across this, in red pencil: If these people could be persuaded to grow potatoes—but what use, if the salt has lost its savour? A great many

Jewish jokes, or rather Yiddish. Solly translated. (He, too, was writing memoirs, called: Patterns of Betrayal. Yes, I feel my life is over, Matty, and when I've finished this book, I shall live on a kibbutz in Israel.) The jokes, he said, might have come out of a joke book; he had cut his teeth on them. Was there a theme or tendency shown in their choice? Not unless there was a theme running through all Jewish jokes, and if so, he'd leave it to Martha to sneer at it. There was a long article about how to run a carp farm. A tributary of the Zambesi might very well be netted off as a carp farm, and the carp used to supplement the Africans' diet. Or for fertilizer? said the red pencil, across this. Stories: "Once there was a man who travelled to a distant country. When he got there, the enemy he had fled from was waiting for him. Although he had proved the usefulness of travelling, he went to yet another country. No, his enemy was *not* there." (Surprised, are you! said the red pencil.) "So he killed himself." To make fish stew in the manner of the Mamonka . . . first catch your fish. If you keep your grain on stilts, to save it from the white ants, why not walk on stilts yourself?

Pages of this kind of thing, damp, musty smelling pages, which Jack and Martha turned, never once saying, at least, not at the start: Well, our old friend Thomas, he was off his head, towards the end.

But that was not all. At last there emerged a sort of pattern, or one could be made. Because, embedded in all this, were stories of the people in the village, a history of the tribe, facts, figures—as if, sometimes, Thomas had intended to produce material for the Survey. Many of the biographies were obituaries. "So and so, 'born in the year of the heavy rains,' aged about thirty. Married. Three children, two dead of malaria. Never seen a white man before myself. Never been out of the Valley. Died this morning." "So and so. I think fifty-odd. His father was once in a town, but I can't make out which. It had 'men of stone' in the streets, which he took to be protective magic figures. Has had two wives. Nine children, three still living. Can understand headlines in the newspaper. Died this morning." Quite sensible, these were, and full of interest. But across them, as across everything else, the notes in red pencil.

The obituaries spread to include ancestors, parents, children, animals. "So and so, born the year the lightning hit the Chief's hut," then the history of the Chief, and what the witch doctor said about lightning. About the birth of the Chief's first son: he was born feet foremost because "he wanted to walk as soon as he was born." About the village of the mother of the first-born, which was across the river, and then about the mother's brother's personal habits—he was

jealous of the old goat *his* mother used to sleep beside, for warmth
on cold nights—there were no blankets twenty years ago; and when
he had his six teeth knocked out, the four incisors and two upper
canines, with the chisel, he had never once uttered a sound, as was
right and proper, but he had a fit, and thereafter the people of the
tribe knew that the gods had not been pleased with him, for the poor
quality of the sacrificed teeth. But he ran down a deer better than
anyone, and no one knew as much about catching fish by the use of
herbs. And so on. Before the conclusion: Died this afternoon, it was
hard to remember who had died; Martha had to leaf through perhaps fifty sheets to find out. And in the middle of all this, slap in the
middle of Africa, Poland: On Wednesday afternoon, I had to take
the horse to the smith for my uncle, and Mira from the school window called to me: Leave the horse and come to the river. So I went
swimming in the pool with Mira, and the horse broke its rein from
the tree and ran away. My father beat me. My mother made a poul-
tice of sour milk. What the father breaks, the mother makes. Even
so I couldn't sit down for a week. These people, these red mud-
smeared savages don't beat their children. Comment across this in
red pencil: It could be said, therefore, that gentleness saves sour
milk.

"Vermin, vermin," said the red pencil, "the world is a lump of
filth crawling with vermin." "Death here. Death there too. Everywhere. Blood on his face where the bullet went in under the cheek-
bone. Death in the bottom of the river. His face, red: the faces of
the Mamonka, red with red mud. His hair: red. Their hair: red.
His red: blood. Their red: mud. Did he have lice in his hair? (A
riddle!) No. Neither do the Mamonka, the red mud keeps lice away.
The backside of a baboon, scaly and red."

Obscenities in English, Polish, Yiddish.

"If flies buzz, buzz harder. There are enough flies here—to kill a
crow. Kill. Crows are more common than eagles, while vultures sit
on the trees around the village smelling our deaths. The vultures
come down from the trees gobble gobble with their red necks, thin
skin of red necks puff and blister like wounds puff in the sun. A
wound made by fire, if a leg is left lying in the fire too long, first
has flies walking over it, then the skin puffs and blisters and walks
gobble gobble. Vermin. Swine. Murderers. Apes. Apes with red blis-
tering behinds. Kill. Kill, my comrades, and make a good meal of it.
The meal is kept on stilts away from the white ants, and so are you."

In the end, there were two versions of Thomas's last testament—
Jack Dobie's name for it. One version consisted of the short biographies and the obituaries and the recipes and the charms and the

tales and anecdotes. The other, typed out on flimsy sheets which could be inserted over the heavier sheets of the first version, made a whole roughly like the original—more or less common sense, as a foundation, with a layer of nonsense over it. But even in the first version, the "sensible" one, was a note of something harsh and repellent. Martha sat holding this extraordinary document, fitting the leaves in between each other, separating them, so that sense and nonsense met each other, as in a dance, and left each other; and meanwhile thought of Thomas, the strong brown man she had known—this was the same person. She felt she should ask the real Thomas, the man she had loved, to forgive her for her obtuseness. Presumably this person revealed to her, in this document, had been there all the time? Yet she did not recognize much of Thomas in this, except (and she did not know why) perhaps in the facetiousness which marred even the most straightforward entries and which, perhaps, was a line forward into the man who wrote "vermin, vermin, we are all vermin?" Yet facetiousness had not been a quality of Thomas's. He had had an abrupt grim humour—yes. For instance, the grimness of the story of when he visited his old teacher, in Israel: And how's evolution with you, my teacher? Is that you, Thomas Stern? Are you still working hard at your Latin?

Jewish. The Jewish acquiescence in suffering. Except that it is everyone's acquiescence in suffering.

What did you say was the theme of the Yiddish jokes you cut your teeth on, Solly?—I shall leave it to you to sneer, Matty, I have no comment.

"But what on earth are we going to do with this thing?" she said to Jack.

"He was nuts, wasn't he? Burn it."

In the end she took it to Mrs. Van, who read it all one night and telephoned Martha in the morning.

"That was a very strange thing to do, copying out all that nonsense on to the flimsies."

"It was the nearest I could get to the original."

"But why on earth should you want to?"

"But it's not honest, otherwise."

"It's a Foundation—they don't want this sort of thing."

"They don't want anthropology either—but if there's anything in this stuff, that's what it's nearest to."

"Lose it, Matty. Drop it into the nearest well."

"I keep thinking of Thomas, going crazy in that village, trying to get messages out."

"The same could be said of anyone in a mental hospital. Be sensible, Matty. Next time some enthusiastic amateur like Thomas asks for money, instead of giving it, they'll say look what happened to that maniac in Southern Zambesia."

"I suppose so."

Martha wrote to the Foundation that the survey material was lost. The bundle of papers lay about the flat, with the manuscript Martha had made of it. She could not make herself throw it away. When it was the only thing left in the empty flat, after she had finished packing to go to England, she threw it into her suitcase and took it with her.

At the end everything happened quickly. The divorce was set down in the High Court two months before they expected, and a berth became available on an earlier ship.

The divorce itself was nothing but a formality, as the lawyers had promised.

Anton and Martha and their lawyers, and Marjorie and Jasmine—just up from Johannesburg to visit her parents—went to Court together. At the Court, Martha was relieved that Mr. Maynard was nowhere in sight, though he might have been: he was now a High Court Judge. The appropriate lies were told, and Martha and Anton came out of the Court together to find Bettina waiting for Anton. She was apologetic about "intruding at such an awkward moment," but she had been unable to get her car, parked some blocks away, to start.

"Well, I'll come and get everything packed later," Anton said to Martha. He hesitated, then kissed her on the cheek, while Bettina smiled as if to say: Of course! Quite right, don't think that I object. The two women were so concerned to assure each other of their magnanimity, that in fact their faces were strained by smiling, and they were both relieved when Anton at last went off with Bettina.

"What a farce," said Jasmine. "However, they make a handsome couple."

Marjorie said, "Who'd have thought it! It has to be Anton who makes a suitable marriage in the end. Are you coming tonight, Matty?"

There was a meeting that night, which Jasmine and Marjorie had promised to attend. Marjorie had said, "It's a crowd of new people—who knows, perhaps this time it really will achieve something?"

"What's the point?" said Martha. "I'm leaving next week."

"Oh isn't it dreadful—no one left. Please come, for old times' sake. There's only me now to do anything—but of course, these new people will take over now, I expect." Marjorie was in tears. Ashamed, she said, "Yes, I know, I'm terribly tense. I'm sorry. If I don't watch out

I'll be having a nervous breakdown—imagine, I always used to despise women like me."

That night Marjorie and Martha went to an ugly office not a hundred yards from their old office in Founders' Street—now demolished.

They were a few minutes late, and as they went up the stairs they joked about their corruption—once they would never have dared to be late.

They stood in the doorway, looking around to see who they knew. No one—they were all strangers.

There was something about all these faces—what was it?—of course! they all looked such babies: they were in their early twenties, while Martha and Marjorie, six, seven years older, were a different generation.

"Thanks for coming," said an intense dark youth. "We are glad to welcome members of the old guard."

Luckily the two guests realized in time that this was not a joke, and refrained from either smiling or exchanging glances. But their sense of shock made them feel as if they had. The young man nodded unsmiling at an already full bench. People squeezed up: Marjorie and Martha squeezed in. As they did so, Jasmine came in, looking far too elegant. She had been at a family dinner with her parents, and yet another suitable businessman they hoped she would marry. Jasmine found a few empty inches on the end of the opposite bench, and sat on it, having examined it carefully for dust. This made a bad impression, and eyebrows went up. Meanwhile the intense youth continued with a speech. He was persuading them into something: he had a vision which he wished them to share—enormous sums of money were involved. When he at last mentioned the final amount, Martha felt Marjorie's elbow in her ribs, and she looked around to see why these apparently sane young people did not throw him out as a madman. He was speaking fast and well, leaning forward, his eyes first on one face and then moving on to the next. He spoke, in intimacy, to one person, as if they two were utterly alone, and then, having established this connection in the eyes of everyone, moved on to the next. But instinctively he knew that Martha, Marjorie and Jasmine could not be absorbed into a public tête-à-tête—his eyes moved past them—not, however, without a small smile which said: you'd trust me if you knew me!

Jackie Bolton. Martha was so strongly transported back to that other office, that other group, she had to look around to see if Anton Hesse, Andrew McGrew, the two sensible solid men whose task it was to calm and oppose, were sitting in their places. And how did Jasmine feel—who had after all loved Jackie Bolton? Both Marjorie and Martha looked to see: Jasmine had the wry look of one judging a younger self; and she, like them, was being careful how she directed her glances of curiosity—for, knowing Jackie Bolton, they knew how passionately this orator would resent infidelities of attention.

Yes, there they were; in a corner sat a square bespectacled young man taking notes, and each time the orator mentioned that fantastic sum of money and spoke of a "nation-wide network" he allowed himself a humorous grimace. And sitting beside the impassioned orator in the position of Chairman (who, should have welcomed them officially—it was not the orator's task at all) sat another silent, judgement-reserving person, in this case a large, dark, rather beautiful girl, in style like a Turgenev heroine.

As for the others, they all leaned forward, absorbed, lost, gone into the speaker's fine, high-winging language. The two silent critics were a minority and knew it. So if history was repeating itself—and why not? If the dramatis personae were the same, presumably the plot was also—this group would not be in existence, these people would not sit all night on uncomfortable benches talking about nation-wide networks which would transform the country, if it had not been for the impassioned orator? He it was, presumably, who had fired them all, fused them all; he was the risk taker, the spark, the vision maker—and the sensible young man in the corner, and beautiful sensible girl might radiate a judicious calm in vain. And if they disapproved, which they did, what were they doing here at all? My dear sensible friends! Martha found herself addressing these two silently: You imagine you are here as representatives of common sense, don't you; and you are having "a restraining influence." Well, don't fool yourselves—he will have his way, set everything in motion, form everything, and in what he forms will be the seeds of its destruction. So you can foretell the end of what you are creating now, if you know how to look for the signs: you find them, my friends, in what you are forgiving this lovable young maniac for, in those irritating things which you meet to discuss (feeling rather disloyal to the group) and decide are not really important after all, the vision's the thing. And, keeping your minds firmly on the vision, as if it were an entity, a thing, quite separate from the minds and personalities which created it, you overlook the lies, the exaggerations, and the sheer damned lunacy, because you know in your hearts that you haven't the spark, you couldn't set anything in motion. While you are sitting around saying: there isn't the basis, there aren't the conditions, it's quite impossible (and you are absolutely right: there never is the basis, it is always impossible—if you leave out of account the recklessness of this inspired young idiot) he has already lit the fire, and things are in full swing, the pot's on the boil—and the fat's in the fire. Of course he, the inspirer, will soon have a nervous breakdown, or be ill in some way, or lose interest and go off somewhere else where, he believes, there will be uncorrupted and whole people who can't ruin his vision—as you are doing, he thinks. It will be you who will try to put in order (a phrase you will use continually) the mess he has left behind. You'll say, oh what a pity it happened like that, "if only" he had not created so much dissension, offended so many people, frightened off so many because of what were obviously lies—in short, created such an atmosphere of intrigue, unpleasantness and unreality. If only, if only . . . then there would have been a fine healthy organization, and the nation would have been transformed. But my dear sensible friends, without the "unreality," "the lunacy" (you'll be using such phrases for years; you two will probably even get married on the strength of your disappointment over the "unreality") there would never have been anything at all, that's the point; it always happens like this; that *is* the point; the "if only" which is so important to you, which you will be muttering to yourself in five, six years' time to soften your feelings of shame, waste, nostalgia for what-might-have-been, well, that "if only" shows you never understood the first thing about what was going on. And never will.

But Martha, having reached this point in her silent address to those sympathetic figures, the beautiful solid girl who bent her dark head over her chairman's notes, the pleasant bespectacled young man who was softening his criticism with a fraternal smile, understood that the orator, sensing the three visitors were absorbed in thoughts unconnected with what he was actually saying, interrupted a sentence in which the word *millions* had already occurred four times, to demand with hostile politeness, "Was he boring them, perhaps?"

"Good Lord no, far from it!" Marjorie exclaimed, with all the energy of her frank charm. She was transformed with new enthusiasm. Martha shook her head, smiling: she knew better than to risk speech. He looked at Jasmine, who said, "I'm sorry I was late. But I want to know, what is this group?"

At once eyes met, communed, separated. A discreet silence.

"Oh well, if it's like that," said Jasmine companionably, and lit a cigarette.

"No one said it was like anything," said a pretty student of about eighteen. She looked with dislike at the three old women—as she clearly felt them to be.

A silence.

"Well," said Marjorie warmly, her eyes shining, "it's awfully nice of you people to ask us old reactionaries around anyway."

At once eyes met again, lingered. Grimaces, silence, hostility.

Martha was remembering an incident from those dead days of eight years ago.

Jasmine had come hot-foot into the office—which? There had been so many dingy, bench-furnished, dust-smelling little offices. She had just met Mr. Forester in the street, and had stopped for a talk, "I was on my guard of course, he might be a spy for all *we* know!" He had said humorously, "Well, thanks at least for acknowledging the existence of an old reactionary like myself." "Imagine," Jasmine had said, in prim shocked tones that nevertheless managed to suggest a sneer, "he wasn't even ashamed of saying it aloud. He actually *said* it in so many words."

Lord, Lord, thought Martha, were we really so awful, so stupid? Thank goodness she was leaving soon and would not have to forgive these young idiots for the sake of her own past.

She said, smiling with what she hoped was a benevolently neutral expression, "It's particularly nice of you to invite me, because I am leaving the country soon."

"If people aren't ashamed to turn their backs on the problems of this country for a soft life in England," said the pretty girl bitterly.

At this, the fair solid young man took a pipe from his pocket and began to fill it, watching his hands at work, while he calmly smiled. Their attention attracted by this deliberate gesture, everyone waited for him to say something. Martha again felt Marjorie's elbow against hers, "Remember, Andrew?" she whispered.

"Some people are much more interested in private conversation than in the meeting, forgive me if I'm wrong," said a young Indian teacher.

The pipe-filler said, "I'd like to remind everyone that a vote was taken as to whether members of the old groups should be invited." He spoke humorously and the Chairwoman said humorously, "I was just about to say the same thing. I hereby bring this meeting to order. Our guests don't even know what it is all about."

"Oh yes, we do!" muttered Marjorie, smiling; but the people who had heard her, frowned.

"This meeting," said the orator humorously but with passion, reclaiming everyone by leaning forward and sweeping them with a fire of hot demanding accusing glances, "is to establish socialism in this country—now!"

Small flattered laughs all around.

The pipe-filler said, "We are a group of socialists—enough said, in present conditions."

More flattered laughter.

"Who *are* we?—if I may ask?" Jasmine persisted.

The Chairwoman said, "You are quite right to ask, but at the present moment all that can be said is: we are socialists, we are feeling our way, and we are very loosely organized. You must understand that we can't say more than that."

"Well, of course," said Marjorie, with a sort of friendly gruffness. But this remark, for some reason, caused general ill-feeling. Eyes met again, and even the Chairwoman seemed upset. It was clear that afterwards people would ask each other, "Who told *her* our affairs—there must be a traitor in our midst."

"I suggest someone sums up—the world situation I mean," said the Indian teacher.

"That is just what I was doing," said the impassioned orator huffily. "Or rather, what I was working up to," he went on, recovering good humour as people affectionately laughed at him. He drew notes towards him and began to speak. It was "an analysis of the situation." "Not a patch on Anton in his heyday," Martha found herself thinking.

The problem for discussion tonight was: what effect would the newly created Communist China make to the world scene?

It turned out, after some hours, that there was complete unanimity about this.

Who would have foreseen it? Everyone spoke, including "the old guard;" they disagreed, they raised their voices, were riven with dissension, agreed to differ, might have gone on till morning, if the Chairman, or Chairwoman, had not said, "I'm going to put it to you: in fact everyone's saying the same thing." They all looked at each other again—not really friendly, this look, for they didn't want to be like each other, to be similar, although the violence of their discussion had in fact caused an underlying good feeling. But they saw it; they had, in fact, been saying, though of course in very different ways, the same thing. They laughed, all together. The laugh made them one.

It was the laugh heard always when a group of people are in agreement but—and this is the point, when they are in agreement against an outside majority. It is the laugh of a minority in the right, the intelligent, forward-looking, informed minority, holding difficult or even dangerous opinions against great odds. It is the self-flattering, comforting, warming laugh heard—but how many times, in how many different settings had Martha heard it! And how many times and in what circumstances would she hear it again?

The good humour was now so great that it was easy for the Turgenev girl to suggest that Jasmine should sum up. Besides, she was a visitor from the Communist Party in the South (though of course it was no longer in existence, it had dissolved itself) and while the people in this room could on no account be considered Communists, there was a sense in which she might, perhaps, be considered a fraternal delegate.

Laughter, and even the impassioned orator nodded.

Jasmine summed up:

"It was unlucky for the world that the first socialist country had chanced to be Russia, because that country's backwardness had branded socialism itself with a barbarousness that had nothing to do with socialism. China, being an ancient country of deep and imperturbable civilization—much more civilized than we are!—" Cries of hear, hear, all round the room—"would restore to Communism moderation, calm, sense, humanity, humour, tolerance, etc.

"The Soviet Union, realizing in the true spirit of Communist self-criticism that she was not as fitted for the task of world leadership as this new unspotted exemplar with her ancient civilization, would stand aside and allow China to lead the world towards full Communism.

"America, having sunk so many billions into trying to prevent the Chinese Communists from coming to power, would probably continue fomenting civil war, there would be another epoch of civil wars, famines, etc., etc., but after all this year, 1949, would be remembered in the world's calendar as the first of the new epoch of benevolent socialism." And so on, of course, but this was the gist of it.

For a moment when Jasmine had finished, there was confidence, elation, general good feeling. If the three guests had not been familiar with such situations, they might have believed the meeting was over, it now being after midnight. But they recognized the atmosphere of "closed meeting" and they got up, one after another, to say good night.

Marjorie was obviously longing to be asked to stay; but while the three were no longer considered enemies, or perhaps even spies, they certainly weren't accepted either. Marjorie would have to wait until Jasmine and Martha left, and she the only member of the "old guard" in the town. She would finally be asked to join on the basis that she was quite a good soul, and useful for running around and doing donkey work, even if theoretically she was quite hopeless, poor thing. "But of course she'll have to work her passage."

Formal thanks for being invited at all were offered and accepted, and the three went down the dark stairs.

They stood together on the pavement. They realized that while they had sat arguing in the stuffy bright little room, the skies had been swept by storms and by rain; it must be raining somewhere outside the city, for gusts of soft damp air came to their faces with a smell of freshly wetted leaves.

Jasmine said, "Well, they're a nice lot, really. If only they weren't so unbalanced about everything. But they'll settle down."

Marjorie said, "Oh, I'm so pleased they are starting. It doesn't make one feel so bad about our failing. And if only they'll learn some lessons from our mistakes . . ." She gave a little laugh which was half a sob. "I've really got to stop being so emotional about everything. Colin says it is driving him mad, and I don't blame him. But of course he's never emotional about anything. Shall I see you before you go to England, Matty?"

"I suppose I should have a party—but who to invite?"

"Yes, who's left? Oh, isn't it awful, when you think . . ."

"Never mind, the young are on the march," said Jasmine. Martha laughed, but Marjorie said, "Oh, don't, don't joke—it's all right for you, but I've got to stay here."

She ran off to find her car. Colin was waiting for her to come home; he was sitting up—one of the children was feverish.

Martha and Jasmine walked up the empty street under the deep glitter of the stars.

Jasmine said, "Poor Marjorie, what a fate. We're lucky, we're getting out."

"Are you really going to stay in Johannesburg?"

"I like the nasty hole. And besides, with the Nats in, one feels as if one really can do something—I mean, it's so terrible, it can't last. I reckon we'll have socialism in five years at the latest . . . Well, so long, Matty. Be seeing you somewhere, some time."

She went off by herself down the street. At the corner she turned to wave, "Barricades!" she said, almost formally, as she might have said, good night, or how are you? Then she vanished from sight.

THE CHILDREN OF VIOLENCE SERIES
FIVE NOVELS BY DORIS LESSING